The

WITCHES *of*
BONE HILL

The
WITCHES *of*
BONE HILL

AVA MORGYN

**ST. MARTIN'S
GRIFFIN
NEW YORK**

First published in the United States by St. Martin's Griffin, an imprint of St. Martin's Publishing Group

THE WITCHES OF BONE HILL. Copyright © 2023 by Anna Sweat. All rights reserved. Printed in the United States of America. For information, address St. Martin's Publishing Group, 120 Broadway, New York, NY 10271.

www.stmartins.com

The Library of Congress Cataloging-in-Publication Data is available upon request.

ISBN 978-1-250-83543-7 (trade paperback)
ISBN 978-1-250-83544-4 (ebook)

Our books may be purchased in bulk for promotional, educational, or business use. Please contact your local bookseller or the Macmillan Corporate and Premium Sales Department at 1-800-221-7945, extension 5442, or by email at MacmillanSpecialMarkets@macmillan.com.

First Edition: 2023

10 9 8 7 6 5 4 3 2 1

For all the witches, both real and imagined,
who taught me how to hold my power

The

WITCHES *of*
BONE HILL

CHAPTER ONE

THE CALL

THEY SAY WHAT doesn't kill you makes you stronger. Cordelia was beginning to think "they" were liars.

She looked up at the gleaming, white-brick two-story and willed herself to feel something, staring at the sun bouncing off the paint until her eyes began to water and her head felt heavy. The first time she'd seen the house, she'd thought it looked immaculate. A paragon of suburban construction, solid and flawless. Her very own ivory tower. It seemed molded to the earth, dominating the end of the cul-de-sac like a modern fortress, rising from the carefully shaped boxwoods and the rows of cheery marigolds and coleus, the menace of black-iron fencing, as if to proclaim its value to anyone passing by. She'd even imagined a white dog behind the gated drive to complete the picture. Something regal—a standard poodle or a borzoi.

And of course, the house had a certain whisper . . .

But over the last several weeks, when she walked into it, she couldn't feel anything except betrayal. The space didn't whisper to her anymore. It was like John's affair had tainted their connection, and she and the house couldn't hear each other.

Looking at it now, she felt only an alarming sense of numbness where the pang of loss should have been. Maybe the grief had spiked when she'd gotten the notice of default from her mortgage company—a herald she'd been quietly dreading from a lender known for property seizure—and then had receded like an outgoing tide. Maybe this was the drawback before the tsunami.

The moving truck angled toward the drive, rumbling in the street. Cordelia simmered with a barely repressed shame, like an evicted mistress with her negligees scattered across the lawn. She hated to think of her neighbors witnessing this. John had secreted away whatever he wanted at her first prolonged absence, along with the money in their joint accounts and the business they'd built together. Cordelia mentally flogged herself again for agreeing to not list herself as co-owner of their agency. It had made so much sense when he explained it to her—him pulling back to take brokerage classes since *her* income was greater, protecting her assets from liability should the agency incur debts, thinking it was all fifty-fifty anyway since they were legally married. *Outsmarting the fine print,* he'd called it. What a gullible fool she'd been.

And then the notices had begun to arrive—maxed-out credit cards, payday lenders frothing at the mouth for instant reimbursement, the accounts he kept opening in *her* name even after he and Allison split for Vegas, then San Diego, Key West, and God knew where else. All on her tab apparently. She'd done her best to explain, to make whatever small, indemnifying payments she could, but he'd poked so many holes in her finances it was like trying to bail the *Titanic* with a colander. She was staring down the inevitable—divorce, foreclosure, bankruptcy, homelessness. They would fall on her like dominoes, one after the other.

A budding tension between the eyes, the initial squeeze of an oncoming headache she'd become all too familiar with in the last six months, forced her to look away and turn toward the street. Her mother's tired face sprung to mind, the sharp intake of air she'd make at the onset of pain, shadows puddling in her eye sockets. Cordelia had been just a girl when Maggie started getting them—*migraines*, the doctors would say, or *cluster headaches*. They would give her hormones and pain relievers and supplements, but still they came without warning, dragging the smile from Maggie's face and the spring from her step, causing her to get as low as she could—the sofa or the floor—and huddle there in the grip of pain.

Cordelia winced at the memory as much as at the ache in her head. She didn't like to think about the things she had in common with her mother or where those things could lead, *had* led for Maggie in the end.

"Where do you want these?" Molly, her new assistant, asked, walking up with a gargantuan arrangement of irises and gladiolas as an angry streak of black and tan barreled past their ankles.

"Hold on," Cordelia told her, turning to jog after what could only be Perry Ellis, her neighbor's Australian terrier. She caught up with him behind the truck, where he had a mover cornered inside. Fifteen pounds of swagger and spite, he looked like a roughed-up Yorkie with mutton chops and made everything on their street his business.

Cordelia bent over and scooped him up, his body rigid as he continued to bark, every shriek hitting her square between the eyes. "It's okay—he's missing most of his teeth," she explained by way of apology to the frightened mover, then marched toward the yard to the right of her own. Mrs. Robichaud was already halfway down the driveway.

"He snuck right past me," the older woman claimed as she reached for him with unsteady hands, resin baubles clacking. Of course, the glaucoma meant that Perry Ellis snuck right past Mrs. Robichaud almost every time she opened the door.

"It's the movers," Cordelia said with a smile, handing him over. "He was just defending his territory."

Mrs. Robichaud glanced at the truck. "Oh, I was worried this day would come. Perry Ellis and I will be so sad to see you go."

Cordelia put on a brave face. She would miss the quiet old lady next door who always invited her in for tea and regaled her with tales of international travel in the seventies. She would miss her monogrammed teaspoons and matching pantsuits, the soft overlap of her curls like duck feathers. Mostly she would miss her kind smile and generous nature. "I'm sorry I won't be able to bring you your groceries anymore."

"Don't you worry about us," Mrs. Robichaud said, batting a hand. "You just look out for yourself." Her puckered mouth scrunched up in distaste. "I knew you were too good for that man, always slinking around with his gold watches and shiny loafers, giving Perry Ellis the stink eye. Thought he was back last night when I saw someone at your door, but this man was far too large to be John. Had Perry Ellis fit to be tied."

"Last night?" Cordelia racked her brain for who might be knocking on her door after dark, but she had no idea. She'd taken to staying in a hotel once it was clear she would have to sell. With the house already in pre-foreclosure and her business yanked out from under her, bills *with interest* piling up in the rolltop desk, this sale was her last-ditch effort to avoid total collapse.

"Walked all around peeking in windows, then left something in the mailbox before he drove away," she said. "These old peepers couldn't make out much, just shoulders like a gorilla." Suddenly, her eyes widened and her face brightened. "I'll bet he was an early buyer wanting to see the property before someone else snatches it up!"

Cordelia felt her stomach drop. She didn't have the heart to tell Mrs. Robichaud that the house hadn't been listed until this morning.

"I'll bet he was," she lied before stepping away. "Don't hesitate to call if you need anything. I may not be next door, but I'm still close enough to help a friend," she added as the old woman turned back for her house. Cordelia watched until she was safely indoors and then scurried over to the mailbox, pulling out the single envelope waiting inside.

She slid a finger to open it before she noticed that Molly was still standing on the sidewalk, the giant flower arrangement trembling in her tired hands. "Oh gosh, Molly, I'm sorry. You can put that on the entry table. Thanks."

Cordelia watched her make her way up the walk in tight, little steps. Unlike the last one, Molly was too eager to please. She lacked Allison's confidence, and she asked too many questions. But she put in the hours and would drive to kingdom come if Cordelia told her to. More important, she lacked Allison's natural blond highlights and runner's legs. Cordelia could still hear the sound of her old assistant's naked ass rubbing against the Carrara marble, John grunting like a wild hog every time she walked into the kitchen. Cordelia would stand in the middle of the living room and take inventory of every surface she thought they probably fucked on. It didn't leave her many places to sit.

Loyalty was what Cordelia needed as she sifted the wreckage of her life, and there was something in Molly's eager-beaver personality that she found endearing. She shared perfectionism and ambition with her new apprentice, qualities needed to compete and succeed in her field, where every house had five agents waiting to list it. Without them, Cordelia never would have gotten as far as she did. And of course, there was *the knack*—an uncanny timeliness and intuitive knowing that Cordelia possessed which couldn't replace hard work but made a sizable difference.

Molly didn't have the knack, but maybe it would rub off on her. After all, hadn't it transferred to Cordelia from her mother after so many years? That's what Cordelia told herself when her hunches and her clients' needs intersected a little too perfectly, leaving her skin bristling with an indefinable tingle. In time,

Molly would get used to Cordelia's inclination to predict the little things like rain showers or an offer about to come in. Some of the mysticism would wear off. Like Cordelia, she would learn to explain it away as an exceptionally perceptive gut honed by experience and evolution. Luck was not genetic, and Cordelia preferred to ground herself in the firmly rational, where things could be explained. *Most* things, anyway.

And then there were the whispers. But Cordelia didn't talk about those, hadn't since she was a small girl of six or seven. And what was there to say? They were so scarcely perceptible she wasn't sure they were there at all. Not everything she'd experienced could be so assuredly minimized.

A sudden hammering jolted her. To her left, Molly—mallet in hand—was pounding the *For Sale* sign into the emerald-green lawn with all the enthusiasm of a drummer in a death-metal band. Once the stakes were a foot deep, she straightened. "Done."

But Cordelia didn't appreciate the finality in her tone. Every stroke of the mallet felt like it was proclaiming her failure. As a wife. As a businesswoman. As a person. She'd procured an image over the years that she could hide behind, but she'd never quite managed the finer complexities of "fitting in"—a relic of growing up her mother's daughter. John's vanilla-wafer mien went a long way toward securing her place in the community and her mind as an exemplar of normalcy. Her impostor syndrome had been in overdrive since he left.

As if to affirm Molly's pronouncement, the largest crow Cordelia had ever seen landed atop the sign, cawing rudely in her direction, pinning her with one horrid obsidian eye.

She scowled at its greasy black feathers as it launched into the air and sailed over her roof, an ominous blight on her perfect specimen of a house. As it disappeared, her gaze dropped to one of the dormer windows, curtains parted. She stood between them, the stern-faced woman dressed in black, a bonnet of white

hair piled on her head as she stared down at Cordelia malevo-
lently, pale as death itself.

Cordelia fell back a step, heart grinding to a halt within her
chest, breath trapped inside as she gave over to little-girl terror.
Not again, she thought, squeezing her eyes shut. *Not again, not
again, not again.*

Her fingers began to buzz with a pins-and-needles effect she
couldn't ignore. She opened her eyes to check her cell phone, the
home screen lighting up with a picture of her and John on their
wedding day—flushed faces pressed together, electric smiles
dazzling. They were probably four glasses of champagne in when
she snapped that shot. It used to be her favorite. Now, it filled her
with equal parts doubt and longing.

The first few chords of Cher's "Gypsies, Tramps & Thieves"
began to play. She used that ringtone for only one person, but it
had been years since she'd heard it.

Cordelia caught Molly watching her with a curious expression, one she'd seen on many faces over the years. She gave a
weak smile, registering that she'd pulled the phone out *before* it
rang, then carefully turned her back, pressing it to her ear as she
walked a few steps away. "Eustace."

"Cordy," her sister breathed into the phone. "I didn't know if
you'd pick up."

"You caught me between engagements." Cordelia wandered
up the drive as she glanced back to the dormer window, now
thankfully empty. Eustace always managed to call in the middle
of important meetings or unexpected crises, as if she could feel
her sister's tension from eight hundred miles away. But after their
falling-out five years ago, she'd remained conspicuously silent.

It was *so* Eustace—showing up late and stoned off her ass,
pretending she knew John better than Cordelia did, a man she'd
barely said five words to, insisting they call the wedding off. She
knew her sister was only trying to protect her after their mother

died, but they had each said things that couldn't be unsaid that day. They'd always seen the world differently, had disagreements and fights. But for the first time, there had been a real disconnect. As if their grief had eclipsed their bond.

Or maybe it was the fear.

Cordelia had meant to reach out after the wedding, but with Maggie *and* Eustace out of the picture, she'd found it so much easier to put everything behind her, to forget where, *who* she'd come from, and pretend her upbringing had been as *Criss Cross Applesauce* as the next person's.

Now, she was wondering what had changed.

"You sound . . . *off*," Eustace replied.

Cordelia had never been a fan of her sister's ability to read her so accurately. She could read houses, but Eustace could take one look at someone and know their whole life story. Or at least think she did. She'd hoped the distance had put an end to that irritating trait. Apparently, it hadn't. "I ate a bad egg at breakfast," she lied.

Without Perry Ellis to stymie them, the moving guys were already in action. Her Victorian walnut console table was resting beside the hydrangeas. Rolled up next to the silk rug she'd ordered from Jaipur. Cordelia wandered into the side yard to avoid them, her reasonable three-inch heels sinking into the freshly watered ground. They were streaked with mud when she pulled them up. Doubly annoyed, she felt the hum of pain radiating between her eyes grow.

As much as she longed for reconciliation, Cordelia couldn't face this conversation today. The *I told you so*s would finish her. And the mysterious envelope from the mailbox was burning a hole through her palm. "Eustace, this isn't a great time. If you just want to catch up, I can call you ba—"

"She died," Eustace interjected. "Aunt Augusta. She's dead."

Cordelia stabilized herself on the concrete. Her eyes crept

up the spotless brick of the house to the empty dormer window where the frightful woman had been, the curtains still parted conspicuously. She swallowed. This was *unexpected*.

"Cordelia?" Eustace asked after a moment. "Did you hear me?"

Molly came rushing out of the house with a pinched expression, waving her hands as she darted toward her.

"Uh, yeah," Cordelia said, eyes shifting to Molly's sack dress. She was really going to have to talk to her about smartening up her business attire. But then, remembering Allison's slinky pencil skirts, she thought better of it.

"Is that all you have to say?" Eustace pressed. "Our great-aunt, the matriarch of our estranged family—the one our mother disavowed with such vehemence we didn't even know they existed until I had that family-tree project—has finally passed into the hereafter, and *Uh, yeah* is your response?"

"Sorry." Cordelia pressed her lips together as Molly approached, a little out of breath.

"I think you'd better come inside," Molly said. "You need to see this for yourself."

She frowned, her head beginning to feel like Molly had pounded the *For Sale* sign directly into her brain.

"It's the bedroom," Molly whispered loudly.

Cordelia placed a finger over the speaker of her phone. "I just need a minute."

"Okay," the girl said, sheepish, but then she continued to stand there wringing her hands with worry.

"Fine," Cordelia snapped, immediately contrite. She softened the edge in her tone. "After you."

"Cordelia? Are you still there?" her sister beckoned on the other end of the line.

"Yes, sorry," she said as she followed the assistant into her house. "There's just a lot happening right now."

"We haven't spoken in five years," Eustace said quietly.

Cordelia sighed, her guilt and shame multiplying like weeds in cow shit. "I know."

She tried to focus on what her sister was telling her. Eustace wasn't exaggerating. They really had thought themselves a genetic island of three for half their childhood. Once the existence of their living relatives came out, it seemed preposterous that she'd never considered them before. But Maggie had been so resolutely mum on the subject, it had never occurred to Cordelia to ask until her sister's project. Even then, their mother had precious little to say about the shadowy aunt and uncle living in Connecticut, no matter how they plied her for information. And it was clear from her crisp tone and shifting eyes that she'd buried her feelings along with the details of their extended family. Whoever they were, Maggie had little use for them and even less regard. And considering their already reduced station, that didn't paint a pretty picture of where they'd come from.

"Okay, Aunt Augusta is gone. Do we need to arrange a burial?" It was the least they could do for their last known living relative, but Cordelia wasn't exactly flush after John's stunts. She was teetering on destitution. She worried her sister would detect the tightness in her voice.

"Not exactly," Eustace said.

She dropped her purse on the entry table beside the irises and slipped off her muddy slingbacks, leaving them on the Italian tile floor, padding down the long hall to the master bedroom into which Molly had disappeared. "Eustace, please. Don't be cryptic. Just tell me what you need."

After a moment, her sister said, "There was a will."

Cordelia stopped just shy of the bedroom and spun around to lean against the wall. For a split second, hope dared to bloom in her heart, until she remembered the sour expression their mother wore whenever they mentioned their Connecticut family. Over the countless occasions they'd needed money growing up, she'd made it abundantly clear they wouldn't find it there.

She watched as the movers carried her pearl chesterfield sofa out the front doors, hailing a silent good-bye. The furniture would be listed online to pay her mounting hotel bill.

"What'd they leave us? The family collection of salt and pepper shakers?" She knew it was wrong to mock the dead, but under the circumstances, she couldn't keep the sarcasm from her voice.

"They left us the house," Eustace told her. "Augusta's attorney contacted me as the eldest."

"The ancestral seat, huh?" Cordelia wanted to take it seriously, but judging by how quickly her mother had fled Connecticut when she came of age, she doubted it was a palatial estate Maggie Bone had left in her wake. Still, property had a nifty way of appreciating, and Connecticut was expensive. Even a backwater hut would buy her some time, maybe allow her to reinstate the loan on the house until she could secure a buyer or get the worst of the payday lenders off her back. Perhaps their estranged family would turn out to be a godsend after all. A tiny sliver of light streamed down on her in the darkened hallway.

"More or less," Eustace said.

Molly tapped her boss's shoulder like a bird pecking at seed. Cordelia put up a finger to hold her off a moment longer. "I'll get a contact for someone in one of the Connecticut offices and have them pull us some comps. We can decide on the list price together if you want, but we can have it on the market in a matter of days if we stick to an *as-is* sale—"

"No." Eustace sighed.

"What do you mean *no*?" It was a word Cordelia had never gotten used to hearing, even from her older sister. Which was another reason she excelled in real estate and struggled in personal relationships.

"I mean, we can't do it that way," Eustace said calmly.

Cordelia rubbed at her throbbing temples, trying to swallow her desperation. "Says who?"

"Aunt Augusta, apparently."

Her headache was mushrooming, and a faint but sickening smell was just beginning to pierce her awareness. She pinched the bridge of her nose. "I don't understand."

"It's all in the will," Eustace told her. "In order to receive our inheritance, we have to go there. Also, to bury Aunt Augusta in the family plot or whatever."

"Go where? Connecticut?" Cordelia was aware her voice had become shrill in that way John had so often complained about. Impromptu out-of-state vacations were not exactly factored into her budget or her schedule. She tried counting to six as she breathed in through her nose.

"To Bone Hill," Eustace replied, beginning to sound a touch exasperated.

"Where or what is *Bone Hill*?" Cordelia asked, feeling pressed between Molly's heightening panic at her back and her sister's maddening nonsense at her front.

"The house. The crypt. All of it," Eustace answered.

Cordelia blinked. It wasn't very common for houses to have names unless they were of a certain caliber. But that couldn't be. "You mean, there's a cemetery *on* the property?"

"Apparently," Eustace told her.

The stream of light widened.

"Eustace," Cordelia whispered into the phone. "How big is this place?"

Molly, unable to contain herself any longer, grabbed Cordelia's arm and spun her around, tugging her through the bedroom door.

"I don't know," her sister answered. "But I guess we're going to find out."

The smell coated Cordelia's mouth and nose in a bitter tide, musty and sour. She looked up to see Molly pointing across the room where the king-sized bed had been pulled back from the wall.

"*This* is what I was trying to show you," Molly exclaimed, her face going all blotchy from the stress.

"I trust you," Cordelia said into the phone, unable to process what she was seeing. "You can tell me all about it when you get back."

"It has to be *both* of us," Eustace told her. "You're named."

"I didn't realize they knew our names." It was one thing for a random attorney to look them up as next of kin and quite another to learn their great-aunt had known of their existence and never reached out.

She approached the wall slowly, holding the phone away from her ear, the smell making her head pound. She could see a bit of gray where the zebrawood nightstand had been. Moving around the linen headboard, she realized what had been giving Molly panic hives. An impressive bloom of black mold was creeping its way up the Sheetrock undeterred, like something from another, darker world bleeding through, a stygian presence and a likely parting gift from the bathroom sinks on the other side.

This would cost her a small fortune to fix before she could list the house, and she wouldn't see a red cent from John.

She stared at the blackened wall. Budget and schedule be damned. She could not afford to lose whatever meager sum awaited her in the Nutmeg State. It would take every penny she could scrape together to remedy this and pull herself out of the pecuniary nosedive she was in. "Connecticut. Both of us. The sooner the better."

"Are you free this weekend?"

Cordelia smiled. "As a matter of fact, I am. I'll get a ticket tonight."

"It's settled then," Eustace said with a sigh.

"See you soon," Cordelia said. "And Eustace?"

"Yes?"

"It's good to hear your voice."

"Same," her sister responded before hanging up.

Cordelia could feel the pressure mounting as she put away the phone, that invisible weight that always preceded a sudden summer storm. Thunder bristled outside despite how sunny it was when they'd arrived. Inside her, a different kind of pressure was building, threatening to spill over into a full-blown attack of feelings.

She looked down at the blank envelope she was still clutching. Lifting the flap, she pulled out a single sheet of printer paper and unfolded it. The handwriting was oversized, almost juvenile, with crooked letters that ran off the edge in slanted lines.

To whom it concerns (this is you—John's wife),

Your husband borrowed a certain sum of money from one of my esteemed associates which he has yet to return. Seeing as we can't find the slippery bastard, it now falls on you to pay his debt. Nothing personal, you understand, just business. You have exactly thirty-one days to repay the loan in full or we'll take it out in years instead of dollars. How many of those you got left?

Don't call me; I'll call you.

—Busy Mazzello
P.S. No point in going to the cops. We own them too.

The envelope and paper slid from Cordelia's hand and wafted to the carpet. She'd heard of people taking business loans from the mob, but she never imagined John would stoop that low. Then again, he always had to have the best of everything—at any cost. Her phone began to buzz, the number *Unknown*. She put it to her ear. "Hello?"

"You get my letter?"

"Mr. Mazzello, I presume?"

"Call me Busy," he replied.

"You realize I have nothing to do with my husband's loans? He's left a string of debt broader than this state in his wake. How am I supposed to repay this?"

"With all due respect, miss, that sounds like a *you* problem."

Cordelia wanted to scream. "Why don't you go after him, huh? Take it out of *his* years?"

The line was quiet for a moment before Busy Mazzello responded, "You're closer."

Cordelia's mouth hinged open like a broken doll's. She felt like she was trapped in a bad eighties movie.

"Thirty-one days," he reiterated. "Don't find me; I'll find you."

Cordelia swallowed. "Wait! You haven't even told me how much."

"Fifty thousand" came the reply, and then the click of a dead line.

She sank to the floor, eyes tracing over the mildewed blotch like it was a giant Rorschach test. She pulled a small prescription bottle out of her purse and swallowed one of the pills dry, grateful that she would get some relief from the headache at least. The way the pattern of the mold fitted itself precisely to the width of their headboard seemed like an omen she'd failed to heed. As if the house itself had been trying to tell her what a liar John was. She wanted to pretend she saw something optimistic in it, like a butterfly or a maple leaf, but as the pain in her head radiated down the back of her skull, Cordelia had to be brutally honest with herself.

She saw nothing but ruin before her.

Ruin . . . and death.

CHAPTER TWO

THE HOUSE

DISTANCE SHOULD HAVE made Cordelia feel better, but every mile only made her feel worse. She was no longer the "closer" one, and she didn't know if or when John's mob contact would realize she left the state or how he might react. It shouldn't matter; he'd given her thirty-one days to come up with the money. How and where she spent that time, what she did to get it, should be of little concern to a man who liked to go by *Busy.* But she didn't ask permission first.

Still, if all went as planned, she should be back home in Texas with a suitcase full of cash inside of a week. All they had to do was bury the old lady, sign a few papers, and get the house listed. At the right price, it would sell itself practically overnight. She just hoped it would be enough. John may have been the one who doused her life in kerosene and struck a match, but it was still *her* life, shambles and all, and she wanted to live the rest of it.

Cordelia wheeled her bag through the throngs of milling people in the Hartford airport until she spotted her sister in the distance. But as Eustace came into focus, the fuzzy borders of her silhouette shrinking against the wall of glass doors, she cycled through a series of emotions, from uncertainty to recognition to concern. Her sister was *much* thinner than when she'd last seen her. On another woman, it might not be alarming, but Eustace lived a kind of fullness other women openly *tsk*ed and secretly envied. She usually radiated health, but she wasn't radiating now.

Cordelia wrapped her arms around Eustace in a hug, certain her shoulders had not been that bony before, and pulled back. "Have you lost weight?"

Eustace's smile faltered. "Five years and that's what you want to lead with?"

She softened. "No, of course not. You're beautiful as ever." She tugged at a strand of her sister's graying curls. "I've missed you," she admitted.

"Likewise," Eustace said.

But Cordelia couldn't shake her concern. The wrinkles around Eustace's eyes had deepened, and her hair didn't glow with the luster she recollected. Perhaps she'd built her sister up in her mind into an idol. Perhaps that's what family members did when they became alienated from each other. Perhaps if she'd made a greater effort, this reunion wouldn't have been such a shock.

"They sent a car," Eustace told her, abruptly switching topics. "The attorney's office."

Cordelia raised an eyebrow. "What kind of car?"

Eustace shrugged. "Let's go see."

She felt unusually suspicious of this gesture, though she couldn't pinpoint why. A strange buzz was building at the base of her spine, an electric tingle she couldn't identify. Cordelia pressed her lips together, swallowing her inexplicable misgivings as she followed her sister outside. She would have to trust Eustace's superior people skills. Maybe if she had before, she wouldn't be wading through a minefield of debt and divorce right now.

At the curb, they spotted a boxy Mercedes sedan in charcoal gray, a relic of bygone decades with hubcaps painted to match and unforgiving lines. The pomegranate interior glistened through the windows like raw organ meat. The combination reminded Cordelia of something rescued from a fire, and the buzz in her spine spiked at the car's hearse-like appearance.

Beside it waited a tall, thin man looking uneasy with his post. Young, with a pasty complexion, he had a weak chin and a shock of white-blond hair, as if he hadn't been allowed to see the sun in years. Sharp shoulders and arms like pool noodles made the blazer he wore look painfully misshapen. Something about him left Cordelia unsettled. He wasn't exactly threatening, but he did little to instill confidence. His absurd height and general lack of color might have been attractive on someone else, but he carried them so uncomfortably she found herself wondering if he was ill.

Seeing them, he opened the trunk and reached for their bags without a word, as if he'd known what to expect.

"*This* is it?" Cordelia asked.

"Looks like it," Eustace said, handing the young man her duffel and a second weekender bag.

Cordelia left her carry-on for the driver. She opened the rear door and leaned down to peer inside the car, searching for anything that might explain the wave of apprehension she was feeling. Both the exterior and the interior of the Mercedes were immaculate, though dated. Chrome accents along the body were polished to a high shine. Inside, the lurid, stitched-leather seating had seen many years, but it was supple and conditioned. The car itself looked to be in good shape, if a little macabre in its taste. And even if it weren't, she could hardly decline. One quick flash of Busy Mazzello's handwriting reminded her of what she stood to lose if she didn't get in—*I'll find you.* She shuddered convulsively.

"Did you lose a contact or are you gonna take a seat?" Eustace asked from behind.

Cordelia shot her a look and slid inside. She preferred not to ride shotgun to the silent, skinny kid who had yet to introduce himself. Eustace slid in beside her.

The drive into the hills was a couple of hours. They tried out some small talk in the beginning. Eustace asked after John, and Cordelia deflected by giving a noncommittal sound and asking about Eustace's business. Legitimizing cannabis was harder than most would believe, cutthroat and expensive. She'd never understood the pull to the industry, but Eustace had a way with plants. And pets. She was always growing or nursing something when they were kids, forever dragging in one stray or another—a puppy with mange, a cat bleeding from its nose, a geranium covered in aphids—only for their mother to immediately turn it out. Even Cordelia found Maggie's rebuttals cruel.

It had been the three of them against the world until she and Eustace went their separate ways geographically—Cordelia settling for Dallas, Eustace "finding herself" in Colorado, Maggie splitting the difference in Oklahoma.

But her sister only responded with a vague "You know how that goes."

They quickly waned to an unsettled silence after that, staring out their respective windows, drinking in the green countryside. It was uncomfortable having a personal conversation with a stranger listening in, and they'd left too many words unsaid for too long.

The young man eventually gave them his name—Arkin. It was as weird a name as Cordelia had ever heard, but then again, she married a *John*.

Curious about the woman who'd left her whole world to two great-nieces she never met, she cleared her throat and leaned forward. "Were you acquainted with our aunt?"

"Yes, ma'am," he replied, not meeting her eyes in the rearview mirror.

She tapped Eustace on the knee. "What was she like?" She imagined one wild rendition after another of her mother's aunt— recluse, hoarder, drunk.

Arkin swallowed audibly. "Imposing," he said with no further explanation.

Cordelia looked at Eustace with wide eyes.

"She was tall then?" Cordelia assumed. Maggie had been a hearty five foot eight, and Eustace was pushing five foot nine, but Cordelia had never made it much past five foot six.

"Not particularly," he said.

This time, it was Eustace's eyes that widened. "Can I ask . . . I mean, how exactly did she die?" she pressed.

Beside her, Cordelia sighed.

It wasn't so unusual a request. She was their relative, after all; it could affect their medical history. For her own part, Cordelia wondered about the headaches she'd seemingly inherited. What caused them exactly? Who had Maggie gotten them from? Did their aunt succumb to them at last like she had? How, then, had she managed to live so much longer? And most important, how could Cordelia circumvent the same mortal fate? She'd raised questions like these with more than one doctor over the years, only to find their answers bleak and vague. The truth was, like her mother before her, Cordelia fell into one of those maddening cracks the medical community preferred to ignore rather than admit the truth—they simply did not know.

But Eustace wasn't worried about blood pressure or hardening arteries or even the headaches their mother suffered. She and Cordelia had graver concerns since losing Maggie.

The medical examiner called it a brain aneurysm, but the sisters knew the headaches had finally killed her. They might have left it at that except for one strange detail. How did the woman on the phone phrase it? *A minor mutilation.*

When they'd found her in a back parking lot next to her car, someone had taken a patch of their mother's skin. Carved away the flesh between her breasts where her tattoo sat like a trophy. It was a bizarre, rudimentary inking of a leafless tree with three branches. Cordelia had never been sure what it meant, and Maggie refused to talk about it. What interest would anyone have in removing it? Did they find her dead and decide to keep a piece, or had the attack brought on the bleed in her brain?

These were questions the county would never answer—Maggie Bone was inconsequential to anyone except her girls. Police could only say there was no evidence of a struggle.

Cordelia had locked her suspicions about what happened to their mother inside with the all the other things she couldn't explain. She was riddled with peculiarities. It almost seemed fitting that even her death was a mystery. Like her past, her taste in men, her hatred for music. Maggie Bone was a puzzle Cordelia grew tired of trying to solve. Until she began having the headaches herself.

But Eustace could never let it go.

Arkin locked his gaze on the road, stiffening in his seat. "She was old," he said, as if time itself were fatal.

"Were there any parts missing?" Eustace asked bitterly.

Arkin's eyes shot to hers in the rearview mirror. "Pardon?"

"Nothing," Cordelia told him, glaring at her sister.

He abruptly turned the radio on. The heady, metallic twang of a Bruce Springsteen hit poured into the cabin.

Cordelia leaned back in her seat, accepting that the Q&A was over. But she could only stand it a few minutes. "Can you turn that off?" she asked irritably. "Please. No music."

"Like mother, like daughter," Eustace muttered.

A distaste for music was admittedly odd. It was like having a distaste for chocolate or puppies. But that was Maggie. She hated any kind of music and any kind of animal, regardless how benign. She never did yard work, detested cooking, and refused to enter cemeteries. She wasn't religious—never even spoke of God—but she thought gambling was a cardinal sin. And she loved bad men. Real drifter types. Men with no ties who would vanish as quickly as they appeared. Not entirely unlike herself.

Cordelia's dislike of music was acquired. The result of having its innumerable mystifying evils pounded into her throughout her childhood. When she was very young, she used to hear strange melodies in her head. They weren't like normal songs, and she never put words to them. She tried to hum a few, but once Maggie caught her she was too afraid to do it again. They weren't even allowed to sing "Happy Birthday" growing up. For Cordelia, the programming had stuck. Eustace however, got right over it while briefly sleeping with the bassist in a well-known rock band.

Quiet fell over them again. Cordelia fixed her eyes on the sweeping terrain outside and tried to imagine telling her sister about John over dinner. She felt strangely lulled by the drive, as if with every mile a vise loosened its grip around her heart. The headache nestling inside her since she'd gotten up that morning, ominous and raw, was miraculously fading against the backdrop of forested hills, farmland, and a clear New England sky. Even the uncertainty she'd felt at the airport had settled from her spine into her hips as a dull restlessness, the result of too many hours sitting in one position.

Cordelia felt a growing eagerness, as if she were going to meet a beloved friend she hadn't seen in a very long time. The feeling seemed misplaced inside her, bouncing around unattached and unfounded.

At some point, Arkin turned off the interstate onto a two-lane road that wound through the rash of trees like an unspooled ribbon. Cloaked in deep green foliage, it seemed a far cry from the usual New England scenery of rolling pastures and autumn colors, sailboats and rocky coastlines. Cordelia had never been

stirred by all that early Americana and Puritan history, the primitive aesthetic—bushels of apples and butter churns—but this
plucked at her heart like a lute even as it set her teeth to grinding.
Shadows were the defining characteristic here, stretching from
tree to tree like jagged holes ripped in the fabric of the landscape, blackening the road ahead and making it hard to discern.
Boughs dripped over the pavement like withered arms, some so
low she thought they'd surely scrape the roof right off the sedan.
And mist seeped from the ground, lingering between twisted
roots and coursing over the road in cloudy streams.

She caught herself wishing she'd paid better attention to the
drive. It would be helpful to know how to retrace their steps out
of here. But she supposed that's what Google Maps was for. And
Arkin, should they need him.

It was along this lonely, winding stretch of pavement that she
first began to hear it—a kind of distant song, like white noise
building in the back of her mind. She thought maybe a stiff wind
had set the leaves of the trees rustling against one another, but
the branches outside her window were still, and Eustace didn't
seem to notice anything. Though she'd grown used to the whispers over the years, this was different. More like a chorus rising
that she couldn't quite make out. She leaned toward the glass of
her window and closed her eyes, losing herself in the pull of it
until Arkin turned the radio back on, flipping to an AM talk station, and the chatter of broadcasters drowned it out.

At an indefinable signal, the Mercedes began to slow and
turned onto a crushed-pebble drive between a pair of wildly
overgrown bridal wreath shrubs spewing clusters of white
blooms. Cordelia felt her heart rate pick up, and her knees began
to bounce.

They wound their way up the snaking drive, the landscape
taking a decided turn toward the cultivated, with dogwood trees
set into green inlets among crab apples and hawthorns, while

maples, birch, and oaks fought for their patch of sky. More of the bridal wreaths could be seen, along with rhododendron, aster, and burning bush in its dull summer green. But everything had an untamed air, as if the gardener had vacated decades ago.

Cordelia was eyeballing what she thought might be an enormous lilac out of bloom when Eustace ribbed her with an elbow. She turned to look out her sister's window, the drive having curved sharply to the left, where the uppermost peaks of a black-shingled roof crowned in ornamental iron cresting were rising from the foliage like a Gothic castle.

"Holy Mother of Christ," Cordelia muttered as the car broke into the sun and continued around a wall of tightly packed Japanese cedars, allowing the house to finally come into view. A coil of chills broke across her skin, dimpling it in goose bumps and causing every hair on her body to stand at attention.

"You're drooling on me," Eustace complained, but Cordelia ignored her. She couldn't take her eyes off the structure. Three imposing stories stacked upon one another in a frenzy of eaves and turrets, scrollwork and dormers. A combination of dark-red brick, graying stone, and chocolate-painted siding, the house sprouted from the gardens around it like a wild briar, tangled and untamed, refusing to come to heel. Darkened windows dozed under sinister spires; Gothic arches and angles crossed like hexes. A jewelry box of confidences, it nestled among the spread of jade and tourmaline greens like a sparkling, gingerbread topaz—a giant, sleeping bat tucked into itself, just waiting for night to fall. A dominating tower with a fourth-story set of windows stared down at them in distaste, and Cordelia felt suddenly underdressed. As if she should have come in cocktail attire, or a vintage gown with jet beads and high collar.

It was a true Victorian manor. But *Victorian* felt like an understatement in this case.

Arkin brought the car to a stop before the wide front porch that wrapped around one turreted corner like a sash made of spindles. Cordelia leaned back and met her sister's eyes. Eustace whistled long and low as Cordelia opened her door and climbed out. She moved around the car so that nothing would be between her and the house, looking up to where the tower pierced the sun, bleeding golden light.

Her heart fumbled its rhythm in her chest. She waited for the whisper to come, wondering—almost fearing—what the house would have to say, but it was mute as it loomed over her. She found it hard to imagine her mother growing up here. Even harder that she had kept it a secret.

"I trust you had a pleasant drive," a smooth, deep voice spoke from the porch.

Cordelia dropped her eyes to a man with silver hair and a dark suit who stood waiting between two columns at the top of the porch stairs.

"Welcome to Bone Hill," he said cordially.

Her sister rushed past her with an outstretched hand. "You must be Mr. Togers," she greeted, clasping his hand and giving it a hearty shake.

"Bennett, please," he replied. "And you are Eustace Bone?"

"The one and only," she declared with her usual flair.

Cordelia could not match her sister's enthusiastic introduction, because she could scarcely tear her eyes from the house.

"And you must be Cordelia," Bennett said.

She forced herself up the steps. Bennett looked to be somewhere in his late sixties or seventies. This close, she could see that his pewter hair was thinning on top, revealing a liver-spotted scalp, and that his cheeks had a slight wobble where they'd fallen over the decades, sinking in the middle to dark pits. His eyes sat over them proudly, though, a steely glint shining in them like a reptile's. He reminded her of a cross between a butler in an old movie and a moray eel. She wasn't sure if he would kiss her hand or bite it. "I'm sorry. This is all just a bit surprising."

"I take it Magdalena never disclosed the family's position to you?" he replied with an uncanny familiarity, as if he didn't simply know *of* their mother, but knew her personally.

It had been ages since Cordelia had heard her mother referred to that way. She'd always insisted on *Maggie*. "No," Cordelia said, squaring her shoulders. "Not exactly."

"Not at all," Eustace clarified.

"Well, then we have much to discuss," Bennett told them. "Unfortunately, I cannot stay to go over it all with you just now. But I will hand over the main key and encourage you to make yourselves at home. The house dates back to the Victorian era, fashioned in the Gothic Revival style. The architect remains a mystery, but some say it may be the famous Alexander Jackson Davis. At any rate, I'm sure you'll find it in working order, if not entirely up-to-date. And, hopefully, quite comfortable."

"Wait," Cordelia interrupted. "You're leaving?"

Bennett smiled graciously. "I assure you I will be back in the morning, and we can discuss whatever questions or concerns you have then. In the meantime, I wish you a most agreeable evening."

At that, he trotted down the steps between them, pausing only to place a large, brass skeleton key in Eustace's hand. At the bottom of the stairs, he stopped and turned. "Do watch out for the bats," he said merrily.

"Bats?" Cordelia frowned. Was he serious?

"They're not dangerous," he insisted. "But they are protected. I'm afraid killing them is out of the question." With that he hopped into the back of the waiting car and rode away, with Arkin at the wheel.

Cordelia gawked at her sister. "Did that just happen?"

Eustace grinned back. "Shall we go in?"

She started for the front door, but Cordelia remained. "Wait," she said, craning her head to listen. "I need a moment."

"Suit yourself," Eustace told her as she turned and walked across the porch to the narrow doors that reached over eight feet to meet the beadboard ceiling.

Cordelia backed down the steps and glanced up. She looked past the places with peeling paint and cracks in the mortar, past the Virginia creeper trying to reclaim one corner of the house and the wavering quality of the old windows. Instead, she listened for the spirit of the place, for the whisper.

The house held its tongue, as if it did not trust this prodigal daughter from another world, another era. But the collective drone she'd felt in the car sounded again between her ears, wrapping itself around her skull, calling from some corner of the property she couldn't place. With effort, she pushed it aside and concentrated on the building before her, this grande dame of brickwork and lace.

And just as Cordelia had given up, Eustace opened the door. A heavy sigh escaped, as if the house had been holding its breath for too long. And with it, the first whisper, like the susurrus of a forgotten woman.

Eustace turned back to look at her, and Cordelia grinned. She grabbed her sister's open hand.

Together, they took their first steps inside.

CHAPTER THREE

THE TOWER

IT WAS LIKE standing inside a secret. From the outside, there was the distinct sense of *more*. Inside, just how much became gallingly evident. Cordelia felt like a violation and a joke at the same time. The elaborate tiles of the vestibule seemed to be mocking her with their pattern, and in the same breath, something she was never supposed to see had been laid bare, cracked open like a banned book, filling her with forbidden words. She couldn't look away.

She lifted her chin, inhaling the house into her. She could smell antique roses—a strong floral scent underscored by peppery, lemony notes. The second she stepped out of the confines of the vestibule, it hit her with such force she sneezed.

"Figures," Eustace said dryly. "We *would* be allergic to money."

Cordelia ignored her and let her eyes wander around the grand stair hall until they began to dry out and she had to remind herself to blink. An ornate hall tree with gargoyles carved into it towered to her left, thick with varnish. A pair of balloon armchairs with emerald velvet hoods sat like empty thrones just ahead. She imagined her and her sister in them as girls, how they might have whispered back and forth to each other from inside their malachite caves. It made her heart thump with longing and betrayal—what they might have known versus what they had. Even the black-and-tan Persian carpet beneath them upset her, too soft and delicate to be real. And yet, it all collided in a minatory impression, a burst of wicked energy just below the surface, like spiders hiding under the rug.

She searched for a flower arrangement to explain the smell, or even a dish of potpourri, but saw none. It was as if the fragrance were coming from the house itself, oiled into the parquet floors at her feet.

"Do you smell that?" she asked Eustace. "Like those old garden roses that came up under our window in the Veranda house?" They called the house so not because it had a veranda, but because it was situated on Veranda Street, which wasn't nearly so lovely as it sounded. "Those dark ones with the squishy centers."

Maggie had tried to dig the roses up. When that didn't work, she hacked them down to the ground. But they kept coming back. She finally just decided to move.

Her sister fingered the anaglypta wallpaper that covered half the wall in a raised pattern, painted so dark it was almost black. The rest of the walls were papered in a rich green floral, with creeping vines and flowers and hidden woodland animals.

"Smells like bullshit to me," she said bitterly, staring up at the massive mahogany door frame to their left, rounding overhead where it was topped with the carving of a woman's face, wrapped in heavy braids and crowned with flowers. "Maybe you smell *her.*"

Cordelia stood beside her sister. Something in the carved expression tugged at her, as if it were capturing a moment in time and wasn't just a generic rendition. She let her eyes fall through to the parlor, every inch covered in crimson velvet or brocade, like it had been hosed in blood. Even the mirror over the black marble fireplace had its own set of scarlet valances trimmed in mauve tassels. It made her wonder what she might see in the reflection if she stood before it.

Heavy furniture grouped in every corner—not a leg was left unturned or a cushion untufted, as if a swarm of grandmothers had been employed in the decorating. She was no expert in antiques, but even Cordelia could point out the spoon-back chairs and the elegant settee in silk moiré, the Regency secretary and the gothic grandfather clock—like something from Dracula's castle. An ornate pump organ stood in a far corner, lonely and soulless, just waiting for someone to pound out the *Danse Macabre*. The combined assets in this room alone were well above her skill for mental calculation.

Passing under the doorway, she felt cold air stir against her skin as the room greeted her like an autumn wind. She wandered around, taking in the fringe and needlepoint, the flocked paper, the jeweled Tiffany glass. It was all so exquisite, and yet it turned her stomach like a child sick on too many sweets. The iron console behind the settee held the curious body of a stuffed fisher-cat, with near-black fur, long torso, and fierce head. It glared at her with glassy, enigmatic eyes, dead but not abandoned, something still flickering there. At a Chinese lacquered table, she dared herself to open a drawer, fearful of what might crawl out. It revealed a deck of well-worn playing cards, fussy with filigree. Lifting them, she found that little smiling skulls had been wrought into the design, but then she blinked, uncertain, and they seemed to disappear, suggesting an instant of face pareidolia.

She was about to drop the cards back inside, not wanting to think about the games played on them, things gambled away, when she noticed it lying there. It must have been beneath the cards when she picked them up. It shone dully against the glossy black wood, crusted with age, like a piece of old candy corn. *A human tooth*. Revulsion pulsed through Cordelia alongside inexplicable curiosity, pulling her toward it like a burning rope. The fingers of her free hand crept over the lip of the drawer, stretching, when the tooth began to wobble, clicking against the bottom like a Mexican jumping bean. Her senses flooded back to her, and she threw the cards down, slamming the drawer shut.

Looking up, she saw a tarnished silver frame with an image of a young girl, straight red hair hanging limp, barefoot in a simple cotton sundress. A waif trapped in time. Cordelia picked up the frame. She recognized her mother's plain face and smattering of freckles, perched on the banister of the front porch like an imp from the nearby forest, more creature than girl, a blitheness Cordelia had never known in her beguiling smile.

She walked out of the parlor and passed the photo to her sister before striding to the opposite doorway, making a silent promise not to open any more drawers. This room was clearly a library, the masculine counterpart to the parlor's feminine mystique, replete with English paneling and built-in cases crammed with thousands of leather-bound volumes, some so old their spines were eaten away at the edges, the gilded or embossed lettering nearly impossible to read. The far corner opened into a turret room, with window seats and lace panels to soften the light. Something about the shape reminded Cordelia of a cell. It felt one great iron door away from holding her hostage.

She stepped inside and danced her fingers over the nearest spine—Lord Byron—which looked like it could be a first edition. Beside him rested William Blake, Thomas Gray, Robert Frost—a cemetery of poetry. Switching on a double-globe lamp, she marveled at the hand-painted vines and small birds in flight. But they were rendered in violet, highlighted in brown and sweeps of gold, so that even the light was gloomy. A taxidermic owl with pointed, ear-like feathers and great yellow eyes stared her down. A pair of worn-leather sofas anchored the space yet looked too stiff to be comfortable. The back wall revealed a gentleman's study through a broad set of pocket doors, with a bust of Homer in one corner and a rosewood desk large enough to be an operating table.

But it was the man's portrait hanging behind the imposing desk that called to her—a somber palette of cracking oils, the workmanship exquisite. Too bad she couldn't say the same for the model. His heavy brows and striking scowl did nothing to soften the lean and angular features of his face. Features she recognized but couldn't place, like an actor in a play she'd tried hard to forget. Looking closer, she saw a silver plaque tacked to the bottom engraved with the name *Erazmus Bone*. His dark mop of hair reminded her of Eustace, turbulent and night-colored, but there was nothing of her mother's delicate beauty in his face, or her sister's radiance. His eyes were a storm—like her own in hue—and they made her uneasy. She felt like a child caught out while misbehaving. Turning, she found her sister standing in the doorway, the picture of their mother hanging limply in her hand.

"We'll need to get an appraisal," Cordelia said matter-of-factly, though her voice gave a little. She cleared her throat. "It might be best to contact an auction house. This is a lot of valuable stuff. We can't exactly drag it out and host a yard sale."

Eustace's face was a mask of mixed emotion. "Mom sure has some explaining to do," she said, passing the frame back to Cordelia and crossing her arms.

Cordelia followed her back into the stair hall. "Why would she hide all this? From us? We struggled all those years, and *this* was here the whole time."

Eustace shrugged. "Why did Mom do most of the things she did? Like take up with losers who stole our furniture?"

"Oh God," Cordelia said, recalling. "Remember the one who set fire to the neighbor's garage?"

"How could I forget?" Eustace snarled. "We were evicted

before the fire engine pulled away. She didn't even break up with the bastard."

"That's how we ended up at the Veranda house," Cordelia remembered. "Eventually."

She didn't mention the nights in between, tucked under the sprawling branches of a red oak tree, cold and sleepy, until Maggie found a job at a nearby motel and shuffled the girls between vacant rooms for the next three months, her arsonist boyfriend crashing whenever she'd let him. When they moved into the Veranda house, he moved right in with them. But when Maggie left over the roses, he stayed behind. The place was paid up for the month, after all.

Unlike Cordelia, Maggie never mastered exploiting the *knack*. She had her own uncanny ability to turn up in the right place at the right time, like when she wandered into the motel lobby to inquire about a room just as the previous desk clerk was storming out. The owner took one look at Maggie's open, pretty face and honest smile and asked if she wanted a job. But she never really worked it to her advantage. She just took it for granted when things fell into her lap. Looking around, Cordelia wondered if her mother had never formulated a plan for her life because before leaving Connecticut, it was unthinkable that she would need one.

"She could never just *settle*," Eustace griped. "Like she was afraid to put roots down anywhere."

"Even here," Cordelia whispered. That all this wasn't enough to hold Maggie Bone still seemed inconceivable. And what did she trade it for? A string of hopeless relationships, dead-end jobs, and a couple of tagalong girls.

A slow chill began to creep up Cordelia's arms, wrapping around her throat. *Unless . . .* she thought, recalling the spectacular grimace on the portrait behind the desk. Unless there was a reason Maggie left Bone Hill behind, a reason she never stayed in one place too long, a reason she kept this secret. She might have been a restless enigma of a woman, but she was a caring mother. If she didn't bring her girls here, maybe she didn't think it was safe.

Before Cordelia could voice her thoughts, a low creak sounded overhead where the stairwell wrapped around and met the second story. She started, and the frame she was holding slipped from her fingers, crashing to the floor, shattering the glass. "Who was that?"

"It's an old house. They make noise," Eustace said with a shrug, bending to pick up the picture frame.

Cordelia crouched beside her as Eustace turned it over, pulling their mother's photograph from the jagged glass. "I'm sorry I dropped Mom."

"I'm not. She deserves it." Eustace stood back up with the photo in one hand and the frame in the other, but another picture fell out, landing at Cordelia's feet.

Cordelia reached for it, lifting it slowly as she stood. It was black and white with that soft, yellowed quality vintage photographs often have, taken outside when the light was low. Three ominous figures circled a young woman impossibly suspended between them. Her arms and legs dangled off the ground, antlers grasped in her hanging fingers, the white skirting of her dress draping down. Her head hung back, throat exposed, open eyes staring into the camera. Black powder rimmed them in thick smudges, drawing violent slashes across her face, marking a symbol on her forehead where her fiery hair fell away. But her irises were gone, the eyes rolled so far back only the whites were showing. Her mouth twisted open in an ecstatic cry.

"Get a load of her," Eustace said, looking over Cordelia's shoulder. "Who is that?"

Cordelia gaped, unable to process what she was seeing. She

turned the picture over. A hasty inscription in black ink was scrawled across the back. *The Bone Witches, 1959.*

The picture began to tremble in Cordelia's hand. She turned to look at Eustace, who stepped away.

"I had a friend who was Wiccan once," Eustace said. "She used to carry crystals in her bra and burn a lot of incense." She took another step back, glancing around the stair hall, taking in its dark furnishings with new eyes. "But she never did shit like that."

"Maybe they meant it metaphorically," Cordelia suggested weakly.

"Does that look metaphorical to you?"

Above them, the same low creak sounded again, longer this time.

Eustace bolted for the majestic staircase, pausing only a moment at the curling newel post topped with a bronze woman riding an owl, her left arm clutching the base of a giant glass torch that rose above her—a lamp.

"Is someone here?" she called as she started up the first flight, craning to look higher. When no one responded, she glanced back at Cordelia and pointed, indicating she was going to check the second story, before rounding the corner and disappearing.

Cordelia stood there trying to shake the feeling that she wasn't alone in the hall, the haunting picture still hanging from her hand. Remembering it, she dropped it suddenly, backing away from where it landed among the broken bits of glass. That's when she noticed the inlay at her feet, an eight-pointed star in pale wood with a dark outline and bands of dark wood between each spoke. Everything seemed to radiate out from its center like it was the navel of the house.

Cordelia walked slowly around it. She'd seen medallions in floors before. Like grained compasses, they lent a sense of direction and order as much as they did flourish. But something about this one, like so many of the details in this house, wasn't quite right. She wondered where each spoke would lead if she dared to follow them but quickly decided she'd rather not know. If she stared long enough, she feared the design might suck her into its heart and hold her there, the way a spider sticks a fly in its web, every desperate move to escape only tangling it further.

The sound of footsteps overhead indicated someone was making their way to the third story. Had Eustace decided to climb higher? She looked up and realized she could see all the way into the tower, where an ever-narrowing staircase rose to a fourth, foreboding platform.

"Is that you?" she called up to her sister, but got no reply. "Eustace! Is that you on the stairs?" she tried again.

Cordelia took a step back and peered into the musty shadows of that highest reach, a nest for wayward corvids. She thought she could dimly make out a figure—just an arm really, white and graceful, the trailing hem of a long skirt—ascending along the railing. What did they call those things? A widow's watch. The name caused her to recoil. There was a reason for names like that, and it was never good. She imagined the tower as a forsaken woman, the windows her many eyes peering out, waiting for some lover's return. Eustace had to be crazy to go up there. Who knew if those boards were even stable? It's doubtful their aunt had climbed them in the last thirty years.

"Eustace! Don't go up there! It's not safe!" Cordelia yelled into the shadows, cupping her hands around her mouth.

"What are you shrieking about?" she heard her sister ask with irritation from the second floor as she appeared over the rail.

"I—I thought . . ." Cordelia tried to say when she saw a second figure lean over the railing much higher up. She could make out the slender form of a woman, the pale oval of her face, the shape of her hair tumbling down, the grip of her hand on the smooth mahogany. She raised a finger to ashen lips, bidding Cordelia stay quiet.

Cordelia's heart shrank, withering like a fig left out in the sun. The whispers she had learned to live with, even prize, using them to her advantage. But the things she'd seen were a different matter. In dark halls and spare closets, curling against the far corners of empty rooms, passing by open doorways. Those were harder to swallow.

Now all those breathless childhood moments came flooding back. The things she didn't understand that her mother refused to explain.

Close your eyes, Cordelia, her mother would say. *Don't look at them.*

But more important, *Never,* ever *speak to them.*

"Really, Cordy. I know that picture has you spooked, but the way you're acting, no one would know you do this for a living. It can't be the first old, vacant house you've been in. Anyway, this floor is clear. Must have been one of the bats," Eustace teased before stepping away.

Cordelia watched, rooted to the floor, as the woman opened her hideous mouth to speak. But no sound emerged. Her eyes burned with invisible fire as she glared down. Then she wrapped both hands around her throat and squeezed.

A feeling of cold dread washed over Cordelia, her own voice frozen in her throat, lodged like a block of ice. She saw the house with the blue shutters again, the one where the nightmares started, where the woman with the tangled black hair and the brain matter dripping down her shoulder, the off-white bra and panties strapped around her sagging flesh, wandered from room to room. And then the screech sounded outside, the little boy prone in the street, their mother's latest boyfriend shrieking that it wasn't his fault. She was five when they came to that house, five when they began to show themselves to her, five when her mother pressed her back against the rough siding of the shed—the one populated with rats and orb weavers and other things formed to frighten little girls—and told her the three rules she must never forget. Don't look at them. Don't speak to them. Don't sing for them.

Bad things will follow. They'll come for you, she'd threatened if Cordelia forgot, if she broke the rules even once. *They'll take you away.*

Cordelia's eyes had widened then, her fear running down the leg of her overalls to think the ghosts could separate her from her mother and sister, her only comfort in the world.

They'll drag you back to their hell, Cordelia Bone, and there won't be a damn thing I can do to stop them.

After that, whenever Maggie caught her daughter with that fixed, faraway look in her eyes, she would raise a finger to her lips in warning, and Cordelia would force herself to blink and look away before bolting for the nearest bathroom.

Now, without her mother there to stop it, Cordelia felt the house and all its fixtures, the world of Bone Hill, pressing in on her in a flood of horror. Unable to scream, she did the only thing she could.

She ran.

SOMETHING IN CORDELIA'S chest was collapsing, and she couldn't breathe. If Maggie had taught her anything, it was this—there were parts of herself that simply couldn't be trusted. Parts that would be her undoing if she ever looked them in the eye. Behind the shed that day, she'd promised her mother she would never break their rules. And it was a promise she intended to keep. John, for all his faults, had been a boon in that regard. He'd kept everything that didn't fit—inside and outside of her—at bay.

The last five years had been blissfully ordinary. Of course, she'd felt less and less herself with John. But then, wasn't that what she wanted? To be less Cordelia, less like her mother, less a Bone?

Her head hammered with sudden ferocity as she crashed through a door beneath the stairway into a dining room. There was a table long enough to seat fourteen and a chandelier dripping in crystals. An enormous fireplace with a mirrored mantel ran along one wall, while on another hung portraits of what she could only assume were her own family members.

She didn't pause to investigate. She circled the table and pushed through to the kitchen, complete with an enamel gas range checkered by more doors than she owned pots to cook in. A back exit caught her eye, and she bolted for it.

If she was seeing them again, seeing them *here,* then she knew why Maggie never wanted to come back to this place. This house was like the one with the blue shutters—a place of unrest. Here she would never be free of them, never safe from their clutches and the things inside her they could unleash. She'd kept her promise; she'd pretended not to notice when they staggered past, and she'd moved on as quickly as possible until she found somewhere blessedly vacant of them. Now she'd do what she had to to get Busy's "associate" his money, because her neck depended on it, but then she'd get the hell out of here. Because after all, one could only pretend for so long.

Cordelia had hoped the door she slammed through would lead outside. Instead, she found herself in an iron-and-glass solarium crowded with overgrown tropicals. Palms did their best to block out the light, raining over her like weeping giants, and everything was sticky with vapor as if she were trapped in a glass-and-iron lung. A moody pond brooded at the solarium's heart, spotted with lily pads bigger than dinner plates. She half expected that some kind of water-dwelling cryptid lived under its surface, a kelpie or lake monster. It was the kind of superfluous space only the Victorians could appreciate, and on a normal day, Cordelia might have found it enchanting. But there was nothing normal about this day *or* this house, and she was as revolted by the conservatory as she was pulled to it.

Something burned up and down her nerves. Something deeper, colder than a whisper. It drove her on. She didn't trust her own vision or voice, didn't trust the sounds licking at her ears. She didn't trust the plants crushing in around her, lolling like sick tongues, leering without eyes. Her feet tripped over the cobbled walkway as she slapped at fronds, unsure what waited behind each drooping, oversized leaf and curl of steamy mist, desperate for a way out.

She was just rounding an Elephant Ear palm, hand pressed anxiously against her head, when she slammed into something hard. Her eyes focused on a broad chest and two bulging arms that grabbed for her, gripping her shoulders like beastly paws.

Cordelia screamed.

The man released her, raising his hands in surrender. "Whoa. I was just trying to keep you from falling."

She flinched and shrunk back. He was the largest man she'd ever been confronted with. Taller than John by half a foot and rippling with muscle, hiding his face behind hanks of wild, black hair. But she couldn't miss the wide, sculpted brow or proud nose, the way his cheekbones bowed like hammered iron, sweeping down the planes of his face to a perfectly squared jaw. His eyes were dark, flashes of Baltic amber in them, and they hovered over her pitilessly. Like a man from an ancient windswept battlefield or the keep of some nightmarish castle, he seemed to hold the world up with his shoulders. Atlas unleashed. Thunder in a body.

"Who the fuck are you?" she demanded, a mix of fear and magnetism goading her. She was only aware of her tone a beat too late, but grateful her voice had returned.

"Gordon Jablonski," he told her, defensive. "I live here. I should be asking you that."

Cordelia felt her temper flare, a hot pulse under her skin, as the pain in her head spiked. She disliked being questioned in her own home, but nearly as soon as she registered the thought, a fresh wave of panic washed over her. Bone Hill was not home, these strange apparitions not her family.

Beneath the anger, a giddy hunger raged, the way she felt right before biting into a hundred-dollar steak. She crossed her arms and tried to steady her voice. "I'm Cordelia Bone—proprietor." It might have been the only time that having Bone as a last name truly served her.

"The niece," Gordon replied under his breath.

The way he said it made Cordelia feel judged, as if there were something distasteful in the way she handled the role. It stung with unexpected rejection. "Pardon?"

He ran an enormous hand across the back of his neck, his black T-shirt looking like it had been painted onto his formidable biceps, arm bulging with every movement in a way that made Cordelia's blood run fast.

She knew women were supposed to swoon over men like Gordon, but so much testosterone in one package usually made her uneasy. She had ideas about men like that, and yet, she couldn't ignore the long lashes framing his eyes or the fullness of his bottom lip, the way he looked a little lost in her presence, as if she, of all creatures, were able to disarm him.

He cut his brown eyes away from her and pulled a handkerchief from his back pocket. "I'm the groundskeeper," he said. "I guess Togers forgot to mention me."

Cordelia ran a weary hand over her brow, head still pounding. "He forgot to mention a lot of things."

Gordon's square shoulders rounded a bit; his lips pressed into a line. "I'm sorry if I frightened you. I was coming in to treat the pond."

She glanced back to where she'd left the low stone walls and brackish water.

"The algae gets out of control if I don't put some bacteria in it regularly."

"Charming." She resisted pulling a face, his *niece* comment making her want to bite back. "My sister and I are here to see to the arrangements," she explained. "For our aunt."

Gordon's head bobbed in understanding. "Sorry for your loss," he said awkwardly, as if they both knew better.

She smiled tightly, casting her eyes to the ground. "Yes, well. We weren't close." It was an understatement in the extreme, but she was growing tired of trying to explain the eccentricities of their family arrangement to others. "You probably know that already."

His flash of a smile told her he did but wasn't going to point it out.

It looked good nestled amid the strong contours of his cheekbones and the strip of dark hair on his chin, that smile, though it didn't last long. *Too* good. She was in no fit position to seduce a man, especially one who looked like he might run her over with his motorcycle as soon as make love to her. The very fact that she was thinking about it made her question her sanity and sent a jolt of desire and shame through her gut. That's when she began to notice the tattoos—a giant ram's skull wrapping his neck and the coils of a snake curled down one arm. On his other arm, a demonic woman with white eyes and black hair backlit by a pale moon and a flock of ravens.

Then she noticed other details like the silver chain he wore with a wolf's head pendant and *hell fire* inked across the knuckles of his hands. She resisted the urge to take a step away from him as she placed a hand at the base of her throat. Beneath her palm, she felt her chest grow hot and tight, adrenaline spreading under her skin. *Fear,* she told herself. But she knew that wasn't all it was.

"You looking for something?" he asked her. "You seemed in a hurry."

Cordelia cleared her throat. "I was just going to step outside. I needed some air."

"There's a door through the Australian tree ferns," he told her, throwing a thumb over his shoulder.

"Thank you." She started to brush past him, but his touch reignited all of her nerve endings like a high-voltage shock, causing her to pause and take a breath. "I think the place will go quickly," she said nervously to detract from her behavior. "It's what I do—real estate. We'll list it right."

She sincerely hoped it would, at least. She needed a windfall in the worst way. Molly had already texted to say the mold remediators were calling the bedroom wall *the tip of the iceberg.*

Just tell them to get started, Cordelia had texted back with no idea how she'd pay the invoice. She only knew she couldn't sell without that mold gone, and she couldn't save herself if she didn't sell both properties soon.

Gordon's eyes narrowed, his large brow lowering. He crossed his bulging arms. "*Go?*"

Cordelia froze. She had a habit of speaking out of turn when she was anxious. "Maybe I shouldn't have said. It's just that my sister and I plan to put this place on the market in a matter of days," she clarified. "Whoever wins it may have their own people. I will put a word in for you if you want to stay, but we can't force them to accept a tenant."

Gordon stared her down, and Cordelia began to get restless, knowing she'd put her foot in her mouth. They were alone in this solarium. Would Eustace even hear her if she screamed?

But it was more than his size that unnerved her. Those

cognac eyes and layers of gold sunbaked into his skin . . . He was the kind of guy John would point out with a disdainful laugh. He was also the kind of guy who could stomp John into the ground. Which, under the circumstances, endeared him to her. As much as she wanted to turn and run, she also wanted to lean in and breathe deep.

"I guess what I'm saying is I hope you have somewhere else lined up just in case," she continued.

"Somewhere else?" He looked so perplexed Cordelia thought she'd made a mistake. Maybe he lived in the nearby town.

"I'm sorry. You said you lived here. I assumed you meant on the property. That *is* relieving if you don't. I hate evicting people." She'd had enough experience being on the receiving end of that equation growing up. It made doing it especially distasteful to her.

"I do live here," Gordon corrected. "In the old carriage house. And I can't leave. Not yet."

Cordelia drew back and gave her head a little shake. The temperature in the room dropped by several degrees. She was making a terrific mess of this. "If there was a contract, perhaps we can buy you out of it once the house sells? I'm sure you can find another arrangement. My sister and I will happily give you a reference if that's what you're worried about."

Gordon turned away from her, hands on his hips as he breathed audibly. "Togers never said anything about selling." His voice was low, angry.

"Well, it's not really up to him, is it?"

He gave her a hard look. "You do realize this property has never belonged to anyone besides your family? The White Lady would be none too pleased."

"The White Lady?" Cordelia asked, confused, her mind filling with images of ghostly women—in her window, on the stairwell, floating in that disturbing photograph.

"Your aunt Augusta. I called her that on account of all the

white hair. Though she wore mostly black. She used to say we could share a closet," he said.

Cordelia's blood slowed as the woman looking down from her dormer window flashed across her memory. White hair. Black dress. No smile. *Imposing* was how the driver, Arkin, had put it.

Cordelia didn't like being filled in on her relatives' preferences by strangers, but she had her own mother to thank for that. It wasn't Gordon's fault. "To be fair, we haven't actually *told* Bennett yet. But we'll inform him tomorrow when he comes by. It's all very standard, this estate business. I'm sure Augusta would understand."

Gordon eyed her as if she'd just said the stupidest thing he'd ever heard. "I wouldn't count on that."

Cordelia frowned. She took a step back before turning to walk away. Her aunt would have to get in line behind all the other people, dead and otherwise, who wanted a piece of her these days. What concerned her more was the hulking groundskeeper and his bedroom eyes, the things he wasn't saying more than the things he was, the effect he had on her. Men like that didn't roll out of the womb covered in ink and defiance—they were damaged somewhere along the way. And Cordelia hated to admit just how much she yearned to know what his damage was. Considering how her marriage had turned out, she didn't have the best track record for picking winners. But at least when it came to John she could plead deception.

Gordon, on the other hand, wore his troubles like a surgeon general's warning, and Cordelia was certain he was going to be bad for her health.

CHAPTER FOUR

THE CRYPT

SOMEONE WAS SINGING. She could hear it behind her eyes like a memory, behind the pain that instead of lessening with the sky and space and sun seemed to grow. Stepping out of the cloistering atmosphere of the house was like taking the lid off a pot of rice. Everything boiled down to an essential simmer, except her headache. Cordelia tapped the bridge of her nose and listened, the song trailing to some distant point like a car driving away with the windows rolled down. She could just be imagining it. But after everything she'd already witnessed, she somehow doubted that. She headed into the garden.

She'd expected something formal with right angles—the remains of a hedgerow, a green and growing maze. Perhaps some topiaries. Instead, enormous shrubs and decorative trees mounded and clumped in a dizzying array of foliage. Fat, furry bees glided over brightly colored blooms, and weeds sprung up unhindered in a frenzy of life. Narrow paths spiraled through the chaos in no particular direction. Cordelia would start down one, straining to hear the voice up ahead, and find herself at a dead end. She'd turn back and take another only to arrive where she started.

It was messy and random, but there was a certain wild appeal not unlike the groundskeeper himself. A rough-around-the-edges type—*real* rough by her standards. She didn't really do unpolished, not after all those years watching her mom drag home one fixer-upper after another that just wouldn't fix. But something about Gordon made her curious. She assumed that, like a pendulum, she was swinging as far away from John on the male spectrum as she could and resolved to put him out of her mind.

Finally hitting a walk crowded with allium and lupine that spilled onto a wide-open lawn beyond the garden, Cordelia made her way down a set of slipshod stone steps among the dotted cherry trees and dogwoods in bloom, blissfully free of the choking plants and gingerbread. Here, the song spread out around her as if coming from many directions at once. Cordelia spun in a slow circle. "Hello?" she called, not really expecting an answer.

The voice dropped, the glade around her going unnaturally silent. Even the birds fell quiet, the grass running away from her in long, green stripes. Her eyes skirted the dark woods along the perimeter, and she shivered beneath the watchful gaze of the forest, reminded of the photo hidden in the broken frame. The trees seemed to reach for her, crowding together along the edge like men fighting at a fence, their limbs thrown out over the grass recklessly, grasping. Something about the lines in the grass meeting the upward sweep of their trunks distorted her perspective like an optical illusion, causing the land to bend and buckle, the trees to move in menacing arcs. Fighting the urge to shrink back, she looked away and willed herself forward.

Clearly, a lack of sleep, the long drive, and the shock of where they found themselves were sending her imagination into overdrive. She would feel infinitely better when she could put this whole sordid trip behind her. But a chilling question hovered in the back of her mind. What if this was her only chance *to know*? In Texas, even if she paid all of John's debts—and that was a big *if*—her mother's fate still waited for her, every headache an unsettling maternal reminder setting off alarm bells in her mind. Cordelia had no intention of treading in Maggie's mysterious footsteps, yet despite her best efforts, it seemed to be the very path she found herself on. One with a dark, distressing end. This place, with its gothic sensibility and family history, might hold the only answers she could hope to find about who and *what* their mother was, why she left, and what happened to her. Answers that Cordelia might not survive without. Answers that terrified her as much as the questions which spawned them.

It was here that Cordelia felt the strange hum from the car return. Radiating up her calves from the earth, it called to her in a kind of throaty vibrato, like singing without words. Not the voice from the garden, but queerly familiar, it was subtle but growing, making her legs itch with the desire to move and her head buzz with a burgeoning awareness, an idea taking shape inside it, coming together like bits of rolled clay.

She closed her eyes and followed the sound, shutting everything else out, letting the sensation carry her forward. Heady with trance, she realized it wasn't some*one* as it had been before but many, a harmony of wordless voices, without shape or context, throats without tongues. Across the back of her eyes, she saw the swiftly passing clouds of a brilliant sky, bluer than the water that reflected it, sharper than the mountains straining to pierce it, and she felt the tingle of winter on her cheeks, like freckles of ice. It was so vivid that she forgot herself entirely until she crashed into something pungent and prickly, backed by hard earth and cold stone.

Her eyes flew open, and the chorus she'd been hearing with her bones, the vision she'd been dreaming while awake, vanished as swiftly as they'd arisen. She was standing before an enormous hill. Too big to simply be a part of the natural landscape, it emerged from the glade like an unwanted growth, a pox on the land. It was shaped and mounded like a giant's sandcastle, primitive and pagan, a shrine to things unholy. Their very own Silbury Hill, with beautiful doors of iron grating set into it and bricks of stone to either side holding up a wide, peaked roof. Chiseled beneath the roofline was her surname—*Bone*. Chilling when set adrift, detached from the people who humanized it. And beneath that an inscription in Latin: *Silens in vita, in morte vocalis*. Dead languages always did give Cordelia the creeps, amputated from their time and place in history. The immortal past lumbering on, undeterred, as out of place as a butterfly in the snow.

She was looking at the family crypt. *Her* family crypt. But the usual symbols of comfort that adorn cemeteries could not be seen here. No angels or crosses or doves. Epitaphs to lives well-lived. Suggestions of a bespoke afterlife, sweet as cream, carefully arranged like furniture. Just those letters, gouged from the stone, and the unfeeling hill rising over them, and the rosebushes scrabbling up either side that she'd walked into—dark with squishy centers. The very same that sprung up at the Veranda house when they were girls, seemingly overnight.

Cordelia huddled in the shadow of the hill, dwarfed by the scale of the mound and the secrets festering in its dark. She imagined lancing it like an infected pustule, fearing what might pour out—curses and grave dirt, crimes of passion, the sins of all their fathers. But an unmistakable fact was also occurring to her, one she couldn't reconcile with the disconcerting place she now found herself. Her headache had miraculously dissolved, as if an invisible hand had reached out and cleared the cobwebs in her skull. She couldn't remember ever having one go away so quickly before, and certainly not without drugs. To draw some kind of connection was irrational, and yet she couldn't shake the sense that there was one, buried here with all her relatives, like cable under the ground.

Emboldened, she climbed the low stairs to the doors. Wrapping her fingers around the unseasonably cold iron, she gave a hard tug, but they were locked fast. Darkness greeted her inside, and a faint, musty smell—the echo of rot. She pressed her face against the bars, squinting into the woven-linen blackness, looking for explanations. She could see only the cut-stone walls and negative space, the mausoleum ambling into the shadows as if it went on forever, no horizon line to anchor it.

Why hadn't their mother asked to be laid to rest here with her family? Why deny them even that opportunity to know who they were, to have someone beyond each other?

Eustace had taken her ashes when she was cremated. They couldn't bring themselves to bury her after her lifelong avoidance of cemeteries. She'd spread them in the mountains of Colorado, closing that dark chapter of their lives.

Cordelia stepped back and picked a petal from one of the roses, crushing it between her fingers before rubbing it beneath her nose. It was late in the season for them to be blooming, too late really. Veranda Street wafted back to her, hot and sour and full of bad memories, like orange juice after it's turned.

A chill pushing through the woods beyond the hill snaked under her collar, making her feel vulnerable. Her eyes scanned the dark brush warily. Something about the tops of the trees in this part of the property made her uncomfortable, the way they rustled without wind, scraggly and disordered. She decided it was time to go back to the house.

She turned to leave, but a stroke of movement inside the tomb caught her eye, like someone passing behind the grated doors.

Cordelia stumbled back, but it had evaporated. *An animal,* she told herself, disbelieving, briskly walking in the direction of the house. It was only when she dared a look over her shoulder that she realized the hill of the crypt had no peak. It had been leveled off at the top, flattened as if shorn with a mighty ax. Beheaded.

For what, she couldn't imagine.

CORDELIA FORCED HERSELF up the stairs, casting her eyes down to the baseboards. It was an uneventful climb, but she was still grateful to get off at the second story. She wandered down the hall, bobbing her head in and out of opulent rooms until she found Eustace behind a door at the very end. Her sister was standing before a dressing table covered in old photographs, so engrossed she'd scarcely noticed Cordelia's absence.

Eustace lifted the nearest frame and held it up. "Do you think this is Augusta?"

Cordelia recognized the woman instantly. She was younger then, but still past middle age, poised elegantly on the parlor settee, a swath of stark white hair pinned atop her head. Her face was full, shaped more like Eustace's. But she was pale, with a dour quality to her expression, which lacked a smile. Her black turtleneck cloaked her square shoulders and long neck. Beside her stood a slender man with a receding hairline. He had her same heavy lower lip and blank expression, but not her strength or severity. Gordon's term—The White Lady—came sharply into focus. It was the same woman she'd seen in the window back home.

"Yes," Cordelia told her. "That's Aunt Augusta."

She scanned the collection of images, fearful of more surprises hiding behind them. In one, she recognized Maggie's small nose and Augusta's proud bearing, a woman who couldn't have been a day over twenty. Her hair spiraled around her face like Eustace's but had their mother's ginger coloring. Her eyes were laughing here as she smiled into the camera, but only moments ago Cordelia had seen those same eyes white and glassy like pale marbles. It was the levitating girl, her face now clean and familiar. She had to be their grandmother, who, according to their mother, hadn't survived Maggie's birth.

But it was another picture that stood out to her, of a thin woman in a drop-waist dress, a flash of pearls clutching her neck, dark hair knotted behind one ear. She held a strange animal in her arms, with a thick black coat and beady eyes, a pointy nose and long tail—the fisher-cat from downstairs, clearly still alive when the photograph was taken. Her face was serene with sensitive, shadowed eyes.

Cordelia picked the picture up.

"Who's that?" Eustace asked.

"I'm not sure." Though she knew she'd seen her already, leaning over the stair railing, squeezing her own throat. She quickly put the photo back where she'd found it.

All these faces she couldn't name, with eyes like hers or a jawline like her sister's, a chin that matched their mother's. It would take time to sort them out. And time went against everything Cordelia had planned on her way here. It should be a quick listing, a fast, *as-is* sale. She intended to be back in Texas next week, paying Busy Mazzello to stay as far away from her as possible, which didn't leave room for poring over family albums.

And yet, something in her *wanted* to know them, wanted to know why her mother had left them all behind.

"Do you think this was *her* room?" Eustace asked suddenly, indicating their great-aunt.

Cordelia could smell Augusta in the space with them— jasmine and black pepper—obvious as a forgotten word you've spoken hundreds of times before. She opened a top drawer and nodded. It was full of folded cashmere sweaters, all black except for one that was such a dark purple it may as well have been. "It would seem so."

But it wasn't just their aunt clouding the space around them. Another presence lingered beneath that one, lower down, sinking like carbon dioxide, odorless, invisible but no less real. Cordelia ran her fingers along the edge of the dresser, past one shining frame after another, until they stopped before a brass box, twitching like they did right before she got a call. She tapped the elaborately etched lid, a pattern of twining flowers so thick they reminded her of the wild garden outside.

"What's that?" her sister asked.

Cordelia picked the box up off its dainty feet and carefully lifted the lid. The notes poured out slowly, hauntingly, a trickle of music old and revered, a tune she knew she'd heard before. It reminded her of the holidays and heartbreak and wine poured from tall decanters, with necks like giraffes.

"'Greensleeves,'" her sister whispered.

Cordelia snapped it shut. "What?"

"It's 'Greensleeves'—an old English folk song. They used to play it in our high school orchestra."

"How do you know?"

"I slept with one of the cellists," she said with a shrug.

Cordelia set the box down and opened it again, the melody encircling her like an embrace, a choke hold. Inside, a small packet of Polaroids had been tied together with black velvet ribbon, a lock of orange hair tucked beneath it. She pulled them out, tugging at the bow, letting the ribbon drop to the floor, lifting the hair to her nose—traces of cinnamon and viburnum: *Maggie*—and then setting it aside. Shuffling through one photo after the next, she could feel the blood draining from her face, throbbing in her fingertips.

"What is it?" Eustace asked, leaning in.

"It's Mom," Cordelia said, closing the lid to stop the music and laying the pictures on top. "This belonged to Mom."

Eustace scowled. "Let me see." Her hands made quick work

of the pictures, no more than five or six. She held the last one up. "Are you kidding me?"

Cordelia felt the wind go out of her and slide back in again, her lungs slack as old rubber bands. In the image, their mother was around twelve or thirteen, wearing a simple gingham skirt and bikini top with a lopsided smile, a raggedy black cat hanging from her arms, floppy and tame as a cloth doll and clearly just as beloved. Someone had written *Magdalena & Atticus* at the bottom. Behind them, the crypt loomed, the roses blurring to a magenta mass.

"I guess she wasn't always opposed to pets," Cordelia said weakly. "Or cemeteries. That's the family crypt behind them."

"Or music for that matter," Eustace said with a pointed glance at the box, flipping through the Polaroids again. She held up another one for Cordelia to see, a teenage Maggie staring back at her, laughter rimming her mouth, eyes lit like fireflies. Beside her stood a man, rail-thin, head turned, transfixed.

"Who is that with her?" Cordelia asked. He wasn't familiar exactly, but something in the way he was looking at their mother felt familiar, as if she'd seen it before.

Eustace frowned. "Who the hell knows? But does that look like a woman who is suffering to you?"

"Well, no," Cordelia concurred. "But it's just a handful of pictures. Moments really."

"Happy moments," Eustace said sharply. "Not a sickly little girl with blistering headaches or someone being abused."

"No," Cordelia agreed. "Not those things."

"So why leave then? Why deprive herself and us?"

Cordelia rubbed her arms up and down as if she were caught in a snowdrift. "Something must have happened to change her. Something in this house." Something that made Maggie hate animals and dead people and standing still. Something that ripped the music out of her, the health, the joy.

She turned away from the dresser, eyes crawling around

the room, lured by the dusty old pillows spilling along the bed and the sable comforter, needlepoint and frayed lace. Cordelia walked over and sat down on the edge, gripping the mattress. "Do you think she died in here? Aunt Augusta?"

Her sister cast a wary look around, eyes falling on the bed accusingly. "Probably."

Cordelia wanted to ask if her sister felt the house breathing the way she did. If she sensed the company it kept. But outside of her own mind, the words didn't make sense, and she couldn't bring herself to speak them. Instead, she turned and picked up one of the throw pillows, small with flowers knotted into it. Then she picked up another and another and another. She pulled and pulled until the last of them had been tossed to the floor.

Her eyes narrowed. "Look at this."

Eustace placed a knee on the bed, leaning toward the wall where Cordelia was reaching for the beadboard.

"Do you see it?"

"See what?" Eustace asked.

"That," she said, pointing to a series of scratches in the wood.

Eustace leaned closer, squinting. "Probably just from something she was wearing."

"To bed?" Cordelia asked.

"Or maybe a pet?" Eustace suggested. "I had this cat—you remember Clawdius Germanicus—that completely destroyed the bamboo flooring in my guest room."

"Only you would name a cat after a Roman emperor," Cordelia said, ignoring her sister.

"He had a regal bearing."

Cordelia looked closer at the wall. The marks were deep, the shape too intentional to be an accident. "It looks like . . . a letter? A *Y* maybe. Was she trying to spell something?"

Eustace shook her head. "The lines at the top are too close together."

Eustace was right—the top two lines didn't vee far enough out to look like a letter *Y*. But to the right, a tiny line was just emerging, cut off before she could finish it.

"Eustace?" Cordelia asked in a whisper, her throat suddenly too dry for proper sound. "Does this remind you of something?"

Eustace started to roll her eyes and wave her sister off, and then froze as if struck. Slowly, she turned back to the wall. "Mom."

"Her tattoo," Cordelia clarified, meeting her sister's eyes. The one that had been cut from Maggie's body at the time of her death.

Eustace took a step away from the bed.

But Cordelia drew closer, her nose nearly touching the paint. She saw something sticking out of the scratched groove and reached for it, gripping it between thumb and finger. It came away easily and she laid it in her palm, immediately regretting that decision.

"Cordy," Eustace asked in disbelief. "What is that?"

She looked up into her sister's face. "A fingernail."

Eustace knocked it from her hand, and it landed somewhere among the pile of pillows. "Well, that confirms it. I'm not sleeping in here tonight."

Cordelia rubbed her palm on her thigh and stood up. She gathered the pillows and replaced them on the bed, covering the scratches. "Maybe it's just a coincidence," she stammered. "Would they even know about Mom's tattoo? Wasn't that after she left?"

"Beats me," Eustace said. "But what are the odds? It has to mean something."

"What do you think happened to her?" she asked, moving away from the bed. "Our aunt?"

Eustace shook her head. "Maybe the same thing that happened to Mom."

"Mom had a brain aneurysm," Cordelia corrected. "You heard the driver: Augusta was old."

Eustace rolled her eyes. "So the coroner says, but I don't think women with brain aneurysms get flayed in parking lots. And I don't think old ladies who go peacefully in their sleep claw messages into the wall beside the bed first."

Cordelia's throat felt like it had been coated in sawdust. She was suddenly desperate for a glass of water.

"You don't think"—Eustace looked at her sister, eyes flashing white and gray and blue—"we'll be next?"

"Don't be absurd," Cordelia rasped, though she felt a wild streak of suspicion rise in her own breast. "She probably had dementia. I'm sure if we do a little asking, we'll find there's a perfectly reasonable explanation for this."

"Right," her sister agreed. But Eustace didn't look reassured as she turned for the door. "Guess we better pick a different room for the night."

Cordelia followed her to the hall. "Eustace, you can't be serious. We can't stay here."

She spun around. "Why not?"

Cordelia's mouth fell open. "Do I have to spell it out for you? Our aunt *died* in this house. And no one has yet to tell us why or how." She took a step toward her sister, pitching her voice low as if someone might overhear. "Not to mention that picture we found downstairs."

It went without saying that she had no intention of sharing a roof with the ghastly woman on the stairs.

"You just said there was a perfectly reasonable explanation for it all," Eustace threw back at her.

"And there probably is," Cordelia backpedaled. "But until we find one, we should sleep somewhere else. I'm sure there's an affordable hotel in town," she suggested, though in truth, the only thing she could afford at the moment was *free*.

"There probably is," Eustace told her. "And how exactly do you propose we get there? In case you didn't notice, the attorney fled before sundown, taking the only car with him."

"Then I'll call and tell him we need suitable accommodations. What's his number?" She pulled her phone from her pocket, prepared to dial.

Eustace sighed and began to rattle it off.

Punching it in, Cordelia waited, but instead of the customary ring, her phone shot back an error message. Cordelia checked her signal and frowned. "There's no service."

"Hold on," her sister said, dragging her own phone out. "You can get away with one of those cheap providers because you're in the city. I can't cut corners like that in Colorado."

Cordelia started to argue until she saw the smirk fade from Eustace's face. "What? What is it?"

Eustace held out her phone. "I don't have any either."

The air rushed out of Cordelia, leaving her hollow. They were stranded.

"It's just one night," Eustace told her. "What's the worst that could happen?"

But before Cordelia could answer that, the house shuddered like a dying engine, groaning as all the lights snapped out at once, plunging them into darkness.

CHAPTER FIVE

The Night

IF A ROOM could scowl, she was certain this one was. It didn't seem possible to sleep here. It didn't seem safe. Cordelia reminded herself she only had to make it until morning. Then the gray-faced attorney would return, his insipid nephew, willow-thin, behind the wheel of that unsavory car, and she could sign whatever needed signing and insist on a ride out of here, find a comfortable queen at a nearby bed-and-breakfast, fly home the next morning, put the past behind her.

She gripped the collar of the lamp with sweaty fingers, flames flickering, kerosene sloshing as she held it high to peer inside. At least if they had to be trapped in a haunted house with no power, they were in one old enough to be littered with candlesticks and lanterns. The room stared back, watching her with Mona Lisa precision, unscrupulous and unapologetic.

It could have been the bedroom of the man in the library portrait, with its distinct masculine aesthetic and heaviness, a certain weight in the shape of the furniture, the fall of the drapes, the hang of the air. The overall disregard it seemed to hold for her, its only occupant in how many years? The bedroom reminded her of Christmas in a sinister kind of way, painted a rich forest green, dominated by a tall sleigh bed with a carved stag's head emerging from it, a red-and-green coverlet more like a tapestry than a blanket. A huge ebony wardrobe brooded in one corner, the kind children could get lost inside, and the windows were hidden behind thick drapes the color of port wine.

At least there were no taxidermic animals to speak of.

She sat on the edge of the impressive bed, putting the lamp down on the bedside table, lifting her feet off the floor like she did when she was young. Children knew to be wary of the things that slid under beds. Cordelia felt like a child again in this house, trapped, powerless. Tomorrow, she'd call the Hartford agency and get a list of comparable properties and their selling prices, unload it on some unsuspecting buyer as quickly as possible. Though taking in the gloomy, overstated decor that surrounded her, she couldn't imagine there were many comparable properties for them to go on.

Malevolent spinster might not be her favorite aesthetic, but there was nothing mediocre about this house, and Cordelia could respect that. Bone Hill had a dark regard; it carried itself with formidable grace and an iron bearing, not unlike their late aunt. Despite her reservations, it filled her with an unexpected sense of pride.

But keeping the estate was a ridiculous idea. Even Eustace would know better. Living here would be like stepping back in time. She would show respect in how she dismantled it, though, locate an appraiser and a reputable auction house. It was the least she could do for the family she'd never known.

Beneath her, the bed suddenly moaned. Cordelia jumped up and spun around, threw the covers back and ducked to look beneath the solid frame, but she couldn't make out anything in the stifling black. Feeling like a schoolgirl, she opened her bag and was greeted by the pills she used to manage her headaches. She set them on the bedside table, that little brown bottle all that stood between her and her mother's deterioration. Her head felt fine at the moment, but her symptoms had been erratic all day— dull and foreboding in the morning, the way her headaches so often started, only to recede on the drive up, return in a flash of pain with the apparition on the stairs, then ebb once again as she neared the crypt.

The unpredictability was new, and she worried what it might mean. Their mother had suffered a decline steady enough to plot on a chart for years, but in her final weeks, she began to complain of a mercurial shift in her symptoms—unexpected increases and decreases in pain, abrupt onset and random triggers, even waking her from a dead sleep. Then came her sudden turn for the worse one unforeseen night. Maggie was made of sterner stuff than either of them, and Cordelia secretly feared she had less time than her mother.

She closed the door and changed, assuming she and the room had agreed to a truce for the night, leaning gingerly on the bed as if she might anger it again, the kerosene lamp her only consolation, the stag's head casting beastly shadows up the wall. She was loath to twist that knob, watch the fire shrink and die, feel the darkness press in on her, a living thing writhing with foul intentions. But the room was still, and at last she breathed deep and nestled into the embroidered sheets, killing the light in one swift motion.

She wondered if John was sleeping alone somewhere tonight. She tried to imagine him in a hotel room like the one she'd left behind, surrounded by so much beige, sad and bored. But it was impossible to see John that way—regretful, lonely. If she pictured him at all, it was laid out next to another woman, lithe and spent. And she marveled that it had never occurred to her before how striking that was.

Irritated, Cordelia wondered brazenly what kind of bed the groundskeeper slept in. She envisioned something with black leather and studs, maybe flame stitching or a giant pentagram. Or perhaps he slept in a coffin like a vampire. It was all so ludicrous she practically giggled. Until she imagined him pulling his too-tight shirt over his head and tugging the band from his long, jet hair. And then she felt herself blush acutely, as if the dark itself were scandalized by her secret imaginings.

On the edge of sleep, Cordelia had the distinct sense Bone Hill could take care of itself, *had* taken care of itself for decades, like something possessed, a place with its own heartbeat. And then the feeling faded, and she dreamt of dark shutters and parquet flooring, trees that bristled without wind, her mother's laugh, and the satiny white of her aunt Augusta's hair and eyes and bones. Above all else, the bones, smooth as polished driftwood and rattling in their sockets.

It must have been hours later when the sound of a creaking door finally stirred her, sleep holding on stubbornly, sucking her down, suffused with repetitive dreams. She thought she saw a soft light spill into her room through the open crack, but just as quickly it went out. And that couldn't be right, because the house had lost power hours ago, even without a storm to justify it. Too frightened to move, she whispered into the darkness. "Eustace?"

But her sister didn't respond.

Her fingers tightened around the bedcover. A floorboard cried out softly, mewing under the weight of some invisible stranger just outside her door, followed by a scuffle as if someone had hurried away. Cordelia swallowed. And then she heard the high-pitched chitter above her, like mice on the ceiling.

In a whoosh of blinding illumination, a flash as sudden and unexpected as dry lightning, the lights in the house flared back to life, bathing her room in a jaundiced glow as a shadow swooped low over her head. Cordelia screamed and leapt from the bed as another glided across the room. She looked up. The air above her was writhing with small, furry bodies and black wings. Here and there, a gruesome face could be seen, nose-less and fanged with tiny, pinprick eyes and bald ears. They seemed confused, crawling all over one another, flying into the windows and the walls, leaving speckles of blood before they hit the floor. Some stayed down, but others darted up again, tearing at her hair and gown, driving her from one end of the room to the other as if she had invaded their space and not the other way around.

Cordelia raced for the door, slamming it behind her. She tore into the hall and, for the second time in twenty-four hours, ran straight into Gordon, who was barreling in her direction from the stairs. He caught her in his giant arms, wrapping them around her before she could pull away, holding her against him. She started to scream, and he flattened a hand over her mouth.

"It's okay. I'm not here to hurt you," he said into her hair, his breath warm against her ear and neck.

When she stilled, he slowly peeled his fingers away from her face and let her go.

Cordelia spun on him, shoving him back a step, angry at being manhandled and flustered by his nearness. "What are you doing here?" she pressed, wrapping her arms across her chest, aware now of the paper-thin cotton of her nightshirt, the pants she wasn't wearing. He towered over her in a dark sweatshirt, flannel pajama pants, and boots, long hair left to fall over his shoulders. "You shouldn't be in the house this late."

The creaking door that had woken her, the sound of someone just outside her room before the power snapped back on, sparked questions in her mind, blanks that he seemed to fill. It was too suspect to be a coincidence, his presence at just this hour, unwanted, unannounced. Cordelia didn't like the idea of him sneaking around the property, continually turning up in her path like a dead end, this brick wall of a man.

"I was out walking when I saw the house light up. I was worried. Thought there might be a fire or—" He looked over his shoulder at the closed door, the chaos of fluttering within. "Is everything okay in there?"

She put herself between him and her room. "Don't go in there. Don't open that door."

His eyes met hers, and for a split second she thought she registered a slice of fear in them.

"We lost power," she said, explaining the lights he claimed to have seen. "Earlier this afternoon. It just came back on. The carriage house didn't?"

He shook his head. "No, but they're on separate circuits. A breaker must have tripped."

How convenient. "What were you doing out walking this late?" Her eyebrow cranked skeptically. "In the dark?"

He sighed, massive shoulders drooping. "I couldn't sleep. It's a thing I do to clear my head. And then I saw the shadow."

She drew her arms tighter around herself, a new twinge of anxiety triggered by his words. "What shadow?"

"A silhouette passed in front of the first-story windows. Looked like someone running away from the house. I would have gone after them, but I was more worried about you and your sister. Wanted to be sure you were both okay first."

Cordelia stared up at him, weighing the possibilities. What were the odds he was lying, maybe covering his own tracks? The odds that he was telling the truth and two people had been skulking around this behemoth of a house in the middle of the night? He leaned an arm against the wall, eyes continually flicking to the door behind her, where muted thuds sounded. She supposed if he'd wanted to hurt her, he had every opportunity to right now. She didn't trust him exactly—that would be foolish—but she begrudged him the benefit of the doubt, at least for the moment.

"Could have been a mistake," he offered quietly. "It's late. It's dark. Maybe it was just a deer or something. Anyway, are you all right?" he asked now, concern skating the dark corners of his eyes.

"They're in my room," she whispered, that scuffling she'd heard playing up and down her spine.

"The shadow?" He pushed off the wall, tensing.

"The bats," Cordelia replied. "*All* of them."

A grin winked at her from the edges of his mouth, quickly cleared, suggesting he found something in her answer amusing. Maybe he enjoyed her fear. "They're harmless, you know."

She ground her teeth together. "So everyone keeps saying."

But he hadn't just seen them like she had, crazed and frenzied, gathered atop one another. She burned with humiliation and the feeling of being targeted, as if the bats were a message meant just for her. It was paranoid to think so, but it gnawed at her sanity, fraying the edges. She felt an intense longing for her old bedroom, now sick with mold, and the white fortress she'd left behind where she'd once felt nothing could hurt her. Her skin smoldered under the groundskeeper's enigmatic gaze as if she were naked.

"Sleep somewhere else tonight," he said, forcing his eyes to meet hers. "I'll come by tomorrow to chase them out of there, make sure they can't get in again."

"Thank you." Relief flooded her, cool and fluid, nearly causing her eyes to water. If she never stepped foot in that room again, it would be too soon. "Could you direct us toward accommodations in town? I don't intend to spend another night on the property."

He clucked the corner of his mouth. "Well then, you'll have to drive back to Hartford, I'm afraid. The Bellwick Inn closed its doors a decade ago. No one's taken up the mantle of restoring and reopening it."

Cordelia swallowed. "You mean there's nowhere? Not an Airbnb or a drive-in motel or anything?"

He shrugged. "We don't see a lot of tourism here. Most people head for the coastline or the better-known towns like Greenwich."

She stood awkwardly for a moment, processing her predicament. Even one more night was too high a price. But Busy Mazzello's thick voice, like glue being poured into her ear, taunted her; she figured the man must have a tongue like a beaver tail. She couldn't go back without his money. With all he was putting her through, she hoped John choked on a scallop in Key West.

"I should get back, try and catch some sleep before the sun rises," Gordon said, attempting to extricate himself.

"How did she die?" Cordelia blurted, drawing herself up, refusing to let another person get away without at least one solid answer. "Aunt Augusta?" The scratches from the room were emblazoned in her memory. He might know more, since he lived here.

He paused, confusion knitting his brow, before relenting. "In her sleep, or so I'm told."

Cordelia breathed in. It sounded innocuous enough, but how did they explain what they found? "She wasn't sick then? Or demented?"

Gordon squinted at her. "She kept to her room toward the end. But she was sharp as a tack. Not the sort to go soft—you know, up here." He tapped his temple.

"Oh." Cordelia mulled that over. It dashed at the flimsy explanations she'd erected to dispel their fears. "You're the one who found her?"

He shook his head, hair tousling in shiny, black waves. "That was the Togers boy. The nephew."

"Arkin?" What was the driver doing in her aunt's bedroom?

"He came to take care of the house most days after my mother . . ." He let this last bit fall off, a look of regret paining him.

"Your mother?" Cordelia asked, a little shocked.

"She worked here in the big house," he clarified. "Briefly. A maid and a cook."

Cordelia noted the past tense. Her eyes met his, searching.

"She passed," he said without emotion. "Not long after getting on here. She suffered from an autoimmune disease but . . ."

Cordelia waited for him to finish.

"She talked about being afraid of someone before she died." He eyed her quizzically. "Someone on the property. She never told me who. You should be careful is all."

She flailed for the right thing to say, half-dressed in the middle of the night. She felt bad for him. "I'm so sorry," she finally responded. "We lost our mother almost six years ago. It was . . . *sudden.* You don't really get over it."

Gordon eyed her strangely, as if he didn't trust this gush of empathy, big arms tightening over his broad chest. "Try and get some sleep," he said finally, signaling their conversation was at an end, before turning and heading back down the stairs.

Cordelia shivered alone in the great hallway, the door behind her gone quiet but no less threatening. He'd told her to sleep somewhere else, but she couldn't imagine trusting another room now, especially after his shadow story, even if it was just a deer, which she doubted. Turning, she spied the room her sister had chosen and scurried past her own door toward it, inching inside.

In the dark—her sister's light had apparently not been on when the power failed—she made her way to the bed, carefully pulling the blankets back and slipping inside.

Beside her, Eustace groaned and rolled over. "Cordy?"

"Shhh. Go back to sleep."

"What's going on?" her sister asked, rubbing at her eyes.

"Nothing. Just some bats. Possibly a shadow. And then the groundskeeper . . . I'll tell you in the morning. I just need to sleep in here if that's okay."

"Seriously?" Eustace asked sleepily.

"They are like rats with wings, Eustace," Cordelia shot back at her.

"Fine, but if you pull the covers off me, so help me God, Cordelia Bone—"

"I don't do that anymore," Cordelia grumbled, adjusting her pillow and sinking down, her back to her sister.

"Can John vouch for that?" Eustace asked.

"Not exactly."

Her sister sat up. "Why? What's wrong?"

"Nothing. Can we talk about it tomorrow?"

"Cordy, I can hear it in your voice," Eustace insisted.

"I am not doing this with you at—" Out of habit, she tried to check her wrist, then sighed, realizing she'd left her watch and her phone back in her room. "Whatever o'clock," she muttered.

"Okay," Eustace agreed, lying back down. "But this is not going away. Tomorrow . . . we talk."

"Yeah. Sure. Whatever. Can we just sleep now?" Cordelia hated the way her sister could make talking sound like a death sentence. It was a gift she'd inherited from their mother.

"Good night," Eustace whispered as Cordelia closed her eyes.

Too late for that, Cordelia thought. She couldn't remember the last time she'd shared a bed with her sister, but for the first time in weeks, the terrible pall of loneliness that hung over her seemed to ease. She hadn't realized until this moment how alone she'd felt these last five years, even when things were at their best with John. Maybe trading her sister for a slice of suburban pie hadn't served her so well after all. Whatever their history, she determined to do things differently with Eustace from this point forward. Before she fell asleep, she squeezed her sister's hand.

CORDELIA WOKE AND was greeted by a hooked beak and two beady black eyes inches from her face.

"Christ." She recoiled in shock, remembering with sudden force where she was.

"Morning, princess," Eustace drawled. She stood beside the window in her bathrobe, looking out over the back garden.

Cordelia leaned her head against the cool iron of the headboard and eyed the stuffed bird anxiously. A raven, it appeared to be. Two, in fact. One on a driftwood perch and the other leaning down to inspect unsuspecting sleepers.

"Did they really think the bedside table was the most appropriate place for this?"

Eustace grinned. "I like them. I've named them Hocus and Pocus."

"You would," Cordelia grumbled.

"You were snoring," Eustace told her. "I thought you'd never wake up."

"Don't be ridi— What time is it?"

"Almost nine," Eustace told her. "That's practically noon in Cordelia hours."

Eustace was right. She never liked to be caught in bed past six in the morning. Another quirk John couldn't understand. "What are you drinking?" she asked her sister, zeroing in on the ironstone mug in her hand.

"Tea," Eustace told her. "English Breakfast. I found it in the kitchen. No coffeemaker to speak of, I'm afraid."

"What?" Cordelia's voice pitched unnaturally high. Even the bats hadn't solicited such a reaction. "How is that possible?"

Eustace shrugged. "You're not going to go into withdrawal, are you?"

"Yes," she told her with conviction, sitting on the edge of the bed, trying to gather her thoughts. Instinctively, she reached for her pill bottle, expecting a headache to bloom at the mere mention of no caffeine, only to remember she'd left her pills in the room with the bats last night.

"Maybe he'll loan you some coffee," Eustace said with waggling brows.

"Who?" Cordelia rose and went to the window.

"The groundskeeper is pruning the hydrangeas," Eustace said with a purr.

Cordelia looked out over the haphazard arrangement of garden beds and found Gordon in a familiar black T-shirt taking some shears to a plot of spiky hydrangea stalks. His long hair was loose again this morning, curling against his shoulder blades.

She gave her sister a withering look. "Have you been watching him all morning?"

Eustace nodded. "I haven't had a view this nice since Roberto moved out."

"What about Emily?" Cordelia asked, hoping it wasn't as touchy a subject as it used to be.

"Emily never did yard work," her sister replied.

Emily was the closest her sister had ever come to marriage—an outdated convention Eustace didn't put much stock in. She was good for Eustace, grounding her wilder tendencies, giving her focus and direction. Emily was the reason she'd started her own grow room. Cordelia liked Emily's domestic flair, though she didn't miss all those hand-knits at Christmas. But she was ten years Eustace's junior, and she wanted things Eustace didn't— most significantly, a family. Cordelia understood her sister's reluctance to commit to parenting after their own childhood, but it was hard to explain that to people who hadn't lived it with them. And Emily, in the end, didn't understand either. That breakup crushed Eustace for a while. But she slowly pulled herself back together, pouring everything into her business—a coping mechanism she'd learned from her sister.

Roberto, on the other hand, had been one of a number of casual engagements Eustace used to fill the time and her bed before and after Emily. Cordelia never minded that her sister enjoyed herself, but "revolving door" didn't seem a healthy relationship model.

"Come on," Eustace said, elbowing her sister. "You've got to admit, he's *very* easy on the eyes."

"I don't have to admit anything," Cordelia muttered, watching the way Gordon's arms stretched over the hydrangeas, pulling his muscles into leanly knotted cords. "There are just so many tattoos."

Eustace snickered. "I knew you thought he was hot."

Cordelia rolled her eyes. "What are we? Fourteen?"

Her sister shrugged a shoulder. "Oh, Cordy, even *your* loins aren't completely devoid of feeling."

Cordelia frowned. "He looks like one of those satanists or someone from a motorcycle gang."

Eustace shot her a withering glance. "Because you've met so many?"

"John is more my type," Cordelia said, unable to peel her eyes away just yet.

"John is not a type."

"What's that supposed to mean?" she asked.

Her sister sniffed. "He looks like he belongs in a Rolex ad."

"So?" Cordelia felt suddenly defensive. "Those men are attractive. They're models."

Eustace dropped her chin and looked over her mug at Cordelia. "No one wants to go to bed with a Rolex ad."

Cordelia stared out at Gordon gathering up the branches he would need to haul off. "But they want to go to bed with bikers and devil worshippers?" she asked, affronted.

"When they look like that, they do," Eustace replied, sashaying away from the window just in time for Gordon to look up and spot Cordelia watching him alone in nothing but her flimsy nightshirt.

Cordelia flopped on the bed.

"How exactly do you know this guy worships the devil?" Eustace asked her.

"His fingers spell out *hell fire*."

Her sister frowned.

"He has a giant goat's head wrapped around his throat! That's not exactly altar boy material."

Eustace grinned. "You've been living in the suburbs too long. There's a whole field of gray out there between altar boys and devil worshippers. You should sample it sometime."

Cordelia rolled her eyes, but secretly she knew her sister was right. The Dallas suburbs had limited her human exposure to soccer moms, church deacons, and corporate commuters.

"So, when did John leave?" Eustace asked quietly, curling up in a brocade armchair. She pulled out a small glass pipe in a spiraling design and held a lighter to it, inhaling deeply.

Cordelia deflated. There was no point in hiding it anymore. "About five months ago."

Eustace pushed the pipe toward Cordelia as the smoke poured out between her lips.

She waved it off. She'd never taken to cannabis the way her sister had. She didn't like how loose it made her feel, like she might unravel where she stood and puddle on the floor. "Go ahead. Gloat. You never liked him. Turns out you were right all along."

Eustace tucked the pipe back in the pocket of her robe. "I didn't like him because I knew he would hurt you. There's no joy in that for me. It's not a victory."

"Well, he's not the only one. You hurt me too."

"I know," Eustace said quietly. "I'm sorry for that. After Mom—I felt responsible for you. And you fell into him so quickly. Master manipulators are charming in the beginning. I wanted to protect you."

Cordelia rolled her eyes. "You can't just ride in at the twelfth hour and demand I break up with someone because you got a 'vibe.'"

"I was scared," Eustace told her, shrugging. "Someone had just butchered our mother in a parking lot. I didn't want to lose you too."

Cordelia sighed. She understood her sister's fears better now than she did at the time. The headaches had made her vulnerable in a way she wasn't then.

Eustace frowned. "Tell me what happened."

Cordelia glanced at her, weighing how much to spill. It was humiliating admitting to all the ways he'd deceived and used her, and she didn't want to drag her sister into her problems. Especially when her problems came with an Italian surname and paid muscle. "Allison."

"That kitten of an assistant you had following you everywhere?"

She tucked a knee under her chin. "So much for loyalty. I was always worried she would strike out on her own with another agency. That someone would steal her from me. Just not my husband."

"I should have been there." Eustace shook her head sadly. "Your mandar is so out of whack."

Cordelia raised an eyebrow skeptically. "My *what*?"

"Your man radar," Eustace told her. "It's always been off-center. It's not your fault. You were just born that way. Another thing you can thank Mom for."

Cordelia scowled. "Are you saying I am genetically hardwired to have bad taste in men?"

"Pretty much," Eustace told her. "But it's okay now."

"How is it okay?" Cordelia asked. "My marriage has gone down in a spectacular burst of flames."

"It's okay because you have me. I won't let someone come between us ever again. I mean that." Eustace stared at her.

Cordelia nodded, annoyed but grateful. She'd missed her sister terribly over the last five years. Missed her bossiness and explosive laugh, her wry humor and down-to-earth wisdom. Missed the way Eustace saw her like nobody else. Missed the things they held between them, unspoken. It was a heavy burden to carry alone, being a Bone.

"I will be your seeing-*guy* dog," Eustace announced. "But you have to listen to me next time. When I tell you he's a dud . . . *he's a dud.*"

Cordelia laughed despite the tears springing to her eyes. Her sister tossed a pillow at her, and she dodged it. "You want to know what the worst part is?" she said quietly. "After everything, he left *me.*"

"Oh, Cordy." Eustace rose to sit beside her and wrap an arm around her shoulders.

"I knew I should have kicked him out, but I was so scared of being truly alone. He wasn't even sorry. He acted like it was my fault. I asked to go to counseling, and do you know what he said?"

Eustace shook her head.

"*What for? You're never going to change.* And then he left." Everything John had done to her—the affair, the gaslighting, the outrageous debts, torching her reputation, stealing their clients and her identity . . . Cordelia still couldn't believe she'd let it all happen.

The shrill ring of the doorbell echoed up the stairs, interrupting their moment of closeness.

"What is that god-awful noise?" Eustace asked, rising. "It's murder to the ears. Is that supposed to be a doorbell?"

Cordelia nodded. "Sounds like we have a visitor."

Her sister wrapped her robe tight. "Must be Mr. Togers, the attorney. I'll get the door. You get dressed."

Cordelia looked down at her bare legs. All her clothes were in the other room, the one she'd begun her night in. There was nothing for it; she'd have to go get them.

Padding down the hall, she reminded herself that bats were nocturnal. They should be tucked safely away by now, crawled back through whatever chink they'd found in the plaster, though it did little to ease the fisted nerves in her stomach. But when she reached the door and tried to open it, there was resistance, like pushing against a crumpled rug. Cordelia leaned into it with a shoulder, determined to get her things, and with effort finally shoved it open. She immediately wished she hadn't.

The room was littered with their dead, limp bodies, scattered across the floorboards and bed, piled against the door. Dozens of glassy eyes reflected the morning light, and brown, leathery wings were spread at wrong angles or tucked stiffly at their sides. A sharp, skunk-like smell pervaded the air, backed by the beginnings of rot. The evidence of last night's frenzy stained the walls and cracked the windows, even the mirror over the washstand.

Cordelia began to quake, a prick of pain flaring to life inside her skull, like the *tap, tap, tap* of a sharpened fingernail from the inside. She tried stepping over them, the honey-orange glow of her pill bottle calling to her, but it was impossible not to feel the give of flesh and tickle of fur beneath her bare feet. Horrified, she stumbled forward squealing, catching herself on the washstand, clutching it for dear life. She squeezed her eyes closed.

There was something unnatural about so much death in one room. The floating woman in the photograph they'd found the day before etched herself anew across Cordelia's mind.

Had her own presence done this? That thing deep inside her she could never let out? Had it drawn them here, possessing their tiny bodies and minds, sending them into a collective paroxysm, driving them to their end by some invisible means?

When she opened her eyes again, she read the answer in the mirror before her, her heart icing over. In the blood dripped and spattered across the opposite wall, righted only by the reversal of its reflection, one gruesome, gut-twisting word had formed.

Witch.

CHAPTER SIX

THE TRUST

R EADY TO JOIN us?" Bennett called like a teacher scolding a tardy student as Cordelia slunk down the stairs. Eustace was at his side near the vestibule. "I trust you had a restful night's sleep?"

"Not exactly," Cordelia said under her breath. Without her morning dose of caffeine, she was in no shape for this meeting.

"These old houses can take some adjustment," he countered with an indulgent smile. "Should you need anything, I can send my nephew, Arkin, to fetch it for you. In the meantime, I've brought a basket of supplies to get you started." He lifted a large, handwoven bushel basket overflowing with produce and food items. She prayed there was coffee in there.

Cordelia wasn't sure she wanted Arkin fetching her anything. She tried to imagine these men in the same family, the aging, overly cordial attorney and his taciturn nephew, pale as skim milk. *What a gene pool that must be.* "I think we can manage our own groceries."

"Of course." Bennett puckered, then forced an agreeable smile. "In due time, I'm sure Bone Hill will grow on you."

"Due time?" Cordelia asked, wrinkling her nose. "I'm afraid you don't understand the arrangement here."

"Arrangement?" Now it was the attorney's turn to wrinkle his nose, as if the word left a bad taste in his mouth. He pressed his lips into a thin line and glared at her.

Sensing the tension, Eustace quickly jumped in. "Mr. Togers was just telling me that it was our great-great-great-grandfather who commissioned this house. What did you say his name was again?" she asked.

"Erazmus Bone," he drawled with a hearty nod.

Cordelia quickly recalled the glowering man in the study portrait with the little plaque.

"His father and uncle were born here after his grandparents immigrated with the Scottish," Bennett told them. "They were very industrious men, but Erazmus was the one who really built the family fortune in America."

"Surely they weren't Scots," Cordelia wondered aloud. "With a name like *Bone*."

"They came from England," he answered.

"You seem to know a lot about our family, Mr. Togers," Eustace said.

"*Bennett*," he insisted a little less warmly than the day before. "Yes, well—my father was an attorney before me. He worked for your great-grandfather, Linden, handling the estate. So, you could say much of the Bone history has been passed down."

Cordelia thought it strange they should both work for the same family. And yet, isn't that what small-town people often did? Follow in their parents' footsteps, inherit the family business? Wouldn't a family like hers—the most affluent in the area—provide the most work?

"You'll find the house has many details alluding to your history," the attorney told them both, smiling broadly and turning toward the parlor. "The image carved over the door here is said to be a likeness of your fifth-great-grandmother, Winter

Bone. It was commissioned by Erazmus himself in honor of his beloved mother when he fashioned the house."

Cordelia felt a shiver pass through her as she stared into the wooden face, remembering how it struck her yesterday. She felt like she was on one of those historical tours of a famous person's home, like a president or an author. Only, this was *her* family estate. And Mr. Togers' droning was solely for her and her sister's benefit.

"And you'll no doubt have seen the portrait of Erazmus that has hung in his study since the mid-1800s," Bennett added.

Cordelia nodded.

"In the dining room," he called as he walked toward the door under the stairs, "you'll find several more portraits, including your great-grandfather, Linden, and his sister—your great-great-aunt Morna."

Bennett stopped in front of two portraits hanging side by side—a young man and woman. He had golden-brown hair and blue eyes with a pale suit and waistcoat, standing before the library mantel. She was posed in the garden, in a long, pleated dress of teal silk, and though she was every bit as fair of face and skin, her dark auburn hair and warm brown eyes were in stark contrast to her brother's. Cordelia knew her right away, despite the peachy cheeks and demure stance. It was the woman she'd seen on the stairs.

"Morna," Cordelia said softly.

Bennett hung his head. "Yes. I'm afraid her life was quite tragic. She was rather afflicted. It took her from her brother in the end."

"Afflicted?" Eustace asked. "With what?"

Bennett cleared his throat. "*Melancholy* is what they called it at the time."

"Depression," Eustace clarified.

"And suicide?" Cordelia followed.

Bennett nodded. "Unfortunately. Only a few years after your aunt Augusta was born. It was a terrible tragedy for the family. But Linden carried on, and here you both are." His smile tightened.

"Who's this?" Eustace asked, sliding over to the next painting of a handsome young man with golden hair in a frock coat and burgundy ascot, also poised before the stately library mantel.

"That is Roman Bone. Linden and Morna's uncle. Erazmus had four children—Roman was his only son," Bennett informed them.

"He looks quite dapper," Eustace noted. "I'm sure the ladies went mad over him."

Bennett smiled sadly. "He was quite the socialite in his prime, that's true. Though, he changed dramatically after he lost the twins."

"Jesus," Eustace said. "These are bleak. Can you point us to a happy one?"

Bennett moved to the next portrait, featuring a man and woman in the parlor. She was seated in a spoon-back chair, and he stood behind with a hand on her shoulder. "Your great-great-grandmother, Opal, and her husband, Theodore. A very proud woman, I am told, who inherited not only her father's estate but a great deal of his sense and drive as well."

"And his scowl," Cordelia noted.

"Yes, well. I'm afraid it wasn't a pleasant union," Bennett informed them. "Your great-great-grandfather was a drunk and a gambler and carried on with a good number of women during their marriage."

"You need to freshen up on the meaning of *happy*," Eustace told the attorney before shooting Cordelia a *What gives?* look.

Bennett smiled flatly and moved through the kitchen to the solarium. "Here you'll find the herbaceous heart of the house.

Erazmus had this solarium built for his young bride, Arabella, who took great comfort in its beauty."

Cordelia and Eustace glanced around skeptically. Though full of plants, the solarium had a grim, diluvian air, manifested in the unseemly pond at its center. And the glass dripped with condensation, as if the greenhouse itself were weeping.

Eustace raised her eyebrows. "Of course she did."

Cordelia had to hide a chuckle in her sleeve.

Bennett frowned. "Shall we tour the second story?"

"After you," Eustace told him.

He led them up a spiraling iron staircase in a corner of the solarium that entered a back door to one of the bedrooms. "This was Arabella's personal suite," he told them, his arm unfolding to indicate the four-poster bed hung with heavy, mauve Dupioni curtains and the adjoining sitting room, large enough for a matching settee and two armchairs. The wainscoting had been upholstered in the same rose silk as everything else.

"I've never seen pink look so depressing," Eustace whispered in Cordelia's ear.

"She didn't share a room with her husband?" Cordelia asked.

Bennett shook his head, and his jowls wiggled. "It was not so uncommon in that time for couples of a certain position to keep separate rooms."

"And yet she had four children," Eustace quipped in a bawdy tone.

There was an untraceable flash in Bennett's eyes before he changed the subject. "Your aunt, of course, took the room across the hall." He opened the door and gestured but made no move to show it to them.

Cordelia stepped through the door, and Eustace followed. Bennett started to press on.

"Shouldn't we see it?" Cordelia asked him. "Our aunt's room?" She'd been in there already, but he didn't know that.

He paused, clasping his hands in front of him. "If you must," he said, before moving to open the door. "It's plain enough. Your aunt had rather simple tastes. Though it was another's room first," he added with a marked look at the music box. "Your mother's, in fact."

Cordelia had felt as much the day before, but having it pointed out by Mr. Togers bothered her. It was the second time he'd hinted at an intimate detail of their mother's life, and it felt a shade too close for someone technically outside of the family. She turned and smiled tightly at the old attorney. "Can you tell us what happened to our aunt?"

"Her heart stopped," he said patently. "In the night."

"A heart attack?" Eustace gave him a curious look. "I didn't know heart disease ran in the family."

"That's because it doesn't," he told her, closing the door. "It was not a constriction of blood flow to the heart muscle, but a cessation of all function." He started again down the hall. "It was rather unexpected, but the medical examiner insists she did not suffer."

It sounded plausible, and yet Cordelia couldn't shake that dislodged fingernail from her mind. Was that the action of a woman who wasn't suffering? "The groundskeeper said she didn't leave her room."

Bennett stopped abruptly. He turned to stare at her. "Did he now? Yes, well, she was rather tired toward the end, quite on in years, as you both know. Time does take its toll."

"Sure," Cordelia agreed, casting her eyes downward. "On the mind as well. We wondered if senility ran in the family?"

Bennett studied them before responding. He cleared his throat. "As not only her legal counsel but a lifelong friend, I can assure you your aunt was of sound mind until the day she died," he told them. "You'll find nothing to contest to that end. And her wishes would be respected in any court of law."

Cordelia realized he thought they were questioning the will, though they had yet to learn anything about it. "Oh yes, of course," she said to reassure him. "We're really just curious about our own medical history, you understand?"

He nodded perfunctorily, before striding off again.

"Did she ever complain of headaches?" Eustace asked, picking up Cordelia's inquiry as she tried to keep pace with him.

Bennett's teeth gleamed in the gloomy hall. "Headaches? Heavens, no. She was fit as a fiddle. Just weary when it came down to it," he said, escorting them on.

Moving to the room Cordelia and Eustace had shared, he opened the door and told them, "This room belonged to Morna, from the portrait downstairs."

Cordelia and Eustace peered into the space through new eyes. The shades of blue seemed grayer somehow, sadder, everything a touch more dismal.

"She was a great lover of animals," he added dryly.

"That explains a few things," Cordelia said, indicating the stuffed ravens with a nod of her head. It seemed Eustace wasn't the only one in the family with a penchant for animal husbandry.

Turning back across the hall, Bennett smiled. "And this was the bedchamber of Erazmus Bone himself." Before Cordelia could stop him, he flung open the door, revealing rich green paint now spattered red and the stag bed cluttered with furry, lifeless bodies.

"Good heavens," the attorney exclaimed as he looked inside. "This is most unusual."

Cordelia cringed as she saw the morbid scene for the second time, and looked away.

"Wasn't this your room last night, Cordy?" Eustace asked.

"Before the bats chased me out. But they were most definitely *alive* then," Cordelia told her, voice going flat.

Bennett closed the door and turned to face them with wide

eyes. "I suggest you choose a different room tonight," he said gravely. "I'll get someone to take care of this."

"I've already spoken to Gordon about it," Cordelia told him. "He's going to come by later."

Bennett looked waxen. "Just so. I apologize if this was distasteful for you. The house has a way of making its will known, you'll find."

Cordelia's eyes narrowed. "You're saying *the house* did this?"

The old man's face fell. "I have worked for your family a long time," he said. "And my father before me. And while I consider myself a man of reason and education, I must admit, there is much about Bone Hill I have witnessed over the years which cannot be rightly explained. It is a fine house, and a peculiar one. I'll say no more than that. Not within these walls."

The marrow in Cordelia's bones went cold and runny.

Bennett turned for the stairs with a wary glance toward the door he'd just closed. "We should resume our discussion in the library, I think. Keep to the first floor for now."

"Wait," Eustace interrupted. "You only mentioned choosing another room for tonight. Why? What happens after tonight?"

"Your aunt will be interred, of course," he told them. "Tomorrow morning."

"Oh, but we haven't spoken to anyone yet. Do we need to contact the funeral home?" Cordelia asked.

"By no means," he said, ushering them back toward the stairs. "Everything has been arranged. Preparations are already under way. Your aunt has left specific instructions. Your presence will be required, of course, as part of the family. But beyond that, the best thing you can do is stay out of the way."

As they headed down the stairs, Cordelia had an idea. "It would be great, Mr. Tog—I mean, Bennett, if you would be available to give these historical tours on showings."

He stopped abruptly and turned to face her. "Showings?"

"Yes. I mean, only for those we know are serious. We'll take them by appointment, of course. No surprise visits. History can really drive a sale."

Bennett's face seemed to sag even farther, like a melting candle. "Sale?"

The man reminded Cordelia of a sick parrot. "Yes. My sister and I intend to list the property as soon as we can."

Here, he smiled assuredly, suddenly understanding her meaning. "I'm afraid that won't be possible," he said before turning around and starting back down the stairs.

Cordelia shot her sister a surprised look. "What do you mean?" she called.

Bennett stopped again, this time at the very base of the staircase. "Your aunt has left you a modest inheritance, but it is in fact bound to the estate through a trust."

"A trust?" Eustace asked.

He grinned, steepling his fingers in front of the lapels of his dark gray suit. "In order to receive the Bone inheritance, you must maintain the estate within the family line."

"You mean live here?" Cordelia pressed. This was a wrinkle she had not been prepared to iron out.

While inheriting a house just as she was losing another might sound like a miraculous solution, Cordelia did not want to share space with the haunts of the estate. She'd gone well out of her way as an adult to avoid properties with lingering inhabitants. It was the only way she'd kept from going out of her mind with terror. And she needed every penny to get John's creditors off her back.

Her fingers began to twitch at her side. *It can't be possible,* she thought. Only yesterday they'd had zero service, but a technological *ping* quickly confirmed a message. She turned and glanced at her phone. Connecticut is nice this time of year. Minus a day for the time zone difference. 27 and counting.

The number was yet again *unknown.*

Cordelia nearly swallowed her own tongue. *That's not how time zones work,* she wanted to scream, but it didn't matter. Busy and his associates were watching her, and they made the rules.

"Indeed," Bennett informed them. "That is how it has always been done since your great-great-great-grandfather, Erazmus, built the house here at Bone Hill."

"What do you mean by *modest*?" Cordelia asked. She needed a *lot* of money. *Modest* was not what she was hoping for. "How much is this inheritance?"

He leveled a patronizing smile at her. "As the trustee, I determine when and if you should be informed of the specifics, and sums are not what's important right now. I'm sure you'd agree, with your aunt so recently departed."

Cordelia shut her mouth, adequately chastened.

"Surely there's another way . . ." Eustace plied the attorney.

"You can, of course, forfeit the inheritance," he said plainly.

"What happens then?" Eustace asked.

"We get nothing," Cordelia told her, finding her voice as she deflated. If she stayed, John's loan sharks would come for her, but the inheritance might be just enough to pay the worst of them off. If she walked away with no inheritance and no sale, however, there was an aluminum baseball bat waiting with her name on it. She needed this too much to refuse.

"Quite right. Everything would revert to the contingency laid out in the trust," he told them.

"Contingency?" Cordelia asked.

Bennett smiled, and Cordelia felt a little chill creep its way down her back. "Nothing that would, at that point, concern you."

Her phone *ping*ed again. Cordelia looked down at it.

If you don't come back, we'll take
the debt out of your neighbor.

Though I doubt she's got enough
years left to pay.

An image followed, the black and tan face of a dog, ears flattened and whale-eyed with fear. It was Perry Ellis.

CHAPTER SEVEN

THE TRUTH

CORDELIA'S GUT TWISTED with guilt as she stood in the vestibule watching the attorney drive away, peering through the narrow windowpanes in the door, the ripples in the cylinder glass distorting his shape, morphing him into something unrecognizable. It wasn't just her life on the line now, but an innocent woman's. Someone she called a *friend*. She'd never intended to entangle anyone else in her sordid marriage and financial problems, least of all her kindly neighbor, Mrs. Robichaud, but her sudden departure must have looked like an escape attempt. If they'd been watching her for a while, which she now suspected, then they'd seen her with Claire and her beastly little terrier. They knew where her soft spots were.

And that meant it was only a matter of time before they realized she had a sister. She turned back to Eustace, who was standing in the stair hall, a packet of papers for them to sign clutched to her chest.

"Do you believe all that?" she asked her sister. "About the trust?"

Eustace shrugged. "He'd have no reason to lie."

Cordelia nodded. Of course, her sister was right. It was just such a strange caveat. She'd never heard of an inheritance being bound up with the estate through a trust. As if the house were more important than the heirs.

"Do you?" Eustace asked. "Believe him?"

She bit her bottom lip. "Yes, but . . ."

"There's something he's not saying," Eustace finished.

Cordelia exhaled. "Yes. That."

She didn't think the old man had a dishonest bone in his body, but she did get the feeling he wasn't telling them everything. Maybe it was for their own good. Or maybe he didn't want to overwhelm them. Or maybe he was bound by his word and legal obligations to their aunt. Cordelia didn't know. She only knew that she felt like she and Eustace were missing the punch line to a joke everyone else was laughing at. "He called the trust *modest,* but nothing about this place is modest."

"Isn't that how generational wealth goes?" her sister asked. "It gets squandered by your forebears until eventually there's nothing respectable left but a name."

"You heard what he said," Cordelia told her. "We'll get nothing if we refuse to live here. Not even the house."

"As though we aren't even family," Eustace concluded. "As if our genetics can be erased with a few legal documents."

But their genetics weren't at stake right now—their inheritance was. And Cordelia needed money more than blood. With the house tied up in the trust, she could lose both—her share of whatever money her aunt left her and the considerable amount they stood to make on the sale of the property. Under her current circumstances, Cordelia couldn't think of a worse outcome.

"So, what do we do?" Eustace asked.

Cordelia chewed her bottom lip. "Nothing. For now. I'm going to have these reviewed by another attorney—someone not connected to the family. We need a second opinion."

Bennett Togers' first allegiance was to their aunt, after all. To seeing her final wishes carried out. But Cordelia and Eustace needed someone on their side, someone who could put their interests over those of their deceased relatives.

"What do we do when he comes back? You heard him—the funeral is in the morning. He's going to expect these," Eustace said, flipping through the papers in her hand.

"We stall," Cordelia told her. "We stay here just until we can get our own legal counsel and sort this out. There has to be a loophole."

Eustace walked over and dropped the papers onto the bench of the hall tree. "I don't know. Maybe it would just be easier to move."

Cordelia rounded on her. "Permanently? Don't you have a life waiting for you back in Colorado? What about your business?"

Though her own life was technically in tatters, the sale of the house stood to provide more than the trust if Mr. Togers were to be believed, and she needed that money badly. Her eyes crept across the room. She would do what she had to in order to protect Mrs. Robichaud and pay off John's debts, but she couldn't take up residence here forever. She'd stay just long enough to sort the estate, get what they came for, and maybe learn a thing or two about their mother in the process.

Eustace shrugged, evading her eyes as she glided into the parlor. "Businesses can be moved. They can be closed. They can be sold. New ones can be started. I'm just saying I think it would behoove us to stay fluid right now. To be open."

Cordelia followed her sister, frowning. "After all the work you've done? You would abandon your plants, that strain you've been working on? What about your employees? Their livelihoods, their families? This doesn't sound like the Eustace I know at all."

Her sister leaned her elbows on her knees, face calm but unyielding. "It's been five years, Cordy. Maybe I've changed." She sounded tired, as if her vim had deserted her. "This house is the only family we have left. By all means, contact an attorney, get that second opinion. But don't presume to speak for me. I make my own decisions last I checked, and I haven't made up my mind about this place yet."

Cordelia knew only one person on the planet who could be more stubborn than her and their mother combined, and that was her sister. It was easy, after so many years of Eustace's carefree, permissive lifestyle, to forget that when she wanted to, she could be the most bullheaded of them all.

"Of course you do," Cordelia told her, softening her voice. "You surprised me, that's all. I didn't realize you cared about this place so much."

"There are a lot of things you don't realize," Eustace said without meeting Cordelia's eyes.

Cordelia took a breath. She'd carried her own secrets here, but she could see now that if she didn't confide in her sister, she wouldn't be able to get the help that she needed. "Speaking of which, there's something I didn't tell you about John."

Her sister leaned back, listening.

Cordelia felt the tears rise as the whole ugly truth spilled out of her—the debts she'd only started to see once he'd left, the credit accounts he'd opened in her name over the years, the call from Mr. Mazzello. The shame was almost more than she could bear, as if they were her sins, her crimes, and not his. Finally, she told Eustace about the text message she'd received in Mr. Togers' presence.

"And you're sure this guy is connected to the mob?" Eustace asked.

Cordelia sniffed. "I don't think *Busy* is a very common name for bankers, do you?"

"Fair point." Her sister frowned. "I hate to think how he got that name. What was he *busy* doing?"

"If I don't come up with the money in twenty-seven days, I don't know what they'll do. But if we don't sell, how will I get it? The inheritance is minimal at best, and it's bound to a trust which Mr. Togers has control over." Cordelia forced herself to stop sniffling. "I know it's a lot to ask, and I haven't been the best sister over the last few years, but maybe you could lend me just enough to pay off Mr. Mazzello? You can take it out of my half of the equity when we sell this place. I'll come up with the rest on my own."

Eustace stood and began pacing the long parlor. "*If* we sell this place," she corrected.

Cordelia's mouth hung open. "Eustace, did you hear what I said? They are threatening to *kill* me. And my neighbor."

"I knew John was dirty, but this is foul even for him," her sister muttered.

"Eustace—"

"Just let me think!"

As far as Cordelia could see, there was nothing to think about. She would have given her sister the money in a heartbeat if she had it, and she wasn't half as generous as Eustace had been growing up. Something about her sister's reluctance didn't add up.

"I'm going to take a shower," Eustace announced out of the blue. Before she left the room, she met her sister's eyes. "We'll figure this out, I promise."

Cordelia watched her head toward the staircase. Once she could no longer hear footfalls on the stairs, she sunk onto the settee in defeat and bewilderment. It had taken courage for her to ask her sister for the money, but she'd never considered that Eustace would say *no*. "What was that?" she asked the empty room as if it could answer.

In response, she heard the water kick on, rushing through ancient pipelines in the walls, loud as a herd of cattle. Cordelia rolled her eyes. Who knew when the plumbing was last checked? That alone could cost enough to sink them. She could understand the allure of Bone Hill perhaps, but this estate was a monstrous responsibility whatever one's means, and it was crawling with family secrets. Maybe her sister was having a midlife crisis.

They had no choice at the moment, however. If they left with papers unsigned, that could be seen as forfeiting their stake in the trust. Cordelia tried to comfort herself with the reminder that they could find another lawyer and make another legal arrangement. Once they established a divide between money and property, they could make their own choices. If Eustace wanted Bone Hill that much, she could buy Cordelia out of her share. That should be enough to pay the worst of John's debts.

She sent Molly a quick text asking for the contact info of an estate attorney she'd worked with. One positive thing to come from Mr. Togers' visit—the WiFi password.

Stomach growling, she made her way to the kitchen to poke around in the basket he'd left behind. She sampled several packs of crackers and a wedge of expensive cheese but sadly found no coffee to speak of. Refusing to give up, she raided the cabinets for a coffeemaker or a tin of Folgers. What she found was more like an enamel teapot with a lid and a strainer. It didn't even have a cord, for pity's sake. It would either be the best or the worst cup of coffee she ever made, but she would need to get some grounds first. Her head was already starting to pinch.

Cordelia heard the water shut off and the pipes rattle in response, followed by a bang so loud it made her flinch.

"Eustace!" she called to the ceiling, imagining her sister tripping over the edge of the claw-foot tub and cracking her skull on the tile. "Is everything okay?"

She didn't respond.

Pursing her lips, Cordelia dashed up the stairs and knocked on the door.

"Eustace?!" she called through the thick wood. "You all right?"

There was still no reply. Eustace could be obstinate, but they were just getting their relationship back on track. Cordelia worried at a pick in her sweater, wondering what her sister was thinking after her full confession. "Eustace, please," she tried again, banging on the door. "Don't be angry with me."

Cordelia was beginning to feel an increasing sense of concern. What if whatever had killed those bats had gotten to her sister? Or worse? Hadn't Mr. Togers said the house had a will of its own? They were nonsensical thoughts, but she couldn't put them aside. She placed an ear to the door. Beating on it a third time, she called, "Please just say something so I know you're okay!"

She gripped the knob, but it wouldn't turn. Cordelia rattled it to no avail. It was jammed fast, the door locked from the inside. Frantic, she beat against the wood with the flat of her hand, calling her sister's name, begging her to open up.

Cordelia wrapped both hands around the knob, pushing and pulling, shaking the door in its hinges. Panic surged through her, a shot of dazzling, electric energy that gathered in her chest, pressing against her heart and ribs, demanding action. But her head felt like it was shrinking, squeezing her brain, causing her to squint her eyes and reel with dizziness.

Her body began to tremble as she continued to jostle the knob. Beneath her, the house rumbled in kind. The window at the end of the hall shook against its frame as if something were beating to get in. Cordelia glanced at it in fear, but all she could think about was getting to her sister. A swell of power shot from her feet to her throat as the window flew open, practically knocking her out of her shoes. Cordelia opened her mouth to scream, and a blast pushed through her, an explosive wind that blew the door open, splintering the wood of the frame and flinging one of the pins from the hinge, causing it to slam against the wall and hang at an odd angle.

Eustace shrieked, grasping a nearby towel to clutch to her chest, barely missing the swing of the door as it burst inward.

But not before Cordelia saw—the sharp, bony shoulders, sunken chest, and countable ribs, the angry scar cutting across her left breast, leaving it tucked and misshapen where a large portion had been cut away, and the horrified look on her sister's face.

"Y-y-you weren't answering," Cordelia tried to explain, one hand on her head, where the excruciating pressure of a moment ago was already dissipating. Her body felt strangely empty, like a balloon that's been stuck with a pin. But something remained, something delicious, a ripple of power Cordelia could feel sparking along her insides. It made her weak in the knees, the way she felt after a really good orgasm, wrung out and on fire all at once.

"You could try knocking first," Eustace snapped, anger contorting her face. She looked at the lopsided door, the shards of wood littering the floor. "What the fuck did you do?"

"What do you mean? I was calling your name over and over. I practically beat the door down before I got it open," Cordelia tried to tell her. She still wasn't clear on *how* she'd gotten it open, but she would deal with that later. "I kept shaking the handle, trying to get in. You didn't hear me?"

"I didn't hear anything." Eustace eyed Cordelia skeptically. "The water's not even running. How would I not hear all that?" She gave the door a little push, and it creaked pathetically on its remaining hinge. "Cordy . . . what happened exactly?" Then she really looked at her sister, saw the hand pressed to her temple. "Are you all right? Are you hurt?"

Cordelia shook her head. "It's nothing. Are you going to tell me what I just witnessed?"

Eustace's face fell. "I've been trying."

"Well, try harder," Cordelia insisted. "Because it appears you had surgery, and the only reason I can think of for breast surgery is c-c-c . . ." She couldn't bring herself to say the word *cancer*.

"I wanted to tell you," Eustace said, wrapping the towel around herself. "It just never seemed like the right time."

"I'd say now feels pretty right," Cordelia responded.

Her sister frowned. "I know it was wrong to keep it from you. But we weren't really speaking, and I didn't want to worry you unnecessarily."

"I would call cancer necessary, Eustace," Cordelia argued. "When were you diagnosed?"

"In June," she told her.

"You've been living with cancer for eleven months and didn't even bother to call?" Cordelia knew she was sounding indignant, but she couldn't help it. They'd been at odds, but she still thought of them as close enough to face a potentially fatal disease together. She felt guilt-stricken that her sister had faced this crisis all alone.

"The surgery was in July," Eustace told her. "Followed by a year of chemo. I have two injections left."

"So, I wasn't wrong. You have lost weight. That's due to the chemo?" Cordelia asked.

Eustace nodded. "It makes me nauseous, kills my appetite. It could be much worse, really. I'm one of the lucky ones."

"I'd hate to see your version of *un*lucky," Cordelia muttered.

Eustace sighed and pushed past her sister, stepping over the splintery mess and heading toward the bedroom. Cordelia followed on wobbly knees, lowering herself into the nearest chair for support while her sister changed.

"I can't believe you went through this all alone," she reiterated, her eyes beginning to fill with unexpected tears. "What if I'd lost you?"

"You see? This is precisely why I didn't call. And you didn't tell me about John," she chided.

"That's entirely different," Cordelia bellowed.

Eustace scowled. "I hate when you act like this."

"Like what?" Cordelia asked her. "Concerned?"

"Look, it's done," Eustace grumbled. "There's no going back and there's no changing it. I'm sorry your feelings are hurt, but it's out now. You know. So maybe you'll understand why I'm not so ready to leave this place, and why I can't help you."

Cordelia felt like she'd been knocked in the head, the truth registering in sickening waves. It wasn't that her sister didn't want to give her the money, it was that she couldn't. She didn't have it to give.

"It's not exactly cheap paying for surgery and drugs and monthly hospital visits," Eustace told her.

Cordelia placed a hand over her mouth. "Didn't you have insurance?"

"I'm a business owner—or *was*. An entrepreneur in the cannabis industry. So no, I didn't exactly have a benefits package to keep me afloat. Even if I did, the co-pays are enough to sink anyone poorer than Warren Buffett."

"Oh, Eustace," she whispered. "Tell me you didn't?"

Eustace dropped on the end of the bed. "What choice did I have? I sold off everything I could just to keep my treatment going. There's no use crying about it. I'm alive. That's what matters."

"Of course," Cordelia agreed. "Of course. It's just . . . all your hard work."

"I know," Eustace said quietly. "Let's not dwell on it. I'm still adjusting to my new reality."

Cordelia nodded.

"But I need some time," she said now, meeting her sister's eyes. "A place to lay low. To *rest*. I'm so exhausted, Cordy. This opportunity came up at precisely the moment I needed it most."

"I'm not sure *opportunity* is the right word for what this is," Cordelia told her, taking in Morna's dismal room.

Eustace furrowed her brow. "Then what is it? I was just starting to make my peace with what happened to Mom when I was diagnosed. And now we come here and find the same mark on our aunt's wall. And that photograph. Are we even going to talk about that?"

"I'd hoped I'd imagined it," Cordelia admitted.

Eustace reached into the pocket of her robe on the foot of the bed and pulled it out. "Think again," she said, wiggling it in Cordelia's face.

"Don't wave that thing around." Cordelia ripped it from her fingers, laid it in her lap. She looked down at its eerie imagery with dismay.

"It's not staged," Eustace told her. "Photoshop wasn't a thing back in 1959."

Cordelia pursed her lips. "It's disturbing."

"It's proof," Eustace corrected.

"Of what?"

Her sister took her hands in her own. "Of everything. Mom. You. Me. The tattoo. Don't you see? There's something *different* about our family. Mom knew it but would never talk about it. It's why she left. It's why we're here. And it's at the bottom of what happened to her."

The scope of the moment ballooned around Cordelia, convex and reflective, slippery as mercury. "Actually, I'm here for the money," she joked.

It was true, of course, but her sister's logic wasn't lost on her, especially after whatever had just happened in the hall, her body still floppy as string from it, the absence of a headache more notable for once than the presence of one.

"Wouldn't it feel good to finally put some of the goddamned pieces together?" Eustace asked her. "Don't you want to know?"

"If we're witches?" Cordelia passed the photograph back to her sister.

The blood-dripped word she'd seen in the mirror hovered between them. She hadn't told Eustace about that. Now, she didn't feel sure she'd really seen it at all. But she wasn't about to go back and check. Her head gave an unsolicited throb at the memory. With effort, she kept any expression of pain from her face. She was beginning to wonder if doing what she always had—repressing the difficult things: the scary, inexplicable, unnatural things—wasn't precisely what had led her here, to this point in her mother's shadow, a few headaches away from her own "brain aneurysm." But it was all she knew.

Maybe her sister was right. Maybe the answers she needed—to put an end to the headaches, understand things seen that shouldn't have been, lay their mother's memory to rest once and for all—were already here waiting for them. Maybe with Eustace's help, she could dig herself out of the hole she was in, get her life and her health back on track. She took in her sister's diminished appearance. Eustace already knew her secret shame about the debts, but she couldn't bring herself to tell her about the headaches, to send her already compromised sister over the edge with worry. Those she would have to get to the bottom of on her own. Once she learned how to eliminate, or at least manage, them, then she would tell her sister the *whole* truth.

She'd been raised to believe some secrets were best left buried, but that had gotten her here—at a dead end in her marriage, career, and finances with her life and health on the line. Like it or not, Bone Hill was the only way forward. For *both* of them.

"What else do I have to lose?" she told her sister, rising, steadier than she was before.

"So, you'll help me?" Eustace asked, brightening.

"Do what exactly?"

"Dig!" Eustace insisted. "Investigate. Turn this place over until we find enough clues to fill in the blanks between this photo, our mother's death, and the family she made sure we knew nothing about. This time is a gift, Cordy. This place . . . it brought us back together. What if that was for a reason?"

"Okay." She couldn't deny her sister after leaving her to face surgery and chemo all alone for the last year. And she could no longer deny herself. Whatever the cost of knowing, it couldn't be higher than *not* knowing. Could it? "Just promise me one thing."

Eustace beamed. "What?"

She pointed at the photo. "You'll never ask me to wear that much eye makeup."

CHAPTER EIGHT

The Funeral

"THAT'S THE LAST of them," Gordon said, eyeing Cordelia darkly as he carried a black trash bag through the kitchen, heavy with the lifeless bodies of her assailants.

Feeling culpable, she took a step back. "Thank you for taking care of this."

He nodded briskly. "I'll have to report this to the wildlife department."

"Why?" Eustace asked, emerging from the pantry. "We didn't do anything. We just found them like that."

"That's exactly why," Gordon told her. "They're a protected species. They'll want to investigate, see if there's a new virus or disease that could be responsible. Something they need to protect the other colonies from."

"They sort of did it to themselves," Cordelia supplied, knowing it sounded ridiculous even as she said it. But he'd heard them that night beating against the door. She needed him to believe her.

He stared at her, one brow cocked, appraising.

"It was a mass suicide," Eustace said plainly, and Gordon's eyebrow arched so high it practically disappeared into his hairline.

"What she means is they seemed driven by something. In a frenzy," Cordelia rushed to clarify.

A shadow passed across Gordon's face, unreadable.

"Do we need to . . . I don't know . . . fumigate the room or something?" Cordelia asked him, rubbing her hands together.

He ran a palm over his flanneled chest. She couldn't help noticing how the sleeves strained to contain his arms. "No, nothing like that. There's a vacuum on the third floor if you want to give the room a cleaning. But I would warn you against sleeping in there again just in case the disease is zoonotic."

"I doubt I can bring myself to go back in that room at all, let alone sleep in there," Cordelia told him.

"I set the rest of your personal things in the hall. In case you felt that way."

She looked down, flustered to know he'd handled her things.

"I, uh, couldn't help but notice the bathroom," he said now, and waited for either of them to respond.

"Oh that," Eustace said with a nervous laugh.

"The knob was stuck," Cordelia chimed in. "Eustace couldn't get out."

Gordon didn't respond, but his expression was layered heavily with skepticism.

"I was trying to shoulder it open," Cordelia attempted to explain, suddenly aware of how dainty her shoulders seemed.

"She pushed when I pulled," Eustace added.

"Yes," Cordelia said. "It was both of us."

His eyes narrowed, pinging between them.

"Can you fix it?" Eustace asked him.

"When I come to paint the bedroom," he said with another curt nod, heading into the solarium.

The second he left the room, Cordelia sagged onto the counter, head in hands.

"He's not the only one wanting an explanation about that door," Eustace said, low. "I was there. I didn't have a finger on it when it flew open like that, and neither did you!"

Cordelia looked into her sister's face. "It just *happened*."

Eustace scowled, crossing her arms. "Am I to believe house tornadoes are a thing now?"

Cordelia withered under her sister's scrutiny, but before she could respond, Gordon ducked back into the kitchen. The sisters immediately straightened, Cordelia clearing her throat and Eustace grabbing a dish towel, pretending to wipe at something that wasn't there.

"I, uh, almost forgot," he said, inexplicably awkward, his stoicism cracking. "I brought you this." He pulled a small paper bag from his back pocket, handing it to Cordelia. "It should be enough to get you through the next few days."

Cordelia took the bag and felt the familiar give of coffee grounds. She immediately lifted it to her nose and inhaled deeply. "Oh, you're a lifesaver," she told Gordon, something small and imperceptible shifting between them. "How did you know?"

"Your aunt never touched the stuff. I figured Togers would forget." A small smile played across his lips. "See you in the morning, then. For the funeral."

"Is it in town somewhere?" Eustace asked.

His brow wrinkled. "Didn't he tell you? It's here."

"Here?" Cordelia shrieked. "But we aren't prepared. We didn't know we were to host anyone."

"You aren't," he said plainly. "There are no guests except the two of you."

Eustace stepped toward him, dropping the dish towel. "Didn't she have friends? People in town who would pay their respects?"

He shook his head, refusing to meet their eyes. "Not exactly."

Cordelia stared at her sister. A family so long-standing in such a small community, and no one wanted to see its matriarch laid to rest? To bring over flowers or casseroles? To reminisce about old times? "But you—?" Cordelia started to ask.

"Pallbearer," he told them. It was obvious why he was chosen for the job. "See you at five," he said, turning to leave.

"Five A.M.?" Eustace caterwauled.

Cordelia rolled her eyes. Twelve years of public schooling and Eustace had never quite adjusted to getting up to an alarm. But her sister was right—it was an unusual time to plan a funeral. The sun wouldn't even be up yet.

Gordon shrugged his meaty shoulders. "Something about the dawn."

CORDELIA STOOD IN the doorway of Arabella's room, the saddest shade of pink she ever did see, like rose-colored tears. The second story housed six bedrooms plus one large bath, a morning room, and Arabella's secret boudoir. With one room occupied, one room haunted, and one room potentially harboring a fatal disease, she'd wandered the hall with her suitcase in tow, sighing repeatedly.

There wasn't a room on this floor that didn't reek of its previous tenants. They hung in the air like a film, so thick she could nearly smell them. Even without Bennett to point them out, she could guess which room had likely belonged to whom, now that she knew a few faces and names. Here was the room of Morna's brother Linden, and probably later Claude, with soft gray stripes and the scent of tobacco clinging. Here was Opal and Theodore's room, the floral wallpaper a bitter burgundy, the angles of the turret sharp and accusing. And here was her great-great-great-grandmother's room, a wilted flower.

With a final sigh, Cordelia wheeled her suitcase inside. It hardly mattered which room she chose; she would be uncomfortable regardless. She wondered how Eustace slept in Morna's room without feeling the slow surrender to madness. And then she recalled the pungent pineapple scent of Eustace's pipe and realized how.

She readied herself for bed and climbed between the heavy drapes, propping up against a pile of pillows so thick she felt like the princess and the pea. But she dared not turn out the light. It felt as if the room were breathing the soft, gentle breaths of a woman sleeping. She could feel a wreath of disappointment about her, like a stain splattered across the walls.

When she finally managed to sleep, she dreamt she woke to see a woman glowing like the moon at the foot her bed, with pale hair and gentle eyes, a delicate frame that held too much grace for this formidable house. Cordelia watched as the woman leaned over her and put a finger to her lips, then wafted through the boudoir and out the door to the solarium.

She woke with a chill running over her like ghostly fingers and found the solarium door standing open, the cold stairs beyond empty and silent.

"ARE YOU READY for this?" Cordelia asked her sister as the coffee finished dripping and she poured a cup. She'd brought a black, belted dress for the occasion but felt unprepared.

Eustace looked through the window to the solarium. Her face was wistful. "Seems a shame this is the closest we'll ever come to the woman. Who might we have been if we'd been allowed to grow up here? Or even visit?" She turned to face Cordelia. "I've been thinking," she said. "About Mom. The headaches, the way she died."

Cordelia winced, knowing she'd been keeping her own symptoms a secret.

"I think there's a connection," Eustace told her. "With this place."

Cordelia set her coffee cup down. "Are you saying the house killed our mom?"

"No," Eustace told her, ruffled. "But I can't unsee that mark in the wall, the way it resembles her tattoo."

"But what does that have to do with the headaches?"

"You always said the medical examiner would have no reason to lie to us," Eustace reminded her. "So then there has to be a connection between the aneurysm and the mutilation. And if there's a connection between the tattoo and this place, then it stands to reason there's a connection between the headaches and Bone Hill too. Like a triangle."

Of speculation, Cordelia thought, but she couldn't deny that they were only scratching the surface of a vast network of family secrets. She wasn't sure the headaches were a mystery Bone Hill could solve—hers had only gotten worse since arriving—but she desperately needed it to.

A knock sounded, and they saw Gordon filling up the doorway in a striking black suit. His hair was slicked back into a tight ponytail, and his neck tattoo seemed to leap off his skin against the stark white shirt and black tie. Cordelia reflexively looked away, a rise of panic and desire warring within her. He looked damn good in that suit, commanding and dangerous.

"The others should be arriving soon," he told them as he came in.

There was only the faintest hint of light outside, filtered through a miasma of fog, so that the trees and plants were as vague as smudges of charcoal.

"I thought you might like to have this," he said, passing them an embossed, hinged frame. A small button at the side released it, revealing a pink lining and dreamy tintype—a portrait of a young bride. Her face was framed in silk rosettes and her dress cut straight across her shoulders, a bouquet of ribbons over her heart. The skirts were a whipped-up froth of chiffon. But it was her face that caught Cordelia's attention. Heart-shaped, like her own, and guileless, with a rosebud mouth and coy eyes. Cordelia knew her instantly as the shining woman at her bed last night—Arabella.

"Where did you get this?" Eustace asked.

"I found it in the carriage house when I was remodeling it," Gordon answered. "I tried to give it to your aunt, but she told me some things were better left where they lie. Whatever that means."

"Thank you," Cordelia told him. "I know who this is."

The screech of the doorbell signaled the arrival of Bennett Togers, his nephew, Arkin, the hearse bearing their aunt, and a gentleman from the funeral home. The headlamps of the hearse cut a line through the gloom, illuminating murky swirls.

Cordelia swung the front doors wide, but Bennett refused to enter.

"We'll proceed from here," he told her. "On foot." He waved in the direction of the men.

Cordelia shot Eustace a wary look. It would be a long way to carry a coffin in the dark, but how could she argue?

Gordon moved past them, and the men pulled their aunt's casket from the vehicle, resting it gently on the ground before the porch steps like a dish being served. The shape struck Cordelia— long and narrow, wide at the bottom like a treasure chest, a foot at each corner carved into talons.

Bennett pulled a folded satin pall from inside his suit jacket and unfurled it over the casket. It was embroidered with a skull sprouting wings and the words, *Silens in vita, in morte vocalis.*

Cordelia recognized them from the crypt. "Your family motto," he told them, before gesturing to the men again. With Bennett and Gordon on one side, Arkin and the third man from the funeral home on the other, they lifted the casket from the ground by iron rings welded to the sides. Without a word, they began walking.

Cordelia gripped her sister's hand as she and Eustace followed mutely, Bennett the head of their meager procession.

A loud caw startled her, the shape of a crow in the branches of a nearby tree. Soon, she spotted more crows and numerous other birds, large and small, lighting in the trees overhead, circling and flitting like shadow puppets against a slowly brightening sky.

Cordelia's head began to buzz, and she cursed herself for forgetting her pills. She tugged on her sister's sleeve, pointing up. Eustace squinted at the gathering flock and breathed in sharply.

The procession wound a serpentine trail through the congested gardens, stalks and flower spikes emerging from the gloom like spears, Bennett knowing instinctively which paths to take until they found themselves beneath the cherry trees and dogwoods, birds filling up the branches like stuffing in medieval pie. Just as the hill came into view, he gestured and the men stopped, setting the coffin on the ground. To Cordelia's surprise, they turned to face her and Eustace, then picked it up again, proceeding backward to the crypt.

Burning with a million questions, she squeezed her sister's hand. But her tongue was stuck fast to the bottom of her mouth, awed by something she couldn't define.

The trees moved beside them, crowded by feathered bodies. The rising sun took the sky from black to gray to eggshell. The fog parted around them, thick with eyes. Beyond the pain, Cordelia could feel the familiar hum, low and deep like a note held at the base of the throat. The hill loomed, stoic, the roses so vibrant they hurt her eyes.

Some quantum of blood within her understood that this was the denouement of a great and commanding woman. This white-haired lady boxed in black that hovered at the edge of her life like a conjured spirit. A shift was taking place. A changing of the guard. As day gives way to night, sun to moon. And she and her sister would be forever changed by it. Beside her, she sensed that Eustace felt it too.

As they entered the shadow of the crypt, the breeze danced in whorls around them, causing the birds to flap their wings with irritation. The crypt doors blew open as the men set the casket on the ground before it. Cordelia gasped, and Eustace clutched her arm.

The man from the funeral home stumbled back a step, and Arkin flinched, but Bennett held steady, as if it were all unfolding on cue.

Recovering the casket, they hoisted it high onto their shoulders, backing into the darkness like they'd been swallowed whole.

"Jeez," Eustace muttered. "How big is it in there?"

But Cordelia was fixated on the open gates and her deep need to know what lay inside, the hum radiating up her spine clashing with the pain behind her eyes. She wanted to enter; and she wanted to run. Her foot rose to the first step, and Eustace yanked on her arm, but Cordelia shook her off as she climbed.

Then Gordon appeared in the doorway, wide as a boulder, ushering her back down. "I'm sorry. The rest must be carried out privately."

Behind him, Arkin and the other man emerged, the first rays of morning sun breaking over the hill. Only Bennett remained behind, the heavy doors closing over his secrets as Gordon pulled them to.

"But we're family," Eustace insisted.

"This is how The White Lady wants it," he assured them.

Cordelia took a step back, still hovering on the stairs, her eyes drawn to the darkness beyond. Whatever Mr. Togers was doing in there, she felt it like the pull of a magnet. It called to her—this place, this day, this moment—like the tingle she'd felt after the bathroom door exploded. The birds began to circle the hill.

"You can go back to the house," Gordon told them. "I'll wait here for the stonemason to come and seal the burial shelf."

But Cordelia couldn't bring herself to leave. She didn't like being shut out of her family's crypt by this man who seemed to know their history better than they did, even if he was carrying out her aunt's final wishes. She didn't like that so little had been disclosed to them beyond the funeral march. She didn't like that he controlled the trust and the estate, holding them there like some kind of warden. And she didn't like that he was in there with her aunt now, doing God knows what. It was morbid. And strange. It didn't fit in the real world. Like they were witnessing—or *not* witnessing—some ancient rite handed down through generations. And off-putting as it all was, it was also *hers*. And it called to that part of her she knew was inside, buried under a mound of resistance.

Something slammed against the inside of her skull, and her pulse quickened. Cordelia bolted past Gordon for the doors, swinging one wide as she stumbled inward. Straining to focus, she could just make out the shape of Bennett Togers near the far-left wall. His arms rose as he muttered something she couldn't hear.

"What are you doing?" she called, stumbling forward. She felt drunk, affected. Inside the cool, stone cavity, the thing thrashing in her head calmed.

His arms dropped as he spun around, a white blade clattering to the floor. "Get out," he hissed, wholly unlike himself. "You don't belong here!"

Gordon rushed in behind her, grabbing her by an elbow as Eustace stood in the door.

"He has a knife!" Cordelia told them, pointing to where the dagger had fallen, though she didn't see it now. It was only then she noticed the birdcage, the trio of doves. She couldn't stop picturing the flesh ripped from her mother's chest. Cordelia shook her head. "What's going on? What are you doing to her?"

"I'm sorry," Gordon told the attorney. "She bum-rushed me."

Bennett schooled himself, approaching Cordelia with a suddenly placating expression. "Your family, Ms. Bone, is very old. It has customs for the deceased. Customs you may not understand. Customs it is not for us to judge. Customs you are not trained to carry out."

"But you are?" Cordelia questioned, shaking all over.

"Indeed," he said coolly. "Your aunt saw to it herself, knowing that your upbringing made you strangers to this place and its ways. It's not your fault," he said now, patronizing. "You are but a product of your mother's foolhardy choices."

"Hey!" Eustace objected, taking a step forward.

Bennett *tsk*ed, placing a hand on Cordelia's shoulder. "Now, now. We mustn't question your aunt's authority. Even Mr. Jablonski understands. Don't you, Gordon? He was a witness, you see."

Cordelia turned to Gordon, who raised both palms in peace. "Your aunt called me to witness her giving her final wishes to Togers—*sealed*. All I know is that I was to be a pallbearer, and that no one, except the stonemason and Togers himself, should be permitted entry to the crypt."

"Cordy," Eustace said, reaching for her. "Come on. If the man wants privacy so he can put our aunt's body to rest, we'll give it to him."

Cordelia rounded on her, shocked after all of Eustace's outrage over their mother's death, her burning speech the day before about putting the pieces together.

"She's already dead," Eustace said, tugging on Cordelia's arm. But as Cordelia allowed herself to be pulled away, Eustace leaned down and whispered where only she could hear, "We'll come back. Tonight."

CHAPTER NINE

The Dinner

CORDELIA FELT SUDDENLY exhausted upon returning to the house. Normally, getting up at 5 A.M. wouldn't be a problem for her. All she could think was that the confrontation at the crypt, the surrealness of the morning, had drained her.

"I'm famished," Eustace exclaimed as they trudged into the kitchen. "I feel like I haven't eaten in weeks."

Cordelia eyed her sister. "Yeah, well, I don't think I can hold my eyes open a moment longer. I'm so tired I can barely stand."

Eustace was already rummaging through the pantry like a hog rooting for food. She poked her head out, a box of Danish biscuits in one hand. "You go rest," she said, pupils dilating as she bit into her first cookie. "I am going to prepare a feast in honor of our aunt!"

Cordelia looked at her strangely. "You? *Cook?* Your idea of *epicurean* is adding cannabutter to your Kraft Macaroni and Cheese."

Her sister pointed a half-eaten cookie at her. "I resent that. I make a mean pizza burrito. Best cure for the munchies in a thousand square miles. Besides, I'm feeling inspired."

Slumping across the island, Cordelia's eyelids were drooping as if there were lead weights in her mascara. "I've got to go lie down. I'm heading upstairs for a short nap." She trudged past her sister in the pantry.

"You do that!" Her sister called through a full mouth. "I'll wake you when the food is ready."

Cordelia lifted a weary hand and dragged herself up the stairs. *Have there always been so many?* she wondered as she stumbled down the hall. By the time she made it to Arabella's room, it was all she could do to kick off her shoes and climb onto the enormous bed, grabbing one of her pills and swallowing it dry in the process.

Her eyes began to close, the thrum in her head dulling at the edges, and Cordelia could just make out a crowd gathering at the boundary of her vision, their blurred forms staggering toward her, but she didn't have the energy to tell them to get out. Someone bent over her, a head full of dark reddish hair and sad eyes, and Cordelia lifted a finger to say, *I know you,* but the words didn't make it past her lips. She was out before she could even mouth the name, *Morna.*

She woke to the smell of something savory and fragrant. Her sister's humming echoed throughout the second floor, as if the house were magnifying it through the rooms. She knew the house was old, but sound didn't carry normally there. Things that should be loud were quiet, and things that should be quiet were loud. She still didn't understand how Eustace had never heard her outside the bathroom, banging to get in.

Bleary-eyed, she made her way downstairs. Her head was no longer hurting, but it felt as though it had been stuffed with cotton in her sleep. The light filtered through the tower windows like liquid gold, as it did when the sun was sinking. Cordelia frowned and headed for the kitchen.

It was a mess. Pots were bubbling on the ancient stove, flour coated everything, empty boxes littered every surface—cookies and crackers and cans full of nuts, jars of old jam, bags of goodness-only-knew-what. Cordelia lifted a mostly eaten can of deviled ham and sniffed. It smelled of cat food. She made a face and set it down.

Eustace bustled in from the solarium, fistfuls of something leafy and green in her hands. A ragged apron was tied around her waist.

"I'm sorry," Cordelia said, staring at her. "Who are you and what have you done with my sister?"

Eustace laughed. "You're up! That's excellent."

She glanced around the room. "Eustace, what is all this? You didn't eat *all* this food, did you?"

But before her sister could answer, Gordon strode in. He was still wearing his white dress shirt from that morning, though he'd lost the jacket and unbuttoned the top, rolled the sleeves to the elbow. He had a bottle of wine in one hand. "My mother taught me never to come empty-handed," he said.

"What are you doing here?" Cordelia blurted, realizing how rude it sounded after it was out.

His eyebrows rose.

"I invited him," Eustace told her. "So be nice." Turning to Gordon, she added, "You're just in time."

Cordelia's brow wrinkled. "Invited him to what?" She felt like she'd woken up in *The Twilight Zone*.

"To dinner," Eustace said, as if it made all the sense in the world.

"*Dinner?* What time is it? How long did I sleep?" She reached up to check her hair and could feel the tangles her waves had made. She tried to run her fingers through it, to little avail.

Eustace checked her phone. "Ten and a half hours, by my estimation. That was some nap!"

Cordelia shook her head. That couldn't be right. "You didn't wake me?"

"I've been busy," Eustace told her, gesturing with a wooden spoon around the kitchen.

"Doing what? Eating everyone's feelings?" Cordelia couldn't quite get a handle on what was happening.

Eustace scowled at her. "I told you, I was *hungry*. Now, you two go in the dining room and open that wine, let it breathe," she commanded. "I already set the table."

Gordon did as he was told. Begrudgingly, Cordelia followed, but not before turning to hiss at her sister, "You could have warned me!"

Eustace only grinned and smacked her playfully with the spoon.

Sure enough, in the dining room her sister had set out several tarnished candleholders and lit tapers of varying lengths. Three plates with black trim and coral roses were set alongside matching bowls, etched flatware, and a trio of crystal coupe glasses. Cordelia picked up one of the glasses and stared at it.

"Those are all wrong for wine," Gordon said, pulling a corkscrew from the long sideboard. "You can't swirl with no headspace, and the scent just leaks out of those wide rims. I hope you like Riesling."

"Well enough." She sat and tried to find somewhere safe to put her eyes. She'd not really pegged him as a wine drinker. Blood, maybe. Ox horns brimming with dark beer. Viking mead out of the skulls of his enemies. Something less . . . *couth*.

"The food smells good," he added as he poured her glass, then Eustace's, then his own.

"Yeah, it does," Cordelia said with a touch of awe. She was still struggling to clear her head. The nap-turned-coma had left her out of sorts. She finally allowed herself to meet his eyes. "Sorry, I didn't know anyone was coming. I would have, you know, changed clothes at least." She was still in the black, belted dress she'd worn for the funeral, now wrinkled from a full day of sleeping in it.

"She wouldn't take *no* for an answer," he said. "And after this morning, I felt like I owed you both an apology. I, uh, don't like being caught in the middle like that."

Eustace burst into the room carrying a loaf of crusty bread and a brick of butter for the table. She returned with a soup tureen and a salad bowl, and then again with two stoneware casseroles and a cruet of homemade dressing.

Cordelia surveyed the spread before her with wide eyes.

"Don't look so shocked," Eustace told her. "It's rude." Raising her glass for a toast, she said, "To Aunt Augusta, for saving my ass."

Gordon gave Cordelia a quizzical look as they clinked glasses.

"To Aunt Augusta," Cordelia added awkwardly.

"To The White Lady," Gordon echoed. They were all quiet for a moment before he said, "So, tell us what's on the menu."

"Yes, by all means, elucidate," Cordelia said dryly.

"Well, I whipped up a salad with most of the produce," Eustace began. "The apples and parsnips I roasted together with some spices. The asparagus I sautéed in lemon. The soup mixes I combined with wild rice. And the bread I baked myself. Oh, and the vinaigrette is a simple garlic balsamic." Her cheeks were pink with exertion, but she didn't seem tired in the least. In fact, she was brimming with giddy energy.

"You baked bread? *You?*" Cordelia asked in disbelief.

"Who else?"

"Am I still sleeping?" Cordelia asked out loud. "Is this a dream?"

Eustace ignored her. "Dig in! I am simply famished." She began loading up her plate.

Cordelia didn't understand how Eustace could still be hungry after unburdening the pantry of nearly all its contents. Maybe it was a side effect of nearing the end of her chemo treatments, a signal that she was returning to health. In fact, looking at her now, Cordelia thought Eustace looked better than she had in the last decade. Her cheeks seemed fuller. Her shoulders rounder. Her lips softer. She knew her sister needed to gain back the weight she'd lost, but even a full day of eating wouldn't show up that quickly, would it?

She sniffed a crust of bread and took a bite. "Gordon here was just apologizing," she said with unconcealed sarcasm.

He choked on the wine, setting his glass down quickly.

"For what?" Eustace asked.

"Presumably for barring us from our own property," Cordelia answered, dipping into the soup, surprised by her bluntness.

"I was only following orders," he told them.

"Yes," Eustace said. "I seem to recall you saying you'd been asked to witness our aunt's final wishes."

Gordon chewed on an apple slice with a faraway look. "She called Togers and me into the library, where we received separate envelopes. I didn't get to read what was in his, mind you, just my own, but his was significantly thicker." He tugged at his collar. "I don't think either of us expected it."

"Funny, that," Cordelia cut in. "Because you told me our aunt didn't leave her room in the end."

"She didn't," Gordon agreed. "This was not long after I came to work here. Before she became bed-bound."

Eustace set her wineglass down. "You're telling me our aunt readied her final wishes almost a year before she died?"

"Not *almost*," Gordon told her after taking another bite. "A year to the day, in fact."

Cordelia shot Eustace a serious look.

"She was in good health at the time," he explained. "She couldn't have known. She just said that Togers, as her legal counsel and trustee, would see to everything, and that no one—she really emphasized that part: *no one*—should interfere. She trusted him implicitly. This is delicious, by the way," he said, gesturing to his nearly empty bowl.

Eustace added another ladle of soup to Gordon's bowl. "What changed?"

He scooped up several mouthfuls of soup, then shrugged. "Nothing for a long while. Then she went from her usual self to being unable to leave her bed practically overnight. She even stopped talking. And then she was gone. It was only a couple of weeks before it was all over." He looked from Eustace to Cordelia and back to Eustace again. "Togers' own sister, Diana, came to nurse her," he said.

Cordelia turned her wineglass around and around, thinking. "Bennett said she died in the night. That her heart stopped suddenly. But what you're describing sounds more like a stroke. Like she was paralyzed first."

Gordon flinched, then quickly wiped the anguish from his face, but not before Cordelia noticed. He pushed back from the table. "I think I've had enough," he said with a silent belch.

But Eustace only ladled more soup into his bowl. "Eat," she encouraged. "Before it gets cold."

Slowly, he scooted toward the table, as if the promise of another bowl of soup was more than he could refuse. But he scowled as he ate, and a tense lull filled the room, broken only by the scrape of silverware against the china.

Cordelia felt her limbs loosening with every bite. She'd avoided drinking too much wine, and yet she felt like she'd polished off a bottle by herself.

"You know, we used to dare each other as schoolchildren to ride by this property on our bicycles," Gordon said.

"You grew up in Bellwick?" Cordelia set her spoon down.

He nodded. "I was as curious about this place as I was frightened by it. I've never told anyone that."

Eustace smiled. "Have you always lived in Connecticut?"

"I moved away after high school to pursue music," he said. "I joined a band, did some touring, had a messy relationship with our lead singer. Generally aspired to rock godhood."

"Anything we would have heard of?" Cordelia asked, thinking that explained the tattoos, long hair, and wardrobe devoted to black.

"I doubt it," he said, paying her a cursory glance. "You don't look like the type who listens to a lot of Slavic folk metal."

"That's a tad presumptive," she complained, taking a sulky sip of Riesling. "Never judge a queen by her tiara." She'd done the same with the wine, but at least she'd been civil enough to keep it to herself.

Eustace leaned on the table. "But you came back to Bellwick? *Why?*"

He sat back in his chair. "I had an injury, followed by a bad breakup. I needed a change of pace. Support."

"Support?" Cordelia studied him. It was hard to imagine this man needing anyone.

"It was a dark time," he said with sudden vulnerability. "And then my mom died. Here."

"You mean, *here*?" Eustace topped off his wine, and he took a long sip.

Gordon nodded. "They found her in the woods, her clothes dirtied and torn like she'd been crawling. Every joint in her body was so swollen and misshapen from the rheumatoid arthritis, they could hardly identify her. When I left, she was managing her symptoms. Something happened to advance the disease. They said she just stopped breathing right there in the leaves. Her lungs were horribly scarred. The worst the ME had ever seen." He looked at them each in turn. "That's when your aunt took me on here."

Cordelia fell back in her chair as Eustace let out a low whistle. "I'm so sorry," she told him. "It sounds awful."

"If it makes you feel any better," Eustace said ruefully, "someone cut a piece of our mother off and kept it for a souvenir."

Gordon's eyes widened.

"She had an aneurysm," Cordelia tried to explain. "But they found a piece of her, um, skin missing when they found her body."

He looked horrified.

"They did find yours with all her bits, right?" Eustace asked.

"You don't have to answer that," Cordelia snapped.

"There was nothing like that." He cleared his throat. "Will you, uh, be leaving soon?"

"Not soon enough," Cordelia muttered, Eustace shooting her a nasty look. "My sister has taken a shine to the place," she said. "And there seems to be a hang-up with the trust. So we're here until we can sort out some things." She didn't go into what those things were.

"You'll have to excuse Cordelia," Eustace said. "She's leaving behind a once-booming business and a douchenozzle husband to be here." She pressed her fingers to her mouth. "Sorry. I probably shouldn't have said that," she added with a punctual hiccup.

"*Ex*-husband," Cordelia emphasized with an embarrassed glance at Gordon. "Or soon to be, at least." She hiccupped suddenly also.

Gordon opened his mouth to say something, but all that came out was another booming hiccup. Quickly, he shut it again.

"Are we soup-drunk?" Cordelia asked between *hic*s, giving her bowl a distrustful look. "Eustace? Have you put something in this?"

Her sister smiled lazily. "No, of course not. It must be the wine."

Cordelia glanced at her nearly full glass. "But I've barely touched my wine."

"I feel it too," Gordon said, looking alarmed. "I never talk about what happened to my mother. I—I don't know why I told you all that."

Cordelia felt the blood rush to her face. "My sister is in the cannabis industry," she explained. "Please forgive her. She has a habit of believing a little too strongly in her own product."

"I feel better than I have in ages," Eustace exclaimed. "But I swear I didn't cook any herb into the food. At least not that kind. Just love. And a little old-fashioned sincerity. Oooh, and tarragon."

"Surely Mr. Togers . . ." Cordelia questioned.

Eustace gave her sister a playful shove. "Lighten up, Cordy. The attorney didn't roofie the produce."

Gordon stood suddenly, upsetting his chair and knocking the table. "I'm going to have to run," he said, rubbing the back of his neck. He turned to Eustace. "This has been . . ."

Cordelia thought he was going to say *nice,* but then his eyes met hers.

"Attractive," he said. Startled, he tried to recoup. "I mean, appealing." He closed his eyes in frustration. "Appetizing," he tried again. "I'm just gonna go now," he said before storming out.

Cordelia slid her chair back from the table. "Eustace, what is in this? Did you cook up some kind of truth serum?"

"Not exactly," Eustace admitted.

"What is that supposed to mean?" Cordelia blazed.

Her sister shrugged. "While I was cooking, I just kept thinking how helpful it would be if we could get some answers out of someone," she said. "I think it kind of crept into the food."

Cordelia ran her hand down her face. Maybe there was more to that photo inscription than she wanted to admit. Her sister, who had never cooked a real meal a day in her life, had just pulled a three-course meal out of a gift basket and some old dry goods and used it to interrogate the groundskeeper. It was doubtful they'd get anything from Gordon after this beyond a curt nod and a safe distance.

"I'm going upstairs to take a shower and sober up," she said with a sigh, looking down at her hopelessly rumpled dress. "You take care of the kitchen. And then we need to get ready."

"Ready?" Eustace asked.

"Yes," Cordelia reminded her. "We have a grave to burgle, remember?"

CHAPTER TEN

THE GRAVE

CORDELIA PULLED A cardigan over her nightdress and tiptoed down the hall to Eustace's room, knocking softly on the door.

It swung open, and her sister stood before her in cotton pajamas, patterned in bright green marijuana leaves. She held a brass lantern in one hand with a lit candle inside.

Cordelia frowned. "Nice, Eustace."

Her sister looked at the lantern. "What? It came with the room. I thought it might be useful."

"I meant your pajamas," Cordelia corrected her, starting for the stairs. "You're not exactly incognito."

Eustace whispered behind her. "Well, excuse me for forgetting to pack my ninja spy clothes. Oh, wait . . . I don't *own* any ninja spy clothes."

Cordelia flashed her an irritated look over a shoulder.

"It's not like I was expecting to go grave robbing in the middle of the night when we got here," Eustace added.

"We're not stealing anything," she corrected. "We're just investigating."

"We're literally sneaking into a crypt in the dead of night. If we get caught, no one's gonna care how we label it," Eustace retorted.

By now, they'd reached the stair hall and were making their way to the dining room and kitchen.

"It's technically *our* crypt. We're allowed inside," Cordelia reasoned.

"It's no one's at the moment," Eustace countered, "if you want to get technical about it. We haven't signed anything yet."

"You know what I mean," Cordelia said with a huff. "It has our name on it. That's got to count for something." She paused at the pantry door and Eustace bumped into her from behind, giving an audible *oof*. "Shhh . . ." she insisted with an angry swat, turning the handle carefully.

Eustace looked annoyed. "What are we shushing for? There's nobody in here but us."

Cordelia doubted that. She hoped the restless spirits of the house were tucked away in their respective corners till morning. She had no intention of alerting them to what she and her sister were about to do. In the pantry, she fumbled around in the dark until she came out clutching a butcher knife and a steel spatula.

Eustace gave her a flat look. "What are we gonna do with those? Flip her over and check to see if she's done?"

"No," Cordelia replied defensively. "I don't know. We might need tools."

Eustace narrowed her eyes. "What exactly are you planning?"

She shrugged. "Who knows what we'll encounter in there."

"They're not zombies, Cordy."

"I know that," Cordelia snapped, starting toward the solarium.

They trekked through the overgrown plants and across the slick tiles in silence, and as they stepped out into the night air, a noticeable chill crept along the ground, swirling around their bare feet and up Cordelia's nightgown. The moon hung like a broken ornament in the sky, silvery and waning. It coated the branches of the trees in white light so that they crackled across the dark like disjointed phalanges. The grass was velveteen against her feet. Even with the chill, the skeletal trees, she liked the feeling of nothing between her and the property, the connection she made with the earth her family had walked for generations, the sense of being anchored.

When they reached the front of the crypt, its towering hill stern and shadowy, a vault of riddles, they both stopped. The roses bloomed ever brighter, devoid of all respect for time of day or season. Cordelia took a deep inhale and gave her sister a solemn look. "What Bennett Togers doesn't know won't hurt him."

Eustace nodded, handing her the lantern before moving up the steps and reaching for the heavy chain around the doors.

"I was hoping they hadn't locked up after the stonemason," Cordelia complained.

Eustace gripped the padlock tight and pulled the skeleton key from her pocket, but it was too large to slide into the keyhole. Frustrated, she yanked, but the lock didn't budge. It looked to be about a hundred years old, made of dark metal and heart-shaped.

"Let me see," Cordelia said, stepping up beside her sister. She set the lantern down and reached for the lock, still in her sister's hand. Her palm warmed at the touch of the metal despite the night air, and the shackle parted easily from the padlock body, swinging open on the chain.

"What did you do?" Eustace asked as they both let go.

She shrugged, baffled. "I—I don't know. I just touched it. You were already holding it. It came undone on its own." She pulled the chain from the doors. "The lock must be faulty."

She was about to set the chain on the ground when Eustace said, "Let me see that."

Cordelia passed it to her, and Eustace pulled the lock from it, tossing it into the woods. "No one is going to keep us out of this place anymore. Not Mom, not Bennett Togers, not anyone."

Cordelia nodded silently, and they each pulled an iron door back from the mouth of the crypt. A rush of stale air greeted them.

Inside, Eustace held the lantern high as they turned slowly in place. Thick, rough-cut stones blocked the burial shelves, some of which were marked with oxidized metal plaques bearing names. Others, however, had either lost their plaque or simply never been fitted with one, rendering the inhabitants a mystery. Here and there, a stone jutted from the wall, a natural shelf where personal effects had been left, mementos of the dead. An empty vase stood sentinel on one, on another a beaded necklace, heavy with dust. A favored blade. An old timepiece. A child's doll. Striking hallmarks of the humanity that was.

The interior cavity was deceptively large, bigger than any private mausoleum Cordelia had seen in a cemetery. A handful of stone pillars held up the heavy slab of roof. Altogether, she counted twenty-one burial shelves.

Whatever shadows she'd seen pass here before were still now. The driving hum that brought her to the gates that first day lay quiet. Cordelia set the knife and spatula down as she walked to the back wall, tracing her fingers over the rock. Between the burial shelves a section of blank stone stretched to the ceiling, wider than she was, like a sheet of unused paper. Odd that they chose not to bury anyone there, but her eyes were soon drawn to the plaques on either side.

She stopped before two set atop one another, as if the people had been buried together in one slot. "Agate Lula Bone," she read aloud when Eustace held the lantern close for her to see. "And Briony Mae Bone. The dates are the same."

"The birth dates or the death dates?" Eustace asked.

"Both," Cordelia said, turning to her.

Eustace swallowed. "The twins."

"Who?"

"Remember? Bennett said Roman was never the same after losing the twins. This must be them."

"Tragic," Cordelia whispered. How could two twelve-year-old girls die on the same day? "I didn't know twins ran in our family."

"How could you?" Eustace reminded her.

She moved to the wall where they'd seen Bennett that morning, searching along it for anything that might tell them what happened after they were ushered out. But the shelves here were empty, the rock unreadable. The cage of birds was gone, but Eustace found the dagger Cordelia had seen Bennett drop, wedged between two stones at eye level.

"That's the knife he had," Cordelia said, looking at the strange white edge, wiped clean. The polished grip was smooth from use, the same material as the blade.

"What is it?" Eustace asked. "Some kind of mineral?"

Cordelia shrugged. "It's definitely not metal."

She turned back to the wall, running her hands along the grooves until her fingers met wet mortar and pressed in. "I found it! I found Augusta's final resting place. This is where he put her."

But Eustace was entranced by the knife. She kept turning it over and over, studying the material. "It seems so familiar," she said.

Cordelia dug in with her fingers, flinging wet mortar from between the stones until her hands and gown were dotted in gritty, gray clay. "Help me," she told Eustace.

Her sister dropped the knife, its white blade clattering at their feet. Cordelia looked up at her.

"It's bone," Eustace said, her face draining of color. "The knife. It's *bone*."

"A relic?" Cordelia asked.

"An heirloom," her sister responded with a shudder.

They stared at the knife together, neither willing to bend down and retrieve it. After a moment, Cordelia kicked it to the side.

Eustace noticed the flecks of mortar covering her sister's skirt and coating her hands. "What are you doing?"

"Digging her out," Cordelia said matter-of-factly.

"Whoa, whoa, whoa." She looked horrified. "Are you out of your mind?"

Cordelia held a finger before her lips. "Don't you want to know what he did to her? How did you think we were going to find out? Osmosis?"

Eustace blanched. "I thought we were just going to look around. I didn't realize we were going to exhume her!"

Cordelia ignored her sister's outrage and bent down, gripping one of the stones, trying to wriggle it from the wall. "What happened to all that blathering about us being here 'for a reason'? Do you want to know what the connection is between Mom and this place or not?"

"Of course I do," Eustace fumed.

"Then why don't you help me instead of just standing there."

Eustace choked on her indignation before finally relenting, working her fingers between the stones and pulling until they began to slide out. They stacked them neatly to one side, working without another word until they'd opened the full shelf. The end of their aunt's casket glinted inside. Together, they reached for it and dragged the dragged it out.

Cordelia wiped at her brow with the back of her hand. She met her sister's eyes.

"After you," Eustace said dryly.

Cordelia nodded and reached down, pulling off the pall with their family motto and gripping the lid. *Now or never*, she told herself before sliding it open.

Augusta's lifeless body lay supine and pale, her white hair coursing over her square shoulders and black dress. Even in death, her face looked unmovable, a woman not easily taken to compromise. Cordelia respected her for it. She felt in that moment as if something very precious had been stolen from her—the chance to know this grand lady, to learn from her. Maybe if she had, she wouldn't have made quite so many mistakes. Augusta did not seem the sort to ever be taken in by a man like John.

"She looks peaceful, at least," Eustace said quietly.

There were no apparent gashes across her face or hands that they could see, only the smudged markings of strange symbols—crossed and angular—drawn in ash over her brow and down her throat, along each of her long fingers, the tops of her feet. On her lips, though, the markings changed from the gray smudge of ash to the red-brown of blood. The shapes were similarly angular, a bizarre alphabet, but these were unique. And they'd been more hastily drawn, scrawled ragged over her mouth like cuts.

"Look at these," Cordelia said, pointing her to aunt's mouth. "Why are they the only ones like this?"

Eustace shook her head. "Is that blood?"

"I think so," her sister confirmed with a nod. "Must have come from the birds."

Augusta was intact, at least. But Cordelia could not say the same for the doves. Over her aunt's heart, a pair of wings had been crossed, atop which sat something dark and small. Cordelia reached to pick it up and shrunk away as soon as her fingers made contact. "It's an organ of some kind," she said, revolted.

"The heart," her sister told her.

In the jugular notch between her aunt's clavicles, the head of the dove had been placed, torn from its body. And emerging from the white tangles of her hair, Cordelia could see two other doves, both dead, nestling on each of her shoulders. At her feet were the intestines and other organs, things Cordelia didn't recognize. Starkly white feathers were scattered along the sides of her aunt's body, striking against the dark fabric.

Eustace looked a little green. "Why the birds? And what do all these symbols mean?"

Cordelia shook her head. "It seems like something from another time."

She traced the symbols down her aunt's neck with a finger, all the way to her chest, where she could see three branches just emerging from the hem of her dress. She tugged the fabric and feathers back to reveal more and sucked in a breath. "Eustace! Look!"

There, on their aunt's chest, the markings ended in a final sigil, a *Y* with three lines, like a leafless tree.

"Just like Mom's," Eustace whispered. "And in the same place."

Cordelia pulled her shaking hand away.

"Maybe Mr. Togers knows what it means?" her sister suggested.

"If he does, he's not telling," Cordelia whispered. "You saw him today. His loyalties are to her, not to us."

Eustace sighed and rubbed at the bridge of her nose. "Well, at least we know she wasn't desecrated like mom. He just gave her a weird makeover."

Cordelia wasn't sure what she'd expected to find when she opened that lid, but this wasn't it. Was the aging attorney carving pentagrams into her aunt's chest? Shaving off bits as someone had done to their mother? It seemed farcical now, the image of an elderly, educated man poised over their aunt's corpse with a knife, enacting some necrophiliac perversion. She had to remind herself that she was here because of what she'd witnessed when they'd barged in. She glanced again at her aunt's face, the rash of lines drawn over it, remarkably similar to the levitating image of their young grandmother. It may not have been what she feared, but it was still frustratingly inexplicable.

She sagged against the wall, letting her eyes skip around the crypt. "Do you think they're all here? The people in the portraits and the photographs?"

"You mean, our family?" Eustace clarified. She looked around too. "Yeah. I think they're probably all in here. All but Mom."

Cordelia flinched. It suddenly bothered her, the notion of their mother being elsewhere. *Displaced.*

"It was her choice," Eustace said, reading her mind. "We could have brought her here if she'd only told us. She didn't want to come back."

Not even in death, Cordelia thought, a shiver running through her. Wordlessly, she closed the lid to her aunt's casket, trying to commit some of the symbols to memory. She laid the pall gently overtop. "What do you think it means? *Silens in vita, in morte vocalis?*"

"I don't know," Eustace told her. "But I'll find out. Now, how do we get her back in? Think your spatula will help?"

Cordelia narrowed her eyes, but she was secretly glad to hear her sister's sarcasm. It was the only predictable thing in this whole damn place. She dragged the casket back just a bit and began stacking stones up to the opening like a staircase. Too many years staging the homes she listed had taught her a thing or two about moving heavy objects.

"Help me get it up onto the first one," she said, and together they lifted the head of the casket, angling it against the stone. Moving around back, Cordelia pushed as they slid it toward the opening, and then lifted to push it inside. They stacked the stones back in their places, but with no mortar, they didn't fit quite as well as before.

"We'll have to get a new stonemason," Eustace said.

"A discreet one," Cordelia agreed as she bent to retrieve the bone knife and slide it back into its hiding spot.

Eustace moved toward the doors. "Time to let the dead lie."

But Cordelia only made it a few steps. She could feel the hum beginning to run through the stones beneath her feet, like bees in an underground hive. The crypt was waking up. "Do you hear that?"

"Hear what?" Eustace asked.

She closed her eyes. "That feeling."

"How do you hear a feeling?" Eustace asked.

But Cordelia was losing herself to it, slipping into the stones below, moving through the earth toward . . . *something*. "With your legs," she told her.

"You're not making sense," Eustace said, wrapping an arm around Cordelia's waist. "I think you've overexerted yourself."

Cordelia opened her eyes and looked to the back wall. She could feel it, whatever it was, coming from behind and below, but when she walked over and pressed against the stones, there was nothing. No door, no opening, no secret passage. Just the voices calling her.

"Cordy," Eustace said, going to her side, attempting to pull her back. "Come on. It's late. We both need to sleep."

Cordelia pressed the side of her face to the stone, feeling the hum reverberate through her cheekbone and jaw. She closed her eyes and listened.

"Cordy, you're scaring me," she heard Eustace say beside her. "Let's go."

Suddenly, it stopped. Cordelia's face went still against the cold stone. In the silence, a heavy thump sounded from the other side. Her eyes shot open.

It sounded again—a terrific knock from behind the wall. Cordelia jerked away, feeling it echo through her. "Did you hear that?" she asked, breathless.

Eustace stared at the wall with wide, white eyes. "*That*, I heard," she whispered.

The sisters backed up a step, waiting in the dark. The knock sounded a third time, causing both of them to start.

Eustace gripped Cordelia's wrist. "We need to get out of here," she insisted, dragging her toward the doorway.

Cordelia could feel her trembling as they backed away. She wanted to stay. To press herself hard against the rough grate of stone until she could bleed through it to whatever—whoever—waited on the other side. But Eustace's nails were digging into the thin skin of her wrist.

She let Eustace drag her from the hill and across the lawn, past the dogwood buds and the pointed lupine, to the hidden door of the solarium. Upstairs, she helped Cordelia wash the mortar from her hands and legs and put on a new nightshirt. Neither spoke.

"Interesting choice," Eustace said when she escorted Cordelia to her room and the big four-poster bed. "I didn't think pink was your color."

"It's not," Cordelia told her, still fuzzy. "But it's hers."

"Whose?"

"The blond lady. The bride from the picture. The one who walks here at night. Our great-great-great-grandmother—Arabella."

"Uh-huh," Eustace replied skeptically.

"She has a secret," Cordelia said as her eyes began to droop. "One of these nights, she's going to tell it to me."

CHAPTER ELEVEN

THE RUMORS

CORDELIA TRIED TO put on her friendliest, award-winning Realtor smile. She'd woken with a regret hangover, the night before coming back to her in fits and starts, a dodgy blur of over-sharing and breaking and entering. She'd dressed with a moan and helped herself to one of the sticky buns her sister was just pulling out of the oven, the scent of cinnamon and butter heavy in the air, then downed a quick cup of coffee before marching toward the carriage house, a plate of buns in hand.

West of the main house and near the road, it had a small timber carport that gave cover to a black truck. As she approached, she could see that the original carriage doors had been swapped for a set of contemporary, steel-framed French doors, and she remembered Gordon's remark about remodeling. She knocked awkwardly at the glass, not sure if she should lean against the frame or turn around. She'd practiced a sultry, come-hither grin in the mirror that morning to go with her tight jeans but scrapped it when she realized it made her look drunk instead of seductive.

When Gordon answered, she held out the plate brightly, feeling like a Girl Scout. "Peace offering."

He stared at her.

"Ummm . . ." She tried not to let her eyes trail past his navel.

It was hard with his shirt thrown on unbuttoned. "Look, I know last night was uncomfortable for everyone, but I really need a ride into town to get some groceries after my sister wiped out most of the walk-in pantry. So, I was hoping we could start over. Maybe pretend yesterday didn't happen?" She thrust the plate of buns at him. "I'll start. Hi there! I'm Cordelia Bone, newly minted owner of the world's creepiest estate and soon-to-be divorcée. You?"

Gordon took the plate and looked past her, as if he expected a camera crew to jump out of the bushes. Seeing no one, he scratched his head. "Shouldn't you call Togers for that? I'm sure he'd be happy to arrange a delivery for you."

Cordelia dropped her arm. "I can get my own groceries. I just need a ride."

His mouth opened and then closed and then opened again. He obviously wasn't comfortable agreeing to drive her and wasn't sure how to say it.

Cordelia groaned. "You know what? Never mind. Maybe I can get an Uber out here. We just don't have great service on the property, and the WiFi is spottier than a bowl of Raisin Bran. But I shouldn't have asked." She turned to walk away, pulling out her phone and raising it over her head, searching for those glorious bars.

"No," he called behind her with a sigh. "I'll take you. Just wait here while I get dressed."

"Thanks," she said. The amber light that filtered through the trees made her feel as if she were in an Italian Renaissance painting, stealing her breath. She lifted her phone to snap a picture. A noise sounded behind her and she turned, thinking it was Gordon. But his door stood open, empty.

Cordelia hesitated, then wandered inside. The first floor was open and airy, making the space feel larger than it was. Modern cabinets and appliances lined one side, marking the kitchen, while a sleek sofa and wood-burning stove set apart the other. It was eerily quiet. "Gordon?"

She gravitated to the stairs, tried calling his name again. When he didn't reply, she went up. "Just checking on you. I thought I heard something."

His room was empty. She glanced around, noting the desk and computer, the workout equipment, the bed she'd imagined more than once over the last few days. It was a rumple of dark blue sheets. She walked over to it and reached down, rubbing the cotton between her fingers, a starless sky. And then, like a woman under a spell, she lifted the sheets to her nose and took a deep, delicious breath. Cedarwood and nutmeg filled her. Her eyes flitted closed as she held it in.

The bathroom door flew open to her right.

Cordelia shrieked and dropped the sheets, jumping back from the bed as if it bit her.

Gordon's mouth hung open. Slowly, he moved toward her and reached down to pick up a shirt that was partially buried under the top sheet. He slung it on over his broad shoulders. "If you wanted to see my bed, all you had to do was ask."

Cordelia smoldered with embarrassment. "I was checking your thread count."

"With your nose?"

Her eyes shot to his. "Your detergent smelled nice. I was curious—"

"I bet you were," he cut in.

She huffed and breezed past him, storming down the stairs. But he rushed behind her, catching her arm and spinning her around before she could get out the door. "Cordelia, wait! I'll stop, I promise."

"It isn't what it looked like," she fumed, though it had been exactly that.

"I'm sorry if I jumped to conclusions." He grinned.

She crossed her arms, her face hot enough to melt candle wax. "Well, you did," she replied, still mortified. What had come over her? "I thought I heard something. You didn't answer when I called, so I decided to check on you."

"You were worried about me?" He seemed genuinely surprised.

"*Worry* is a strong word for it," she said stupidly. "I had some vague concern."

He smiled. "I can work with that. Let's try this again. I'm Gordon Jablonksi, *ex*-musician and groundskeeper of the world's creepiest estate," he said in a parody of her introduction moments earlier.

Despite herself, she put her hand in his.

He gave it a hearty shake. "Still need that ride?"

She nodded.

"You have a list?"

Cordelia lifted her phone.

"All right then. Come on," he said, heading for the truck. He paused just before the driver's-side door. Turning, he looked her in the eye. "You sure you want to do this?"

For a second, Cordelia faltered. She'd thought his reluctance was due to the conversation they'd had last night and the confrontation at the funeral. This felt like he was hesitating for her benefit rather than his own. "Of course," she said after a moment. "Why wouldn't I?"

His big shoulders rose and fell. "Suit yourself," he said, and climbed in.

CORDELIA TRIED NOT to notice how close Gordon was to her on the bench seat. If she put a hand down and spaced her fingers just so, she would touch the dark denim of his jeans. Her stomach squeezed at the thought.

"What was it like growing up here?" she asked him, desperate to put something between them.

"Typical, I guess." Then, pausing, he said, "No. That's not true. Bellwick is idyllic, quaint. A pocket out of time. Most people would kill to grow up here."

"And you?" she asked.

He shrugged. "Its charms weren't lost on me, but it could feel suffocating at times, like we'd been forgotten here. Like we weren't connected to the rest of the world. I was pretty anxious to leave by the time I graduated."

She expected a troubled past. An absentee father. A mother who drank too much. Maybe even an arrest or two. Something more traumatic behind the rock career and alternative exterior than a small-town upbringing, some kind of reason or excuse. An *explanation*. But Gordon wasn't giving up his story easily, one more conundrum she couldn't puzzle out.

"Still, must be nice," she said under her breath, feeling the taint of envy creep over her. "Our mother—she struggled. Bad relationships. Health issues. She would get these terrible headaches. We moved around a lot."

She'd never told John about her childhood, and he'd never asked. He'd just assumed she'd grown up with the same upper-middle-class privilege he had—well-to-do family, decent schools, suburban morals. She'd liked living in his fantasy of her. She'd kept the truth to herself.

"Sounds rough," Gordon replied.

Cordelia stared out the window, watching the trees thin along the road as homes began to spring up—Colonials with white planking, black roofs, and colorful doors or little farmhouses dotted with shutters and long, lazy porches. "I had Eustace," she said quietly. "At least."

"Family is everything."

"Is it?" Cordelia asked absently, thinking of all the relatives she'd never met. "I wouldn't know."

Rolling into Bellwick, she understood what Gordon was saying. Redbrick storefronts with wide, paned windows and old-fashioned streetlamps greeted her. Stone steps with iron railings. Painted hanging signs. American flags waving. She asked him to stop in front of a small coffee shop next to the grocery store—A Bean Come True.

"It looks like a movie set," Cordelia said as they got out of the truck. Across the street, a pharmacy with green-striped awnings had been plucked from the 1950s. Her little-girl heart burned to think this could have been her childhood instead of the dirty motel rooms and bad boyfriends, the microwave dinners and string of new schools. "It doesn't look real."

Gordon laughed dully. "It's plenty real. Bellwick has its issues like any other town, but overall there's not too much to complain about. Except . . ."

"Except?" she asked as they started toward the coffee shop.

"Except the uncanny family living just outside of town," Gordon told her, squinting in the sun. "The Bones never mixed much with everyone else. Over the years it's bred . . . *superstition.*"

Her smile faltered. It was an interesting choice of word. Rumors were common enough. They were human. But *superstition* made her nervous. *Superstition* belonged to the supernatural. To witches.

"I just want you to understand if people seem a little standoffish," he said.

"Gordon?" she asked, stopping to face him. She placed a hand on his arm. "How standoffish are we talking?"

He looked away.

"Wow. That bad."

She looked toward the coffee shop, painted a cute tan and black. It had felt good to believe that maybe there was someplace they belonged, somewhere they would be more than the weird girls with the funny name and the pretty mom who never seemed to age or settle down. But even here, in the place her family had chosen to stake its claim generations ago, being a Bone created trouble for her.

Cordelia lifted her chin and squared her shoulders. She started walking toward the red front door. "You might want to roll those windows up," she called to him, glancing at the cellophane sky. "Feels like rain."

Inside, she strode up to the counter. An older woman, with hair nearly as white as Augusta's and cropped close to her head, was busying herself with one of the machines. "Can I help you?" she asked, turning, and Cordelia saw that her face was full and friendly. She sighed with relief.

"I'd like a latte, please," Cordelia told her. "With hazelnut syrup if you have it."

The woman set to work, setting a paper cup with plastic lid on the counter a minute later.

Behind them, Gordon entered, and the door jingled. "Morning, Gladys," he said with a tight smile.

"Gordon! Lovely to see you! Hold on . . . I've got your favorite." She turned and rifled through a warming cabinet, pulling out a golden, oversized muffin. "Blueberry butterscotch," she told him. "I just put them out."

"I would dream about these muffins when I was on the road," he told Cordelia.

"And who's this?" she asked him. "A new girlfriend? In from the city, dear?" She smiled at Cordelia.

"Oh, no. I'm Cordelia Bone," she said, painting on her friendliest smile for the second time that morning and extending a hand.

Gladys froze, her own smile slowly fading, the pair of steel tongs in her hand beginning to tremble.

"Cordelia is Augusta's niece," Gordon told her. "She's here with her sister to see to the estate."

Behind her many wrinkles, Gladys's skin grew pasty, her once-merry eyes hard as flint. A haggish pucker stole across her face, twisting the features nearly beyond recognition. "A Bone girl," she said darkly.

"Cordelia's from Dallas," he argued for her. "She didn't grow up around her family."

Cordelia cleared her throat, wiping her hand on her jeans. "Did you know my aunt?" she asked, desperate to lighten the mood.

"Augusta Bone never stepped foot in here," the woman spat.

Cordelia looked at Gordon, who flinched. "Your aunt let Togers arrange all of her shopping," he told her.

"*All* of it?" she whispered back.

He nodded.

"Done a dark deal, those two families," Gladys croaked out, eyeing Cordelia and Gordon with obvious distaste. "Long time ago. Everyone knows that."

Cordelia was shocked by the venom in her voice.

Gladys shook her tongs at Gordon. "You're too young to re-member what the rest of us do. I was alive when Violetta Bone dared to go to the hospital to have her baby. Young and beautiful she was then, like an electric storm. So full of life she couldn't be contained. And that boy, Alton Crane, talked her into it. He was always skulking around there, mooning over that girl. Said it was the only way she'd be safe. Said that midwives were for puritans and hippies. He was going to be a botanist. He believed in science. He didn't listen to the murmurs around town. And away they went. But when she came back, it was in a hearse."

Cordelia recognized the name of her grandmother, but she'd never heard the story of her death or her mother's birth.

"Bled right out in front of a whole team of doctors and nurses who couldn't stop it," Gladys went on. "My parents whispered about it for weeks. It was proof, they said. The old stories were true. Cursed with a dark power that place is. Augusta never set foot off that property since."

"Because she was grieving," Cordelia supplied, defending her great-aunt.

"Because she couldn't," Gladys insisted conspiratorially. "Don't know what your momma did to keep you alive this long someplace else," she said, sizing Cordelia up. "But it can't have been easy. And I'm willing to bet money she met with a bad end all the same."

Cordelia picked up the cup that had been waiting for her on the counter and dropped a five-dollar bill. "Thank you for the coffee," she said hoarsely before walking out.

When Gordon caught up with her, she was standing in aisle seven of the grocery store, staring at a display of canned soup.

"Don't let her get to you," he said, handing out her change.

Cordelia dropped the money into her purse. "I can't decide if I should get chicken noodle or tomato," she said, pointing to the cans. She pulled one off the shelf and held it up. "Maybe split pea? Sounds like something only freaks would eat."

Gordon took the can from her and put it back. "When people don't understand something, they make up stories about it. In this case, that happens to be your family."

"What stories exactly?" she asked him.

He looked away. "Well, there's more than one. That you're all deranged. That your ancestors did a deal with the devil. Some of the kids think you're werewolves."

She gave him a hard look.

"The rest think you're witches," he finished.

At that, she coughed, practically choking on her latte.

He sighed. "But I guess the most prominent belief is that the Bones can never leave their property, or they'll die a horrible death."

Cordelia stared at him. "What? Like we're cursed?"

Gordon rested an elbow on a nearby shelf. "There was a rhyme the kids would say when we were growing up. *They never drink; they never eat. The Bones are never fed on meat. They never age; they never toil. The Bones are fed on blood and soil. They never die; they never rot. The Bones can never leave their lot. So never stray onto their coil, or you'll become their blood and soil.*"

"Oh. My. God." Cordelia gaped. "That makes us sound like vampires!" She started to walk away, then turned back to him. "Is this why you didn't want to bring me shopping? You knew I'd find out that everybody hated us?"

"They don't hate you," Gordon corrected her. "They're just scared of you."

"How is that better, Gordon?" she asked, irritated, as she stomped back down the aisle. If the Bones were a family of witches, then just what kind of witches were they to spawn such terrible rumors? Cordelia remembered the photograph and shuddered.

"Obviously none of it's true. You're living proof of that," he said, following her.

"Why wouldn't we be able to leave our property?" she asked absently, wondering where such a thing even started. She grabbed an empty cart and began throwing things into it, piecemeal. They couldn't have all been shut-ins before her mom, could they? No wonder Maggie left. Bone Hill was impressive, but Cordelia couldn't imagine being stuck there day in and day out. And she couldn't imagine facing the vitriol in this town if you dared to leave.

"Something about the earth being soaked in blood," he answered.

Cordelia scowled. Did her family practice blood magic? "Right. *Blood and soil.*"

Gordon laughed nervously. "It's the kind of stuff kids make up to scare each other after dark. It's a small town. People get bored. Your family has been the most interesting thing around here for twenty decades." He stepped in front of the cart. "Look, no offense, but the Bones aren't exactly normal."

Cordelia glowered at him. *This.* This had been the thing trailing her for her entire life. *Not normal.* And she knew it better than anyone. She didn't need a glorified, inked-up gardener to tell her so. She remembered it well enough every time a shadow flitted by in an empty room and that chill crept over her like an unforgiving mistral and her skin prickled with otherworldly sensation. Every birthday she couldn't sing over her cake. Every Christmas she couldn't sing carols at the school party. And every time she thought about someone standing over her mother's body, cutting part of her away like it was a sacred relic.

"Do I have to spell it out for you?" he asked. "You're rich, you're eccentric, and you've had more than your share of tragedy. I mean, you heard Gladys. Your grandmother died in childbirth. Before that, someone committed suicide. Earlier still, twin girls stumbled into a nest of bees in the woods and went into anaphylactic shock. Every family has its stories if you look hard enough. Yours are just more legendary."

Cordelia kind of doubted that every family had a pair of twins who died on the same day from a bee allergy. "And all that stuff about Mr. Togers? A *dark deal*?"

Gordon ran a fist through his hair. "The Togers family have been the only people brave enough to set foot on your land in who knows how many years. Of course they're mixed up in it."

It sounded reasonable, but Cordelia couldn't shake the eeriness of it. One story on its own might be explained away, but together they felt like more than coincidence. And then there were the things he didn't know. Morna's ghostly face swam before her mind's eye, the photo of her grandmother hanging like a corpse on a line. She didn't think she could take much more.

At the same time, she wanted to drink the stories in like good wine, let them ferment inside her, build a history where she had none, fill up all those empty spaces. How ironic to come from a family who could never go anywhere and a mother who could never stand still.

Cordelia touched a hand to her head, where the beginning of a roaring migraine was making itself known. "Can we just get the groceries and get out of here?"

He moved away from the cart, and together they worked their way from frozen foods to produce, tossing things into the basket. Eustace had texted Cordelia a list, but it was nothing like she expected. There wasn't even a mention of corn chips or ra-men noodles. Instead, it was a rambling assortment of dry goods and herbs, something called *ghee*, a lot of eggs, odd things in jars, and nearly everything from the produce department.

"What is with her?" Cordelia wondered aloud.

"Who?" Gordon asked.

She stared at the cart cynically. "My sister is suddenly the love child of Wolfgang Puck and Ina Garten. You'd think she spent her whole life in a kitchen."

"At least you won't have to cook while you're here," he told her.

He was being uncharacteristically agreeable. While Cordelia appreciated the crack in his shell, she couldn't help but read it as pity. She turned to him, an apple in her hand and a strange feeling creeping its way up her limbs, crawling over her back, wrapping itself around her head like spider legs. "You're very levelheaded for a guy that has *hell fire* printed across his knuckles," she said before the pain seized her unexpectedly and the apple dropped to the ground.

She crumpled, but Gordon caught her against his broad chest. "Hey, hey! Cordelia," he tried, patting her cheek.

She attempted to open her eyes, to tell him about the medicine she had back at the house, to explain that the headaches happened all the time, but it was no use. Her stomach roiled, her head swam, and everything went wonderfully, blissfully black.

CHAPTER TWELVE

The Legacy

She came to in the seat of his truck as they were just pulling up in front of the house, the rain beginning to fall.

"I called the doctor," Gordon told her. "He said he'd meet us here. I wanted to take you to the emergency room, but he was so insistent. Claimed I'd be risking your life, that it was too far. Dr. Mabee has an excellent reputation. Your aunt swore by him. I figured I'd better listen."

Cordelia tried to sit up. The pain was easing by the second, but she still felt woozy. "The groceries."

"Hey, take it easy," Gordon told her, putting out a hand to steady her. "They're in the back. Hugh had a sacker load them while we got you to the truck. He says we can pay later." He gave her a worried look. "Does this happen often?"

She pressed her fingers into the flesh between her eyebrows. "I get headaches," she told him. "But I've never passed out before."

"Like your mom?" he asked, concern rimming his features.

"Hmmm?" She was still trying to put it all together—being at the store, turning to say something snarky, and then the way it hit her so hard and fast, like she'd slammed into a wall.

"Earlier you said your mom would get headaches when you were growing up," Gordon reminded her.

Cordelia mentally kicked herself. "Right."

"It's genetic then?" he asked.

"I guess," she said, daring a glance into his gold-brown eyes. "Listen, you can't tell my sister about this. Eustace has been through a lot recently. She doesn't need one more thing to worry about."

He looked dubious. "I already called to tell her we were on our way."

Cordelia moaned as her sister came running down the porch steps, opening the door. "I'm fine, Eustace," she said, stepping out. "Just a case of low blood sugar."

"Like hell you're fine," Eustace argued, insisting on helping Cordelia up the stairs and into the house. She deposited her on a sofa in the library.

Gordon brought her a glass of cold water after unloading the groceries in the kitchen, where Eustace was now quickly putting them away. Cordelia took it and eyed him. "Why are you being so nice to me?"

He shrugged and gave her a small smile, maybe the first *real* smile he'd let her see. "Turns out I'm a pretty nice guy," he said. "For someone with *hell fire* printed across his knuckles."

She rolled her eyes.

She had to wonder why he was even there, in the place where his mother had died horribly, with the family everyone in town thought were murdering cannibal recluses. He'd defended her today to Gladys. And he'd tried to help her calm down in the grocery store. She believed him when he said he was a nice guy, despite the tattoos and the black clothes and the metal-band past. But she had the distinct sense that underneath all of that, he had a reason for being there. Quite without knowing it, she and her sister had come to Bone Hill looking for answers. Maybe Gordon had too.

Then again, given her track record, she could be completely wrong.

Eustace stomped back into the room, face creased with worry.

She pressed a cold compress to Cordelia's head, and not gently. "I can't decide if I'm more angry or more concerned."

"It shows," Cordelia grumbled.

"Gordon told me about the headache. How long?" she asked, foot tapping.

"Don't," Cordelia told her. "It's not like Mom."

Her face fell. "That long then?"

Gordon rose to his feet as if to leave.

"You never picked up the phone, not even once, to tell me?" Eustace shot at her.

Cordelia furrowed her brow. "Okay, *pot*. Nice to meet you. I'm *kettle*."

The doorbell rang, saving Cordelia from having to say more.

"That's Dr. Mabee." Gordon looked grateful for the excuse to leave. "I'll let him in."

Cordelia stared up at her sister as he left the room. "There's something you should know."

Eustace sat down. "I'm listening."

"We aren't exactly beloved by the locals." She gave her sister a pointed look. "Our family has a history of being generally eccentric and standoffish. And that has not gone unnoticed over the—oh, I don't know—centuries? So, yeah. People here pretty much hate us."

Eustace dug her fingers into her wild curls, pushing them back from her face. "So, we're like the Boo Radleys of Bellwick?"

"I mean . . ." Cordelia searched for the right way to put it. "*Werewolves* has been tossed around. *Vampires. Satan's concubines.* That kind of thing."

Eustace dropped her shoulders. "And I thought *witches* was bad."

"Yes, well, that's been mentioned too," Cordelia told her. "I just thought you should know before this doctor comes in. In case . . ."

"In case he treats you with holy water and three Hail Marys?" she supplied.

Cordelia started to nod when an exceptionally short man with a ring of ashy hair and a small mustache breezed into the room.

Dr. Mabee's medical bag was nearly as big as he was. The nervous type, he was given to a number of unnecessary gestures—brisk hand-wiping and twitchy fingers, too many blinks. He quickly set up shop on the heavy rosewood desk in the study and had Cordelia come sit on the edge of it like it was an examination table, squinting into her face from behind bifocals. "Yes, I think I see the likeness—around the mouth, the line of the neck, and so on," he said. "Remarkable."

She frowned and touched her head, her symptoms all but gone now. She wasn't really in a hurry to be reminded of her mother's suffering or her own, the resignation she felt toward her own undoing. But she was losing her ability to judge the timing and severity of the headaches since coming here, and that frightened her.

"Sir," Eustace stated with a snarl, leaning against the edge of the desk next to her sister. "My sister was out cold in a grocery store. I think we're less concerned with how much she resembles our aunt and more concerned with what the fuck is wrong with her."

"Of course," he acquiesced with a little cough. He shined an ophthalmoscope into one of Cordelia's eyes and then the other. "Did you experience any symptoms prior to syncope?"

"*Sin*-what?" Cordelia asked.

"Fainting," he clarified. "Did you notice anything unusual before you passed out, Ms. Bone?"

"A bit of a headache coming on," she said, carefully avoiding Eustace's gaze. "I was late getting my caffeine fix. You know how that goes."

Beside her, Eustace went brittle as old cheese.

"Uh-huh," Dr. Mabee said, checking each of her ears. "And do you get them often? These headaches?"

She hated to answer that in front of her sister. She could lie if she weren't so terrible at it, and if Eustace weren't a human polygraph. Better to have it out now. "Daily since coming here. A couple of times a week before that."

"*Since* coming here?" he reiterated. "You mean they've gotten worse with your arrival and not better?"

Cordelia nodded.

Eustace sucked in air. "Oh, Cordy." Her eyes watered, shining like silver coins.

Dr. Mabee fitted Cordelia's arm with a blood pressure cuff. "Are your parents still with us?" he asked bluntly.

"I don't know my father," Cordelia told him. "Our mother died of a brain aneurysm."

He emitted a small grunt.

Cordelia sat still while he listened to her heart. Putting his stethoscope away, he pulled out a butterfly needle and a blood collection tube. "It's just as I thought. You're perfectly well, Ms. Bone. *For now.*"

Eustace narrowed her eyes. "I've been around enough doctors in recent months to know when one is holding back, Dr. Mabee. So, what *aren't* you saying?"

The doctor smiled. "I made regular house calls for your aunt—your entire family, in fact. Checkups and such. Though we lost Claude some years ago. It's been just Augusta for so long. I was surprised when Gordon called from the supermarket and told me who you were. I'd not been informed of your arrival. I expected any future Bones would come under the same arrangement," he explained.

"Arrangement?" Cordelia wasn't sure what he was talking about, but he seemed to think she would be.

"Yes, well. I suppose you've been away. Haven't you?" He said more to himself than her. "Most unusual."

"What's so unusual about us being away?" Eustace pressed.

"I suppose Mr. Togers hasn't had an opportunity to explain how things are done yet. I'm on a retainer, you see. Available to come to the big house when needed. Anytime, day or night. It's an agreement that's been in place here with my predecessors for some generations," he told them.

Gordon entered with a tray and several cups of tea. Setting them down, he stood back. Cordelia smiled up at him.

Turning promptly to him, the doctor said, "Mr. Jablonski, would you be kind enough to step out of the room? These are private, *family* matters and I must not violate my oath."

"Oh, sure." Gordon gave her a reassuring grin before sliding the pocket doors closed behind him. Cordelia listened for his retreating steps but was immediately distracted by the poke of the needle.

Once the doors slid shut, the smile dropped from Dr. Mabee's face. "These *maladies*," he began, "have plagued your family for a great many years. To varying degrees and effect for each person, but as I understand it, it is a hereditary defect."

"I'm sorry," Cordelia interrupted him. "What *defect*?"

He leaned in. "Ms. Bone, I am taken into your confidence as I was your aunt's to a most dedicated degree, as I am paid to be. But I can only extend to you that which was extended to me by my predecessor here, circumscribed by your own family's discretion, and under the careful oversight of Mr. Togers. Your family's *condition* is of a discreet nature. My understanding of it is limited—a collection of what I have been told and my own practical experience. I don't pretend otherwise, and no more has been asked of me."

Eustace folded her arms. "Did our aunt have these headaches too?"

His smile puckered like it was screwed on. "Your aunt suffered debilitating migraines on the rare occasion she left her property. As did her father before her. Though I understand some in the family experienced other symptoms—clonic seizures, persistent emesis, serious arrhythmias, dangerous asthma attacks, and so on. Your uncle Claude, for example, was given to fits of such severe bronchospasms that he nearly died on two occasions. One when he attempted to go into town. Another when he wandered past the property line by accident during a walk in the woods."

Cordelia felt her own airway tighten. "Our mother had the same headaches."

"I am not surprised," he continued. "How she lasted as long as she did is a mystery I would truly like to unravel. Within it lies the seed to understanding your family's unique affliction."

"You'll pardon me if I don't quite understand," Eustace said. "It sounds like you're saying you don't medically know what's wrong with us, but that all these disparate symptoms are somehow connected."

Dr. Mabee slid a hand into the pocket of his coat. "That is precisely what I'm saying, Ms. Bone. And your reaction is not unlike my own when I first took over here for Dr. Welsh—a fine practitioner I had much respect for. I won't pretend to know what's at the core of your family's issues. I have taken blood samples and performed as many perfunctory tests as possible, but I have only been allowed to prod so far. Nothing has proven revelatory. And it has not been my job to unravel your condition, but to treat it."

"And how have you treated it?" Cordelia asked. "I've been prescribed medication, but the effects are limited."

Dr. Mabee frowned. "Not surprising. I would assume that even if it is working now, the disease will eventually overcome the cure. My treatment, Ms. Bone, is simple enough. Have you ever heard the old saying about telling the doctor it hurts when you do this and the doctor then replying not to do that?"

Both sisters nodded.

"It's that basic. A prescription of strict adherence to the confines of your own property. Think of it as modified bed rest," he told her.

"You're telling us not to leave the estate?" Cordelia was baffled. Were the town rumors true? Had their mother suffered needlessly because of a stubborn refusal to return home? *Blood and soil,* she recalled with disquiet.

But that did not explain the headaches she'd experienced *on* the property. She'd felt relief on the drive to Bone Hill, but that was shattered when she saw Morna on the stairs. And she'd suffered headaches when her sister was locked in the bathroom and during the funeral outside the crypt.

"Yes. That's exactly it in a nutshell. On-site, you will find your energy and health restored, your symptoms will fade entirely, and you will excel in all manner of well-being. Off-site, there is little I can do for you." He looked grave.

"But . . ." Cordelia looked into his face. "You don't understand. I'm still having headaches. *Here.* Not just when I run errands. At the house. On the grounds. Worse than before. More painful, less predictable. They're . . . changing."

Dr. Mabee gripped her head and began palpating her skull, fingers prodding like sniffing dogs. Fully convinced everything *outside* her head was normal, he dropped his hands. "That simply cannot be."

Eustace glared at him. "But it is. You heard her."

He shook his head worriedly, wringing his hands. "With everyone else in your family, I had only to come by twice a year to record vitals and give a routine exam. And though I was available for more, I must tell you, in all those years, I was rarely needed for it."

"You're saying they didn't get sick?" Cordelia clarified. "Not a cold, not a stomach bug—as long as they were on the property?"

"No," he told her. "Not a cold. Not a stomach bug."

"But our aunt died," Eustace countered. "*Upstairs*. Gordon made it sound like she suffered a stroke. If the property is so damn good for us, then how did she pass? And why are my sister's headaches getting worse instead of better?"

Dr. Mabee lifted his brows. "I saw no signs of a stroke," he told them, tucking Cordelia's blood samples into his bag. "However, the natural course of life cannot be altered. There is pregnancy and its many issues to contend with, though I am told that most of your female relatives experienced little problem with that, home births being the order of the day. The occasions when that was not observed, unfortunately, were not so productive.

"And you will age, of course, and experience the usual decline of the body, though if your aunt is any indication, you should find yourself stronger than most throughout that process. And yes, you will die, like the rest of your family members. A sudden and easy passing, painless and without months of anguish and waste. At least, that's how it should be." He glanced at Cordelia, apologetic. "Why it's not so for you, I cannot say. Perhaps your time away has altered the condition's expression in some way."

Cordelia pressed on the cotton ball tucked into her elbow.

"So that's it?" Eustace asked. "We should be fine until we die as long as we don't leave but maybe not and there's nothing you can do or say about it?"

The doctor leveled a cool gaze at her. "I suggest, Ms. Bone, if you are so curious about your family's syndrome and how it is or is not impacting your sister, that you seek answers among them. I have told you all that I know. I will run some tests, but my abilities are limited where the two of you are concerned." He added in a low voice. "It is my observation that your family has certain *abilities* of their own. Perhaps it is time you employ those."

"You're telling me to ask the dead?" Eustace was apoplectic.

"And if we seek a second opinion?" Cordelia asked, taking a cup of tea.

"I don't recommend it," he said bluntly. "The risk will far outweigh the benefit. But of course, it's up to you."

"My sister has cancer," she divulged.

"Cordy!" Eustace gasped.

Cordelia ignored her. "Will she get better here? Can she finish her chemo treatments?"

Dr. Mabee gave Eustace a sympathetic look. "Unfortunate diagnosis," he said. "And one that is likely to remedy itself if you remain put. How do you feel?"

Eustace's scowl was out of line with her answer. "Great since coming here, thanks for asking."

He pursed his lips, gathered his bag of supplies. "At least the legacy is working for one of you."

But Cordelia had one final question. "I don't mean to offend you, but there seem to be stories in town about our family affliction. Have you or any of your staff ever—"

"Let me be frank," he interrupted. "I have been paid handsomely by your family for my services and my discretion. I would in fact be laughed out of my profession if any of this were to leave this room, and I would lose my medical license. I do not involve my staff in these visits, and your files are locked in a private cabinet. So, no, I am not responsible for the local folktales. But people are observant, Ms. Bone. And your family has lived here a very long time. However exaggerated over the years, most tall tales spring from a kernel of truth. You would be wise to remember that."

With that, he gave them both a brisk nod and turned to go, leaving a card with his private number on the desk.

CHAPTER THIRTEEN

THE SECRET

CORDELIA FELT THE brush of cold fingers over her cheek and opened her eyes. The enormous pink bed surrounded her. A black figure was passing through the door as she sat up, the ruffle of a skirt barely audible in the darkness.

"Hello?" she whispered.

Standing, she stepped into the hallway, where she caught sight of square shoulders and a dark shawl rounding the banister to the stairs.

"Who are you?" She followed on quick feet, always one bend behind the folds of black fabric, the loops of white hair glowing like moonlight, trailing like fog. "Answer me!"

The frigid parquet floors numbed her toes as Cordelia watched the person glide across them into the library.

"Wait." She dimly recalled her mother's warning never to speak to them—the shadows that walk. But it seemed far away and unimportant now. She was here. Her mother wasn't.

She slipped into the library, smelling of moths and old leather, as the woman sailed into the study, circling the slab of desk, crossing before the picture of Erazmus like a thick wind.

"Please stop." Cordelia rooted to the carpet, blocking the doorway.

The shadow jittered in the corner, rotating slowly as if on pinion gears until she was facing her niece. Augusta's blanched hair fell long over her shoulders. Her face was pale as mist, marked with luminescent lines of ash, a horrible, unreadable mask. She worked her jaw, trying to speak, but her lips would not part. The red symbols stretched over them like cords of blood, binding her mouth shut. She clutched helplessly at her throat.

Every hair on Cordelia's body rose as if the room were filling with static charge. "I know you," she whispered.

Augusta raised a knotty finger at her, the knuckles shining like points of light. The curve of nail was a polished white, slick as opal.

A bolt of energy struck Cordelia between the breasts, passing through her like a bullet. She doubled over, chest caving, mouth caught between a twist and a scream, her lungs crumpling inside her like torn wings. Stumbling back, she met her aunt's glistening wet eyes.

Augusta turned, a flourish of black, and dove into the bookshelf, disappearing in a spray of sable mist.

Cordelia sat up in a flash and switched on the lamp. She was not in the library at all, but in her sad, pink room, her sad, pink bed. The door stood open to the hallway, and across its threshold lay a dark, woven shawl.

Quietly, she slid from the bed and made her way to the door. She crouched, touching the threads like they might sting, the wool of an asp. When she was certain they wouldn't, she picked the shawl up and balled it against her chest, then held it to her nose.

Jasmine and black pepper.

She looked up and saw that the door to their aunt's room was ajar as well.

Cordelia rose to her feet and stared into the stillness across the hall. Slowly, she closed her door. And this time, she locked it.

IN THE STUDY, Cordelia switched on the banker's lamp and stared up at the portrait of Erazmus. His prominent scowl turned her stomach. The dream last night had been so vivid, so real. She could practically see her aunt Augusta still standing in that far corner, mute and imposing, rippling with dark energy. Cordelia had felt certain there was something the woman wanted to say, something she was trying to convey to her, but then she'd felt the power pierce her chest, that accusatory finger aimed at her heart, and the breath had flowed from her body in a rush and all she could sense was the heightening of her own fear.

This morning, she'd returned, drawn by her aunt's restless spirit and the secrets whispering from every surface of this room.

"What do you know that you aren't saying?" she asked the portrait, drawing close and staring into the blue-gray strokes of his eyes. She let her fingers dance over the texture of the canvas, let the things trapped inside the paint begin to inform them. It was time for Erazmus Bone to give up a secret or two.

At first, Cordelia could feel only his protectiveness over the space, the invisible weight of his confidences, the skeletons hiding out in his closets. She could feel the way her fingers tripped over them like stones under a blanket, the shape of things unsaid, the bulges and gaps glanced over. And then she could feel something else—*urgency.* It rose like a panic through the paint, pricking at her fingers like thorns on a briar. Maybe Gladys was a little off her rocker, and Dr. Mabee's theories were questionable, but the town's suspicions weren't entirely unfounded. Because if Cordelia could hear one whisper in this room, it was simply this—Erazmus Bone *was* hiding something. And her aunt Augusta. And every relative in between. And she needed to know what it was. *Now.*

Turning, she ripped open the desk drawers and began shuffling through whatever she could find—straight-faced photos and old letters, clippings from the town newspaper, even some hand-written receipts. As she was rifling through a pile of random papers, a folded bit of buttery newsprint dropped to the floor. Cordelia stooped to retrieve it, carefully laying it open across the broad desk. A grayscale photograph of the house instantly caught her eye. Before the long porch stood a stern woman with broad shoulders and thick arms, her white pinafore and nurse's cap crisp. It was from *The Bellwick Courant*, dated August 1937.

The headline screamed *Heiress Dies in Fatal Fall.* Cordelia felt her stomach drop. It was the suicide Gordon mentioned, and it confirmed Mr. Togers' account of their great-great-aunt's battle with depression. Several large water stains blurred the text. Cordelia read what she could. The heiress was listed as *Morna E Bone, aged 33 years.* She quickly came to realize the woman in the picture had been Morna's nurse, a Martha somebody—the rest of her name obscured.

The nurse described Morna as "deeply disturbed," "given to fits," and "unable to speak." She'd been in the tower with her at the time she jumped, apparently trying to stop her. But it was the nurse's depiction of Morna killing her own pets and drawing "unnatural things with their blood" that chilled Cordelia to the bone, the message of the bats cloaked in a newly sinister layer.

This was worse than Morna's being a little *melancholy,* as Togers had referred to it. Her aunt was seriously unbalanced, a truly broken woman capable of violence. Cordelia felt sorry for her, but more than that, she felt a growing alarm over her encounters with Morna's ghost. If she was trapped here, confused and deranged, what might she think of Cordelia and Eustace's presence? How might she act out, this woman who had even turned on her own beloved animals?

She snapped a picture of the article and folded it up as she'd found it, returning it to the drawer. Turning to the bookshelves, she noticed a series of handwritten ledgers dating all the way back to the late 1800s. Their marbled covers were worn at the edges. They detailed the expenses of the property, from quarts of vinegar to bushels of oats to pairs of shoes. Other ledgers accounted for investments of the family—early bonds and their dividends, businesses acquired and sold. Cordelia marveled at the exhaustive means by which her ancestors had recorded their debts and assets. But none of them gave her the answers she was looking for.

Eustace stood in the doorway, a wooden spoon in one hand. She surveyed the piles of books and documents Cordelia had stacked around the room. "What on earth are you doing?"

"Investigating," Cordelia answered. "Like you said we should. There's something here."

"What, exactly?"

"I don't know," she told her, glancing up. "But I'll know it when I find it."

Gordon peeked in. "I'm here to treat the pond. I'll be in the solarium if either of you need me."

Cordelia turned. A morning shower had dampened his hair and shirt, little droplets caught in the glossy strands, making her knees want to buckle. "Wait. Before you get to that, I need you to take care of the bathroom door and repaint that bedroom upstairs—something cheery this time, yellow or white."

A surprise text from Molly had come through last night with the mold contractor's whopping invoice, which she currently had no way to pay. Thinking on her feet, she asked Molly to dig up a contact for a reputable appraiser and auction house nearby. Maybe she could unburden the Bone estate of a couple of its treasures, make a payment of good faith to Busy to get him off her neighbor's tail and tide the mold remediators over so she could sell her house in Texas. She didn't need contractors breathing down her neck along with everyone else. But she didn't want to give the appraiser any reason to lowball her. If he got so much as a whiff of desperation, she couldn't trust a word he said. The house needed to be in tip-top shape.

"Cheery?" Gordon repeated.

Cordelia stopped pilfering to meet his gaze. "Yes. To brighten things up a bit. Cover up the blood at the very least."

He pulled a face. "I know what you mean. It's just, your aunt didn't like anyone making cha—"

"My aunt isn't here anymore," Cordelia said adamantly, last night's dream causing her to be firmer than intended. She refused to let her gaze linger on his warm eyes or the way his shirt stuck to his skin. "It's up to us to update the image of this place and our family. Now, are you capable or do I need to call someone in?"

Gordon looked wounded, and Cordelia realized that yesterday they'd nearly felt like friends, and now she was treating him like an employee, and not a very valued one.

"What I mean—" she tried to say.

But Gordon didn't stay to hear the rest. "Consider it done," he said curtly as he left the room.

"What was all that?" Eustace asked, crossing her arms.

"Nothing." Cordelia sighed. "I'm just a little tired after yesterday."

Cordelia could feel her head beginning to throb. The dream from last night, the scowling portrait, the confrontation with Gordon—they felt like bricks pressing down on her. She reached for the pill bottle in her pocket.

"Another one?" Eustace asked.

"It's not bad," Cordelia told her. *Not yet.* She turned back to the books and ledgers on the shelves, the papers strewn across the desk. "Why do you think he didn't tell us?"

"Who?" Eustace asked.

"Mr. Togers. You heard Dr. Mabee—there's supposed to be

some kind of arrangement. One he should have filled us in on. So why didn't he say anything? Let us risk getting sick or hurt or worse?"

Eustace sighed. "He's an attorney, not a doctor. I highly doubt he knows why the arrangement exists. He probably thinks our aunt is a hypochondriac from a long line of hypochondriacs who are spoiled and lazy and can pay a doctor to come running at their every whim."

Cordelia leaned against the desk. "Maybe you're right." Remembering the article, Cordelia passed Eustace her phone. "Here, look at this."

Eustace studied the picture, zooming in to read the legible parts, then handed the phone back. "You found that in here?"

"Aunt Augusta was in my dream last night," she confided. "Just like we saw her in the crypt. And she led me here, to *this* room, before she vanished."

"Why didn't you say so?" Eustace dropped low and started pulling books off the shelf.

"What are you doing?" Cordelia asked.

"Helping."

Together, they worked their way along the length of the back wall until every book and object had been pulled from the oiled wood and laid or piled along the chairs and floor. When there was nothing remaining, Eustace stepped back.

"I haven't come across anything more exciting than a stack of letters from someone named Hyacinth to her mother back in Virginia," Eustace told her.

"Letters?" Cordelia echoed, blowing a strand of hair out of her face.

"Don't get excited," her sister said. "There's a lot in there about bridge, the weather, and the care and keeping of chickens. Apparently, you have to up their protein intake in the winter while they molt. Or some such thing."

Frustrated, Cordelia ran a hand through her hair. They'd been all over this room, and while the things they'd found were intriguing, they did not amount to much. What were they missing? Running her fingers along the empty shelves, she ended at the corner where her aunt had been. "She was right here. And then she was gone."

"She disappeared from that corner?" Eustace asked to be certain.

"Yes." Cordelia faced the shelves. "She just kind of dove into them." She made a motion toward the wood, and something nebulous caught her ear. Cordelia leaned in, trying to track the whisper.

"What are you doing?" Eustace asked.

She raised a finger to her lips and pressed her face between two shelves. "It's behind here," she said. "I can hear it." Running her hands over the grain, straining, she noticed a small, dark gap between the leg molding and the base molding where one shelf met the next.

Cordelia stood back and surveyed the line of shelves. All the other moldings were flush with their counterparts. But something at the far-right corner was ever so slightly off. "Do you see this?" she asked Eustace.

She dropped to the floor and put her face next to the seam. She could feel a drafty tickle against her cheek, in the distance, a muffled sifting of air, like speech. *Whispers.* Her head eased, the pill kicking in sooner than anticipated.

"Help me," she said, jumping up. "Something's back here!"

Cordelia gripped the carefully trimmed molding that capped the leg between shelves. Eustace stood beside her and together they pulled. As they did, the shelf began to groan, sliding open along a hinge hidden on the other side.

When they'd opened it as wide as it would go, both sisters stood back and stared into the blackness that waited.

"This is straight out of Scooby-Doo," Eustace said as Cordelia shone the light from her phone into the forgotten staircase.

It was extremely narrow, so that they would only be able to descend one at a time. The interior walls were exposed brick with crumbly mortar and streaks of dust-laden cobwebs. Overhead, a single light clung to the back wall, unused, its metal shade covered by a layer of grime so thick you could barely see the green paint it once bore.

"Hello?" Cordelia called into the dark.

The sound of a rock skittering across the floor echoed back. "Probably just a rat," she said over her shoulder.

"What do you think is down there?" Eustace asked.

"The basement," Cordelia told her. "Obviously."

"Then why hide it behind a false door?" Eustace asked. "Isn't it basically just cold storage? Do turnips and potatoes really need to be so carefully guarded?"

"Maybe it wasn't turnips and potatoes they were storing," she said with a gulp.

"Are you going down there?" Eustace asked.

"Of course." Cordelia bristled. "And so are you. This is what Aunt Augusta was trying to show me last night." She snatched her sister's hand in hers and descended the first step.

"You realize this is the point in the movie where someone starts yelling at the screen for the stupid girls not to go down the stairs or they'll die?" Eustace pointed out.

Cordelia ignored her. "We're not girls anymore, Eustace."

With each step, a little more of the stairway came into view, until they could finally see the bottom. While the basement was roughshod to be sure, there was a stone floor in place, and the walls appeared sturdy enough. Cordelia shone her phone flashlight on a maze of piping, beams, and walls that gave the space an uncomfortable, ambling feel, with too many corners for things to lurk around. She could see some old canvas tarps, rope, crowbars, and garden tools—shovels and spades so anti-quated they appeared to be fashioned entirely from wood.

She walked toward them and crouched down, running a finger along the blade of one shovel lying on the floor, smooth from use. The finger came back brown with dirt.

"Have you ever seen a wooden shovel before?" Eustace asked her.

"Not necessarily," Cordelia said, picking it up by the long handle, worn glossy from countless hands, and setting it right with the others. "Doesn't seem like it would be very effective."

Eustace pointed to the crowbars nearby. "Those are metal. Why use shovels that aren't?"

Cordelia shook her head, turning to shine the light on a pile of several dozen empty glass jars, before angling it deeper into the corridor before them.

"Come on," Cordelia told her sister, moving ahead.

"This level of creepiness isn't enough for you?" Eustace asked from behind. "Did you see the jars?"

"Canning, Eustace. They're for canning. Pickles and such."

"You don't *know* that," Eustace insisted.

Cordelia spun to face her. "What happened to *It's an old house, Cordy? Have you ever seen a bat, Cordy? Let's investigate, Cordy?* You were all balls and bravado a few days ago."

Eustace sniffed. "I realize this is a novel experience for you, having lived in Texas all your life, but I call Colorado home now, and I know what kinds of things take up in basements. I don't *do* basements."

"You do now," Cordelia told her, spinning back around and heading into the dark.

Eustace quickly caught up once she realized her sister was taking the light with her.

To their right, a wall opened into a crowded room used for furniture storage—some stacked chairs in need of refinishing, a small table with a busted leg, several headboards and footboards and pairs of rails to mattresses long gone. Amid them, a dark wicker pram with a curling handle and huge wheels held court ominously.

"Well, that's not disturbing at all," Eustace said in Cordelia's ear.

"It's clearly out-of-date," Cordelia noted. "I'm sure they just put it down here because they upgraded to a newer, safer one at some point."

"Keep telling yourself that," Eustace said dryly.

"I just don't understand why it's all sectioned off like this," Cordelia continued. "Why all the little rooms and passages? It makes no sense."

"Unless you're running an illegal business out of the basement," Eustace suggested. "This would be perfect for a grow room. You could get a whole operation going down here."

Cordelia rolled her eyes. "You are not starting an illicit cannabis farm in the basement of our great-aunt's house."

"Just a suggestion," Eustace said coolly. "Don't decide right now. Medical marijuana *is* legal in this state."

"You may be onto something, though," Cordelia said. "What if our relatives were into bootlegging or something like that? It might explain where the money came from. Maybe that's what all those jars were for."

"If you're right, then I bet they falsified the ledgers upstairs to cover it up. I'll try and find some entries that allude to whatever they were up to," Eustace volunteered.

"Good idea," Cordelia said, nearing a yawning doorway to their left at the very back of the basement. Here, farthest from the staircase and its overhead light, the darkness became all-consuming.

Cordelia began to feel a familiar tingle tracing its way through the air, similar to the feeling that would come over her near the crypt, only fainter. If she took the vibrating chorus she felt before and spread it out, she could tease each voice from the next, like singling out a hair. That was what she was feeling now—a single call echoing through this basement. A single voice. A single note.

Rounding into the room, Cordelia stopped as she let the light fall on each wall and corner.

"What the holy hell?" Eustace asked, stumbling in behind her.

The middle of the floor was clear, with everything pushed against the walls. Symbols, like the ones they'd seen drawn across their aunt's face, were etched into the stone in a spiraling pattern. The immediate wall was lined with old shelves, crammed with items barely recognizable in the dark—a reserve of candles, used and unused, the leaning spines of unmarked books, bunches of twigs, jars of ingredients long forgotten, and piles and piles of animal bones. Some were haphazardly thrown onto the shelves, and others were still arranged—in whole or partial skeletons. Cordelia couldn't miss the splayed wings and tiny ribs of a fully constructed bat—bones like jointed white spider legs.

She reached for a disconnected jawbone, missing several teeth, though one powerful incisor remained. It was no bigger than her hand. "Cat?" she asked, shoving it back on the shelf in disgust.

"Or raccoon," Eustace figured. "But *why*? And why so *many*?"

Cordelia couldn't answer that, wasn't sure she wanted to.

Looking away, she shone her light against the far wall where a high table stood, stacked with bowls and various containers and an assortment of peculiar, handheld tools. She recognized the large earthenware mortar and pestle, the copper and brass cauldron dulled by years of dust. But others, she did not.

"What is that?" Eustace asked, pointing to a ring with several chains ending in hooks hanging on the wall above.

"Or that?" she said again, pointing to a silvery saw with a thin blade, open in the middle.

"Or that?" she questioned further, gesturing to something that looked like a long clamp that opened in reverse.

"Eustace!" Cordelia scolded her, her sister's mounting anxiety fueling her own. And then her flashlight fell on the farthest corner. "What is *that*?" she asked quietly.

"Oh sure. Now you want to play," Eustace grumbled, crossing her arms, until she saw what the flashlight was revealing.

A cast-iron stove—squat as a toad and blacker than tar—stood in the corner on four stout legs, its heavy door marked by giant hinges and bolted closed. A fat pipe ran from it up the wall to vent the room. Beside it, a cobwebbed pile of firewood and tinder lay forgotten.

"Looks like some kind of heater," Eustace said.

"An oven," Cordelia corrected, taking a deep breath. She knew appliances, new or old. She'd seen some doozies in her day, but nothing quite like this. "It's an oven."

"Witches indeed," her sister whispered low, and Cordelia could see by the way Eustace bunched the fabric of her shirt in her fists that she was scared.

"But what kind?" Cordelia asked. They both gaped at the oven as if in a scene from "Hansel and Gretel." Her burgeoning headache threatened to pulse back to life as she took in the room, her mind filled with candy-house horrors.

Cordelia moved the light away from the corner to the wall opposite them. Her eyes took a minute to refocus. Painted black as the stove, it was marked with an elaborate mapping system in chalky white. She stepped closer to it, studying the writing. *Omen, Corvus, Laurel . . .*

They were names.

Moving back, she searched until she found it. *Magdalena*—their mother.

"I think this is some kind of family tree," she said to Eustace, who was now flipping through a leather-bound volume she'd pulled from the shelf.

And then she took another step back, shining her light a little lower, and the skin along her arms and neck began to crawl.

Eustace, it read.

Cordelia.

She gasped and stumbled back, accidentally bumping into her sister, who was cupping something in the palm of one of her hands.

"Great," Eustace griped. "Now I dropped half of them."

"Half of what?" Cordelia asked, sinking low so she could help her recover whatever she'd fumbled.

"They're some kind of stones," Eustace was saying. "But I couldn't really see because you had the light. I think they have those same symbols we saw on our aunt and the floor carved into them."

Cordelia held up her phone so they could make out what Eustace was holding.

"Shit," her sister stuttered.

"Those aren't stones, Eustace," Cordelia told her. "They're teeth."

"From the raccoon jaw?" she asked, horrified.

Cordelia shook her head. These were no animal teeth. These were human.

Suddenly frantic to be rid of them, Eustace began trying to funnel them into the pouch she'd dumped them from, spilling half a dozen or more back onto the floor.

Cordelia spotted one glowing softly against the dark stone and picked it up. Hadn't she seen one like it upstairs? The second her fingers closed around it she felt a cord of ecstasy pulse through her. With it, the knot in her head unraveled. The symbols were a match to those on the floor, those on their aunt's corpse. She wanted to know what they meant, why they triggered something powerful in her. Reluctantly, she dropped the stone back in the pouch her sister was holding.

Eustace threw the pouch onto the nearest shelf. "Let's get out of here," she said, turning for the door.

"Wait," Cordelia said, not quite ready to leave. But the light of her phone went out, and both sisters were swallowed in black.

"Cordy," Eustace whispered frantically. "Are you fucking with me? Because it's really not funny."

"No," Cordelia insisted. "It's the phone. I guess the battery died. I thought it had plenty of charge when we came in here."

"I take it back. Not Scooby-Doo. Definitely a horror movie," Eustace said with a tremble.

"Stay calm," Cordelia told her, feeling her own heart begin to pound. "It's trying to come back on."

She entered her pass code when the screen loaded and expected to see the same wallpaper image of herself and John on their wedding day, even though she'd vowed to change it. But instead, her photo gallery opened, and she was greeted by the lawn beside the carriage house, green and gold and marked by trees.

"What the heck?" Cordelia wondered aloud.

"What is it?" Eustace asked, scooting closer in the dark to peer over her shoulder.

"A picture I took," Cordelia said absently. "But there was no one there that day."

"What day?" Eustace asked. "Let me see."

There, poised lithely between two trunks as if she were simply on a stroll, was the silhouette of Arabella Bone—their great-great-great-grandmother. Her light blue dress was washed out, streaked across the screen like paint, and her fair hair was smudged around the pale heart of her face. She was looking directly into the camera. Cordelia stared, her eyes watering from the light.

"Let me see," Eustace said again, reaching for the phone and tipping it out of Cordelia's hand.

As the light emanated away, it revealed a ghostly white face framed by reddish-black hair hovering right in front of her. The dark eyes were melting, the mouth an open gash.

Morna. There and gone.

CHAPTER FOURTEEN

THE BOOK

CORDELIA LEANED BACK against the bookshelf door as she caught her breath, making sure nothing followed them out of the basement. Eustace leaned over the desk, gripping the edge with one hand. Both women were huffing from their race up the stairs, and Cordelia's head was pounding anew with the effort. She grasped it with both hands.

"The medicine not working?" Eustace asked between breaths, her voice hitching with fear.

Cordelia dropped her hands. "I just need to catch my breath." But inwardly she shared her sister's concern. If her pills were already proving ineffective, she couldn't have much time. "I saw our names down there," she told Eustace, as much to change the subject as anything else. "On that wall."

"Which wall?" Eustace asked.

"The one with all the writing. It was painted black. I think it was, like, a family tree. I found our mother's name and then mine. Yours, too."

Her sister stood very still. "Not the most conventional way of tracking your genealogy."

Cordelia shook her head. "No, it was different than that. It was simpler, more straightforward." She thought about it, recalling the names she'd seen. She remembered the name *Opal* on the wall, and Bennett talking about her when he showed them her and her husband's portrait in the dining room. But there was no *Theodore* beside it. Just like there was no name beside their mother's. "I think it's just direct descendants. Not a tree as much as a . . . *bloodline.*"

"Maybe we really are vampires," Eustace said humorlessly.

"Or blood witches," Cordelia whispered. "Do you think they practiced some kind of sacrificial magic? All those bones . . . And you saw the oven."

"I don't know what I saw," Eustace countered.

"What if that's why Mom left? What if they wanted her to do things she didn't think were right? Unnatural things. Murderous things. It would explain her never wanting to come back here, even if it was the only way to save her life. And why she never wanted us to know about this place. She might have been afraid they would suck us into it too. It would explain the rumors." Cordelia leveled her gaze on Eustace.

"Into *what*?"

"Black magic," Cordelia whispered.

"You're jumping to conclusions," Eustace told her. "We don't know anything for certain yet."

"Am I, though?" she pushed.

Eustace eyed her sidelong. "A couple of days ago you told me the landscaper worshipped the devil. Remember that? And then we found out he had a music career. I know what it looks like down there, but I think we should reserve judgment until we know more."

"It looks positively macabre," Cordelia said. "What did Bennett say in the crypt? Something about our family being very old and having all these *customs.*"

"Don't remind me," Eustace said, tugging a vape pen from her pocket and taking a drag to settle her nerves.

"Do you think he knows about that room? The wall of names?

Our bloodline?" Cordelia questioned. "Do you think he knows they were witches?"

"*We're* witches," her sister clarified. "You said our names were on that wall too."

Cordelia's head thumped with pressure, as if it were swelling.

Eustace slammed something down on top of the ledgers they'd left strewn about.

"What is that?" Cordelia asked, straining to see.

Her sister rested a hand on it. "I'm not sure. I was trying to look at it down there, but you had the light. It was in my other hand when you dragged me out."

Cordelia took a step closer. On the cover—a wormy, brown leather with raw edges—was burned the same oddly formed eight-pointed star from the stair hall floor, its center uncomfortably mesmerizing, drawing and repelling her at once.

Eustace ran her fingers over it. "What do you think it means?"

Cordelia shook her head. "I have no idea. I thought it was just a standard medallion at first. You know, like a compass design. But now I'm not so sure."

Eustace peeled back the cover. Rough, rag-laid pages were marked with tight lines of cryptic writing. Cordelia recognized many of the same symbols they'd already seen. Some of the lines ran vertical instead of horizontal.

"Jesus, that would give anybody a migraine," Eustace complained.

Reflexively, Cordelia lifted a hand back to her head, but the gnaw was quieting.

Eustace eyed her but didn't comment. "What language do you think it is?"

She shrugged. "High gibberish? It looks like hieroglyphs, or maybe just pieces of them."

Eustace nodded, flipping through. On the final page, she pointed to some numbers at the top. "Is that a date?"

"Seeing as there's not a sixteenth month or a sixty-fourth day, I doubt it." Cordelia started organizing some of the ledgers and books they'd left in the ransacked room, returning them to the shelves.

Eustace screwed her mouth to one side. "Cordy, this has to be what we've been looking for. If we can translate this book, we can figure out what they did in that room. We can decode those symbols on our aunt's face and Mom's tattoo, the scratches in the wall. Maybe we'll find a way to stop your headaches in here."

"Yeah, if we can figure out how to read it," Cordelia told her. "Here, open it for me." Holding her phone out, she took a photo of one of the simpler symbols. "I saw this same one on the floor in the basement and in the crypt on our aunt."

It looked like an *F* with broken arms. Using a reverse image search, she waited to see what the internet had to say about it.

"Well?" Eustace asked.

"*Ansuz,*" Cordelia read. "That's what it's called. It's part of something called the *Elder Futhark.*"

"The what what?"

Cordelia scrolled up the screen of her phone, scanning for the most pertinent information. "They're Nordic runes," she told her sister.

"As in Vikings? I thought Bennett said our ancestors came here from Britain."

Cordelia shrugged. "Could just be a cipher, a way of coding so it can't be easily read."

"Maybe," Eustace agreed, but she didn't look convinced.

In truth, Cordelia wasn't either. Had she seen the symbols only in the book, perhaps that explanation would be plausible. But why on the floor of that disturbing room? Why across the face and throat and hands of her aunt? There had to be a deeper reason.

"What does *Ansuz* even mean?" Eustace asked.

Cordelia read for a bit. "God," she said.

Eustace appeared puzzled. "I kind of doubt he drew the Lord's Prayer all over our aunt's face before burying her."

Cordelia read some more. "It's someone named Wodanaz, er . . ."

Eustace leaned in.

Cordelia met her sister's eyes. "Odin."

EUSTACE DROPPED THE book on the breakfast table, causing Cordelia's coffee to vibrate in its cup. "I was up all night with this thing," she grumbled. "There's a reason I skipped college, you know. Now I understand what the term *all-nighter* means. I always thought it was just about sex."

"Did you crack it yet?" Cordelia asked, trying to steady her coffee mug.

"One does not simply learn ancient Viking in a day," Eustace admitted. "But I have made progress. I found a surprising number of books on Norse mythology in the library, and I can tell you that this Odin guy is kind of a big deal. For starters, he's the god of the dead. A necromancer, in fact."

Cordelia put down her coffee mug, the fine hairs across her knuckles and the tops of her arms beginning to stir. Speaking to the dead was the main thing she'd been reared not to do. And yet the dead kept finding her, kept turning up where they weren't wanted, complicating her life in ugly ways.

"And get this," Eustace continued. "He would go around waking up these poor dead witches to ask them questions. A *god*. And not just any god, but the head honcho."

"What's your point?" Cordelia asked, finding her voice.

"My point is that the witches were the ones with all the answers. Even in death. Even for the gods. That's a pretty prominent role to hold in a culture." Her sister gave her a pointed look. "A respectable one. Whatever they practiced, it was valued. *Highly.*"

She could see what her sister was driving at, but Cordelia wasn't ready to drop her suspicions because of some myth found in a dusty old volume in the library. Plenty of ancient cultures practiced rituals that would be tantamount to a crime today. Whatever their family was up to, it was obvious their mother was not on board. And that was damning in and of itself. "You saw what I did down there. In what context is that respectable?"

"It's not always so black and white, Cordy," Eustace reminded her.

Her sister wouldn't understand until Cordelia told her everything. They needed to be on the same page if they were going to figure this out, but she was afraid talking about the spirits would only make things worse, maybe as much as talking *to* them. She toyed with the handle of her mug, sighing.

Eustace went on. "Anyway, he's credited with discovering the runes—the symbols we keep seeing. But unlike our alphabet, the runes are considered more than a written language. They're magical."

"So, you're saying our family encrypted their memoirs in a magical language discovered by an ancient god?"

"Keep up, there's a lot to unpack here," Eustace shot back. "The Elder Futhark has twenty-four runes, which can each represent a different letter of the alphabet, but they also have their own meanings—whole words or phrases. Kind of like they encapsulate their own ideas, their own energy. You follow?"

"I think," Cordelia answered with skepticism.

"When I started trying to figure out how they're being used here, I realized there are many more besides the original twenty-four. I think in some cases they're combining them." Eustace opened the journal to a page and spun it to face Cordelia, pointing.

Cordelia studied the symbol beneath her sister's finger, a complicated array of lines and angles. It reminded her of Chinese characters and how they are combined to form more complex words. She could almost pick out some of the basic runes within it.

"That's not in the Elder Futhark or any other runic alphabet far as I can tell. But the Elder Futhark may be in it," Eustace said, flipping a page in the journal and pointing again, this time to a symbol resembling their mom's tattoo, the very same one they suspected their aunt was carving into her wall before she died. "Guess what *is* in the Elder Futhark, though. *This. Algiz*—the elk rune. It usually means *protection,* or *defense.*"

Running her fingers over it lightly, Cordelia felt a shock, as if the symbol were charged. "Protection from what?"

"Or who?" Eustace sighed this time. "Maybe whoever cut it from her breast? Do you think Mom had a stalker?"

"I don't know." Cordelia rubbed at her eyes. "She dated so many weirdos. If she did, she didn't say. Maybe never knew."

"Well, I think it definitely means she knew this magical language," Eustace said. "And that means she was part of it, at least before she left."

"Part of it?" Cordelia echoed.

"The family craft," Eustace said. "Some of these pages are diagrams and drawings. Others, like this one, look almost like recipes." She flipped to one page with a column of writing that did indeed appear to be laid out like a modern recipe.

"Aunt Augusta's top-secret Christmas cookies?" Cordelia joked.

Eustace smirked. "Decoding this book is the key to understanding what kind of witches we are, what our family was doing when Mom left to drive her away, and what made her so sick and vulnerable. This is how we help you, Cordy. I know it is."

Cordelia stared at the markings on the page, alien and alluring, hungry to understand them and also afraid.

"I also figured out a couple of other things last night," Eustace told her, closing the book. "Those teeth we found? They're rune stones, an ancient practice of divination. You would throw them or drop them and read the future in the design. Usually, they were made out of wood or rock. Ours are just more gross."

Cordelia winced.

"And our family name," Eustace went on. "The Viking thing got me thinking, so I started digging online. Miraculously, the WiFi held up. I wanted to find out if *Bone* was British or Nordic, but it came up as Old French. Possibly from the word *bon*, which means *good*," Eustace told her. "Also, I looked up that motto, which is in Latin."

"A British American family with a French name in a Victorian house who writes in Nordic runes and has a Latin motto. We are so much weirder than I realized." Cordelia hung her head. "What does the motto mean?"

"It's creepy. Don't say I didn't warn you." She bit her lower lip. "*Silent in life, vocal in death.*"

The words passed through Cordelia, kicking up something she had tried for years to keep down. A current of understanding wound its way around her mind. The necromancy thread brought up a moment ago tightened like a garrote.

"You have that look on your face you used to get whenever you did math homework," Eustace said, getting up to pull a tray of dough from the fridge.

Cordelia stood, pacing the kitchen. She'd divulged so much already—and this was Eustace, after all—but her last secret was also her darkest. The hardest to explain. Where did she begin? She'd been harboring it since childhood. *Of course,* she thought. She knew where to begin. *The house with the blue shutters.* "Do you remember the house on Rocket Street?"

Eustace peered up at the ceiling, thinking. "You had the worst nightmares at that place."

It was the first house where Cordelia really remembered the whispers. Long nights lying awake waiting for them to stop, only to fall asleep and hear them in her dreams. But it wasn't just the rooms or the beams or the floorboards that were speaking to her there. She'd always kept them to herself growing up, the ones who didn't belong. Once, it was her only secret from Eustace. "I saw someone there—a woman. She terrified me. It was the same day Kenny T. hit that little boy on the bike out front of our house. I thought I was the only one who saw her, but . . ." Cordelia looked at Eustace, who was brushing egg whites over her dough.

Eustace paused, waiting for her to finish.

"Then I saw Mom. *Watching* her." Cordelia swallowed. "That's when I knew she could see them too."

"*Them?*" Eustace laid her pastry brush down. "Cordy, what are you telling me?"

Cordelia suddenly understood. It wasn't the woman or the whispers that were haunting her. It wasn't the shadows that walked or the Rocket Street house or the things she heard when a room was silent that made her feel so petrified. It was their mother. Maggie was what scared Cordelia most. Deep down, Maggie was the reason Cordelia couldn't sleep at night. She closed her eyes, rabbit heart sprinting. "That night, she took me behind the shed out back," Cordelia said, remembering.

Eustace stared at her, dumbfounded. "Where the rats lived?"

"That's when she gave me the rules."

"Rules?" Eustace looked lost. "Honey, what are you talking about?"

Cordelia forced her eyes open, met her sister's wide gaze. "There are three rules when the people who shouldn't be there show up: Don't look at them, don't speak to them, and don't sing for them. She always emphasized that last one. *Never sing for them, Cordelia,* she would say. *Never sing, period.*"

Her sister gaped. "Why have you never told me this?"

"Because you didn't see them like we did," Cordelia told her honestly. "And she said it had to be our secret."

Eustace sucked in air. She slipped her dough into the oven.

"Is that where the singing thing came from? Her hatred of all things musical? From this . . . *vision* you both had?"

Cordelia shrugged, leaning back against the counter for support. "I don't know. She never told me why the rules were what they were. Never made sense out of any of it, but I have my suspicions. I think engaging with them activates something, changes the energy between us and them. Draws them in. I think it gives them power."

Her sister swallowed. "Or us."

"I don't know," Cordelia told her. "I just remember feeling so ashamed. Like I *brought* them there. Like it was my fault."

Eustace brushed Cordelia's cheek, a flash of anger crossing her face. "Mom was batshit."

"No. That's just it," Cordelia said. "I don't think Mom was crazy. I think she was scared. I just didn't understand it then." She looked at her sister. "The motto—think about it, Eustace. *Silent in life.* That's what she made me be."

"And *vocal in death*?"

"That's what *they* are." Cordelia felt a release deep inside, like bubbles rising from an open soda bottle. "It isn't a family motto; it's a family trait. It's *inherited*. This is what's at the center of their witchcraft. It has to be."

"Then why haven't I ever seen them?" Eustace swallowed. "I smoke, like, a *lot* of weed, Cordy. If anyone should be seeing things, it's me."

"Maybe that's just part of who we are. Maybe we have different roles within the bloodline. I just know this place is changing me. It's changing *us*. Look at you. You couldn't even heat a frozen corn dog right half the time. A few days here and you've got a . . . a . . ." Cordelia waved a hand at the oven.

"A pumpkin sweet bread," Eustace supplied.

"Right. Thank you. A pumpkin sweet bread in the oven. Don't you think that's weird?"

Eustace poured hot water over a tea bag. "Of course I think it's weird. Everything about the last few days has been weird."

Cordelia moved to the window, staring into the gloomy solarium. "I've never stopped seeing them, you know. It was better for a while with John. But coming here . . . There's something about this place. They're everywhere."

Eustace slowly stopped stirring her tea and set the spoon down gently, fear igniting behind her eyes. "Who?"

Cordelia rubbed her hands over her face, a sick kind of sense beginning to form. "The women who died here."

CHAPTER FIFTEEN

THE SEANCE

"FOR THE RECORD," Cordelia took the opportunity to say as she watched her sister light the last of the candles she'd gathered on the parlor table, "I think this is a terrible idea."

"Noted," Eustace replied, barely glancing at her as she turned off the antique pendant chandelier. "Relax. We're doing exactly what the doctor ordered—we're asking the dead. We need answers, Cordy. And everyone who has them is deceased. If we find even one thing out tonight, it could blow the lid off this predicament we're in. You said yourself this place is full of ghosts. And not just any ghosts, but our family. They have to be showing themselves to you for a reason. Maybe they can help."

Cordelia was skeptical about that. In her experience, the dead had only caused problems, not solved them. And even if she didn't understand them, she believed her mother gave her the rules for a reason: to keep her safe. This seance her sister had talked her into flew in the face of that. But they were growing more desperate by the day. And it was no longer her life alone hanging in the balance. She recalled with a pang of guilt her sister's twisting scar and sweet Mrs. Robichaud being stalked by the mob.

If she'd learned anything over the last few days it was that the peculiarities they were facing might look distinct on the surface but were intricately interwoven beneath it like fine lace. The trust required they live in residence at the estate, and so did their health. The headaches were connected to their mother's death, and so were the runes. And all of it was linked to this place and the spirits that walked it.

"Do you even know how to do this?" Cordelia pressed, certain they were about to make a dreadful mistake.

"Of course," Eustace said, brushing off her concerns. "I googled it."

Cordelia rolled her eyes from her seat at the game table, a fussy burr-walnut. "Well, by all means then, let's proceed with summoning our unstable, occultist ancestors from the grave."

Eustace frowned, the flickering candlelight causing the shadows on her face to dance. "Don't be such a wet blanket. This is our calling. It's in our veins. What happened to the woman who dug our aunt's corpse out of a wall a few nights ago?" She sat the photo of the floating woman on top of the book from the basement room beside the candles.

"What are those doing here?" Cordelia said, feeling instantly more nervous. "We can't even read that thing yet."

"Something personal to help us connect," Eustace replied.

Cordelia shook her head from the spoon-back chair. "No. I don't think that's wise. We don't know what that book says. Who knows what it might conjure up."

Eustace narrowed her eyes. "A moment ago, you were worried this wouldn't work. Now you're worried it will work too well? I can't have your waffling, ambiguous energy stinking up my seance."

Cordelia's brows lifted.

"Hold on! We need one more thing." Eustace ran from the room.

Sitting in the dark parlor by candlelight—they'd waited until after sundown to start, at Eustace's insistence—was not exactly

Cordelia's idea of a chill evening. The house had enough activity without them trying to wake the dead. But she knew as well as Eustace that they needed answers. She just couldn't help wrestling between her desire to know more and her fear of what it would cost.

A telltale pang sprung to life inside her skull. She moaned and dropped her head into her hand.

Eustace returned, breathless from climbing the stairs. She stopped just inside the parlor door, something behind her back. "Don't freak out."

Cordelia lifted her head. "That is only going to make me freak out more."

Her sister had a long history of inconvenient surprises, like the time Cordelia found a rotten bird's egg in the toe of her patent Mary Janes. The smell had eventually overtaken the whole room, tipping her off. She had become cynical about phrases like *Don't freak out* and *It's not what it looks like* where her sister was concerned.

Eustace sat a tall, rectangular box polished brown and black on the table near the candles.

"Eustace . . ." Cordelia asked, feeling a hum of energy radiating from the container. "What is that?"

"Mom. I lied about the mountains."

Cordelia's mouth dropped open. "You sent pictures for Christ's sake!"

"I did go," her sister was quick to explain. "And it was a beautiful day. The way the light was playing with the trees. The weather was just right—not too hot, not too cold. Mom and I had such a good time that I couldn't go through with it."

"So, you put her in a box and kept her—where? Under the bed?" Cordelia raged, pressing her hands to her head. "I don't believe what I'm hearing. *You and Mom had such a nice time?*" Cordelia glared at her sister. "She's dead."

"Only in a manner of speaking," Eustace told her. "You yourself said you see ghosts. Look, I know I was supposed to. I just couldn't do it. I opened the bag and there she was, reduced to grit. I couldn't let her go. Not with so many questions still."

"She can't answer you, Eustace! She's in a box!" Cordelia replied, slamming her hands against the table and making the candles jump. *What's one more woman haunting this place?*

"Stop saying that." Eustace looked wounded. "It's not a box. It's an urn. Poplar wood and powder-coated metal. It cost me six hundred bucks."

Cordelia cast her a seething glance.

"Now she can be with her family," Eustace told her. "After tonight, we can place her in the crypt where she belongs. Even you feel the wrongness of her not being here."

"Except she didn't want to be. Are you forgetting that? She explicitly left this place out of everything she ever told us, crypt and all." Cordelia shook her head. "I have a bad feeling about this, Eustace."

"Which part, Mom or the seance?"

"All of it!" Cordelia answered.

"Just breathe," Eustace told her, taking a seat across the game table. "We have to be calm for this to work." She took a deep breath in and let it out slowly. "Follow me."

She placed her phone on the table with the screen facing up. Cordelia could see the wikiHow page open to step-by-step instructions on communing with the dead.

"Really, Eustace?" she snapped. "WikiHow is your infallible source?"

Her sister shushed her and opened one eye. "Just breathe in," she said calmly. "Do what I do."

Cordelia pursed her lips, then caved. She closed her eyes and inhaled deeply, letting the breath fill her chest and stomach before releasing it again in a slow stream. For a second, she allowed her eyes to part, but the upside-down face and dead eyes of their levitating grandmother stared up at her from the photograph, and she instantly shut them again. As she concentrated on breathing, the fear in her heart would soften, her head going slack like shot elastic. But then the reality of what they were doing would spread inside her like a subcutaneous injection, and Cordelia would seize, awash with agony.

Eventually, Eustace told her to open her eyes and place her fingers on the top of their mother's urn beside her own. Reluctantly, she did so.

"Is there anyone in the room with us right now?" Eustace asked the darkness.

The candle flames guttered, snapping back to attention, smoke spiraling up from them in a galaxy of particles, and Eustace's eyes went wide. *Did you see that?* she mouthed. She placed the fingers of her other hand atop the book and photograph, motioning for Cordelia to do the same.

Cordelia pulled her free hand from her lap and laid it by her sister's. A twitch of anxiety ran up her spine like mouse feet.

"Can you tell us who you are?" Eustace asked this time. They waited a moment and then Eustace tried again. "Are you a relative of ours? Did you die in this house?"

A tremble ran through the floorboards beneath their feet, vibrating up the table legs, causing the candlesticks to tap a little rhythm against the table. Cordelia curled her toes inside her flats, feeling besieged.

"That's a *yes*," Eustace whispered. She ground her jaw in determination. "How did you die?" she asked the room.

The heavy curtains along the front window billowed as if a gust had passed through it, but it was shut fast. Both sisters turned sharply as the fabric resettled, unrecognizable shapes milling in the undulating drapes like moving sculptures. A French bud vase pirouetted to the floor on their right, crashing upon the rug, rolling back and forth on its side as if teased by invisible fingers.

Cordelia tried to draw her hands back, but Eustace held them fast. "Don't let go! It's working."

"I don't like this," Cordelia told her. "It doesn't feel right."

"Did someone hurt you?" her sister asked the room, ignoring her concerns. "Like they did our mother?"

Cordelia's head began to swim as she blinked her eyes, trying to shut everything out. Around her, the room was speeding up, turning in dizzying circles, making her sick. Everything she'd spent a lifetime running from felt like it was crowding into the room all at once—every spirit, ever nip of fear. They all wanted something from her, their own pound of flesh, and the noise was deafening, like a thousand languages being spoken at the same time. She couldn't breathe.

"Can you help us?" Eustace asked, louder this time. "Can you save my sister?"

A key on the pump organ dropped and a booming note filled the air. Cordelia swooned.

"We call on Maggie Bone!" Eustace roared, encouraged to a near frenzy. "Mom! Are you here? Tell us what happened to you! Who hurt you?"

Several keys on the pump organ pressed down, releasing a devastating noise, loud and dissonant. Between her slitted eyelids, Cordelia could see the shuffling energy of hundreds of spirits crowding into the room like a wall of pearly vapor. Faces vied for their position in the mist—a row of jutting teeth, a protruding nose, an open, empty mouth, angles that could be elbows or shoulders, the press of a palm. She shuddered as they rolled into and out of view, squeezing around her and Eustace, brushing against her ear or the back of her neck, every touch a cold sting.

And through them all, a voice she knew too well: their mother, Maggie, calling with such distress Cordelia thought it must be the sound of her very death.

Something in her head snapped. Cordelia jerked her hands free of her sister's and the candle flames between them all snuffed at once. She couldn't be here in this room, with their frigid, sucking presence, like leeches from the grave, and with the helpless dread in her mother's voice, an echo of her final moments.

Leaping from her chair, she upset the table and urn, the book and photo and candlesticks all plummeting to the floor. She pushed past her sister and bolted out the front door into the night, leaving Eustace calling her name.

She didn't stop running until the soft lights of the carriage house swam into view.

Before she knew what was happening, Cordelia found herself pounding on the glass of Gordon's door.

He opened it, concerned. "Cordelia?"

"Can I come in?" she asked, pushing her way inside without waiting to hear his answer, gripping the door frame, then his arm, then the table as if she were drunk.

He slid the door closed behind her, searching the night for answers. Then he turned. "What's going on? Are you okay? Your sister?"

She pushed herself off the table, standing awkwardly in the center of his room, arms wrapped around herself. "I'm sorry. I just . . . I don't know why I came here. Or if I can talk about it. Can I get a drink?"

Looking baffled, he approached her slowly, her legs and torso tensing. He lifted her chin with a finger, looking her over as if the imprint of what had happened were stamped across her body. She trembled under his careful glare before pulling her face away. "I'm not hurt."

"You're scared," he said bluntly, and an angry vigilance flashed across his face.

"How about that drink?" she asked again, not wanting to re-live it.

Reluctantly, he walked over to the kitchen and pulled a glass from the cabinet. "Is water fine? You want ice?"

She forced a smile. "Do you have something stronger?"

Gordon lowered the glass to the counter. "Stronger like Pepsi?"

"Stronger like bourbon," she said.

"Is that wise?" he asked before reaching into another cabinet and pulling out a bottle of Old Fitzgerald. "Will this work?"

"Bless you," she muttered, practically ripping the lowball glass from his hand as he passed it to her. She sipped deep, finally able to catch her breath through the burn.

"That kind of night?" he asked after a minute.

"You have no idea." She took another deep sip.

"You gonna tell me what happened or drink all my good bourbon and leave me in suspense?" The words were light, hu-morous, but his tone deepened with wary intensity. Her torment clearly upset him.

"Eustace happened," she said bitterly.

"Ah." He nodded in understanding. "I take it you two aren't seeing eye to eye about the house."

Cordelia sighed. "Don't get me wrong. I love my sister. But when she gets an idea . . ."

He grinned then, relaxing a little. "I can imagine."

"I'll be fine," she told him, taking another swig of bourbon, not sure if she needed to convince him or herself. "This has all been a lot to process."

He leaned against his counter, watching her. "Why didn't your mom ever bring you here? I know it's none of my business.

It seems an awful lot to turn your back on, though—family, fortune, heritage. She must have had a good reason."

Cordelia stared at the bourbon in her glass, the smoky gold liquid reminiscent of Gordon's eyes. "I wish I knew," she told him. She took another sip. "Our mom kept a lot of secrets. Sometimes, I'm not even sure she knew why she left. I always figured there must have been some kind of falling-out, but lately . . ."

"You think it was something else?" he asked.

She looked at him. "I think there's more to it than that." She cupped her glass against her chest. "Why don't you believe the stories in town—blood in the soil? Seems a dark place to work."

His eyes narrowed as he studied her. "I told you my mother worked here," he said. "That she died here."

"That's right," she confirmed.

"What I didn't tell you is that she changed before she died." He took a breath. "My mother was the wisest, kindest person I knew, but the rheumatoid arthritis made her life difficult. When I started touring, I made her quit working. I was traveling a lot with the band—Marzanna; that was our name—and I couldn't keep an eye on her. I worried. I didn't need much for myself, so I saved what I made to take care of her. Until . . ."

Cordelia waited for him to finish.

"Everything fell apart at once. I got a stage injury. The medication became a problem—an opioid for the pain. I was supposed to ease off the pills after my procedure, but I found them hard to let go of."

She was surprised he was admitting this to her.

He folded his arms. "This stuff got ahold of me. I was a mess. There were personal issues playing out as well. I was involved with our lead singer—Leila. The relationship was volatile. The pills made everything worse. A couple of months later, they asked me to leave."

Cordelia sighed. "That must have been so hard."

"The worst part is," he continued, "I stopped talking to my mother during that time. I didn't want to hear that I was an addict. I was supposed to be sending her money." He looked up at Cordelia from beneath the thick mantle of his lashes.

She understood now. His mother took this job because he'd stopped supporting her. "Is that when she came here?"

He nodded. "I came home, but I couldn't kick the addiction on my own." He rubbed his hands over his face. "So, I went into a rehab facility in Greenwich. It took all my savings and then some. This job was all she had to take care of herself *and* me. I was so close to leaving the facility when she started slipping."

Cordelia stared at him. "I don't understand."

"She started forgetting things, getting confused. She would go into town and rant to people about things that didn't make sense, mostly to do with this place, your family. She left me voice mails I could barely understand. It happened so fast. One minute she was the woman I always knew and loved, the next she was paranoid and hysterical. She shouldn't have been on her own. Before I could check out, she was gone."

Cordelia remembered he'd told her his mother had been afraid of someone on the property before she died, a person she never named, but this sounded more like delusion, less like reality. She held her drink out to him. "I think you need this more than me."

"You asked me if I believe the stories," he said darkly, ignoring her offer. "I don't. Not exactly. But I believe this place changes people. It changed her."

She swallowed, the bourbon firing her throat. "Then why are you here?"

He shrugged. "My mother is gone. My relationship is over. The band replaced me. I have no family left in Bellwick—my dad died years ago—but I need to be here. For the same reason you do."

"Which is?" she asked, wondering what he thought she was doing here. She wasn't even sure herself most days.

He neared her, taking the cup from her hand. He swallowed a sip of bourbon. She watched his throat move, overcome with the longing to run her fingers over it. This close, he towered over her like a god, too bold to be real. He handed the cup back to her. "Answers."

She held her breath until he stepped away.

"I don't like to talk about what happened, how she ended up here," he said. "People think less of me."

"Someday I'll tell you all about my failed marriage and doomed career. It'll make you feel better. Promise."

Gordon laughed. "It's a date."

She liked how that sounded a little too much. "Can I crash here tonight? I, um, don't think I can go back in that house before the sun rises."

He faltered.

"The couch is fine," she was quick to add, not wanting the memory of her face buried in his sheets to make him think she was asking for anything else.

"Sure," he said quietly, moving up the stairs. He came back down carrying a pillow and blanket. "But tell your sister. I don't want her to worry."

CORDELIA LAY IN the dark trying to ignore the fact that the man she desired beyond all reason was in the house, just above her. Sleep was slow to find her when her heart kept thumping at her chest, her mind wandering up the stairs, her legs itching to go to him. She turned from one side to another on the couch, hoping that with time her body would give up this foolish want.

It must have been near midnight when she heard the first notes drift down the stairwell. Just a whisper of strings, the hush of an electric guitar unplugged. She didn't recognize the tune, but it had a mournful quality that pulled at her. Her mind tripped over melodies long forgotten, sounds she heard as a girl in her heart, songs that could not be sung. The headache that had sent her winging from the house, dulled by the bourbon, finally unclamped itself from her skull.

Rising on bare feet, she made her way up the stairs, pausing between each one to listen. At the top, she stopped and watched him, his naked shoulders draped over the instrument, hands light as swallowtails. His head hung, nodding gently, dark, loose waves falling in deference. The ink on his skin moved with him, crawling like living shadows. She could see the enormous tattoo wrapped around his chest—a rib cage twining with flowers, the heart strapped to it with thorny vines.

She lowered herself onto the top step as he played, unaware of her presence, and soaked him in, losing perspective on where Gordon ended and the music began. Her heart skipped like a pebble on the surface of water—bounding, touching down, then bounding again, a rhythm all its own.

She didn't know how long she sat there before he finally glanced up, eyes meeting hers, hands slowing to a still. She stood, walked toward him, vaguely aware that she was in nothing but a white V-neck and panties.

"Did I wake you?" he whispered.

She didn't respond, just reached down and brushed his hair back with her fingers, cupping his wide jaw in her hands. And then she gently lowered her face, letting her lips graze his, feeling them part beneath her, the hungry slip of tongue. He slid the guitar aside and wrapped arms big as tree roots around her, pulling her onto his lap. Her hips rocked against his.

"Cordelia," he whispered into her neck, her hair, lyrical.

Every cell in her body screamed that she wanted this—to taste him, feel his weight inside her. But the sound woke something in her mind, something uncertain. The tabulator inside her stirred, disgruntled, exacting.

"I'm sorry," she said abruptly, unhitching her legs and backing away. "I can't."

Gordon rubbed his large hands over his face.

"I don't know what I was thinking." She hadn't been thinking. She'd been instinctual, feral, possessed by the music and the shimmering dulcet heat of him. She turned to go back downstairs.

"No," he said. "Stay here. Take the bed." He stood and gripped the neck of the guitar, struggling with his own arousal. "I'll sleep on the couch."

"Oh no, I couldn't," she tried to say, but his eyes were hard and treacherous when they met hers.

"I can't sleep anyway," he muttered, breezing past her, leaving her alone in his room.

Pitiful and unsettled, Cordelia stretched out across his bed, her muscles eventually releasing to the rub of his sheets, his musk around her. She felt confused and embarrassed by what she'd done. As her eyes drifted closed, his words taunted her— *This place changes people.*

Her dreams were heavy and full of whispers, the faces of the dead. She saw a woman with thick, dark hair falling to the ground, her body curling in impossible ways. And she saw Morna stroking a pair of ravens on a tree stand, whispering low into their feather-covered ears. She watched Arabella twirl her way through the garden, face lit with a stolen smile. But it was her mother that shook her—young, winding through the trees, palming the rough bark until she stood at the edge of the street, staring at the asphalt like it was a river that could carry her away.

And then her mother was old, walking through a dim parking lot, mind elsewhere as she dug through her purse. The quiet clap of soles on pavement. A shadow emerging from the puddles of dark. Arms around her mother's throat, grappling her, both of them writhing, and the ripping sound she would never forget, a patch of limp flesh held high, a garbled, maniacal laugh, and her mother's earsplitting scream, the kind made with a dying breath.

Cordelia jumped out of Gordon's bed so fast she toppled over his desk as she hurried to the stairs and barreled down them, fumbling for her jeans on her way to the door.

He rose from the couch, eyes weighty with sleep. "Are you all right? I heard a crash."

Outside the morning was slate gray, the sun just a promise.

"No." She reached for the door. "It's my sister. I heard her scream."

CHAPTER SIXTEEN

The Rune

CORDELIA COULD STILL hear that scream ringing in her ears—a ravaged shriek, primitive and wild—as she tore across the property to the big house, chest heaving. As she neared the main house, she could see it was dark inside. The front and vestibule doors were flung open, swaying on their hinges. She entered gingerly, the stair hall black as pitch and uncomfortably quiet.

"Eustace?" she called. The low croak of an old board sounded on the stairs, as if someone had made a wrong step.

Cordelia took careful steps forward. Something slick caused her to slip, but she recovered and inched toward the nearest switch plate, flicking on the light, blinking in the abrupt change.

Her gaze dropped.

It began at the base of the stairs, dragging across the wide hall and into the vestibule, where it finally pulled to an end just before the open door. A harsh, *red* line, wet and glistening in the lamplight, with a smaller stripe slashing through it at a downward angle like an off-kilter cross.

Near the doorway, the smudge of her own footprint, where she'd stepped into the mark.

Cordelia didn't know what it meant, but she knew it wasn't good.

"Cordy?"

She turned to see her sister on the stairs, looking just as fearful and wild-eyed as herself but otherwise unharmed.

"It's not even six in the morning." Eustace made her way to the bottom step, eyeing the mess. "What is it?"

Cordelia's body trembled and her stomach lurched. A pungent smell like medicine and metal met her nose. Smears of red had followed her across the floor. She bent over and wiped at the sole of her foot with her T-shirt, lifting it to her nose, teeth gritting. "It's blood."

Eustace's eyes widened.

"Not mine," she quickly reassured her.

"I thought I heard a scream," Eustace said. "I thought it was you. I ran to your room, and you weren't there."

"I know." Cordelia had texted her sister to tell her she was at Gordon's but had never mentioned that she was going to stay, only that Eustace shouldn't wait up. "I heard it too. All the way from the carriage house. I thought I was dreaming."

Eustace's eyes slid back to the symbol painted across their floor, the slash and haste of it, the blood rimming her sister's feet and shirt.

Cordelia felt like a girl again, standing in an empty room, staring at a woman in her underwear, brain matter dripping down her front. The threatening message she'd received from Busy crossed her mind. *I doubt she's got enough years left to pay.* If something happened to Mrs. Robichaud, if this was *her* blood, she'd never forgive herself. "What does it mean?"

"It's called Nauthiz—the need-fire. It's a war rune. A symbol of lack or poverty." Eustace gave her a hard look. "It's an ill wish."

"A bad omen." Cordelia felt her stomach twist.

"A curse, Cordy," her sister said ominously. "Someone doesn't want us here." Her eyes darted to the hall tree. "The papers Togers left for us to sign—they're gone."

This was too creative to be the work of the mob. The article she'd found about their aunt Morna came rushing back to her, the accusation of things drawn in blood, the word scrawled on the bedroom wall—*witch*. Eustace was right—someone didn't want them there. Someone *inside*.

That fucking seance, she thought ruefully. They'd woken the dead all right.

Cordelia's eyes lifted to the tower, inscrutable, fear sloshing over her. She knew of only one person capable of such an act, alive or dead.

"I'm sorry," her sister breathed. "You were right about last night. I got carried away."

Cordelia shook her head. "You've always been the one who took the risks. And I've always been the one who played it safe."

Her sister exhaled. "Both of which got us here."

Gordon suddenly appeared, a thin shirt thrown on, catching himself against the doorjamb before he stepped in the blood like Cordelia had, eyes rounding.

"What happened?" He took them both in—Eustace on the stairs, Cordelia's bloody feet and shirt. "Are you hurt?"

Eustace shook her head. "We're fine. There was a scream, like a woman's. It woke me out of a deep sleep. I thought it was Cordy." Her eyes rolled across to the floor to the open doors and Gordon. Her lips pulled into a sharp line. "If it's not ours, whose blood is it?"

Cordelia's heart tumbled over itself. Someone's life was poured out at their feet. She looked at Gordon.

"Whoever it is, they'll need help if they're still here." His face glistened with sweat, paler than she'd ever seen it. She knew then he was thinking of his mother, imagining her suffering, her final moments on this estate, alone. "I'll search outside," he said, and pounded down the porch stairs.

Cordelia's heart lurched. In a moment of heightened concern, she ran after him into the dawn, tripping over unexpected dips and rises, heart thudding frantically. "Wait!"

But the garden's twists and turns seemed to carry him farther and farther away from her, spinning her in directions she didn't want to go, the dim light making it difficult for her to tell one path from another. Before she knew it, she was spilling onto the promenade, racing beneath the blushing trees, calling Gordon's name until she found herself face-to-face with the crypt, its shorn peak shrouded in mist.

Cordelia doubled over and tried to catch her breath. It was only when she rose to her full height again that she realized the iron doors were standing open, not closed and wrapped with the chain as they'd left them. Distraught, she climbed the steps cautiously, ducking her head into the crypt before entering. It was empty, everything untouched, mementos resting peacefully. But on the back wall, between the burial shelves, a smear of blood, a handprint wetting the stone.

They had been here too, whoever was in the house, whoever left that mark for them. And they wanted her to know.

She was shooting down the stairs and across the promenade when Gordon caught up to her. "There's blood in the crypt," she called, as he ran toward her, shielding her with his arms. "I didn't see anyone," she told him. "It's empty now."

His face tightened. "You shouldn't have come out here on your own."

"I was worried—" she started to explain when a wail pierced the air between them, fraught with memories of the night before. They bolted for the house.

"Eustace!" Cordelia screamed as she charged through the

doors behind Gordon. She should never have left her sister on her own, she scolded herself, last night or this morning. He stopped short, and she skirted around him. Her sister's back rounded in the hall light.

Eustace turned, her face a convoluted tangle, streaked with tears. In her arms, a bundled mass of sticky orange fur, foul-smelling and lifeless.

Cordelia stared. "What is that?"

"A vixen," Eustace said. "I found her in the library. She's alive, but barely."

She killed the animals, the nurse had been quoted in the article about Morna. *They were her pets. Loved 'em like her own children. But she killed them. And drew unnatural things with their blood.*

"It was *her* scream that woke us," Eustace said. "It's her blood."

The three of them rushed the animal to the kitchen. Gordon spread flour-sack dish towels across the granite island. Eustace deposited the fox, its body a limp jumble of fur and ick. A large slit ran up the middle of its belly, caked with blood. Her breaths were scarcely perceptible.

Eustace was frantic, gathering towels, water, and herbs. "I need the vodka from the bar in the next room," she told Gordon. "Hurry."

Cordelia stood dumbly to one side, not sure what to do. It seemed preposterous that her sister would treat this animal herself, and yet she knew that look of determination Eustace wore. "I'm sure Gordon knows someone we can call about this. A wildlife rehabilitation place or something."

Eustace glanced up. "She doesn't have that kind of time. We need to close the wound and prevent infection. She's lost a lot of blood. A transfusion would be ideal, but I'll have to come up with something else."

"Do you hear yourself?" Cordelia asked softly. "This is a mortal wound. You can't generate more blood for her. It would be kinder to end her suffering."

"I know I can save her. I have to try," Eustace replied, earnest.

Cordelia didn't like seeing an animal in pain any more than the next person, but this would take a miracle, even for a professional. She was caught in a bad dream, barefoot and bloodied, struggling to grasp what was happening.

"Watch her while I run down to the basement. There are supplies down there I can use." Eustace headed for the door, bumping into Gordon with the vodka.

Cordelia took the bottle from him. "Follow her. I don't want her down there alone."

He nodded, and trailed after Eustace.

She turned back to the island. The vixen lay perfectly still, pumpkin and sable, a mouth rimmed in sharp teeth. With trembling fingers, she stroked a black-tipped ear. The golden eyes fluttered open, long dark whiskers quivered near the nose. A winsome little martyr—she held no hope for it to survive.

Eustace returned with Gordon, arms full of supplies. She threw a long, curved needle down on the table, and another S-shaped one beside it.

"Where did you get these?" Cordelia asked, studying the needles as Eustace began unwinding a spool of silk thread.

"Remember all those instruments we saw? I have a feeling Great-great-aunt Morna did her own taxidermy. Those birds in my room were probably pets first. As were all the other strange creatures around here."

Had their aunt killed *all* these animals? Wasn't that an early sign of psychopathy?

Eustace held up a jar of green and brown bits with a dusty label. "Hawthorn leaf. For the swelling. And oregano oil to fight off infection. Turmeric and honey will help with both, as well as with the pain."

"And the blood loss?" Cordelia asked.

Eustace pointed at a dried bunch of leaves. "Stinging nettle will help her generate more red blood cells; I should be able to harvest more on the property. Now, put those oven mitts on. If she tries to fight, though I think she's far too weak, you'll have to hold her down."

Cordelia did as she was told, but the vixen only twitched as her sister cleaned the wound. Eustace hummed as she worked—an indistinct tune that focused her, the fox stilling beneath her hands.

When the wound was closed, Eustace made a poultice with the honey and herbs. "She needs water. There's a turkey baster in that drawer. Do your best to get some fluid in her until I finish with this."

Cordelia pushed the baster into the fox's mouth, its jaw working against the intrusion, just far enough back to let the liquid slide down her throat.

"Again," Eustace told her, and Cordelia repeated the steps a few more times.

"We'll need more chicken and eggs," Eustace told Gordon. "Some berries and apples too. And a really good blender."

"I have a Vitamix at the carriage house," he said. "I use it for protein shakes. I'll get it now. The rest I can get in the morning." He slipped out through the solarium.

Eustace stood over the fox like a mother shielding her baby. She continued to hum, a rumble behind pinched lips, as she tended her patient with the care of a nurse and the gentleness of a midwife.

"I dreamt of Mom," Cordelia told her. "I *saw* what happened—I saw it all. Like I was there."

Eustace peered at her. "Did you see who?"

She shook her head. "It was dark, but . . . what they did, it ended her."

Eustace took a sharp breath in and looked back down at the fox, now blank as stone. "No, no, no."

"You did your best." Cordelia knew a lost cause when she saw one.

But Eustace wouldn't let go. She pressed her hands against the animal's wound, sobbing, humming, until her whole body was pulsing. Light and heat began to build around her like she was drawing it from the fixtures and the plants in the solarium, the sun outside, and channeling it through her hands. The bulbs flickered in their sockets, sparks crackling from a nearby outlet.

Cordelia could feel the heat like the cast of a hearth fire. And so could the fox. Within moments, her chest began to rise and fall again, her legs and ears stirred, her eyes fluttered. She picked her head up, and Eustace's hands were thrown off by the energy she'd created. She stumbled back, shaking them like they'd been burned.

Cordelia rushed over to the sink and ran a dish towel under some cool water, pressing it to one of Eustace's palms and then the other.

Her sister shook her off, backing away. "I'm fine," she said, wiping her hands across her shirt as if they were covered in blame. But she was suddenly glowing, her complexion radiant in the kitchen light and her hair full of silver luster. Her cheeks were like two blushing apples, and the whites of her eyes seemed brighter, her lips and hips fuller.

The fox was lying on its belly, legs tucked carefully underneath, head raised, ears alert, eyes bright and watching Eustace's every move.

"Holy Neroli . . ." she muttered with awe.

"What was that?" Cordelia pressed.

"I–I don't know? I just wanted so badly for her to live. And I was touching her. It was so warm. *She* was so warm. And for a minute . . . for a minute, I *became* her."

Cordelia shook her head as if she could dislodge those words, keep them from burrowing in.

Eustace was beaming like a strip of neon. "I know it sounds crazy. I slipped into her or . . . we slipped into each other. And there was so much *light*." She stroked the fox between the ears.

Worry festered under Cordelia's skin, hot and itchy, and yet her sister looked better than she ever had in her life. The fox was alive and awake. And Eustace could explain none of it.

Gordon barreled through the door, blender in hand, when the fox stopped him in his tracks.

"Don't move too quickly," Eustace instructed. "You'll scare her."

He made a wide circle around the island. "How is that possible?"

"Eustace did some vet tech training after high school," Cordelia lied, thinking on her feet. "She has a way with animals."

"I just brought the blender to be nice. I didn't think she'd actually make it," he admitted.

He wasn't the only one.

Gordon held up a brown grocery sack. "Change of clothes, toothbrush—the essentials. I'll camp out in the parlor if it's okay with you for a night or two. Make sure whoever did this doesn't come back."

"I'll clean up the blood." Cordelia grabbed a mop and filled a bucket, dragging them to the stair hall. She mopped the floorboards, scrubbing them with an old towel on hands and knees until they were shining and only the rubber and chlorine scent of tap water remained. But she couldn't wash the image from her mind—the crooked cross splashed wickedly before her, the glint of chandelier light on fresh blood, the sagging fox now lying in their kitchen.

She climbed the elegant stairs in wet, bare feet. She would

shower and change. And she would pick a fireplace in the house and burn her T-shirt. And she would check in on her sister and the miracle fox. And then, once she'd managed to eat something and clear her head a bit, she would figure out how to fight back.

CHAPTER SEVENTEEN

THE ACCIDENT

CORDELIA WASN'T PREPARED for company. She was jumpier than usual after their grisly morning, the harrowing night of overturned candles and kisses stolen in the dark. They had just gathered to sit down to lunch when the knock sounded. She froze, posture stiffening.

Eustace cocked an eyebrow. "Expecting someone?"

Her mind whirled over a number of possibilities. She had calls in to an appraiser and an estate attorney through Molly. She checked her phone, but no new texts had come through.

The person rapped again, louder, impatient.

Cordelia sprung from her chair. "I'll see who it is."

Eustace followed her into the stair hall. "Don't answer it. What if it's *them*?"

"I don't think they would just knock and introduce themselves," Cordelia told her.

Banging sounded for the third time, ending with a *whap* from the flat of someone's hand.

Cordelia reached for the knob. "Coming!"

A well-dressed man stood outside with a pale hook mustache and wire-rimmed glasses. "I'm Mr. Browning," he said, passing Cordelia his card. "You were expecting me."

"Sorry, no," Eustace said, coming up behind her sister.

Cordelia glanced down. *E. M. Browning. Appraiser & Auctioneer. Merrin's Fine Auction House.* Molly had come through after all, but apparently her text hadn't. "Mr. Browning—of course." She extended a hand. "Sorry for the wait. Please come in."

She'd had every intention of bringing this up to Eustace, but things had been so upside down. The fact was, Cordelia needed cash *now* to get the mob off her back and protect her elderly neighbor, as well as pay the mold remediators and prevent a lien on her property. She couldn't wait for all the legal mumbo jumbo of the estate to fall into place, not with innocent people mixed up in her problems.

"I'm sorry . . . Why are you here?" Eustace asked the gentleman.

"Mr. Browning," Cordelia announced a little too loudly, "is here to appraise the estate and its assets so we can be sure of its worth in the market."

"Quite right," the man confirmed with hungry eyes, merrily taking in the impressive stair hall and its bedeviled hall tree.

Eustace took a step in his direction. "I'm sorry, sir, but my sister seems to have gotten a little ahead of herself. The estate is still in transition, as it were."

His brows bunched up over the rim of his glasses. "What's that?"

"What my sister means to say is that we're only looking to get a rough estimate at this time," Cordelia interrupted before Eustace could drive him away. "Please come in." She shot her sister a pleading look.

As he stepped inside, Cordelia stole a moment to drag Eustace toward a corner. "Please play along," she whispered, eyes glistening. "I need money, and I'm running out of time. No one will notice if one or two valuables go missing."

"Cordy, none of this stuff is ours yet. What you're doing is stealing," Eustace argued.

"Ho, ho!" the old man suddenly burst out. "Now this is a fine example of late-1800s bronze craftsmanship." He was studying the newel post lamp absurdly closely. "I've never seen one quite like it. Tell me, is the owl significant to your family in some way?"

Cordelia smiled at him from her conspiratorial corner. "I'll be right with you." Turning back to her sister, she whispered, "It's not stealing, it's borrowing. Think of it as an advance. I have to do something, Eustace."

Her sister scowled. "It's risky. What if Mr. Togers finds out?"

"He'll never find out," Cordelia promised.

"And the house?" her sister asked.

"What about the house?" she pressed.

Eustace's lips formed a grave line. "You heard what Togers said about the house making its will known."

A tickle of intuition niggled at Cordelia's gut, but she pushed it aside. "The house is not going to miss a couple of dusty old curios."

"I don't know," Eustace faltered.

Cordelia grabbed her sister's arms. "Eustace, it's my *life* we are gambling with if we wait any longer."

Her sister caved, shoulders and chest sinking. "Fine, but nothing big, nothing noticeable. You hear me?"

She nodded briskly and turned aside to find Mr. Browning salivating at the edge of the library. "Let me give you a tour." Looping her elbow in his, she steered him into it before Eustace could change her mind.

"I'm so sorry about that," she said to him. "My sister and I are taking this on together, and I didn't have a chance to tell her you were coming."

"Ah yes, well, family heirlooms are just that—a *family* matter," he said as he pressed his nose from spine to spine. He picked up an old magnifying glass with a brass frame and mother-of-pearl handle. "You have quite the treasure trove, Ms. Bone, I must say."

The knot in her chest slipped, loosening. If she could let him spirit just one or two things away that wouldn't be missed, maybe that would fetch a sum to tide her over.

"It's a time capsule," he said with awe, eyes bouncing. "Extraordinary."

Near the turret room, he wheezed at a clock encased in glass, its brass workings exposed like spilt innards, sunlight sparking off its cogs and coils.

"My, my," he said, stricken. "May I?"

Cordelia shrugged.

He lifted it delicately. "What a prize," he cooed. "A Victorian skeleton clock, and a James Condliff, no less!"

"Is that special?" She peered into it as if it might start spitting hundred-dollar bills.

He set it back down like a sacrament. "Mr. Condliff was the premier horologist of his day, out of Liverpool, and is known for these skeleton clocks. No two are alike. There are precious few in the world, and I'm afraid they are extraordinarily expensive. It is a fine point of pride for an auction house to feature one of these."

The words *few* and *expensive* pricked at her ears. "You don't say. What would you estimate it at?"

"Just off the top of my head, I'd say this is easily worth thirty thousand dollars, maybe as much as twice that, depending on key details."

Sweat beaded across her lip. Thirty grand should get Busy and his fellows off her neighbor's case. Sixty would clear her debt with them entirely. "What if I make you a little deal?"

He turned to her, twinkling. "Deal?"

"Suppose we let you take this clock today, put it in your auction. If we're happy with the price, then perhaps we'll sit down and discuss a larger contribution to Merrin's. Would that be agreeable?" She watched his face light up.

"Oh, Ms. Bone! That would be most acceptable." He reached

into an interior pocket and filled out a Personal Property Agreement, handing it to her. She signed quickly, and he ripped his own copy off, handing the top one to her.

"Here," she said, passing the outrageously expensive clock to him. "Take this and be on your way. Call me as soon as you have a winning bid, okay?" She herded him, clock in hand, toward the front doors.

"But I haven't finished my tour," he whined. "I can't possibly give you a reasonable estimate without a full accounting—"

"Poppycock!" she insisted, pushing him toward the vestibule. "Consider this a little taste of what's to come. We'll be in touch." And with that, she shoved him outside, patting his shoulder briskly and closing the door in his face.

Leaning a hand against the door, she sighed. Her immediate financial worries were over. What was one little clock? It was nearly impossible to read. Utterly impractical.

"Happy?" Her sister's voice rang from behind.

Cordelia turned to see Eustace, arms folded stubbornly over her chest.

"What did you give him?"

"Nothing. At least nothing anyone will miss," Cordelia told her. When Eustace's worry lines deepened, she added, "Just a clock."

"Will it be enough?" her sister asked.

Cordelia shrugged. "He seems to think so. Merrin's is a reputable auction house. They can fetch as high a price as anyone."

Eustace squared her shoulders. "Finally, some good news."

Cordelia was just starting for the stairs when the door sounded again, brisk and urgent. She turned, opened it a crack, agitated. "Mr. Browning—"

But instead of the man in the neat suit, it was a woman in brown delivery-service garb. Beside her rested several boxes.

Cordelia opened the door wide. Eustace rushed over to sign,

dragging boxes in. "I shipped my personal effects before I left," she explained.

Cordelia stared. "You were always going to stay."

"I was never going to go back. There's a difference."

"There is?" A stray hair tickled her cheek. She curled it behind an ear, smashing waves against her head.

Her sister guided the last box in with a foot. "I didn't know if Connecticut was my future, but I knew Colorado was my past."

"You could have told me." Cordelia's heart tapped in the pause between breaths. Life would never be like it was before coming here.

An enormous crack echoed through the open doors, the world halved like a piece of fruit, followed by a thunderous boom. She felt the floors shake beneath her. A protracted squeal preceded a terrible crunch, steel meeting something more resistant than itself.

"That sounded close," Eustace said.

"And bad," Cordelia added. Mr. Browning's popping eyes and barrel torso flashed across her mind, horror spiked with guilt surging through her. She started across the porch and down the steps, hurling herself onto the massive front lawn, Eustace's words a cruel echo in her ears—*You heard what Togers said about the house making its will known.*

When the road was finally in sight, her legs slowed their pumping as she took in the terrible scene. A white BMW was folded like an accordion against the gigantic trunk of a fallen sycamore less than a hundred yards away. Leaves and branches littered the road, smoke streamed from the hood, and Mr. Browning's carefully combed hair could be seen flopping over the steering wheel.

Cordelia's heart lurched. In her rush to save one innocent, she'd doomed another. But maybe there was still time.

She dashed toward the car, wrenching open the driver's door.

Shaking the man's shoulder violently as she called his name, she realized quickly he was unconscious. Behind her, Cordelia could vaguely make out her sister's calls as she dug a hand beneath each of the appraiser's arms and pulled him slowly from the car to the street. But his weight was too much for her, and Cordelia found it nearly impossible to drag him farther, even as the smoke she feared billowed from around the hood in angry gusts. She leaned over him, trying to check his breathing.

A moment later, Gordon was at her side.

"We have to help him! Do you know CPR?" she asked, panicked.

"He's breathing," Gordon told her over the sound of the car. "Let's get him to the shoulder. It's not safe here." Together, they dragged the unconscious Mr. Browning to where they could lay him free of the road. "Call 911!" Gordon shouted to Eustace, only a few steps behind.

"There's a wound on the side of his head," Gordon told her, inspecting the man. "He's probably concussed. I don't know about anything else."

"Should we have left him in the car?" Cordelia asked, afraid she'd made another deadly mistake. "Until the paramedics come?"

"See that smoke?" Gordon nodded toward the wreckage. "Fire risk. You were right to pull him out."

Eustace trotted over. "They're on their way."

Gordon dug into Browning's pockets and pulled out a wallet. He flipped to his ID. "The paramedics will need identification, medical card, anything like that."

Next to the man's ID, Cordelia saw the folded edges of the paper she'd signed, releasing the clock to him. Lifting onto her toes, she looked toward the car, where the clock sat perfectly unharmed in the passenger seat, its minute hand still ticking away.

Blood pooled in her feet like sediment. A brush of pain

lanced her head as the weight of responsibility swallowed her. Was this the truth of who she was at her core, the reason her mother had taught her to fear herself, her very nature? Because she invited chaos? Because anyone who got near her would suffer for it? Maybe it wasn't their family's magic that was black, maybe it was her. Maybe she tainted the power she'd inherited like a dirty filter.

"You can go back in," Gordon told her. "I'll wait with him. No use in two of you being unconscious."

Cordelia realized she must look waxen, the color of sawdust. She hesitated.

"Go!" He told her. "You've done all you can here. You probably saved his life."

Had she? Or had she cursed it?

She stood on shaky feet, looking down as a roaring rush of heat nearly threw her back to the grass. She looked behind her, coughing, to see Gordon shielding the appraiser with his body, the BMW now engulfed in flames.

"The tires are going," he called to her. "The air is feeding the fire. You need to get back!"

But Gordon and Mr. Browning looked too close to the flames for safety. She clambered to Gordon's side, head splitting from the blow, and tried to convince him to pull the man farther away from the flaming vehicle.

"It's too risky!" he yelled over the sound of the fire. He pointed to Browning's pants, where a dark stain had formed. "He's lost bladder control. He could have a spinal cord injury."

The heat was blistering Cordelia's face, the inside of her skull beating like a hammer on brass. But if another tire went, if the pressure built in the gas chamber, or if the fuel itself burned intensely enough, it could cause a fireball that might engulf them. She couldn't leave them there.

Eustace approached, coughing, grabbing at her. "Cordy, get back!"

Where is rain when you need it? Cordelia glanced to the sky, her mind repeating it over and over. *Where is rain when you need it? Where is rain when you need it?*

Another tire blew, spewing a stream of fire across the asphalt, setting several branches of the fallen tree ablaze. Cordelia reflexively pushed her sister toward safety. Gordon curled over Browning's prone form. Several explosive pops caused her to nearly jump out of her skin. She dug her fingertips into the earth and cried, "Where is the fucking rain when you need it?"

Something tickled her knuckle, and she opened an eye. Beads of water were bubbling up around her fingertips, rolling along blades of grass toward her hands, pushing through the earth like daisies. She didn't know how exactly, but she felt her connection to it, as if tethered by unseen marionette strings. Digging in, she focused on the runnels of water, watching as they gathered in an impromptu stream around her, running toward the men and the car. Cordelia concentrated and darkness crept in, thunder crashing like cymbals in the sky. She felt the first gelid drops sting her face, sloughing away the heat in her head.

"Rain?" she croaked at Gordon.

"Sleet," he told her, disbelieving.

A deluge of slush and water dumped over them. The car hissed as the fire began to snuff out in sections, unable to withstand the onslaught.

Sirens cut through the downpour, lights sparking through streams of smoke like they were in a disco. The paramedics wheeled their gurney forward and pushed Cordelia out of the way.

"You can stop it now," Eustace leaned over and told her as she shivered at Cordelia's side.

She jerked, a delicious tingle coursing through her despite the cold.

Ice gave way to rain and rain to drizzle. It all ended as fast as it had begun.

Eustace flashed Cordelia a shit-eating grin.

She frowned, her understanding of what had just occurred and how she was connected to it still beyond words. But even if she wasn't ready to claim it, Cordelia knew she couldn't deny it anymore. The door and the rain—both had been her doing. Inexplicably, maybe even subconsciously, but resolutely *her* doing.

She walked over to a man placing an oxygen mask on the appraiser. "Will he be all right?" she asked him. But he ignored her.

Another EMT tried to guide her and Eustace toward the back of a second waiting ambulance as fire trucks lined the street. "You should let us check you for smoke inhalation."

"We're fine," Cordelia told him, pulling away. "Just please make sure he gets all the care he needs," she added, pointing at Mr. Browning.

Walking Eustace back to the house, she noticed Gordon watching her as he sat in the ambulance. She knew leaving might look insensitive, but she couldn't breathe, and it wasn't the smoke. She was choking on guilt. Maybe she had saved Mr. Browning's life, but she'd also set this accident in motion, like the bats and the ghosts and the seance gone wrong. Something inside her attracted mayhem and destruction, created it. How else could she explain all the catastrophes she'd been at the center of? It was her attempt to dig herself, and Mrs. Robichaud, out of one hole that had landed her, and Mr. Browning, in another.

The house felt more sinister as they approached it. She knew something in that house had stopped Mr. Browning. Something wouldn't let the clock leave. The same thing that wouldn't let them leave either.

Inside, she sunk into an empty chair, her phone buzzing on the nearby table. A text from Molly had come through, twelve hours too late. The appraiser will be there tomorrow, it read. 11 A.M.

Cordelia felt her stomach drop.

> I sent him a picture of the house.
> He can't wait.

GORDON FOUND CORDELIA sitting on the front porch when he came striding across the lawn, the skeleton clock in his hands. It was nearing evening; he must have left in the ambulance, and someone dropped him off at home. She'd been waiting for him. The house felt too small around her. She was stifled by all that ornamentation, the heavy drapes and musty antiques, things she'd been so ready to slap a price tag on.

"How is he?" she asked, standing at the railing as he walked up.

"No spinal injury. Just a decent concussion and seven stitches above his right ear. He's lucky."

"Looked pretty unlucky to me, traveling up that road at the moment that tree decided to fall." She was angry. Angry at whatever was responsible for nearly killing that man. Angry at herself for bringing him into it.

Gordon looked up at her. "Good thing you were there."

"You pulled him to safety. I just panicked."

"Seems the sky pays attention when you panic." He touched the back of his neck.

Cordelia felt her lips tug down. She was still processing what had occurred at the roadside. Admitting it to someone else—someone besides her sister, someone steeped in the town's unflattering mythology—seemed unnecessarily risky. "I don't control the weather," she said. "No matter how it looks."

Gordon stared at her openly, brow knitting over his amber eyes. "I meant what I said back there. If it weren't for you, for what you did, that man would be far worse off than he is."

"I told you, I—"

"I'm not just talking about the rain," he said, cutting her off. "You pulled him from the car. It was your fast thinking that got him out of harm's way. That took guts and heart."

But it was also her actions that had put him in harm's way in the first place. She crossed her arms stubbornly. "If it weren't for me, he wouldn't have even been here when that tree fell."

"You should learn to give yourself a little credit," he said, watching her. "Bad things happen to good people all the time. And you, Cordelia Bone, are one of the good ones."

Her eyes met his. She wanted so much to see what he saw in her just then, to believe in her own goodness. Maybe there *was* something dark lurking within her, something that kept manifesting itself in all this havoc, but she'd worked against that impetus today. And she'd won. A man was alive because she willed it with everything she had. She couldn't give up on herself, just like she hadn't with Mr. Browning. If she tried hard enough, maybe she could right the wrongs that had occurred. Maybe she could channel what was inside her into something positive. She had to try. In the end, didn't everything come down to choice? She would choose the good, the right, in herself, in the world, and she would keep choosing it. Even if it killed her.

"I saved this for you," he said, passing her the clock, fragile like something from the sea.

Despite the wreck and the fire, it was unblemished. She set it on the ornate wicker chair behind her.

"And this," he said, passing her a folded sheet of paper.

She opened it to find Mr. Browning's copy of the form he'd given her, her signature scrawled there at the bottom, plain as day. She tucked it in a pocket, coloring. "It's not how it looks."

He pressed his soft lips into a hard line. "Not for me to judge," he told her, but his eyes didn't clear the rail.

"I needed money." It fizzed out of her like carbonation. "They're going to hurt someone I care about, a friend, if I don't pay off my ex's debts in the next twenty-two days. And then they'll come for me."

His face flashed with anger. "Who?"

Cordelia shook her head. "I don't know exactly, but I know they're Mafia. The less I know, the better."

He dug a fist into his hair and pulled it out again. "And your ex? Where does he fit into all this?"

Cordelia laughed dryly. "He doesn't. He's squirmed away and left me with the consequences. I've been trying to sell my house in Texas so I could give them the equity, but we found a huge mold outbreak before we could list it. The remediation cost a small fortune that I don't have. If they place a lien on the house, I can't sell. And this place seems bound up in more red tape than the tax code. I'm not a thief. I just didn't see another way."

He looked at her, eyes peaking like gables. "Your sister know all this?"

"Eustace has had her own downslide recently. There isn't a lot she can do." She watched him wrestle with her confession, the implications, for a moment. "You were gone a long while," she said, changing the subject.

"You worried about me, Bone?" he asked, running fingers through his hair.

She went pink inside, like a shell. Probably outside, too.

He held out his phone, an X-ray image of a human spine flaring to life. "I was at the hospital. Sprinting to that car and dragging him to the shoulder did a number on my back."

Cordelia caught her bottom lip between her teeth. "Your stage injury?"

He popped his knuckles one by one. "It acts up from time to time."

"That's how you knew about the man's spine," she whispered. "Earlier, when he lost his bladder, you said he could have a spinal injury."

"I can keep up around here if that's what you're worried about," he told her.

She said, "I'm not worried."

He smiled. "I'm going to clean up, get a few other things. I'll be back before nightfall. Don't wait up for me; I can sleep in the parlor." He started to walk away, then turned back. "What will you do now?" he asked her. "About your ex's debts?"

She sagged against the railing of the porch, let something else hold her weight up for a change. "I don't know."

Without money from the trust or sales from the estate, she had no other cards to play. She would tell Molly to list the house anyway, but if the mold contractors put a lien against it, they would scare any potential buyers off. "Forget I said anything."

"Wish I could," he said, letting his eyes linger on hers a beat too long.

"You worried about me, Jablonski?" she asked, and it was his turn to blush.

"I won't let anyone hurt you," he said before walking away.

She stood there a very long time watching him recede, his words like a bandage around her heart.

Her phone vibrated in her pocket, and she checked it. It was Molly saying the estate attorney in Hartford needed copies of the paperwork on the trust, paperwork they mysteriously no longer had. But Cordelia, being the vigilant professional she'd always been, had been smart enough to take pictures of each sheet with her phone. It wouldn't be as good as a fax or even an email, but she could at least text those images over and get the ball rolling.

That would be one tiny step forward. Every other step she'd tried to take had resulted only in failure or a near-death experience. Fighting back suddenly felt riskier than it had a day ago.

Bone Hill, it seemed, would decide what was to be done with it.

And what was not.

CHAPTER EIGHTEEN

THE NURSERY

THE HOUSE WAS quiet the next day. *Too* quiet. All Cordelia could hear was the infernal ticking of that clock.

When she woke up, Gordon was already gone. She couldn't hear the birds outside through the windows or the gusts beating against the siding. If she was upstairs, she couldn't hear her sister cooing over the fox downstairs. If she was downstairs, she couldn't hear Eustace tromping down the hall upstairs. She had enough experience to know how vocal old houses could be, protesting every tread, every stiff wind, every opened door. Boards creaked. Hinges whined. Windows rattled in their panes like kettles set to boil.

But no matter where she was in the house, she continued only to hear the *tick, tick, tick* like a persistent insect and nothing else.

She'd left the clock on the hall tree the night before and gone to bed. But it woke her sometime after the witching hour, calling like a mewling babe—*tick, tick, tick* . . . as if it were counting down the time she had left.

She'd stomped down the stairs in her pajamas and glared at it darkly, not wanting to wake Gordon, finally stooping to pick it up and return it to the turret room before going back to bed.

It woke her again promptly after seven.

Annoyed, she'd done her best to ignore it all morning, moving from room to room to get out of earshot. She'd never noticed it before, which made her certain it was only her guilt amplifying the sound. But then she became aware of how quiet the *rest* of the house was, as if every brick and board were playing a practical joke on her.

Unnerved, Cordelia found her sister feeding blackberries to the fox under a potted tree in the solarium. She watched her. Eustace kept a string of pets in her adult life, always taking in strays and treating them like children. But Cordelia saw a preternatural bond growing between her and this wild animal. Her sister was besotted beyond reason.

"Something's wrong," she said, stepping out from behind a plumeria.

Eustace grinned as the fox nipped at her finger. "How so?"

"The house doesn't sound right."

Eustace glanced at her. "I don't hear anything."

"Exactly," Cordelia said. "It's too quiet. Except the clock."

"What clock?" her sister asked.

"You don't hear it?"

"I think you're just keyed up after all the excitement yesterday." Eustace was barely able to tear her eyes away from the creature. "I'm calling her Marvel," she said as an aside.

"I'm scared, Eustace," Cordelia told her, crossing her arms. "All that blood . . . What if whoever did that is still on the property? I never told you, but our first night, when the bats went crazy in my room, Gordon said he thought he saw someone leaving the house. And then this happens, and the papers for the trust disappear. We're not wanted here. Clearly, someone wants us to leave, to forfeit our inheritance."

"Whoever has been messing with us is not coming back," Eustace told her confidently. "Not with that tank we've got crashing in the parlor. He's the biggest man around for a hundred miles."

"What if they're not a man—not a person—at all?"

Eustace gave her a quizzical look. "I am very high on life—and a little bit of Acapulco Gold—so you're going to have to spell this out for me, Cordy, because I have no idea what you're talking about."

"The article, remember? *Morna,*" Cordelia hissed. "The animals . . . The blood . . ."

Eustace sucked her teeth, the connections dawning. "Can they . . . *do* that?"

Cordelia remembered the taut lines in her mother's face behind the shed that day. Maggie certainly thought they could. "Remember the seance? The curtains—the vase?"

"But we're family," Eustace countered.

"Are we? You heard Mr. Togers—leaving the estate is like leaving the family. Our mother obviously left some bad blood behind when she moved away, and now we're paying for it."

Eustace's gaze lingered on the fox, her fur clean and bright at this point. "What about Mom? Aunt Augusta? Did Morna do that too?"

Cordelia sighed. "I don't know. I just know that what we read and what we saw sound too close to overlook."

Eustace shook her head, curls sprawling. "I think it's our blood. That's what someone is hunting. Just like the wall in the basement—our line. The fox wasn't the message, or the papers. The blood was."

"Why? What's the connection besides our genetics?"

"The power," Eustace rounded on her. "The *magic.* The way I've gone from skin-and-bones cancer patient to glowing portrait of health overnight. And you—the dreams and the ghosts and whatever that was with the door and the rain. It's what we all have in common. How can you keep denying it?"

Cordelia grimaced. "I'm not denying it. It's just . . . it's different for me, Eustace," she said softly. "Don't you see that? You're some kind of channel for life, beautiful to behold. It's not like that for me." Eustace was thriving while Cordelia was drowning. Everything she touched shattered. "I don't have control over it like you do, and it's destructive, *dangerous*. Mom knew that. It's why she taught me the rules. Inside me there is a door, and death waits behind it. Every time it seeps out, something goes wrong. Horribly, awfully wrong."

"But you saved that man, Cordy—the appraiser. He's alive *because* of you," Eustace argued.

"He was also *here* because of me. If I'm not careful, Eustace, people get hurt. Innocent people. The day I saw that woman in the house with the blue shutters was the same day Mom's boyfriend, Kenny T., put that little boy from down the street in the hospital with his Pontiac Firebird. And look at everything that's happened with John, and now this."

"Kenny T. was a drunk and a moron, like most of Mom's boyfriends, and John is responsible for his own bad behavior. Honey, you're taking way too much credit for other people's bullshit and a whole lotta coincidence. You had nothing to do with that accident, and you're not to blame for your husband's criminally poor decisions. You were a child who experienced multiple traumas in one day, and your mind has drawn connections that aren't there. Now, I'll admit I don't know how it all works, what's going on inside you, but I know you have a gift, sister, and it's there for you to use it."

Cordelia dropped her eyes. It wasn't just the bedlam she saw unfolding all around her. It was also what came after, the inevitable period at the end of the sentence. What would become of her if she broke the rules, if she opened herself and the dead poured through? What hell awaited her then? "What if Mom was right and they can carry me away? What if I lose myself here?"

Eustace wrapped her arms around Cordelia. "That will never happen. I won't let it." She released her. "We have to lean in,

Cordy, not shrink back. Open up, let go, learn to use what this family has given us to help ourselves. Mom was wrong—running was never the answer. It's time for us to set things right. And we start by getting to the bottom of it all, dragging their secrets out into the light."

Her sister didn't know what she was asking. Every day Cordelia spent at Bone Hill, she felt less grounded. She was spinning out. Unraveling. Thirty-plus years of knots coming undone, like an old knit returned to a skein of yarn. But what would be left? If she gave herself over to this place, this power, who would she be?

She left the solarium, intent on trying to check in with the estate attorney in Hartford, but the clock echoing through the stair hall stopped her dead. It bound her skull like a tourniquet, strangling her brain. She could not endure another stroke.

She stormed into the turret room, grasping the clock in both hands. She wanted nothing more than to dash it against the wall, but Mr. Browning's crumpled car made her think twice. Clutching it to her chest, she carried it into the stair hall. The distinct *scree* of a slowly opening door on the third story sounded down— the first real sound she'd heard from the house all day. Cordelia had not yet been that high. And Bennett Togers said that floor was reserved for servants' quarters and storage. Which seemed a perfect place to tuck the clock away. She began to climb.

It was laid out much like the second floor—a suite of rooms, smaller and less polished than those below, with a straight hall dividing it in half. She poked her head into one of the rooms. There was no wallpaper or elaborate trim. The furnishings were spare. Smooth, white walls. A narrow iron bed. A thin, worn quilt. Above it, the dusty outline where a small wooden cross had once hung, leftover from a long-gone cook or maid.

She moved down the hall to a door at the far end standing suspiciously open, clock beating in time with her heart. Figuring this door must be the one she heard from downstairs, she found herself staring into a nursery. A spindly cradle stood empty, a layer of dust over the mattress. A yellow chaise lounge and wood-framed fireplace dotted opposing walls patterned in a small green print. A child's table and chair sat empty beside a plain chifforobe and a wooden horse.

But it was the woman who stood out—the gauzy, green layers of a chiffon peignoir set and that mane of red, spiraling hair. Her arms were cupped before her, but Cordelia couldn't see what she was holding. Humming through her smile, she reached an arm into the crib to adjust a blanket that wasn't there.

It was then Cordelia recognized her. The woman from the photograph. Her grandmother, Violetta. Her other arm was tucked close to her breast as if to hold a child the way Cordelia was cradling the clock, but there was nothing there. Leaning over the crib rail, she deposited her invisible bundle onto the bare, stained mattress, a baby only she could see.

"My little *volva*," she whispered, the word thick with an accent Cordelia didn't recognize.

Her mind rankled. She swung the door wide, but as it hit the wall, the red frizzy hair, the mint-green gown, the smile on her grandmother's face, the sound of her voice—all of it was gone. Cordelia was perfectly alone. She could still smell the powdery scent of violets hanging in the air.

Setting the clock on a table, she sunk onto the chaise lounge and dropped her head in her hands, loosing the emotions she was keeping jarred inside. Fear. Anger. Confusion. Who was she—this woman who ranted about her dreams and shrunk from every shadow and chased every unsettling sound? Certainly not the controlled professional, proud boss, image-conscious sweetheart of the suburbs. This Cordelia imagined ghouls around every turn and refused to leave the house and believed she could command the weather. John wouldn't even have recognized her. She didn't recognize herself.

The rolling scrape of the rocking horse sounded against the thin rug. Cordelia wiped her face with both hands, watching the horse make gentle arcs against the floor.

"What do you want?" she demanded. She imagined Morna hanging over the crib like a funeral shroud. "What do you all want from me?"

There was a tinkle of notes as the old mobile over the crib turned slowly, its vintage music box still functional. The tiny sparrows twisted in circles, their painted wings stuck fast to their sides.

She moved toward it, noticing a disturbance in the dust on the mattress, nearly an inch thick in some places. Reaching out, she grabbed the mobile, forcing it to stop. Silence dropped over her. Even the clock had hushed itself. She looked down. There in the dust was spelled out her answer.

Cordelia crushed her knuckles against her mouth to stifle the scream that was building.

REVENGE

Backing away, she nearly toppled head over heels when her foot hit something small and hard on the floor. She picked it up, examined it in her palm. A band of twisted, tarnished silver, large enough to fit her wrist and open on one side, each end hammered flat between three lines, like a duck's webbed foot. The metal came alive in her hand, glowing faintly beneath dirt and silver sulfide, hissing against her skin. She closed her fingers over it.

Reaching for the door, she swiveled out, pulling it closed behind her.

The bracelet sat heavy on her palm, full of unseen energy. What had their mother done, besides leave, that was so awful her own family sought vengeance for it on her offspring?

She took a step forward and looked up, sucking in. Arkin loomed in the hallway, all long arms and bright hair, his face an unreadable mask, mouth gaping like a sick animal's.

"You scared me," she scolded him, placing a hand to her chest. Thoughtlessly, she slipped the bracelet onto her wrist, pulling a sleeve down over it.

He took a step toward her, working that pathetic chin up and down.

Cordelia was just about to tell him to stop when Bennett Togers rounded into the hall.

"Ah! There you are," he said with a jovial smile. "I feared you'd given up on us already and flown away home."

She did her best to compose herself. "Ah, no. I've just been doing a little exploring. Thought I heard something is all." She started toward the stairs, smiling at him as she neared.

"These old houses, you know," he said with shining eyes. "They always have a point to make."

She pressed her lips together and stepped down, letting him walk beside her. "I'm glad you're here actually," she told him, glancing back to see the glowering Arkin following them. He seemed in a nasty mood compared with their last meeting, and she wouldn't have described him as *jolly* then. "I wanted to ask you a question."

Bennett met her gaze with curiosity. "I will do my best to answer."

"This might be outside the extent of your acquaintance with them, but you told us the other day that our family was from England. However, Eustace and I have reason to believe we might be Scandinavian. And our surname, apparently, is French. So, can you clarify? Are we French, or British, or Nordic?"

His face drew long with thought. "I already told you that you come from a very old family line. They arrived in America after many generations in England. But it is believed they arrived *there* during the Norman invasion some six or so centuries before."

Cordelia paused. "And that would mean?"

"Well, my dear, Normandy is in France," he replied happily, steering them toward the library as they reached the first-floor landing. "Which might explain the name."

She worked it back and forth in her mind like scrap wood, lowering herself onto one of the leather sofas. "And the Nordic connection?"

Bennett approached the far wall and kicked a piece of molding under the shelves. It opened like a cabinet door. From inside, he produced a bottle of fine scotch and two crystal tumblers. "This is where they always kept the good stuff," he said, pouring a bit for each of them. He handed Cordelia her glass. "I can't attest for their *entire* history, of course. I am only the attorney, after all. But I believe the Normans were in fact descendants of Viking raiders who settled the region."

She nodded and took a sip, letting the peat-flavored burn comfort her. She noticed with some distaste that Arkin loitered in the doorway, lowering.

"Now that that's settled," Bennett said. "I thought we ought to talk. It is my understanding that you have met with some misfortune while staying here."

Cordelia froze. How did he know about yesterday?

"I am, of course, referring to your ill health," he said. "Though Dr. Mabee assures me you are quite recovered. Still, I fear you encountered more than you were expecting while visiting our fair town."

"Oh." Cordelia relaxed, taking another sip of scotch. "You mean the rumors?"

Bennett looked apologetic. "I had hoped to spare you both this ugly element of your history. It's hard to dislodge such bitter sentiments once they take root in a small-town atmosphere like this one." .

"Please don't apologize," Cordelia told him. "It's not your fault. People can be so cruel." She set her glass down. "And I'm not sure we would have believed you if you'd told us."

"I hope you won't let it color your judgment of us too much," he told her, moving to look out a front window. "On the whole, the people of Bellwick have been respectful neighbors of your family for generations, if a little superstitious." He turned to face her. "I'm afraid your aunt found it rather unbearable. We did everything in our power to spare her these colorful little run-ins. You will need to cultivate the oily residue of a well-preened duck if you don't want to let it sink you."

Cordelia caught her bottom lip in her teeth. It was apparent their aunt had chosen to keep him in the dark about her inability to leave the estate, using the townspeople's animosity as her excuse. Unfortunately, the "modified bed rest"—as Dr. Mabee called it—had not been so healing for her as it had been her relatives.

"Oh dear." Bennett sighed. "I am too late. You've already made up your mind about us."

"No, no." Cordelia waved off his conclusion. "It's just been a lot to take in—all this." She circled a finger around. Her sleeve slipped down her forearm, revealing the heavy band she wore.

Bennett's eyes locked on the twist of metal. "As I would imagine."

Cordelia self-consciously pulled her sleeve back over the ugly bracelet. "Just something I found," she said offhandedly.

He narrowed his eyes. "Yes. Well, I hate to add to your stress, but I spoke with Mr. Jablonski on the way in. He is tending to the removal of that tree in the street. A most unfortunate incident. So lucky that neither you nor your sister were hurt. He took a step toward Cordelia, and she thought that he might sit, but instead, he continued to stand, looking down on her. "He gave me some news to pass along to you."

"Oh?" Cordelia tried to scoot farther back on the sofa, but the arm was right behind her. She pressed her back into it.

Bennett finished his scotch and set the glass beside hers, still quite full. "It seems he's spoken with the wildlife department."

Cordelia frowned. "Sorry?"

"About the bats," he reminded her.

After everything else that had happened, the dead bats felt like ages ago. "That's right. What did they say?"

His brows drew together to form one gray line. "They could find nothing wrong. Not a virus. Not a parasite. No toxins. Not even a fungus."

Cordelia stared at him, unsure what that might mean. "That's good, right? If they don't have a disease we need to worry about?"

Bennett shrugged ambivalently. "Perhaps. Though it does little to explain their deaths. It seems their diminutive hearts stopped all at once. What do you suppose could do something like that?"

"There must be some explanation," she said, wanting suddenly for him to leave.

"It is a mystery," he said with a hint of bemusement. "Of course, I would understand completely should you decide it unsafe to remain in the house. There are a number of lovely hotels in Hartford. Arkin would happily transport you."

Cordelia gave him a flat smile. "We'll think on it," she lied.

"You do that," he said, nodding. "Nothing is worth losing your life over. Even your mother knew that."

The words hit her with a slap. She couldn't recover in time to respond.

"Well!" Bennett said with an unusually cheery clap of his hands. "I won't take up any more of your time. No need to show me out. I know the way perfectly well. Arkin!" He marched into the stair hall, his gangly nephew on his heels.

Cordelia got up to follow him. But he was halfway out the door by the time she cleared the library. Grinning, he tipped an imaginary hat to her before heading into the sunlight, Arkin clambering into the driver's seat of the old Mercedes.

Such an odd man, Cordelia thought as they started the car. She was grateful, in a way, for his guidance. He was like a bridge to her and Eustace's history, the only thing between them and the family they'd lost. But his familiarity with the house unnerved her at times. The way he came and went of his own accord. She watched him leave, troubled by his words.

It was only in the blistering silence that followed that she realized he'd forgotten to leave the new paperwork. In fact, she had no idea why he'd come at all.

CHAPTER NINETEEN

THE LEDGERS

CORDELIA COULDN'T GET the bracelet off. She'd spent the night before trying everything she could think of—soap, lotion, even olive oil—to no avail. Finally, exhausted, she slept in it and woke to find it still there the next morning. Now, she tugged her sleeve down over it as she called to her sister across the solarium, not wanting to explain the frightening scene in the nursery, reveal what the spirits had written to her. Surely, with a little more work, she would get it off.

Eustace called back from a flowering bromeliad, Marvel emitting rapid squeaks of excitement at her heels.

"Shouldn't she be resting or something?" Cordelia asked, watching the fox, still astonished.

Eustace beamed down at her scrappy new patient as Marvel twirled around her legs. "She's made remarkable progress. And so have I."

"What do you mean?"

"Last night, when I was petting her, we were both just lying there soaking up the other's energy, and it happened again: I slid into her skin." Eustace's face was upturned, remembering, near rapturous.

Cordelia worried about the effect Bone Hill was having on

her sister. She was healing physically, but what if this place sent her over the edge, like it had done to Morna and Gordon's mom?

Eustace grabbed her by the upper arms. "At first, I panicked, and it went away. But then I thought about our conversation. What if we learned how to do these things *on purpose*?

"I closed my eyes and got very still, pouring all of my focus into her. It was indescribable. I could actually feel everything she was feeling. I was seeing the world through her eyes. With a little pressure, I could direct her. She got up and went outside, trotted and sniffed around. We were one being. It sounds bonkers, but I've never felt so real."

Cordelia flashed a gentle smile, but her chest tightened. Eustace had always been a free spirit, though she wasn't usually given to wild exaggeration. Cordelia didn't know what to make of her impossible claims, but she understood the feeling of wind passing through you, the way the earth could sing if you listened just right, the presence of those who should be long gone.

Eustace put a hand to her heart. "I know you might think I've finally lost it, but I swear this wasn't just the high talking. Not like that time I called you from the desert and said I could taste the sky."

Cordelia narrowed her eyes. "Yes, how could I forget?"

"I want to show you something!" She dragged Cordelia to the kitchen, pulling a stack of ledgers off the counter and pushing them across the table to her, holding one back. "I was waiting until I was certain."

Cordelia took them carefully, their pages stiff and stinking of mold. "What are these?"

"The ledgers from the study. I've been trying to put my finger on where the money came from. Look." Eustace opened the one she held and spun it around, pointing to an entry that read *Oct 12, stud fee . . . $90* in a slanting cursive hand. "There are hundreds, maybe thousands, of these listings throughout the earliest ledgers."

"What's a stud fee?" Cordelia asked.

"Horse breeding," Eustace told her. "At this price, it would be the only possibility. Dogs would earn considerably less."

"We're horse breeders?" The idea struck her as incongruent. The only time she'd ever even seen a horse was at a birthday party. The other girls had scrabbled to get in line for a short ride, but Cordelia hung back in fear of something so large and misshapen—all that bulk, legs like toothpicks. She didn't have an equestrian bone in her body.

"I think it was a front. Otherwise, that was one tired horse. I haven't seen barn one on this property."

"Like money laundering? What would they need to cover up?"

Eustace sniffed. "Something illegal. I have a theory, but there's no way to know for sure. Do you remember the wooden shovels we saw in the basement?"

She shrugged. "Sure."

Eustace inhaled deeply. "They were often used in the nineteenth century for, um . . ."

An acrid twinge, anxious and retreating. Cordelia held her breath.

"Body snatching," Eustace finished.

Whatever she was expecting, that was not it. A surge of nausea threatened to revive her last meal. "Does that mean what I think it means?"

"The bodies were dug up using wooden shovels because they were quieter and then sold to universities and doctors for study," Eustace said. "It's kind of progressive, actually. There were some very backward laws then. Doctors were desperate to know more about human anatomy so they could better treat their patients.

Shocking to think we were so primitive only a couple of hundred years ago."

Cordelia gaped. "That's the part you find shocking?"

"Don't overreact," Eustace told her in a steady voice.

She always hated that big-sister tone Eustace would get whenever she thought Cordelia was being hyperbolic. "You just told me our ancestors dug up corpses and sold them illegally to build our family fortune, and you think I'm overreacting?"

"To supplement it, most likely. The year of the ledger I showed you is 1835. The stud fee entries stop sometime after 1890." Eustace picked at a half-eaten cookie on a plate. "Of course, I could be wrong. It could have been something more mundane, like gambling. But who's lucky that often?"

Cordelia was sickened by how calmly her sister was absorbing this. "You saw that photograph of our grandmother same as I did," she said. "You've heard the stories in town. If what you're saying is true, if they orchestrated an underground body-snatching ring, do you really believe it was all in the name of *science*?"

"What are you suggesting?" Eustace asked.

"What if they were using the bodies in their rituals? Think about all of Mom's secrecy and rules, forbidding us from doing anything that would instigate our powers, suppressing her own even when we were in dire need. What if they weren't just stealing corpses, what if they were *making* them? I'm talking about blood magic."

Eustace paled.

Cordelia pressed on. "I've been doing some research online into ancient cults and magical practices. It's not as uncommon as you'd think. Blood is considered the elixir of life. And magic always comes at a price. To get something you have to give something. It's the ultimate trade."

"But I saved Marvel's life. You saved that appraiser's and

Gordon's. Look at me, how I've healed. How can what we have be bad?"

Cordelia shook her head. "The more pieces we collect, the uglier the picture becomes."

"Then I have something else to show you," Eustace said quietly, going back to the solarium and pointing to a pale green fern-like plant under a cassia tree. "Looks like a weed, doesn't it?"

"I would have thought so."

"Well, it's not. It's chervil—a medicinal and culinary herb." She pointed to several other weed-like, herbaceous plants. "The solarium is full of plants like this. The garden is too."

Cordelia glared at the frilly leaves. "I thought the plants in solariums were supposed to be sculptural."

"Maybe Aunt Augusta was into making her own salad dressing?" Eustace suggested. "Among other things."

Cordelia narrowed her eyes. "What *other* things?"

She walked her to a far corner of the pond and pointed out a tall weed in a damp bed with white splaying flowers. "water hemlock. Deadly if ingested."

"Are you implying someone planted that here on purpose?" Cordelia asked her.

Eustace eyed her. "Remember when I told you some pages in the journal looked like recipes?"

She nodded. "Yes, of course."

Eustace started for the kitchen, tugging Cordelia by a wrist, and opened the book on the island. Beside it was a notepad with a bunch of scribblings—her attempts at decoding the entries. "I've been working on unlocking the meanings of some of these more complicated runes," she said. "The ones that aren't part of any alphabet we know of."

"Okay. What does this have to do with the solarium and garden?"

Eustace flipped to a page laid out similarly to a recipe in a cookbook—with a title, a list of indecipherable words, and a paragraph of unreadable instructions. Cordelia assumed it followed a left-to-right reading layout.

Her finger landed next to a complex symbol that looked like an *M, F,* and *B* combined. "The runes have alphabetical meaning—phonetic, like a letter. But they also have deeper symbolic meanings—whole words or phrases. This one, if you tease it apart and break it down, contains these five runes within it," she said, quickly scribbling them out. "The central rune is taken for its symbolic meaning, but the others built around it are used phonetically. This first one represents a bull," she said, pointing to an angular lowercase *n.* "And these, if looked at phonetically, would be *b, a, n,* and *e.*"

"I don't get it," Cordelia said as Eustace finished, looking oh-so-pleased with herself.

"*Bane,*" Eustace told her. "It means *death* or *ruin.* All together it's *bull bane.*"

Cordelia scratched her head.

"Cowbane! It's another name for water chestnut. Because it can kill livestock who feed on it. Understand?" She watched Cordelia with impatient, flashing eyes. "It's an ingredient."

Cordelia backed away from the island. "Why would someone cook with something like that?"

"I don't think this is a recipe for food," Eustace told her.

"Then what?" Cordelia stared at her, knowing already what she would say.

"A remedy, or a poison, or a . . . spell." The word dropped between them with the weight of a cannonball. "And that's not all. I've been cross-referencing the recipe pages," Eustace said, flipping between them. "Their similarity is allowing me to decode them much faster, but there's something strange here I don't understand. Something they all share."

Cordelia stepped back to the island and looked down, the scratchy writing coming into view.

She pointed to a kind of elongated asterisk, a rod with three branches at each end. It looked like the rune on their mother's tattoo, only more rounded and if it were doubled and joined end to end. "This is something personal—something they made up or gave special meaning. It appears to be a variation of *algiz*—which means *protection* typically. Later, it developed different meanings when written upright or upside down—*life* and *death* respectively. But I don't understand why they've joined it here. Or why it's an ingredient in every single spell and potion recorded."

"Are you sure it's in all of them?" Cordelia asked.

"Certain," Eustace told her. "What would be needed for every one of these—from a healing poultice to a charm to ward off pregnancy to a spell for finding love to a tonic to induce visions?"

Cordelia inhaled sharply, her theory about the bodies coming into startling focus. "Eustace, are you thinking what I'm thinking?"

"Soil," her sister said heavily.

Cordelia met her eyes. "And blood."

CORDELIA KNOCKED AT Gordon's door, the ledger Eustace had shown her in hand. When he answered, she flashed him a relieved smile. She wasn't sure he'd answer after the last time. "Are you busy? I was hoping to ask you about something."

Gordon gripped the door, taking a moment to answer. "No, not really. Come on in."

She scooted past him. "You left so early yesterday, I didn't get the chance to thank you."

He smiled, a taut bow. "I wanted to start early on that tree. The county can be really slow around here." He shoved his hands into his front pockets, and for a second Cordelia thought she could picture him as a boy. He tilted his head, set his golden eyes on her in a way that made her want to cover up.

"May I?" she asked, holding the ledger out toward the table.

"Sure." Darting to the table, he scooped up a smattering of papers which he quickly shoved into a notebook with an elastic band, snapping it shut. He tucked it behind his back. "All yours," he said, gesturing to the tabletop.

She eased past him, a flicker of their moment locked together upstairs behind her eyes. Turning quickly away, she noticed how he held the notebook behind him.

Flipping the ledger open to the page she'd saved, she pointed to the entry that read *stud fee*. "Do you know if there are any stables on the property?" she asked. "Besides the carriage house."

He rubbed at his brow, pulling his T-shirt tight across his chest. "There's a small barn on the western perimeter. It's pretty dilapidated. What's this about?"

"I'd like to see it. Could you take me?"

His expression shifted to surprise. "Now?"

"Unless you're busy . . ."

A trace of emotion, unreadable, crossed his eyes. "This way."

Cordelia left the ledger on the table and walked at his side. It occurred to her she hadn't been farther west on the property than his place. Giant oaks spread their branches in an emerald dome, the grass threadbare like a rubbed blanket beneath their shade.

"I guess this isn't because you're interested in horses?"

"No," she said with a laugh. "I'm not much of an animal person. That's Eustace's territory. I thought I wanted a dog once, but . . ."

He waited as she reached to find the words.

"I think I just wanted an accessory." She crossed her arms and looked up at the tangle of branches, the pockets of sunlight bleeding through.

"That's an interesting way of putting it."

She shrugged. "For a while, I believed that if I could just make everything *look* perfect, then it would be."

"And now?" he asked, bending low to swipe at a stem of goosegrass, then twirling it between his fingers.

"Now, I know that really beautiful surfaces can hide very ugly messes behind them." The mold peppered her brain as it had the wall. She eyed him sidelong.

His lips twitched. "The ex-husband?"

Cordelia smiled. "Is it that obvious?"

He shook his head. "You did promise to tell me your story sometime."

She rubbed the back of her neck, eyes trained on the rounded toes of her rubber boots. "It's nothing dramatic. Just another foolish woman falling for the wrong man who has an affair with her assistant, then blames her for it, then steals her identity and tries to take her for everything she's worth, including her life."

Gordon scrunched up his face. "He sounds like a colossal ass."

"He is," she told him. "Unequivocally. But he was charming once, and I thought he was my forever. I don't get things wrong often, but when I do, I have a way of getting them spectacularly wrong."

"Some people can hide their true character until it's too late," he said, a touch of bitterness in his tone, as if he knew firsthand.

"Were you married to John too?"

Gordon smiled, dimples winking as his guard dropped. She'd hardly registered them before. Another irresistible detail. "My ex, the one I told you about. We formed the band together. She's fucking my replacement now."

Cordelia set her fingers against the broad plane of his forearm. She didn't want to tell him that she'd looked his band up online, stared into the catlike eyes of its enigmatic lead singer, seen the toss of long, dark hair, the leather pants and septum piercing, the intensity he'd talked about. "She sounds delightful. I think we should invite them both for dinner. See who claws whose eyes out first."

Gordon smirked. "That's one way to spend an evening."

She let her hand slide naturally down his arm until it rested in his. She stopped suddenly. He turned to face her, staring at their hands together, and she immediately let go. "I think it's really over."

He looked at her, soft with empathy. "Your marriage?"

"My life," she said, voice breaking. "My house, my business, my money, my reputation—it's all gone *poof* thanks to him. Everything I built he's taken from me."

Gordon took a step toward her. "Hey, hey. It's going to be okay."

She looked up at him, and a laugh burbled up her throat. "God, I'm such a punch line. Aren't I?"

"I don't think so," he told her. "I think you're hurting, but you're strong. You'll get through this. You come from tough stock, after all."

"We're going to stay," she said, knowing there was really no other choice. Eustace had made up her mind already, and Cordelia had nowhere else to go. "I want you to stay too. I'd feel better knowing you were here with us." She cleared her throat. "With *me*."

The whole world became Gordon in that moment—his whiskey-colored eyes, the dark hair striping his chin, the ink stippling his proud neck, the curling knot of hair. Everything that wasn't Gordon no longer existed. No trees or grass or sky. And Cordelia could not escape the hammering in her chest or the warming between her legs.

Carefully, he reached out and brushed a flyaway from her face. "We're here," he said with a rough voice, breaking the spell.

She looked up to see the brown, rotting husk of an old barn, many years neglected, in the near distance, with the woods creeping up beside it. Taking a step back, she caught her breath, willed the rumble in her body to settle, then turned and walked toward it.

The old door creaked loudly as she pulled it back. A pair of robins nesting in an exposed crossbeam dove toward her on their way out. Sunlight streamed through holes in the roof. The dirt floor bore tracks of wildlife—coons and rabbits—instead of the U-shaped marks of shod horses.

Gordon pointed at a muddy pile long as her forearm. "Bear scat," he said. "Pretty recent. Must be coming in here to hunt."

A center aisle separated a handful of stalls and what must have been a tack room at one end. Feed and equipment storage was reserved for the open space at the other end. It was practical enough, but not the equestrian finery one might expect for a facility acquiring so many stud fees. This downtrodden structure with rotting boards and weathered cupola fell short.

Gordon looked around. "I told you this place was a wreck."

"You weren't kidding," she agreed.

"You still haven't told me what we're doing here." He raised his eyebrows.

Cordelia walked the aisle between stalls, peering into each as she went. The rusted shell of an old hay feeder could still be seen in one. "Did our aunt ever mention anything about a family business in horses?" she asked him.

"No. She knew the barn was here, of course. Told me I could use it for storage if needed. Why?"

Having reached the end, Cordelia spun around to face him. "The entry in the ledger I showed you. It's from the study. There are dozens of them with these entries for stud fees marked in there—many, *many* stud fees."

His eyes simmered. "This isn't a stud barn," he told her. "These stalls are too small for stallions. And there's not enough reinforced fencing in between. There's no stud shed or place for the breeding to happen—this open end would have been full of hay bales and farm equipment once upon a time. Any paddocks that were once here are long gone, but these stalls don't open out from the back, which would be necessary for a temperamental stallion full of testosterone, rather than leading him through this narrow channel full of other horses."

Cordelia whirled on him. "You know an awful lot about the subject."

Gordon smiled confidently. "My ex. She had a wealthy grandfather who ran a small hobby farm. Quarter horses mostly. We spent a couple of summers there."

Cordelia bit back the jealousy rising at the mention of this woman twice in one day. She wondered if he felt the same when she talked about John.

He glanced around. "They'd have kept the draft horses for pulling in the carriage house. This was likely a place to keep workhorses and a mare or two for pleasure riding."

Cordelia took a deep breath. "It's as I figured then."

He stepped toward her.

"They were a cover for something else, those entries. Some illegal or at least unsavory line of work." She hugged herself, distressed by her family's dishonesty.

"Any theories?" he asked.

She frowned. "Eustace has a couple. They're not very flattering."

Gordon looked at the busted roof. When he looked back down, his eyes were edged with cynicism. "Can't say I'm surprised, considering your reputation in town."

She ran her fingers along the top of one of the only remaining Dutch doors, several others having rotted off their hinges and lying on the ground. The wood was rougher than a jackfruit rind; a long splinter lodged itself in the pad of her index finger. Cursing, she pulled her hand close.

"What happened?"

"It's nothing," she complained. "Just a splinter."

"Let me see," he said.

Cordelia frowned up at him. "It's fine."

"Let me see," he insisted, coming closer.

She leaned back against a weight-bearing pole, still solid, and reluctantly held her hand out. He smiled down and with tender precision gripped the protruding end of the splinter, pulling it swiftly out. Cordelia cursed again.

"There," he said, laughing. "All better."

Cordelia cut her eyes away. His nearness made her unsteady on her feet. She was grateful for the pole.

Gordon leaned an arm against it and looked down, the heat of his breath on her skin, his eyes searching.

A thrill rolled through her, sparking and blooded, eating her control. She touched a finger to the tattooed woman on his arm. "Who is this?"

"Marzanna."

"Your band?"

A wisp of hair fell into his face. She itched to stroke it. "It was named after her. She's the Slavic goddess of winter. My *babci*—my great-grandmother—was from Poland. She would tell me stories about dragons and vampires and ghosts who roamed the streets of Warsaw. She used to tell me about the spring festivals where they would throw an effigy of the goddess into the river to symbolize the end of winter."

Emboldened, she reached for the snake twisting around his other arm and ran her fingers across its scales. "Any special significance for this one?" she asked, turning her eyes up to his.

Gordon shivered beneath her touch. His jaw clenched. "Snakes are the keepers of the underworld," he said, eyes tracing down the slope of her nose, across the pout of her lips. "They're synonymous in many cultures with birth, death, and resurrection."

Her fingers danced lightly up the side of his neck along the great, curling horns of the ram's skull. All the words backed up in her throat.

Gordon closed his eyes, arm trembling. When he opened them again, they blazed with hunger.

She put her mouth to his, feeling the softness of his lips fall between her own, his body pressing along hers, hands gripping her hips, his tongue a sweet intrusion as she yielded to him. Her insides exploded in a rush of desire, mind swept deliciously blank. Gordon filled her senses—his deep, earthy scent, the power in his body, the hardness of him straining against her. Her fingers curled in the loose strands of his hair, and she pushed herself against the pillar of his chest.

She forgot entirely about haunted houses and family secrets and men who hide their cruelty behind a practiced smile.

Until the slam of the barn door jolted them apart.

They both turned to see it bounce open again.

"Stay here," he told her as he went to investigate.

She feared the bear he mentioned was back.

He looked out, listening intently, then stepped into the chickweed. Cordelia held her breath. A moment later, he poked his head back in and motioned for her to join him.

She followed him into the sticky afternoon. There was no bear. No wind. The leaves on the trees were as stiff as if they'd been carved from jade, the air lifeless and secretive.

Gordon rubbed the back of his neck. "Not sure what that was."

In the barn, she'd felt consumed by him, carnal and rapacious behind the screen of decaying wood. Now, under the brazen sun, she felt forward, a fallen woman, serpent-tongued. Even if she wanted to recapture the moment—and certainly something in her did—she wasn't sure how.

Cordelia cleared her throat. "I guess we should be getting back. Eustace is probably wondering about me."

He stepped away from her, and the heat between them cooled like slowly hardening lava. "Right. After you."

As they walked back, Gordon fell farther and farther behind. When Cordelia reached the porch steps, he wasn't with her at all.

CHAPTER TWENTY

THE OATH

CORDELIA READ THE name on her phone with bleary eyes before rushing to answer the call. "Hello? Yes, hello?" she stammered, pushing her hair back from her face.

It had been a week since her trip to the barn with Gordon, nearly two since her phone had last rung. She'd diverted herself with researching their family, looking for more articles, hunting down any birth and death certificates, census reports, or small clues that might string together the pieces of information they had. Eustace was insistent that the spirits Cordelia kept seeing were connected by more than blood or marriage.

They had the article on Morna from the study, but what about the other members of the family? If Cordelia could find out more about them, maybe they could get a handle on why they kept appearing, and maybe that would explain the arcane history hinted at in the photograph, basement room, book, and town rumors, but which they still had yet to fully understand. *That,* they had become certain, was what tied everything together. Unlock their family's craft, and they could make sense of Maggie's murder, Cordelia's headaches, and the strange occurrences that were now terrorizing them.

She'd fallen asleep last night with her laptop open to an online database where a copy of an entry in the local register spelled out the cause of death for one Arabella Bone. It read plainly, *submersion*. She was only twenty-nine years old. Her place of death and burial—the same. Their great-great-great-grandmother had drowned on-site. And Cordelia knew where.

She'd walked to the boudoir, opening the solarium door and looking out over the tropical foliage, the curving stairs. It was late. A smattering of pinhole stars glittered through the hazy glass of the roof. She took the steps one at a time, icy against bare feet, and made her way to the pond. Its lily pads floated like dark, leathery hearts on top.

She'd leaned over the retaining wall, looking into the brackish water at her reflection, a ripple of pale orange hair and paler skin. She could see small markers of Arabella's breeding and gentility there—the delicate nose and high brow, the long neck and heart-shaped face. But Erazmus was there too, flashing in Cordelia's stormy blue eyes, in the rigid way she thrust out her chin.

She'd started to turn away when something caught her eye—a roll of golden hair just under the surface, the flaxen locks wafting deeper and deeper before fading from view like a trailing fin. Cordelia had backed away until she was safely in her room. It was a long while before sleep found her after that.

She'd intended to be up much earlier this morning.

It was Molly. "I have bad news."

Not even a Good morning *first.* Cordelia rubbed at her tired eyes.

"I know we only just got your house listed, but I had to take it off the market."

"I don't understand." Cordelia needed the equity from that sale to fend off the foreclosure, pay the mold contractors, keep Molly on staff, and buy important things like *food* until this estate business was handled. This is not what she needed to hear right now.

"Your husband has applied for home rights and an occupation order," Molly said.

"*Ex*-husband," Cordelia stressed. "But John isn't on the title! He doesn't even live there. He hates that house, for Christ's sake."

"I'm just the messenger," Molly stammered. "But until this is resolved legally, you can't sell. And, well, they've already started moving their stuff back in. As soon as the mold remediation was done."

"*They?*" Cordelia fumed. "Did you see them? Are they there?"

"No. Just a moving truck with a crew that started unloading a bunch of new furniture." Molly hiccupped on the other end. "Sorry. I tend to get the hiccups when I'm nervous."

"Excellent." Cordelia fell back on the bed. "I can't imagine who's paying for that." She made a mental note to call her attorney, start checking for any new credit accounts opened in her name, particularly with a furniture store. If Busy or his goons saw that, would they think it was her? That she wasn't taking John's debt seriously?

"There's something else." Molly took a deep breath.

Cordelia moaned. What else could possibly go wrong?

"I've been offered a full-time position with an agency in the city," she said between hiccups. "And I've decided to take it."

"But you can't! I mean, of course you *can*. But I can't do this without you, Molly. Not from here."

Molly *hick*ed into the phone. "I'm truly sorry. You know how much I respect you. It's just, I'm not sure when you're coming back. You rarely take my calls or get my emails. Without you here, the few clients you were hanging on to have dried up. And if you can't sell your own house . . . well, to put it bluntly, I don't know how you'll afford me. As it is, you owe me two weeks' pay."

She wanted to argue, but Molly was right. She couldn't keep asking her to hang in there. "I understand," she said begrudgingly. "And I'm always here as a reference should you need it."

"Thank you," Molly told her. "If you ever do make it back to Dallas, I'd be honored to work for you again."

"I'll keep that in mind," Cordelia said sourly. Dallas seemed very far away right now. "Could you do one more thing for me?"

There was a pause. "Sure."

"Could you ship my personal effects to this address?" She supposed it was time to face the music. They weren't getting off the estate anytime soon. They needed time to sort the inheritance and trust and get to the bottom of why they couldn't leave the grounds without fatal consequences. Eustace was looking and feeling better than ever, but Cordelia still needed to find a way to make the estate work for her the way it was supposed to. "I left them boxed in the garage at the house."

"Of course," Molly agreed. "I'll take care of it first thing."

Cordelia sighed into the phone. She was not leaving Connecticut anytime soon. Maybe not ever.

She'd only set the phone down a minute when it rang again. She pressed it to her ear without looking. "Molly?"

"Ms. Bone?" the voice on the other end of the line questioned.

"Yes, it's me." She pulled back the phone to look at the screen—Elliott, Gould & Associates, the law firm in Hartford she'd sent the paperwork images to.

"I'm calling on behalf of Mr. Gould. I'm his paralegal, Allen. Thank you once again for the documents you texted. We've been able to make physical copies, and Mr. Gould has given them a substantive read," the man said politely. "You'll be receiving a full letter from him shortly."

"And?" Cordelia asked, hope fluttering in her chest.

"While Mr. Gould himself will be happy to go over any remaining questions that you have, he wanted me to call and give you his immediate findings. I am sorry to report that there isn't much he can do at this time. The jurisdiction of the will is rock-solid. The dynasty trust—though old—is explicitly prepared and has been carried out with no dispute for generations. Mr. Bennett Togers is named as legal guardian and trustee of the estate in your aunt's incapacitation. His remaining so, like your residence at the property, is a condition of the trust. You could challenge the will in court, of course. But it is our emphatic opinion that that would fail to bring you the desired result. And the fees could become quite burdensome." The man cleared his throat as he finished, and Cordelia could hear the telltale sound of him swallowing a drink of water.

"I see," she said, sinking. "And there's really nothing further he can do?"

Allen spoke plainly. "Ultimately, it is your decision whether to pursue this in a local court. He would file for you should you choose to do so. But it is not his express recommendation."

Cordelia sighed. "Allen, is it? So, what exactly are you suggesting? In the simplest terms possible."

This time, it was Allen's turn to sigh. "Ms. Bone, can I be frank?"

"Please," she told him.

"While the conditions of your aunt's will and the family trust are unusual, they are legally sound. Courts are limited in their ability to craft solutions to estate cases like yours. That is why we so often attempt to resolve these cases outside of the litigation process. It will get expensive and adversarial, and there is little likelihood you will emerge pleased with the results," Allen told her.

Cordelia took a deep breath in. It sounded like litigation had the potential to drain whatever was left of their meager family fortune, effectively making the battle over the trust moot. "If a lawsuit isn't ideal, then what does he advise?"

"At this time, his best advice is for you and your sister to sign the trust," Allen told her. "Perhaps in time, with the proper resources behind you, you can unravel this from the inside out. We would certainly be happy to help you try."

Resources, she thought. Where the hell was she supposed to find those if she couldn't sell the house and its belongings? She sighed.

"But right now," he continued, "you're staring down a deadline that could cost you everything if you don't act quickly to secure your claim on the inheritance."

"A deadline?" It was the first she'd heard of it. Bennett hadn't mentioned any kind of time limit.

"It's why I called. Mr. Gould didn't want to leave you waiting on such a time-sensitive matter. You have four weeks to make your claim. That's quite generous, actually," Allen told her. "That timing began with the date of your aunt's death, which means you have less than two weeks left."

"I see," Cordelia said. Another ticking clock. "Can I ask why all the red tape for what is considered a modest inheritance? It seems a bit pompous."

Allen scoffed on the other end. "Ms. Bone, have you taken the time to actually *read* these papers you sent us, to look into your aunt's assets?"

She was embarrassed to say she hadn't. But in her defense, there had been a terrible lot going on. "Not in detail, no."

"*Modest* is not the word I would use to describe your late aunt's estate. Her holdings are some of the most remarkable we've witnessed—varied and extensive. Stocks, properties, businesses. Her investment portfolio is beyond impressive. The numbers are staggering, to be honest."

Cordelia began to tingle in a strange way, the tips of her fingers going numb. "*How* staggering?"

"Your aunt—soon to be you and your sister—is what is known as an ultra-high-net-worth individual. That title is given only to someone with a net worth in the range of eight figures, *many times over.*"

Her mouth dropped open, emitting a high-pitched squeak.

"Don't short yourself," he said. "Sign the papers and allow the trust to begin funding you here in Connecticut. You can maintain your assets in Texas. Once everything has been put into your names, then we can begin dismantling the dynasty trust if you still wish to sell the property, though it will only continue to appreciate. But I warn you, tampering with a dynasty trust like this one is not necessarily recommended. These generational trusts protect the family's assets from a number of threats over time, including enormous taxes. You may find that it's in your best interest to comply with the trust like the many Bones who came before you."

"Thank you," she told Allen, still in shock. "Let Mr. Gould know I will take his advice under consideration."

"Stay in touch," Allen told her. "We'll be happy to help you however we can in the future. You'll receive an invoice by mail shortly."

She imagined it would be "staggering," in keeping with the figures of the trust.

"One last thing," he said. "Congratulations, Ms. Bone."

Cordelia sat with the phone to her ear long after Allen hung up.

"CAN'T SLEEP?" CORDELIA heard a voice ask.

The kitchen was dark, but she turned to see her sister's silhouette at the table, a shaft of moonlight from the window catching in the silvery threads of her hair.

Cordelia had spent the day working up the nerve to tell her about the call from the paralegal. It was ultimately good news she was delivering, so why did she feel so burdened by it? Maybe because she knew this would seal Eustace's decision to remain at

Bone Hill. Or maybe she was simply overcome by the tangle of secrets plaguing this adumbral estate. Nothing here was ever as it seemed, and even if this was the first *good* secret they'd uncovered, it only added to her insecurity, the feeling that she could never get her bearings here or know what was waiting around any given corner.

"Eustace," she breathed. "You startled me."

"Chamomile tea," her sister said, raising a cup in the dark. She used her foot to push out another chair from the table, and Cordelia spotted the sleeping fox curled up underneath.

She switched on a small lamp and moved to sit in the chair. "I have to tell you something," she said after a moment. "Something I should have told you sooner."

Eustace looked dubious. "Oh?"

Cordelia filled her in on the paralegal's call, his attorney's advice about the trust, the deadline they were facing, and the truth about their aunt's considerable assets.

"*How* much?" Eustace asked again, unable to digest the figures Cordelia was providing.

"Multiple eight figures," she repeated. "He actually congratulated us."

Her sister barked out an unexpected laugh. "Holy shit . . ." Her eyes met Cordelia's. "Holy shit, we're loaded!"

Cordelia smiled. It gave her joy to see her sister so happy, but she didn't share Eustace's elation.

After a minute, Eustace noticed. "I don't get it. Why aren't you happy about this? You're free, Cordy. You can get the mob off your back now. All our problems are solved!"

"Not exactly," Cordelia reminded her.

Money, no matter how much of it they were talking about, could not explain what happened to their mother or what they were doing here. It couldn't make the horrors she'd seen disappear. Or root out whoever had left that threatening symbol in blood spattered across their floor. And it couldn't heal the condition that was trying to rip her head open, on a daily basis at this point. Money couldn't save them. Not from themselves. And she feared money had more to do with creating their problems than solving them, that it would continue to. She told Eustace as much.

"You are such a buzzkill," Eustace told her, wilting. "I have never known anybody who could render tens of millions of dollars completely worthless in a matter of sentences."

She felt herself the half-empty glass, her sister the half-full. "Sorry."

"You know what I don't get, though," Eustace continued. "Why wouldn't Bennett tell us about this? He had us thinking it was some piddly amount. And he never even mentioned the deadline."

Cordelia shrugged. "He did bring us the papers right away. We're the ones who didn't read them, who've been dragging our feet to sign."

"How many days do we have left?"

Cordelia counted to herself. "Ten, I think."

Her sister sighed. "I'll call tomorrow, get him back out here to wrap this up. I've got an online shopping habit to establish."

Cordelia nodded, glad that at least one of them would have some fun with this. She'd thought this whole time that if she could just get out from under John's debts, she would feel better. But this house had stirred up too much within her. She would never be at peace now until she put the pieces together.

She noticed their mother's urn sitting in the center of the table. "Do you think she would be upset that we brought her back here?"

"I don't care if she is," Eustace said. "I'm upset that she kept this from us."

Cordelia looked down at her hands, folded in her lap, useless as lace gloves. Their mother had cheated them out of so much, and here they all were anyway, pawns gathered at the center of the board. "Maybe she just wanted us to have a normal life."

"I might believe that," Eustace said bitterly, "if that's what she'd given us. But it's not."

"There had to be a reason. She loved us. She must have believed she was doing the right thing."

Eustace frowned. "Her stupid rules are starting to make more sense now. No cemeteries. No music. No pets. I just thought she was being a bitch all those years."

Cordelia laughed and had started to drag her hand away when Eustace gripped her wrist.

"What is this ugly thing?" she asked, holding Cordelia's arm up to stare at the bracelet from the nursery.

She tugged her hand away and laid it on the table. "I found it," she said. "In the nursery, of all places. I've tried to remove it, but it won't come off."

Her sister's eyes widened. "Did you use soap?"

She nodded. "Even olive oil. It's stuck fast. I don't understand. It seemed so easy to slip on."

Eustace leaned over her arm, examining the details of the cuff. "Cordy, this is old," she said at last. "*Really* old." Her eyes lit with wonder. "I know what this is. I've read about it in my research, seen a few pictures."

"Did you read about a way to get it off?" She felt suddenly self-conscious. She cradled her wrist against her chest like it was broken.

"This design—the twisted bands—is very common," Eustace began. "But these are different than anything I've seen." She ran a fingertip over one of the duck-footed ends. She looked at Cordelia frankly. "It's an oath ring. The Vikings used them to make promises, swear fealty. Something like this, it's binding."

Cordelia looked down at it, conspicuous only in its crudity.

"But I was alone." Her voice had become a whine. "I tripped and found it on the floor. I didn't make any promises to anyone."

"Didn't you?" Eustace asked.

Cordelia swallowed, the stream of emotion she'd released in that room coming back to her, the dread. The message on the mattress. "I heard something, and I followed the sound. It led me to the nursery. There was a woman inside. But then she was gone. It was our grandmother Violetta. I recognized her from the picture, the creepy one."

Eustace nodded, listening.

"I thought I was losing my mind. And I broke down, started crying. Things in the room started moving—"

"Moving?" her sister questioned.

"By themselves," Cordelia recounted. "I became angry. I stood up and asked them what they wanted. I know I wasn't supposed to—Mom told me never to speak to them. But when I walked over to look inside the crib, someone had written a word in the dust."

Eustace's staccato breath hitched between them. "*What* word?"

"Revenge."

Her sister fell back in her chair, her face a maze of thoughts. "Then what?"

"Then I was backing out of the room when I stepped on this and almost fell. I picked it up, and when I walked into the hall, Arkin was there."

"Arkin?" Her sister's face contorted. "Wait. I'm confused. What does Arkin have to do with any of this?"

"I guess he came with Mr. Togers. I forgot to tell you they stopped by. Anyway, he was being really weird. Weirder than normal, I mean."

"That's saying a lot," Eustace said dryly.

"He was just kind of looming and staring at me like he wanted to grab me or something. I was startled, and the bracelet was in my hand, and in my panic, I slipped it on."

Her sister drooped over the table, head in her hand.

"What?" Cordelia asked, concerned. "What did I do?"

"You agreed," Eustace told her.

"Agreed to what?" By her reckoning, Cordelia hadn't agreed to any of this, not that it seemed to matter to anyone but her.

"Whatever *revenge* means. You put that bracelet on. That's the old Norse equivalent of signing a contract."

"I don't understand," she whispered, staring at the band, a shackle.

"It won't come off until the oath is fulfilled," her sister told her. "The only question now is, do they want revenge *from* you or *on* you."

"How do I do that?" Cordelia pressed, rubbing at her skin around the band. She wanted it off more than ever. "Fulfill the oath?"

Eustace looked at her with tired eyes. "I wish I knew. But you had better find out. Maybe it's time you start talking to ghosts," she said flatly.

"On *purpose*?" Cordelia couldn't believe what her sister was saying. After her confession about the blue house, the fear she admitted to, the trauma, the destructive tendencies of her power. "That's what got me into this mess!"

Her sister stood, looming over her. "If our abilities have gotten us into this mess," she said with some vexation, "then they're all that can get us out. Don't you get it, Cordy? This is a message. They're *talking* to you. They're trying to tell us something. Who is the revenge on, and why? Maybe if we knew that, we would know what happened to Mom and what's happening now. We need their help, sister. It's time for you to start asking questions."

"I don't know how," Cordelia admitted, small, weak, lost

behind the shed. "I'm not like you, Eustace. I don't know how to use my power."

Her sister smiled. "You're not a little girl anymore, Cordelia. Channeling your power is easy—just stop following all of Mom's rules." She leaned over and looked her full in the face. "Start breaking them instead."

CHAPTER TWENTY-ONE

THE VISITOR

CORDELIA SUNK INTO despair. Despite the money they stood to inherit, the knowing she could save herself and her neighbor, she felt defeated. She skulked around the pink room, rarely leaving it, scratching at her wrist, tearing at the bracelet that wouldn't come off despite her efforts. She stopped eating all but a few bites a day, believing if she shed enough weight, the heavy silver would slip over her bones, freeing her. She became the prisoner she believed herself to be, paranoid and holding on to her last shred of control by refusing to leave the room. And her head pounded all the while, a deafening, incessant throb like a mallet with the force to split granite, her pills impotent against it. Her financial situation had turned around, but she was still running out of time.

The end hovered in her periphery.

She could not do what her sister was asking. She simply *could not.* She knew her sister was right—they needed to know more about the bracelet, what *revenge* and why? They needed answers, answers they weren't finding on their own. But trying to conjure her abilities would be courting the dead, unleashing mayhem. It would be tantamount to opening a door inside that she could never close again. A door filled with all manner of dark, unspeakable things. A door she had been warned to never, *ever* open.

It took three days to work up the nerve. Three days of skull-crunching pain before Cordelia couldn't take the beat of her own heart and the joyless pink walls like a washed Cabernet stain, the doom filling her mind. Three days before she wandered down to the solarium, her sister's words clapping in her ears like gongs. *Stop following all of Mom's rules. Start breaking them instead.*

The pond was fouler even than her mood. Gordon had obviously been neglecting his bacterial duties. She stared at the murky green water, spine quickening as she remembered the hair she'd seen drifting in it. How had Arabella managed to drown in these shallow waters? Had someone held her down? The glowering portrait of Erazmus shot through her. She feared they had more than one murderer in the family.

Her head pinged irritably, a sensation nearly as familiar to her as breathing by now. Her reflection was pale enough to note, even in this sullied brew. She knew without seeing that the circles under her eyes had deepened. She was fighting her new reality, and she was losing.

Which is why she stood here now, tired eyes scanning the water. It was either mind her sister or give up. She could see no other way. And Cordelia had always been a fighter.

She tried not to think about sinking bodies or vengeful husbands or the rotten-algae stink. She closed her eyes, attempting to concentrate, her headache ratcheting up by degrees the harder she tried. With effort, she pushed past the pain, hoping to find a way to re-create the magic she'd channeled before. She tried to think about the feeling of power, what it must be like to command the waves and the sky. But that led her nowhere, because Cordelia had spent a lifetime feeling power*less*—with her mother, the spirits, John. So, she switched to thinking about that day by the road when the appraiser's car caught fire. She put herself back into that moment, the urgency, the fear. She tightened her whole body around that feeling and waited. And waited. And *waited*.

Opening an eye, she saw that the water was perfectly still, perfectly unchanged.

Eustace made it all sound so easy. And maybe it was for her. Maybe she just couldn't understand what she was asking Cordelia to do.

She tried to think of a new approach. Eustace had told her to start breaking their mother's rules. But Maggie had never said anything about the weather, about harnessing the elements or blowing open doors or bringing rain. Although, Cordelia now recalled, she had never once been caught off guard with her mother where weather was concerned—never got stuck in the rain without an umbrella, or in the cold without a jacket. Had Maggie always known? Had she manipulated it to her liking?

The one rule her mother had emphasized was to keep her mouth shut where the spirits were concerned. Cordelia ground her jaw and lowered herself, digging her nail beds into the soil. She trained her eyes on the water's surface. She thought about everything she had lost and stood to lose—her life, her sister's, their mother's already gone—and let the need overtake her.

"Help me," she said out loud. The pain in her head spiked with her fear. But she held fast, digging her heels and hands in deeper. *Blood and soil*, she repeated in her mind. And then she let it go as slack as the surface of the pond itself.

She thought of her sister merging with the fox, slipping into its skin, the wet, pulsing feel of it, and allowed herself to merge with the pond—a microcosm of activity, rich and viscous, like amniotic fluid. She became one with wind and water and sky, felt herself soaring over a vast land of craggy mountains and verdant grasses, blankets of snow and miles and miles of sea. And for a moment, Cordelia wasn't Cordelia anymore. She was water. And she was rain. And she was power. And a shape began to form in her mind, through the hurt and the strain, straight like a stick with an angled hook. A *rune*, Cordelia realized. *Magic.*

The slap of the water across her face sent her sprawling back, choking and reeling. Her hair hung lank in her eyes, her chin dripped, her mouth tasted sour and wrong. She sputtered as she staggered to her feet, wiping at her face in shock.

"Did the pond get you?" she heard him ask.

She turned to see Gordon walking up behind her. "I must have gotten too close."

He stared at her strangely. "Right."

"Did you need something?"

He looked down, scuffed a booted foot against the ground, ran a hand over the back of his neck. "Uh, listen . . ."

She didn't like the sound of that beginning. She willed him to look at her.

"There's no easy way to say this."

"Then don't," she suggested, feeling a twinge of desperation. She'd been so careful to avoid him since that day in the barn, just hoping he'd forget the whole thing. "Turn around and walk out of here, and I'll forget this ever happened."

He smiled, and it kind of broke her heart. "I can't do that," he said quietly. "Forget."

"Oh." Cordelia clamped her lips together.

"I'm giving my notice," he said, looking resigned. "I'll pack up and find a place I can lease. Maybe try New York City or Boston. See if I can squeeze back into the music scene."

Cordelia shook her head. "You're leaving?"

"You and your sister will find someone else to help you with this place."

She lowered herself onto the pond's retaining wall. "I can't believe this."

He took a step toward her. "It's just time for me to move on. I've been here this whole past year thinking that if I stayed long enough, I might understand what happened to my mom. But . . ."

Cordelia stared up into his face.

He looked torn, as if there were so much he wanted to say to her. Instead, he took a breath. "There are some things I'm never gonna understand, and the longer I'm here, the more complicated it gets."

She nodded. *Of course.* That's all she was to him—a complication. A misunderstanding. All this time she and her sister had been trying to piece together the sordid puzzle of their family, Gordon had been trying to solve his own mystery. He couldn't help her with theirs any more than she could help him with his. She was just getting in the way. "If that's how you feel."

He looked at her, regret creasing his mouth.

Pity made her uneasy. She folded her bruised feelings into an imaginary envelope and put them away. She should have known. Her sister had always told her her picker was broken. Standing, she brushed the pond scum from her rear and squared her shoulders. "I'll talk to Mr. Togers about issuing a final payment."

He sniffed, stiffening.

"If we're lucky," she said now, a cold storm brewing in her eyes, "he'll be quick about it."

"Don't worry," he said, turning her cattiness on her. "He can mail the check. I wouldn't dream of dragging this out. For either of us."

Cordelia took a deep breath and turned her back. As she marched toward the kitchen, she held the image of the rune she'd seen in her mind, the brackish taste of the water in her mouth, and the anger she felt inside her chest, loosing them together at once.

"Fuck!" she heard him call as she hit the kitchen door, the

sound of water ringing through her, and the image of him standing there dripping wet and covered in scum bringing an evil little smile to her lips.

And that's when she realized that the headache she'd endured ceaselessly the last three days had mysteriously improved.

It hadn't just improved, in fact. It no longer hurt at all.

CORDELIA HAD SCARCELY cleared the kitchen door when she heard his forced laughter echo toward her. Her heart seized, gripped in a frigid fist, before rushing headlong into full panic mode. But her brain held squarely to the belief that she was mistaken in some way.

Because it couldn't be.

It just couldn't.

Swallowing down the bitter dread that threatened to rise with breakfast, she moved through the dining room toward the stair hall, every second drawing out impossibly long. She could hear him explaining himself to Eustace—something about a *personal delivery* and *resolution* and *never too late*. The blood drained from her face and puddled in her feet. With a deep breath, she cracked the door until her head peeked out, eyes meeting her sister's across the room.

Eustace's face was a muddle of anger and apology. "Would you look at what the tomcat dragged in?" she said, blowing Cordelia's cover.

He turned around, and Cordelia spotted the large cardboard box sitting between them on the floor, the ones still resting at the open door. The layers of shipping tape were painstakingly applied as only Molly would do, and the design of it all began to fall into place for her then. Somehow, he'd intercepted Molly's attempt to ship her things and taken it upon himself to bring them.

"Cordelia!" He beamed, his smile like the brights on a car, his skin bronzed across the nose and cheeks from a few rounds of golf, days lying on the beach in the sun.

The very sight of him made her want to gag. She emerged from the dining room and took several steps in their direction. Behind her, she heard Gordon pass from the kitchen to the stair hall door, coming up short when he saw everyone as he entered the room. "Everything all right?"

A thousand different words were piling up in her mouth at once like cars in a freeway crash. If she opened it, she had no idea which would escape first. "What are you doing here, John?"

"Yeah," her sister echoed. "What *are* you doing here, John?"

His face fell, nice-guy smile melting off his chin like cheese dripping through the oven rack. But his eyes never changed, and Cordelia suddenly found it so telling the way he could wear a smile or a frown and never have it reach the cool, glacial gleam of his eyes.

"Is that how you're going to thank me for bringing your things?" he asked, gesturing toward the boxes on the floor. "I drove all night," he said, walking right up to her and wrapping her in an intimate hug, the linen and lemongrass scent of his cologne engulfing her.

Cordelia stiffened in his arms, and John drew back.

"Thank you," she said, all venom. "Now leave."

John glanced from Cordelia to Eustace and back again. "I was hoping I could rest a moment, maybe get a decent night's sleep." He added quickly with a sly glance in Gordon's direction, "I was hoping we could talk, Cordy. Just you and me."

John had never called her *Cordy* before. That was Eustace's pet name for her, and one she would only ever let her sister get away with. Hearing it come from his mouth upended her place in the world.

He smiled. "There. See? I'm not gonna bite." He leaned toward her. "Maybe we could go somewhere private to, you know, work things out?"

Gordon cleared his throat.

"Who is he, anyway?" John asked, dripping with arrogance.

"Our bouncer," Eustace said dryly.

"Always a pleasure, Eustace," John said, tone flat as a pancake. "What has it been? Five years since we last spoke? The wedding?"

She pulled her vape pen out and took a puff, giving him a feline smile through the plume. "Once was enough for me."

Cordelia motioned for John to follow her and started toward the dining room, refusing to meet Gordon's eye. "Let me handle this," she mouthed to Eustace as she held the door open for John. He slipped past her, and Cordelia glanced up to the tower, where a shadow gathered like rain.

"Stay here," she told John once they were in the dining room.

But as always, he didn't listen. He followed her into the kitchen, where she was opening and closing the cupboards, trying to find the big mugs so she might make herself a cup of that chamomile tea her sister had the other night.

"Cordelia, will you just talk to me?" he begged beside the island.

She took one look at him and decided she would need something much stronger. Mug in hand, she made her way back into the dining room to the bar, where she poured two fingers of brandy into her cup and took a long, fiery swallow. She set it down on the oversized table and turned to John.

"Are you gonna offer me one?"

"No."

He exhaled and bent his head to his hand as if she were being the impertinent one. He pulled out a chair. "Can you sit?"

Cordelia eyed him skeptically.

"You're making me nervous," he said, all chivalry and sensitivity.

With slitted eyes, she slunk into the chair. He pulled out the chair at the head of the table, she noted with distaste, and sat down in it, resting his elbows on his knees. "I wish you would talk to me. I'm not a stranger. I'm your husband."

She snorted into her brandy mug. "You'll have to excuse me. The sight of you mounting my assistant in our kitchen made me forget all about our vows."

He winced. "Not this again."

"Yes, John. *This*. Again. And again. And again. As many times as you fucked her, that's how many times I'll bring it up."

His mouth twisted. "You know I hate it when you use that word."

The irony, Cordelia thought, was that she'd heard Allison moaning it over and over as she'd made her way from the front door to the kitchen that night—*fuck me, fuck me, fuck me*. Apparently, he loved when Allison said it.

Cordelia leaned back in her chair. His shirt was unbuttoned at the collar, hair combed through, nails straight and clean as any woman's. The slender pinkness of his fingers, compared with Gordon's rough, workman's hands, struck her. And the tidy smell of him, so civil and boring. His shoulders were more rounded and several inches too narrow. There was nothing of Gordon's rugged sex appeal or honest face or genuine nature. John was a caricature of a man, as unappealing as dry toast. And he did look like a Rolex ad.

"You know you very nearly got me killed," she spat.

He sighed. "Don't exaggerate, Cordelia."

"Exaggerate!" she fumed. "Why didn't you tell me about the debts, about the mob? We could have worked together to figure something out. We could have sold the business or the house, taken fewer trips, shopped and dined less. Instead you took off on a monthslong vacation in *my* name with my assistant."

"I needed a chance to think," he stammered. "To regroup.

Maybe I went about it the wrong way, but my heart was in the right place. I was trying to protect you by leaving."

"You stole my identity," she countered. She was ready to get on with this, put him behind her for good. "Why are you here, John?"

He looked around the room, eyes feasting on the burnished wood and ornate moldings, the prized portraits and candelabras. "I made a mistake," he said ruefully. "*We* made a mistake."

Cordelia resented his use of the first-person plural. She was fairly certain at this point that the only mistake she had made was marrying him in the first place. "You're right," she said after another sip of brandy. "You never should have fucked my assistant, racked up a small fortune of debt in my name, and run off leaving me holding the bag. And I never should have trusted you."

With visible effort, he pushed past her accusation, taking both of her hands in his. "I want to make it up to you. Let me try."

"You can start by moving your shit out of my house. And retracting your email to our clients. And calling Busy up to let him know where you are so he'll leave me alone. I've got his number right here," she said, pulling out her phone and setting it on the table before him.

John dropped her hands and fell back in his chair. "*Our* house," he huffed. "And I was angry. Can you blame me?"

"Yes, John," she answered hotly. "I can and I do blame you. What did you have to be angry about? You cheated on *me*. You left *me*. And you screwed *me* out of everything. You don't get to be angry in this scenario. The anger is all mine!"

"Okay," he conceded. "You're angry. I get it. But that's why I'm here. So we can fix this."

"I'm not a car!" she fumed. "You're not a mechanic. We're past that now. *Long* past. The best you can hope for now is that I don't press charges."

He buried his face in his hands. When he looked at her again, his brows slanted upward like a puppy's, but his eyes were unchanged as ever. "Tell me what I need to do. I can't lose you, Cordelia. Not now."

"Awww . . . what happened? Did Allison find someone her own age to give her multiple orgasms?" She glared at him, enjoying the dig. She knew it was unwise to poke the bear—he already had her over a legal barrel—but Cordelia couldn't help herself. And for the life of her, she couldn't understand what he was doing here at all.

He simpered. "I deserve that," he said, putting on a noble face. "But I'll have you know I haven't been with Allison since you left."

"*You* left!" she insisted, frustrated that he found it so easy to rewrite their history, to rob her of the suffering she'd endured at his hand.

"I did leave. The badgering and fighting drove me away. But I wasn't leaving *you*. I was leaving *the situation*. Stepping back, like that therapist told you. Because things were getting too heated."

Cordelia felt like she was going mad. He'd made it very clear they were over. He didn't want to work it out. He didn't want therapy. He wanted a divorce. So, what had changed? "Look, I don't know what you're on about. Can you just tell me what you're doing in Connecticut?"

"I'm putting an end to the divorce," he said. "You don't want to do this, Cordelia. Neither do I. It's time we come back together and work through this." His eyes skirted the room in a quick sweep. "I have never wanted another woman like I want you right now."

There was that word again—*now*. As if the Cordelia of today was somehow more appealing than the Cordelia of a month ago. She had seen the way he took in the room, how comfortably he seated himself at the head of *her* table, how his arm fell lightly along the carved arm of the chair, how he leaned against the regal backrest of it, at home.

It wasn't her he'd come here for. It was the house. The inheritance. It wasn't enough that he'd taken her business and home in Texas—he wanted this place, too. He would never have come back to all the debt he left behind unless he thought she was worth more than that. He'd take more if she let him, and he'd keep on taking. He wouldn't stop until he'd run through her like a lamp burns through oil. She saw him so clearly all of a sudden. However broken her picker had been before, Bone Hill had mended it. She knew what John was. All he would ever do is *take*.

Cordelia burned with indignation. The word slammed into her hard, with all the force of a lead fist. *REVENGE*. It pulsed through her, white hot and defiant. The women of her family were burning for it. And so was she.

She downed her brandy and stared at him, eyes lit with cold fire. "I'm gonna need you to beg," she said evenly.

"What?" John asked.

Cordelia sat on the edge of her chair and spread her legs, pulling the lengths of her skirt up over her knees. "You heard me, John. I want you to get on your knees, right here," she said, indicating the space between her thighs. "And beg me to take you back."

His face blanched, and she could see pride warring with greed. Which half won would tell her everything she needed to know.

"Come on," she said gently, like she was coaxing a kitten. "Show me how badly you want this."

He cast his eyes from one wall to another. "Are you serious?"

"As a tall man in a lightning storm."

Slowly, taking one knee first and then the other, he lowered himself to the floor and scooted between her legs, a place she'd vowed he would never be again. He looked up at her pitifully and said, "Please, Cordelia. I love you. Take me back."

"Lower your eyes when you speak to me," she told him, refusing to be so easily won.

His gaze dropped to her chest.

"Lower," she said.

It dropped again to her navel.

"Lower," she insisted, voice gravelly.

He coughed slightly and dropped his eyes once more, until he was staring directly between her legs.

"Now," she told him. "Beg."

"Please," he said to her crotch. "Please don't leave me, Cordelia. I need you. I love you. I want you."

She knew that to John this was sexual, some part of him responding in a primal, lustful way to her demands. She imagined that even now he was growing hard down there on the floor between her thighs, thinking he might take her right on this table.

But his fantasy of wooing her, winning her, fucking her would remain just that—a fantasy. Cordelia was taking something back. That was all.

Leaning down, she put two fingers on his chest and tipped him back. John rocked onto his heels and looked up at her with need. In that moment, she knew that for him to humiliate himself this way, the object of his desire couldn't be her. It was the house, the trust, her sudden and unexpected status as a woman of great means. It was the prospect of being set for life and wringing even more from her than he already had.

"Get up," she said simply, leaning back as she watched him stand, her lip curling in disdain.

"Anything," he whispered, erection strained against the front of his chinos. He'd always had a hard-on for money.

Cordelia stared up at him, heady with power. "Now get the fuck out of my house," she said plainly. "And *never* come back."

His face washed red, fists balled white at his sides. He reached for the empty mug on the table. "Goddammit!" he cried, sending it careening against the marble fireplace mantel, a hundred pieces of crockery littering the floor.

Cordelia laughed—a chest-deep, throaty roar burbling up from her gut.

John's face went from red to plum. He lunged for her in the chair, wrapping both hands around her throat, squeezing. Cordelia clawed at his fingers, but his face was twisted with rage, manic with greed, as if he could choke the money out of her. Her heart throbbed desperately against the lack of oxygen as her mind wheeled for purchase. All the fury she felt bottled up inside her strained for release. She forced herself to push it back down through her feet and into the floor, into the earth.

The ground began to rumble beneath them. Everything—the table, the chairs, the glass bottles in the bar—vibrated violently. The candelabras toppled over one by one. The portraits of her ancestors slid down the wall, crashing in their heavy frames to the floor. The chandelier swung wildly in his direction.

Cordelia would bring it all down around them before she'd let him have a piece of it.

"What's happening?' John shrieked. A quake hit the floor beneath them with enough force to buckle his knees. He released her to catch himself.

She jumped to her feet, gasping, as John was knocked sideways into the hardwood table, then to the floor. She reached for a brass candlestick and held it menacingly over his head. Everything stilled as quickly as it had begun. The dining room door burst open, Eustace and Gordon rushing through.

"Our guest was just leaving," Cordelia said looking down at John with more hatred than she knew it was possible to feel.

"Cordy," Eustace said gently. "Put the candle-thingy down."

But Cordelia didn't budge. Beneath her, John cowered.

"You don't want to do this, honey," her sister said. "He's not worth it."

Cordelia glanced at Eustace. Behind her sister's shoulder, she could see the shock and concern on Gordon's face, his dilated pupils.

She glared down at John. "If you ever touch me again," she told him, "I'll kill you."

Then she straightened, dropping the candlestick to the floor, and stepped away.

Gordon rushed forward to help John to his feet. "I think you'd better leave."

"What was that?" Eustace asked now that she'd managed to talk Cordelia out of murdering her ex-husband.

"Earthquake," Gordon supplied. "At least that's what it felt like."

"Do they have earthquakes in Connecticut?" Eustace asked, surprised.

Cordelia pushed her hair back from her face, breathing hard. "They do now," she said, and stepped out of the room.

CHAPTER TWENTY-TWO

THE LETTER

WHEN EUSTACE FOUND her, she was sitting on the steps to the crypt, a plucked rose in one hand, her cell phone in the other. She'd texted the divorce attorney already. Give him everything he wants. The business, the house, all of it. I want to sign as soon as possible.

Let him handle the mortgage company and the mold contractors. She needed to sign the divorce decree *before* they settled the will, so there'd be some delineation. She couldn't let John tie up their inheritance in a yearslong legal battle. She doubted he could win against the dynasty trust, but he could certainly make things difficult—and expensive—for them. She would not let him ruin this life for her too.

"Interesting location to lick your wounds," her sister said.

Cordelia cinched her brow. "He never loved me, did he?"

"The only person that man knows how to love is himself." She sighed, taking a seat beside Cordelia. "I should have let you clobber him with that candlestick. I knew I was going to regret talking you out of that."

Cordelia grinned.

"What happened between you two in the dining room?" she

asked, turning Cordelia's chin this way and that to get a better look at her neck.

"Nothing he didn't deserve," she said bitterly.

"We should get some ice on that," Eustace told her.

She touched the bruises tenderly. "I was so desperate to fit in, to look and feel like everybody else, that I let that man use me. I couldn't have been more blind if I'd plucked out my eyes."

"Don't be too hard on yourself," Eustace told her. "You see clearly now. That's what matters."

Cordelia looked at the rose in her hand, the way its delicate petals lay one atop another, growing stronger with every layer. She did see clearly now. She had changed.

"I have something to share with you," Eustace told her.

Cordelia looked up.

"While you were brooding in that boudoir upstairs for the last three days, I was working on something in the book," she said.

"The book?"

Eustace pulled the journal they'd found from under her shirt and laid it across her lap. She opened to the first page. "It's called a therimoire," she told Cordelia. "A kind of record of magic workings. Like a cookbook for spells and rituals. This one is very old. It came with our ancestors from England."

"How do you know?"

"It says right here," Eustace told her. "*Therimoire of the Bone witches, as transcribed by Omen & Sabina Bone—1776.*"

"Wow," Cordelia said. "You cracked it."

"I did," her sister said. "But there's something else. Something you should see." She flipped to the last page, the final entry. "This one is different from all the rest. Most of these entries are original. Some have been added over the years, which is evident because the script changes, but they still look like they've been in here a very long time. This one, though . . . This one is new. Like, *new* new. The ink, the handwriting, the format. And this is a date, like I first thought, inverted."

"What do you mean?" Cordelia asked her.

"I mean, someone else, or many others, wrote the rest of this. But this last page—our aunt Augusta wrote that." Eustace rapped her sister's shoulder. "She wrote it *to us.*"

"Like, a letter?" Cordelia asked now, finally understanding her sister's excitement.

"Not *like* a letter. It *is* a letter."

"What does it say?" She realized that this could crack everything open, make sense of all the random events, fill in all the blanks she and Eustace had. This wasn't just big. This was huge.

Eustace folded the leather cover back. She cleared her throat and, breathily, she began to read.

"*Your mother is gone,*" she said, raising her eyes to meet Cordelia's briefly. "*Her luck ran out, as I knew it would. You are the future of our line. There is so much you should know, so much we should have taught you. Time grows short. Soon our ancestors will sing me back home and everything will fall to you. You were no more than a seed planted in your mother's womb when she left, Eustace. Your sister was but a distant dream. I would have pursued her, were I able. Though that did not stop me keeping an eye on her. I have been watching you for years, doing everything in my power to keep you safe, even going so far as to have the soil of our home laid outside your window. Your mother sensed my intrusion again and again and slipped away, trying to keep you both from me. But she cannot outrun the power of our family line, our family name.*

"*Your birthright is not a house or a hill, though you will inherit both. Your birthright is so much more. I leave you this gift in place of what should have been. A gift to explain your own. But all gifts* come at a price, and the price for curs is very great indeed. So great, in fact, that even as I write this, I do not know if you will find it before you pay for yours.

Forgive the secrecy. I'm afraid anything we have to say must be protected from those who would do more harm than good with it. Even if they are our own kin. Deciphering this letter may feel like a test. Let me assure you—it is. But it is not your first. And it will certainly not be your last. The trials that await you, I cannot prepare you for. You must make yourselves ready. There are many wrongs to right. But whatever you face, you are precisely where you belong, where you have always belonged.

Bone Hill is your home.

Bone Hill is your family.

Bone Hill is your heritage.

I am watching over you now, as I ever have been. And beyond me, a long and proud line of volvas.

Silent in life; vocal in death.

—Augusta"

Eustace's eyes were glistening when they met her sister's. "It's dated a year to the day before she died."

Questions lapped Cordelia's mind like tadpoles. She dropped the rose. "The roses, Eustace. The *soil*."

"I know," her sister said. "I put it together too."

Cordelia recalled her dream of their aunt, that damning finger pointing through her in the study, the feeling when she woke of being the target of their family's rage. But this letter didn't sound angry or accusing, just sad and afraid. *For* them more than at them. She looked at Eustace. "What does she mean by *wrongs to right*?"

Eustace shook her head. "I wish I knew."

"What was that one word you read? The strange one—*volvas*? I've heard that before."

"I'm not sure," Eustace answered. "But I'll look into it. She sounds fearful, like there are people that can't be trusted. Maybe even in the family."

Cordelia rubbed at her arms, feeling the weight of the oath ring around her wrist. "Who? There is no family. We're it." She turned to glance over her shoulder into the mouth of the crypt. "Aren't we?"

"I guess now we know why Mom never stayed put," Eustace said. "She knew she was being followed, watched. And all those loser boyfriends—I bet she put their names on the leases."

"What did she think would happen if they found us?" Her mother's words behind the shed that day took on new meaning. *Bad things will follow. They'll come for you. They'll take you away . . . and there won't be a damn thing I can do to stop them.* What if she never meant the ghosts at all, but their family?

Eustace shrugged. "Aunt Augusta had an enormous amount of resources at her disposal, from what we can gather. And our mother definitely did not. Which brings us back to the real question—why leave at all? Why take the risk? With her own life and with ours?"

"Whatever her reason," Cordelia said, eyes scrambling over the dark and drafty tomb behind them, "she thought the risk of staying here was greater."

Cordelia went to bed troubled that night. Her mind kept replaying the day's events over and over. Gordon planning to leave. Their aunt's letter. John showing up. The madness in his eyes. The earthquake. The feeling of standing over him with that candlestick in her hand . . . She hadn't wanted to do it, not really. At least, she didn't think she had. But the feeling of having that power over him, all that rage crashing through her—she'd liked it. More than she dared to admit. And that frightened her more than anything else.

She'd half expected to look down once he was gone and see that the oath ring had fallen off. She'd gotten her revenge all right. But the bracelet had stuck fast. Which meant it wasn't her revenge the spirits were interested in.

She leaned back on her feathered pillows and let the dark swim around her. In the dining room with John, she'd called it *her* house. Despite her original desire to sell, seeing him here in *her* space, touching *her* things, wanting to take what had been *her* family's . . . It had cemented something between Cordelia and the estate, giving her a powerful sense of possession. It made her want to lay claim to what she'd waffled over for so long.

And it wasn't just the house.

It was Gordon.

She realized now, alone in the dark, burning for him, twisting in the sheets, that despite the countless arguments she'd made to the contrary, the fear it stoked in her breast, and the life and business she'd been clinging to eighteen hundred miles away, Cordelia wanted Bone Hill and everything that came with it, including the groundskeeper—*especially* the groundskeeper.

Just on the edge of dreaming, she heard a low creak. Her eyes fluttered, taking in the dull pink furniture in the unlit boudoir, the diaphanous form wafting by, tall and feminine, the open door.

Cordelia sat up and saw the ghost of Arabella—blond hair and white silk—standing at the door to the solarium. She turned to look through Cordelia and placed a finger to her lips. And then she passed onto the stairs.

Cordelia rose from the bed and hurried after her on bare feet.

When she reached the stairs, she could see Arabella below her, spiraling around and around in a smooth dance of steps, as if she were gliding on water. At the bottom, she floated to the pond, passing through the drooping fronds and delicate blooms as if they didn't exist, and sat on the low stone wall, looking over the edge. She combed long fingers through her hair and pinched her cheeks, using the water as a mirror. She glowed like Artemis bathing in the forest, a nymph at play.

Satisfied with her appearance, Arabella stood and started down a walk toward the garden door, plucking a hibiscus bloom and tucking it behind her ear. Her body was lean and sculpted beneath the thin fabric of her gown, with small breasts and strong thighs, a gentle swell to the womb that had borne so many children. At the garden door, she glanced back once as if looking for someone, craning. When no one appeared, she pulled the door open and stepped through.

Cordelia rushed to keep up, passing quietly through the solarium to the chill of the evening. Outside, the night was holding its breath. She caught sight of Arabella only paces ahead as she made her stroll across the grounds, stopping here and there to stroke a tree or waft over the top of a waist-high shrub.

Cordelia hugged herself in the dark, nervous to be out so late alone. There were bears in this part of the state. And worse. But she had to know where Arabella was going.

Leaving the garden behind, her great-great-great-grandmother continued across the property, as pale as if she'd been born of the moon. It wasn't long before Cordelia began to recognize where they were headed. In the distance stood the carriage house where Gordon lived, hunkering beneath the trees. She tiptoed behind her as Arabella walked toward it, set on her course. It was here where Gordon had found the picture of her.

When Arabella reached the steel French doors, she pulled one back. Again, she glanced over a shoulder, and this time her eyes met Cordelia's, steady and unafraid. Her lips lifted in a ghostly smile. And then, without a sound, she slipped inside.

Cordelia stood shivering in the dark. It felt wrong to invade Gordon's space, but she didn't want to lose her captor now.

Creeping up to the door, she poked her head in, but Arabella had vanished.

"Hello," she whispered softly, feeling foolish. "Arabella?" She slipped inside and looked around, searching for some vital clue to where the spirit had gone.

A rustle caused her to look up. Gordon stood on the stairs to the loft, dark hair coursing down his shoulders, a pair of black sweatpants sitting low on his hips. His eyes found hers across the room.

"I thought I saw someone," she said, paralyzed at being discovered, the soundless way he was watching her.

He walked down the stairs, his eyes pinning her. When he reached the bottom, her blood hammered with need, sending a throbbing spike of adrenaline through her hips and legs, causing her to forget everything else. "I–I don't want you to leave," she told him.

He reached past her and gripped the door, pulling it gently closed behind them.

Cordelia's lips parted. Her breath came heavy and light at the same time, shallow then deep, as if she'd lost the ability to regulate herself.

Gordon pinched the fabric of her nightshirt between his fingers, pulling her to him. Her nipples bristled against him as she looked into his face, his eyes holding nothing back, a question in them, and deeper still, a command.

Neither spoke. They had passed the point where words held dominion. Here, only touch mattered. And the flare of instinct, of action and reaction, push and pull.

Gordon put his mouth to hers, and his craving flowed into her as their lips crushed against each other—his body firm in the moonlight, hers supple as moving water.

Without a thought for why she'd first come, she let him lead her up the stairs. In the pressing dark, she found him solid and ready, a force beneath her that she scaled with ragged longing. Her body dissolved into chasms of ecstasy, and then they lay beside each other, weak and heaving, each shattered in their own way. Until they found each other again and spent themselves over and over in the dark.

CHAPTER TWENTY-THREE

THE STRANGER

CORDELIA WOKE BEFORE dawn. She tiptoed lightly down the stairs to Gordon's living room and looked out the wide glass doors. All was inky but for a barely perceptible light beginning to infiltrate the mist, washing it gray and gold. She stepped outside, a ridiculous grin glued to her face. With her nightshirt only half-buttoned and her legs still bare, she started across the property. Every step she took, the mist shrunk back, revealing patches of flowering bluets, mounding like silky blue stars at her feet.

She noticed the chill in the air, and the sun burst over the horizon, sending tendrils of warm light streaming high. She stopped to watch it rise, the sky blushing. The forest gilded itself about the edges. Everything came into crystal focus, as if the world were being born before her eyes. Taking a deep, delirious breath, she willed the breeze into motion, bringing with it the scent of cherry blossoms and old roses. It was all tied to her by an invisible silver thread. She could feel the magic weaving in and out, causing the land to gush with life even as her heart was gushing. Eastern bluebirds circled, alighting in nearby trees and landing at her feet to peck the ground before taking off again.

Cordelia knew in that moment, as surely as the sun was good

and the trees were good and the birds were good, that so was her power good. She'd been looking at it all wrong, so afraid to embrace who she really was. Eustace wasn't the light sister and she the dark any more than night was evil and day righteous. They were two halves of a whole, she and her sister, two branches of the same tree. Undivided. Just as death was undivided from life. To her sister had gone the power to heal, to grow, to connect with the plants and animals so deeply she became them. And to Cordelia had gone the power to command winds and call rain and shake the bedrock. To hear that which had no voice. To sing the dead to her side. One wasn't a reward and the other a punishment. Their power was *one* power, flowing as it had for generations, now through two women. They were both daughters of Maggie Bone. Both cast from her mold and made in her image. Her love belonged to both of them. And so did her gifts.

Cordelia was done being sorry, being scared, being ashamed.

She was just turning back toward the big house when a frantic chittering caught her ear. Looking behind her, she saw Marvel break from a stand of trees, barreling in her direction. The fox was little more than a streak of red, and as she reached Cordelia's legs, she practically climbed up them, leaving scratches all over her calves.

"Whoa, whoa, whoa," Cordelia said, trying to calm the animal. "What is going on?"

The fox danced in panicked circles, a cacophony of earsplitting noise.

"Eustace?" Cordelia asked, unsure. She knelt down and reached toward Marvel, who stilled. At the brink of contact, a booming, throaty roar cleaved the morning. She looked up to see an enormous male black bear bounding in their direction. The fox dashed behind her legs in fear.

The world spun around her as he gained ground, a loping boulder of coal fur, tiny eyes, and teeth like a polesaw. Everything she'd ever learned said not to run from bears, but Cordelia wanted to run more than anything. Only, her legs weren't working. Shock and paralysis had taken over. Behind her, the fox wailed.

Its sheer size meant the bear could cross the distance that separated them in no time. Cordelia had only moments to think of something.

She threw a hand up, palm out, and shouted, "Stop!"

The hair on her head and body began to stand on end, crackling. All around her, she could smell a strange, sweet scent permeating the air. The bear sensed the atmospheric changes too. It slowed, casting its eyes about, backing up in fear. Then, refocusing, it took a step in her direction.

A massive bolt of electricity ripped open the world between them in a sheet of white, connecting earth and sky. Lightning sent the bear scrambling back in the direction it had come, thunder loud enough to wake the dead blasting behind it, causing Cordelia to clap both hands over her ears before breaking into a sprint all the way back to the big house, Marvel several paces ahead of her.

Throwing open the solarium door, she let the fox in, and they both dashed for the kitchen. Cordelia had just stumbled inside, panting and clutching her side, when she looked up to see that her sister had done the same from the opposite end. They stood staring at each other across the room, neither able to speak.

"Were you . . . ?" Cordelia finally asked between breaths.

Eustace nodded. "I saw it all."

The fox hastened across the tile to her sister's side.

"I saved her," Cordelia said, just processing what had occurred.

"You saved *us,*" her sister corrected. "All three of us."

Cordelia shook her head, leaning a hip against the counter. "What happened?"

"We were out doing our nightly run," Eustace began. "Marvel likes to forage near the woods northwest of the carriage house.

It was getting close to sunup, so we decided to head back. That's when I spotted him."

"The bear?"

Eustace shook her head vigorously. "No. The man."

Cordelia's heart dropped to her knees. The night of the bats, Gordon's claim about seeing someone outside the house, drifted back to her. "What man?"

"He was strolling across the grounds like he owned the place. I didn't get a good look because it was still pretty dark, but I could tell by his size and stature that it was a guy. I mean, not Gordon-sized. You know, more average. And he was dressed all in black except for a bandage or something on his head. He looked like he was coming from here."

"The house?" Cordelia leaned against the counter, feeling weaker by the second. Gordon had been right that night. It was no animal he saw. Someone very real was watching them, coming and going of their own volition. Someone with an agenda.

"Yep. So, Marvel and I started following him. We were being stealthy, but then this field mouse popped up and I lost control for a minute. Marvel started squawking something fierce. That's when he realized we were there, and he just took off into the woods!"

"You chased him?"

She nodded. "But it's like he knew that Marvel wasn't *just* a fox. I mean, who would run from a fox anyway? We tried to keep up, but he was fast. Must be young—he really gave Marvel a run for her money. Anyway, we lost him somewhere in the forest. And then this black bear comes tearing through the trees at us, and we booked it back. That's when we ran into you, doing your walk of shame."

Cordelia's face flooded with heat. "I don't know what you mean."

"Oh," Eustace said with a chuckle. "You know exactly what I mean. But that's neither here nor there. I suspect our early morning guest is the same person who nearly killed Marvel and left all that blood in here. He must have recognized her and that's why he started running. The bear was just a fluke. But what you did, saving our asses like that with the lightning? That was spectacular!"

Beneath the trouble brewing within her, the fear, Cordelia's power coursed through her in delicious waves. It had kept someone she loved safe. She wouldn't doubt herself again. "So, what was that creep doing back here? What does he want? Is he just trying to scare us away?"

Eustace frowned. "Can't say, but the way he was strolling along, he seemed pretty proud of himself."

Cordelia reached for a glass on the counter. She filled it with water and took a sip. She was just holding it out to Eustace when something caught her eye. There, on the dining table, where Eustace had left their mother's urn, was something tan and leathery, small and marked. Around it, a mess of grayish-brown dust fanned out. "What is that?"

"What is what?" Eustace followed Cordelia's pointing finger to the table. She took a step forward, then another. She put a hand to her mouth. Her face washed green and yellow, like a bruise. "Oh no."

"What is it?" Cordelia whispered, afraid to get closer. A few steps forward and she could make out the pattern in the leather, its unusual grain, the blurred lines crossing it. A strange sort of tree with three branches. Around it, her ashes had been used to draw out several runes in a radial pattern.

Eustace met her sister's eyes, her own beading with tears. "It's Mom's tattoo."

"Tell me again what you saw," Gordon directed.

He'd rushed over as soon as he'd gotten Cordelia's call, wrapping his strong arms around her for a second so she'd feel safe.

She wanted to stay curled against his chest like a fawn, block everything out behind the mountain of him, but she couldn't. Gently, she'd pulled away.

"Not what—*who*," Eustace answered. "I saw someone walking across the property. They were leaving the house, so I followed them. But then the bear came, and that's when Cordy—well, there was this sudden electrical storm . . ."

"Uh-huh." Gordon's brows crinkled over his eyes.

"Anyway, we ran all the way back here. And that's when we found this," she finished, pointing at the dried patch of their mother's skin still lying on the table and the circle of runes around it.

"When was this?" he asked her.

"Just this morning," she told him, exasperated. "Didn't I say that?"

"And who was it that you saw?"

Eustace threw her arms up. "I don't know that! I couldn't tell because it was dark, and they were dressed in black. But I'm pretty sure it was a man," she explained.

"And what were you doing out before sunrise in the dark?" Gordon leaned toward her, suspicious.

"Walking my fox," she said defensively. "In the woods."

"Eustace, what time was this?"

She groaned, frustrated by all the things she *couldn't* say. "I don't know. We were out there a long time, pretty much all night. But it was close to sunrise."

Gordon narrowed his eyes, and Cordelia sighed. This was not going well. "You mean to tell me that you were out all night long walking your fox? In the woods? In the dark?"

Eustace huffed. "Well, it sounds weird when *you* say it."

Maybe involving Gordon had been a mistake, but he was in danger too. They had a moral obligation to tell him, and they needed his help keeping watch. "Look, none of that is what matters right now. What matters is that my sister saw someone on our land. Someone who was in our house. And they left this here for us to find. Don't you see? It's another threat."

This time, she could be certain it was no apparition trying to run them from the house. Morna was not to blame, however it might have seemed so before. This time, their assailant was a flesh-and-blood person—a man.

Gordon stepped over to the table. He stared down at the offending display, crossing his arms in a way that made them bulge. "What is this exactly?"

Cordelia moved to his side. "Our mother's tattoo. It's surrounded by her ashes. That's what the runes are drawn in."

He eyed her skeptically. "You mean, your mother had a tattoo similar to this design?"

"No," Eustace insisted, waving her hands. "That is her tattoo exactly."

Gordon rubbed his jaw. "So, she had a tattoo in this *exact* design?"

Cordelia couldn't blame him. She would be lost too if she wasn't living it all. "Not this design," she said quietly. "This is *her* tattoo, Gordon. On *her* skin."

He took a step back from the table, knotting his fingers on top of his head. "That's a whole new level of fucked-up."

"Whoever did this," Eustace told him, "knew about our mother's tattoo. They knew she was mutilated when she died. They knew this was her urn. And they wanted us to know they knew. They want us to know . . ."

"What?" he asked, eyes widening. "What do they want you to know?"

"We're next," Cordelia told him.

Gordon wiped his hands over his face and pinched the bridge of his nose. "You're telling me your mother had a stalker, who may or may not have killed her, who is now stalking you?"

"You can put it that way. Yes." Cordelia could see the wheels of his mind spinning, trying to place each detail in this bizarre picture, to understand what it all meant.

"That's who you think left the blood in the front hall?" He eyed them both. "This person? The person you saw walking?"

"Yes," Eustace told him. "It has to be."

"But why?" he continued. "There has to be motive. People don't make idle threats."

Cordelia took a breath and met her sister's eyes. "We learned something recently. Something we hadn't realized before."

Gordon's eyes slid from hers to Eustace's.

"It's not just the house we stand to inherit. There's money," Eustace told him.

"A *lot* of it," Cordelia confirmed. "And after the blood appeared that day, the paperwork we needed to sign for the trust went missing."

Gordon shrugged. "So. Even if they kept you from inheriting, that doesn't mean it would go to them, whoever *they* are."

He had a point. Cordelia eyed her sister. "Mr. Togers said something about a contingency."

"Who stands to benefit from that?" Gordon asked.

"He wouldn't say," Cordelia answered.

"You don't think it's him, do you?" Eustace asked. "He knows this family backward and forward."

But Gordon quickly dismissed the idea. "If Togers stood to gain from your loss, he would have taken aim at Augusta a long time ago. He's the trustee, after all. He could have found a way to redirect her assets if he'd wanted to. It's more likely the contingency divides the money between a set of charities your great-aunt selected than that it goes to any one person."

"He did say he'd send another set of papers over," Eustace admitted, eliminating the old man from their suspicions. "So what do they want then, if not the money?" she asked, but

Cordelia still couldn't answer that concretely, though her sister's words rose up in response—*It's our blood. That's what someone is hunting.*

"Something else we inherit along with this place," she suggested. "Something big, or else they would have just stolen it already. They've been inside the house more than once."

"A better question," Gordon said, "is why they would take this from your mother's body. And how would they get it?"

"Souvenir? Identification?" That tattoo being removed had something to do with their mother's aneurysm. Whoever took it knew that. They did it on purpose. They killed her. She just didn't understand how. "They must have been there. They did this to her, or they know the person who did."

"Right. Okay." Gordon turned toward the sink, resting both hands on the edge. "What about that stuff around it? What does it say?"

Eustace cleared her throat. "It's a bind rune—another curse. More complicated this time. They've used Nauthiz again. They really wanna drive that particular point home," she said, pointing to one spoke. "And this one here that just looks like a line is Isa. It means bringing something to a standstill. This is Hagalaz. It means *disruption.*" She sighed. "But these three on the bottom are reversed. They're all facing the wrong way. It indicates an inherently negative meaning. Fehu—which is usually money and status—here means *loss.* Loss of property. Loss of wealth. Loss of reputation. And Kenaz reversed, which means *end* or *ending.* And this is Tiewaz, which should mean *victory*—favor with the gods. But here . . ."

"*Failure,*" Gordon finished for her.

"Right," Eustace said. "As if we're being passed over in a competition. As if we've lost favor of some kind."

"Even our mother's tattoo has been placed upside down," Cordelia told him. "It's supposed to mean *protection,* but they want us to know that we're vulnerable. We couldn't save her, and we can't save ourselves."

"Jesus," Gordon responded, horrified. "This person is sick."

"We thought you should know," Cordelia told him. "Because you live here too."

"What about the police?" he asked, turning to face them again.

"We called you first," Eustace told him. "We wanted you to see it just how we found it."

"I don't want the police putting their hands all over our mother's remains," Cordelia said. "I don't want them involved."

Gordon hung his head, giving it a heavy shake. "I can understand that, but what do you propose instead? We just let this bastard keep terrorizing you?"

She took a deep breath. "No. But I don't think the police can protect us anyway. He's too smart for that, whoever he is. He knows more than we do. He'll be two steps ahead of them as well. We can't hide behind a few small-town officers."

"How do you beat somebody at their own game?" Eustace asked them.

Gordon shrugged. "Learn the rules?"

"Exactly," she said. "You have to be two steps ahead of *them*."

Cordelia saw the twinkle in her sister's eye. "You mean go on the offensive instead of the defensive?"

"That's precisely what I mean," Eustace answered. "We have to start hunting this guy the way he's hunting us. He ran from me last night, and he's staying hidden, pulling his pranks under cover of darkness. That means that beneath his flair for menace he's scared. Of *us*."

"Wait." Gordon put a hand out. "Back up. You chased this guy?"

"Is that so hard to believe?" Eustace asked in a tone that implied that even if that's what he thought, he'd better not say it.

"No," he said, meaning it. "But it's incredibly dangerous and stupid!"

"You're onto something," Cordelia said, interrupting both of them. She turned in small circles, thinking. "What if *we* go after *him*?"

Gordon looked like they'd both lost their minds. "Are you hearing yourselves?"

"And how do we do that?" Eustace questioned, ignoring him. "Since, you know, we don't really know our way around *past the property line*," she added from the corner of her mouth. She knew as well as Cordelia that they couldn't leave the estate.

"We bring him here," Cordelia suggested.

"And *do* what?" Gordon argued. "This person is homicidal."

Cordelia tapped a foot, thinking. "First, we need to identify him. Figure out who this is."

"And then?" he pressed.

"We need evidence against him. Something we can actually take to the police to have him arrested."

"You're talking about catching him in the act," he clarified.

"If that's what it takes," she said. "Or at least collecting something that puts him at the scene, physical evidence that can't be denied."

"You'll need cameras—security. A way to record what's happening," Gordon told her. "A *small* model, so you can hide them from view."

"Can you install something like that?" Cordelia asked.

"Sure," he told her. "But it won't be cheap."

She frowned. They'd have to find a way.

"Say we get these cameras and put them up around the house. How do we get him to come here again?"

Cordelia thought for a moment, eyes squinting as she brainstormed. "I know!" she said, brightening. "We *invite* him."

"That's brilliant," Eustace shouted. "A party!"

Cordelia's eyes lit up. "Yes! A party! Perfect. We'll invite everyone in Bellwick," she said. "He won't be able to resist."

"To celebrate the signing of the trust," Eustace continued. "He really won't be able to say no to that!"

"Once everyone is here, will you be able to recognize him, Eustace? Pick him out of the crowd?" Cordelia wondered.

"I think so," she said. "I know his build, his general size and shape. But more than that, I know his attitude, the way he carries himself. There won't be anyone else like that, I'm certain."

"And then?" Gordon asked. "When this mystery man is exposed as the person threatening you? What will you do? You gonna shoot him on sight? In front of all your party guests? Without a trial?"

"We'll hit him," Eustace blurted, improvising. "With *your* fists."

Gordon raised his hands. "I'm not hitting anybody, not without provocation."

"Maybe there will be another freak lightning storm," Eustace suggested sagely. "Or a hurricane." Her eyebrows curved menacingly high.

Cordelia had to hide her smile in front of Gordon. "Accidents do happen all the time," she said knowingly to her sister.

Gordon pushed himself off the kitchen counter. "I can't be a part of this," he told them.

"Why not?" Eustace insisted, taking offense.

"Because it's half-cocked and crazy," he bellowed. "You're going to lure this guy here hoping to call him out or catch him somehow, but you don't really know what you're getting into. You don't know who you're dealing with."

Cordelia turned to him. "You're right," she said. "You're absolutely right. It is half-cocked. But it's not crazy. We need to know who this person is. There's a good chance he won't be able to resist sneaking around once he's here. If we have the cameras set up, we won't have to do a single thing but turn the tapes over to the police. Even if he doesn't, once we're armed with the knowledge of who he is, we can strategize, lay a trap. Then we can go to the police when we have something concrete. But if we go to them now, we're no better off than we are now—perhaps *worse* off. Please," she said, meeting his eyes so he would see the earnestness of her plea. "Help us."

Without Gordon, she knew, none of this would work.

He sighed, bit his bottom lip for a moment, and then drew a deep breath. "Okay. As long as all we're doing is trying to identify this person, take a little video, nothing more. What do I have to do beyond the cameras?"

"Not much," Eustace said. "Just deliver the invitations."

Cordelia nodded emphatically. "That, *and* convince everyone in Bellwick who hates us to come."

CHAPTER TWENTY-FOUR

THE OFFENSIVE

CORDELIA HUGGED HER mother's urn to her chest. The wooden corners dug into her skin as she stood before the iron gates of the crypt, sad, bitter, and more than a little afraid. They should have done this sooner. Maybe if they had . . .

There was no point thinking about that now.

The memory of the ashes drawn out on the table and the patch of skin tapped a nervous drumbeat down her back. She'd been so certain before that the ghosts of the estate were after her. That the blood rune was their doing. That every mishap to befall them since their arrival was because her ancestors were vengeful, angry spirits seeking her end to satiate their need for retribution. On her mother. On her. But she'd been wrong.

She felt more confused than ever. If her ancestors didn't want to hurt her, what did they want? Why all the dreams and sightings, the strange gestures and voiceless messages? How did the disparate stories of the Bone women tie together? What ending did they seek?

And who was this man that let himself into their house, that waved their mother's own flesh before them, creeping in the shadows, the property a suit he wore better than they did? What did he want?

"I really have no desire to go back in there," Eustace complained beside her, staring into the maw of their family grave. They'd come before dark, at least.

Cordelia sighed. There was still so much she and Eustace didn't understand, but they had a plan. The plan gave them focus, direction, *hope*—and these were things Cordelia thrived on.

"You can stay out here if you want," she told her sister.

"Alone?" Eustace looked pale. "No thanks. I'll take my chances in there with you."

Cordelia nodded. Horrific as the morning was, Cordelia was grateful they could return *all* of their mother to her family's resting place.

"Are we sure this is the right thing?" Eustace asked one last time.

Cordelia reached for the gate and pulled it open. "Does it really matter?"

Their mother had done everything in her power to stay away from Bone Hill and to keep them from it too. And yet, here they all were. Augusta's words echoed in her memory as they entered the crypt—*She cannot outrun the power of our family line, our family name.* What that power was in its entirety, where it came from, they were still uncovering.

A shaft of sunlight penetrated the center of the mausoleum, illuminating stones that knew little but darkness. Cordelia found an empty shelf along the rear wall and sat Maggie's urn there. She stepped back and looked around. Next to her, Eustace was studying the personal effects left for some of the graves.

"Something keeps bothering me," Eustace said, fingering an intricate hair comb.

"What?"

"In Aunt Augusta's letter to us, she uses the runes in a simplified way—an alphabetic way. Except for one." She faced Cordelia. "It's in the line about Mom's luck running out. There, she used a single rune for the word *luck* instead of spelling it out," Eustace explained.

Cordelia wandered around the crypt, studying the little plaques, reading their names—*Gloriana Astor Bone*—always so proud, so unusual. "Shorthand, perhaps?"

"Maybe," Eustace conceded. "But why only that one? It's like she wanted us to notice it. And then I got to thinking, it can also mean *charm* or *coin* or *token*. When I decoded the rest of the sentence, *luck* seemed to make the most sense. But if we use a different word, it shifts the meaning somewhat—before Mom's *charm* runs out."

Cordelia paused and looked at her. Eustace had her attention. "Like a good-luck charm. You mean an object?"

Eustace nodded. "Maybe she found something that made it possible for her to leave, for us to live somewhere else."

Cordelia glanced around at the personal items littering the crypt. "Or maybe she took something. Something she kept close. Maybe even something from here."

"But wouldn't we have seen it?" Eustace asked. "That's the only thing I don't get. How could we miss something like that?"

Cordelia shrugged. "Unless it was very, very small. Like a pin or a button." Looking around the crypt, she didn't see anything matching that description. "What about the room in the basement?" she asked her sister. "Could it be something from there?"

Eustace pushed her bottom lip out. "Could be. It's full of ingredients mostly. And bones."

"Could it be a recipe then? Like you saw in the book? Something she concocted?"

"Then it would have been something they all knew," Eustace replied, shutting that theory down.

But the basement room had Cordelia thinking, with its half-assembled skeletons and bizarre assortment of taxidermy tools and old kitchenware. Of all the items in that room, only one had given her the feeling she had now—that hum of power sunk deep, calling to something within her she couldn't yet name: the human tooth with the rune carved into it.

"I've been thinking too," she told her sister.

Eustace gave her her undivided attention.

"All this time I thought the spirits of the house were terrorizing us, that they wanted to do us harm. That article we found mentioned Morna killing her own animals and drawing with their blood. And then the rune appeared in the stair hall the morning after our seance. I assumed our mother's leaving was at the heart of what they were angry about. But after this morning—the man you saw and chased—it doesn't make sense anymore." She tapped the bracelet around her wrist with a finger. "They don't want revenge *on* us; they want it *from* us. They want us to carry out their revenge on someone else. But on whom? And why? Could it be the person that killed our mother?"

Eustace reached out and squeezed her sister's shoulder. "You're the ghost whisperer."

Cordelia shot her a pinched look, her gift still something she wasn't entirely comfortable with. "Which is why I was thinking, what do all these women have in common? The ones I've seen?"

"Besides that they're all related to us?" Eustace asked.

"They all died tragically," she said. "Think about it. Morna jumped from the tower. We know what happened to our mom. Something *off* definitely happened to our aunt. Our grandmother died in childbirth, hemorrhaging before anyone could save her. And Arabella apparently drowned in the solarium pond."

Eustace paled with disgust. "No wonder that thing is so nasty."

"Even Gordon's mom's death is suspicious," Cordelia muttered. "I thought this place was supposed to protect us, that nothing bad could happen here. My headaches aside, that was the deal, right? So even if you write Mom and Violetta off as the result of leaving the estate, what about the rest of us?"

Eustace thought, tugging at her lip. "Well, Gordon's mom isn't a Bone, so the protection doesn't extend to her. And for that matter, the same can be said of Arabella, who only married into the family. That wall you saw in the basement does not include the names of spouses, only direct descendants. Which means no power and no protection where they are concerned. The two, somehow, go hand in hand."

"Okay," Cordelia said. "But then . . . Morna? Where does she fit in? She's definitely blood-related. She should have been safe here."

"She took her own life, Cordy," Eustace said, squeezing her sister's hand. "You read that article. The estate can protect us from other things—disease, accidents—but it can't protect us from ourselves, I guess."

Something in her sister's logic clicked into place, illuminating a corner in her mind she'd overlooked. "That's it, Eustace!"

"It is?"

Cordelia turned to her. "My headaches . . . The estate can't protect us from *ourselves*. That means the source of my headaches has been inside me all along. It's my magic beating to get out!"

Eustace puckered, piecing her sister's words together.

"They kept getting worse and worse until a couple of days ago, when I finally embraced my power like you said. I started breaking Mom's rules."

It was plain as words in a book. She'd undergone a change of heart about the estate, but more than that, she'd undergone a change of heart about herself. It felt like part of her was just waking up, alive in a way most people weren't. Parings of herself that had left her rindless and exposed were now fluttering back and settling into place. She'd finally stopped fighting who she was, *what* she was, what she wanted. She'd finally stopped fighting the witch inside her.

She grasped her sister. "Mom wasn't suffering simply because she left the estate. She was suffering because she was denying her magic. All those years with us, all her rules, she was keeping the witch locked inside, and it was tearing her apart."

Eustace inhaled deeply, finally catching on. "Does that mean you're going to be okay now?"

"I think so," Cordelia told her.

But then her eyes fell on the dried red pigment of the hand-print on the back wall, and realized that something still felt unsettled within her. How would Morna experience depression at all if she were here actively using her powers? Or mental illness? Weren't those chemical imbalances? Didn't that constitute disease? It still didn't quite make sense.

She walked over to the back wall and lifted a finger to the dried blood. The *blood*. There was something so important about the blood. What were they missing?

"What about murder?" Eustace asked carefully, watching her. "Can the estate protect us from that?"

Cordelia turned and met her eyes. "Let's hope so."

CORDELIA COULDN'T REMEMBER ever feeling so happy and expectant. She should have realized it couldn't last.

For once, things were going her way. Gordon had installed the security equipment, carefully tucking the cameras under the eave of the house so they wouldn't be noticed. There was one in back near the solarium entrance, two in front, and another on the house's west side, where the gardens spilled around. He'd set up a small monitor in the parlor to keep tabs on things.

And her experience staging houses had come in handy with the party planning. She'd thrown their grand soiree together in a matter of days, ordering online anything Gordon couldn't pick up in town. It had to be impressive if they were going to lure most of Bellwick's residents. If nobody else came, neither would their target. So, Cordelia pulled out all the stops for decorations, lighting, and catering. They would host the main event in the back garden, with a little tour through the house for everyone who showed. She had the invitations printed on expensive vellum with a pearlescent backing.

She'd spared no expense to pull this off. But with her savings gone, her checking at an all-time low, and her credit wrecked by John, to get what they needed they'd had to leverage Eustace's good name, and even better FICO score—though her sister had lost everything in her battle against cancer, unlike Cordelia she'd been able to pay every fee, down to the last dime.

With the party and the signing on the horizon, however, their financial woes would be over soon enough. Arkin was due any day with the new set of papers for them to sign. In fact, she'd expected him already, but with so much to do for the party, Cordelia didn't have time to chase the young man down. She'd thrown their plans into overdrive, setting the event date for just under a week away and expediting all the shipping. She'd even texted Busy Mazzello to tell him she would have his money by week's end. His response came swiftly—See you Sunday. The thought of a carful of gangsters pulling up beside the Japanese cedars was enough to give her the sweats, but they'd be signing in three days' time. And then it would all be over.

After toiling in the house and garden each day, Cordelia would slink off to the carriage house at night to feel Gordon's body ripple under hers, hard and insatiable, and to drink in the smell and feel of him. Sometimes they would talk for long hours into the night. Though it had been a challenge at first, Gordon said, the people of Bellwick were coming around to the idea of a party at the estate. Not much happened around their sleepy little town, and most folks were nearly as curious about the Bones and their property as they were afraid.

But everything went sideways one morning early in the week. She woke with her body delightfully sore from the night before. Untwisting her long limbs from the sheets of Gordon's bed, she kissed him on the cheek and tiptoed down the stairs to the kitchen, where she filled the French press with fresh coffee grounds and heated some water on the stove.

Looking for the little spoon he kept in the sugar dish, Cordelia quietly rifled through several kitchen drawers. When she didn't find it, she pulled his cookbook stand away from the backsplash, wondering if it had dropped behind there. She was imagining him trying to perfect his grandmother's recipe for borscht when she noticed the little notebook tucked behind a much larger cookbook. She'd seen him with it when she came over with the ledger. She wondered now if it was where he kept notes on his favorite dishes.

Pulling it out, she spread it open on the counter, expecting to find handwritten recipes, maybe even some of his original plans for the carriage house. Instead, it was full of dated entries, jotted words and phrases all about her aunt, his mom, and the estate.

July 1: Togers shows up unannounced. Why?

September 1: The White Lady surprises me by the barn, tells me to expect a storm, move all equipment to the shed.

October 10: I walked the western woods again. Found nothing. Why was she there? What was she running from?

Cordelia swallowed and flipped back a few pages. Scribbled words covered both sides. In the center, circled many times in black ink, was written, *Beware the pair. Beware the heir.* Beneath that, Gordon had asked simply, *Who?*

The someone his mother had obsessively feared. Not one person, but two.

She was scared to see more. And unable to turn away. Then, she found this entry: *The White Lady has a niece. Correction—a pair of nieces.*

Suddenly, she didn't like the way he kept referring to their aunt as *The White Lady.* At first, she'd thought it a term of endearment, but now it struck her quite differently. As though Augusta was a thing he didn't trust, maybe didn't see as human.

Flipping forward again, Cordelia found an entry corresponding to the date of their arrival. *They're here,* it read plainly. *BEWARE.*

He'd been keeping notes on them all this time. He'd been keeping notes on everyone.

"I can explain," she heard him say from behind.

Cordelia nearly jumped out of her skin. "Now who's sneaking up on people?" she snapped.

He took a tentative step in her direction.

"Who are you?" she asked, voice low and taut. "Who are you really, Gordon Jablonski?"

He placed a hand to his bare chest. "I'm exactly who you think I am," he told her. "Nothing has changed."

She held the book up. "What is this? Are you some kind of reporter or private investigator? What is this?!" The walls of the carriage house shook threateningly at the sound of her voice, and a stiff wind kicked up outside, beating at the windows and glass doors.

"It's nothing like that," he told her, glancing around.

"I'm waiting," she said, refusing to set the book down.

"I told you about my mom, how she wasn't right before she died. All of that was true. I came here looking for answers about what happened to her," he began, holding both hands out.

"You failed to mention this," she spat, wiggling the book at him.

"I know. At first, I didn't know what to think of you. Things had changed so rapidly after I got here. And then suddenly she was gone, and here you and your sister came. As I got to know you, I wanted to say more, but I wasn't sure how. Not without looking and sounding like a creep."

She pointed to the open page. "What does this mean—*Beware the pair*? What do you think I am? Are you sleeping with me so you can learn the family secrets? Because I've got news for you—we're just as in the dark as you are."

He shook his head. "No, Cordelia. You have to believe me. I would never do that. I know what you are. Okay? And I love you for it."

"Bullshit," she raged. "Tell me what it means!" The walls rumbled again, and one of the doors blew open.

Gordon rushed to close it. "It's something she kept saying before she died. It was the last thing my mother ever said to me. I wrote it down because I know it's at the heart of her death. Something was chasing her through those woods. Something did that to her. And I want to know who, and why. Wouldn't you?"

"That's us then? *The pair?* You think Eustace and I did that to your mother?" Cordelia wanted to hurl the book at him. She'd already been married to one liar; she was not about to go down that road again. Whatever his reasons, this was inexcusable.

Gordon slapped his chest. "Of course not. But I'll admit, at first I wasn't sure. Nothing here makes sense. Except you."

"Don't do that," she warned, eyes blinking with fury. "Do not patronize me. I will not be toyed with!"

He dropped his hands to his hips and looked away. "What do you want me to say? I should have told you the second we started sleeping together. But it's only been a few days, Cordelia. I didn't want to scare you away. I was working up to it."

"Too late," she told him, shaking with rage and disappointment.

"Can we talk about this calmly please? It's not like I'm the only one keeping secrets around here."

She glared at him. "What is that supposed to mean?"

Gordon scoffed. "Do you seriously think I don't see what's going on with you and your sister? Do you think I don't notice? The tree, the rain, that earthquake the other day? You walk around here like you expect to get ambushed at any moment. You let yourself into my house in the middle of the night. I took you off the property *one* time and you passed out. First your aunt living here like a recluse, now you and your sister refusing to leave. And those runes that keep showing up?"

"So, tell me, what does it all mean?" she demanded. "Because we sure as hell don't know!"

He narrowed his eyes. "You know a hell of a lot more than you're saying."

"I think you should leave," Cordelia told him, her jaw so tense she practically chipped a tooth on the words. "I don't know you, and regardless of what you think, you don't know me. And we should keep it that way."

He threw his hands up. "Fine. I'll go as soon as the party is over."

She shook her head. "No. I want you gone before noon. Pack your shit and don't come back." She narrowed her eyes into dangerous slits. "You know what I'm capable of if you do."

His mouth hung open. "But-but the party! Cordelia, please. Don't do this. It's not safe."

"We have it under control. We don't need you, Gordon." She glared at him.

"Let me help you," he tried again, lowering his voice, softening his features. He reached for her arm.

She pulled away. "You can't help me," she said coldly. "You're not one of us."

His face fell. "You and your sister can't walk into that alone."

"Watch us," she said, turning for the door.

CHAPTER TWENTY-FIVE

THE TOOTH

CORDELIA SLAMMED THE front door so hard it nearly fell off its hinges.

Her sister emerged from the library with a puzzled expression. "Something wrong?"

"Everything!" she spat, heading straight for the dining room and its well-stocked bar. This time, she didn't even bother with a glass. She just unscrewed the top of the brandy bottle and took a large swallow.

Eustace watched from the doorway. "Lovers' quarrel?"

"Not anymore," she said, panting out the liquor's heat.

"You always do this," Eustace told her. "Push them away. Every time you start to really fall for somebody, you pick a fight. That's how I knew John wasn't right for you. You never challenged him because you never let him get close to your heart."

"I do not," Cordelia argued.

"Do so," her sister countered.

"Do not," Cordelia insisted. "And he started it."

"Well, when you two work it out, send him in. I want him to taste the madeleines I'm planning to make for the party. I'm dipping them in a light champagne icing and sprinkling them with candied orange peels."

"He's not coming," Cordelia told her stubbornly.

Eustace backed up as Cordelia moved through to the hall and then the library, plopping herself on a sofa. She scurried behind her sister, aghast. "What do you mean he's not coming? Cordelia, what have you done?"

"It's not what I did. It's what he did! We don't need him anyway."

"Yes, we do," her sister argued. "Very much so. He has to come."

"Well, he can't," she said, taking another swig of booze. "He's leaving—left. He's gone."

"Stop him!" Eustace shouted at her. "Get him back here. Whatever it takes."

"It's too late for that." Cordelia set the bottle on a nearby table. "We just have to do this on our own."

Her sister shook her head. "Cordelia, in three days' time we are luring our nemesis to this very house under the guise of a party where we will be surrounded by people who despise us, with no protection whatsoever. That gigantic bruiser of a man was all that was standing between us and the person who has been picking our family off like sitting ducks. Possibly for generations! And you just sent him packing? Why?"

Cordelia covered her face with both hands. She would not cry. "I don't want to talk about this now. Can't we just forget him and move on?"

Eustace made an exasperated sound. "We'll deal with Gordon later. Maybe I can find him and talk some sense into him after he's cooled down. Right now, I have something to show you." She motioned for Cordelia to follow her to the desk in the study.

Cordelia skulked after her sister like a dog with its tail between its legs, dragging the brandy bottle with her. On the desk, the therimoire was splayed open.

Eustace pulled the bottle from Cordelia's hand and set it on the desk. "You cannot go to pieces on me right now, Cordelia Hazel Bone."

"Okay, okay." Cordelia crossed her arms. "What do you want to show me? I'm listening."

Eustace's eyes lit up like the sun had risen behind them. She picked up a small pouch that Cordelia recognized but couldn't place and reached inside. "This," she said, pulling something out and dropping it.

Cordelia bent over and saw that it was one of the carved teeth they'd discovered in the basement—the rune stones. It landed facedown on the book's open pages and then quickly righted itself. Her eyes widened. "Did I just see that?"

Eustace nodded emphatically.

"Do it again," she said.

Her sister snatched up the tooth and dropped it again. This time it rolled off the pages onto the desk, once more righting itself after it had stopped.

"Do they all do this?" Cordelia asked.

"Not all at once, but yes. Watch." She turned the whole sack over this time and the rest of the teeth fell out, rolling here and there before they all eventually stopped. Several landed faceup, but of those, a few turned themselves over after they had stopped moving. And of the ones that fell facedown, three turned over to face them just as the first one had.

"Are they supposed to do that?" Cordelia asked, amazed.

Eustace shook her head. "Usually someone just reads them however they land. These are different, *special*. It was so dark down there that day we found them and I dropped a bunch on the floor, we must not have noticed if any of them turned over."

Cordelia studied the teeth whose runes were exposed. "What do they mean?"

Eustace leaned closer. "This one here is the symbol for *man* or *friendship*," she said. "Or in some cases it can mean *cooperation*."

Cordelia looked at the weird little *M* with a bow tie on top.

"And this one means *water*," Eustace said. "But it can also mean *intuition* or *dreams* or *fears*."

"It's not a very precise method, is it?"

Eustace shrugged. "Divination is more art than science."

Cordelia pointed to another with two bent lines facing off. Whereas the first two Eustace had explained were close together, this one had landed far from those and stood alone. "What's this one?"

She bent low to examine it. "It represents time and cycles— the polarity and dance of nature, give and take, push and pull. It can mean *change* or *completion*."

"Why is it way over here?" Cordelia asked. "The first two are right next to each other."

Eustace bit her bottom lip. "I couldn't say."

Cordelia moved her finger to one with an arrow carved into it.

"*Battle*," Eustace answered automatically. "Or *justice*. The fight for what's fair."

"And this?" Cordelia asked about the final tooth, its sideways symbol open on one side.

"*Fate*," Eustace told her. "And *secrets*. Something deeper than what's on the surface."

Cordelia closed her eyes, letting the runes spin behind them. It was clear they were trying to get a message across. But *what*?

"These first two, if taken together, plus the third one, could mean the end of a friendship," Eustace supplied, as if reading her sister's mind. "An instinct about someone that proves to be true."

Cordelia opened her eyes and stared at her sister. "You're good at this," she said. Reconsidering the last two, she added, "Maybe these indicate a showdown with the person, something about them that will be revealed."

Eustace nodded. "Makes sense. But why tell us this now? And who are they talking about?"

Cordelia sucked in, violently aware. "Gordon," she whispered. "That's exactly what happened today." She filled Eustace in on finding his notebook and the argument that ensued.

"Perhaps," Eustace conceded, reserving a bit of doubt.

"Perhaps?" Cordelia gave her sister a hard stare. "He's not what he seems. You always tell me my picker is broken, and then that notebook just falls into my lap and lo and behold, he's a creep!"

Eustace narrowed her eyes. "I thought you took the notebook from its hiding place after snooping through his kitchen."

"Semantics," she responded acerbically.

"Why would they go to all the trouble to tell us this after it's already happened?" Eustace put to her.

She shrugged. "Confirmation. They're letting us know I was right to send him away."

But Eustace didn't look convinced. "What if they're talking about someone who will be at the party?"

"You don't think he'll show up, do you?" Cordelia asked, half-hopeful and half-disgusted at herself. "After I expressly forbid him to?"

Eustace sighed. "I don't know. This just feels like it could be a warning rather than a confirmation. Maybe we should cancel, especially since you just fired the bodyguard."

Cordelia dragged a hand down her face. "And say what? *Just kidding? Practical joke?* Everyone in Bellwick will hate us even more than they already do. This is our chance to figure out who's behind those threats. Gordon or no Gordon."

Eustace started to scoop up the teeth and return them to the bag. After a minute, her face twisted with confusion. Her lips started moving as she mumbled to herself.

"What is it?" Cordelia asked her.

"There are only twenty-two runes here in total," she said, looking up.

"How many should there be?" Cordelia asked.

"Twenty-four," Eustace replied, putting the last few in the bag.

Suddenly, Cordelia's memory in the crypt came into blistering focus, and then another followed of their first day arriving at the estate. "Wait here!"

She charged across the stair hall into the parlor and pulled open the drawer of the lacquered table. There, she found the tooth resting beneath the deck of cards where she'd left it. The rune carved into it was blackened from years of dirt; it looked like a diamond with legs. She held it to her. Something beat in this ancient incisor, yellow at the root like summer squash. Something Cordelia wanted to understand. She'd felt it when she'd first laid eyes on it that day, and she could feel it now.

An idea began to form in her mind. She made her way back to Eustace. When she reached the desk, she placed it on the wood.

Eustace picked it up. "You kept one?"

"I found this in a drawer the day we came here," she admitted. "I was drawn to it. But then it started acting strange, wiggling or vibrating in place. I got scared, and left it there and closed the drawer, then forgot all about it until we were at the crypt."

Eustace reached out slowly and laid a finger on the incisor, then picked it up when it didn't respond. Holding it, she studied the inscription up close. "Othala. *Possession*. It also means *inheritance*."

The irony was not lost on Cordelia. "Which one is missing then?"

"Missing?"

"You said there were twenty-two but there should be twenty-four. This one brings it to twenty-three. One is still missing."

Eustace inhaled deeply. She pulled the teeth out one by one, checking their inscriptions. When she'd at last considered them all, she put them back and met her sister's eyes. "*Algiz*," she told Cordelia. "*Protection*."

Cordelia's suspicion grew. "Like Mom's tattoo."

Eustace nodded.

"Could it still be down there in the basement room? Could we have overlooked it when we were picking them up that day?"

Eustace opened a desk drawer and pulled out a large chrome flashlight. "I'm game to check."

Together, they crept down the tight staircase into the darkness, the beam from the flashlight cutting through it with brilliant precision. They didn't waste time looking around, but made their way straight to the little room, last on the left. Eustace sat the flashlight upright on the table against the far wall, pushing some picks and scrapers over to make room. The light bounced off the ceiling and rained back down, creating a dull circle of visibility. Both sisters scoured the dusty floor on hands and knees, but came up short.

"It's not here," Eustace said. "We'd have found it by now."

"I thought that might be the case," Cordelia told her, standing up and dusting herself off. "These teeth are different than everything else in this house. I could feel it that very first day. They're powerful, and they're *old*. That's why she took one."

"What are you saying?" Eustace asked her.

Cordelia grabbed her wrists. "*This* is what Mom took. One of these teeth. A very particular one. That's what allowed her to leave and stay alive away from the estate, for a time at least." She gripped her sister's hand containing the pouch. "These are the charms."

Eustace looked down at the open bag of teeth she was cupping in her hands. "Of course," she said, eyes rounding. "But where did she keep it? And why the tattoo?"

Cordelia shook her head, releasing her sister's hands. "She must have kept it close somehow. I don't know how it all ties together, I just know this is it."

Eustace frowned. "Well, it's gone now. Who knows what she

did with it?" She started pacing the odd little room. "We're missing something. I can feel it. It's like it's right in front of our faces and we're just not seeing it."

Across the room from them, a skinny bone the length of Cordelia's hand—the humerus of some animal—clattered in its place on the shelf and dropped to the floor.

She ran over to pick it up. Staring at Eustace, she fumbled for the truth.

Her sister picked up the flashlight to shine it Cordelia's way. On the shelves behind her, the bones glowed softly white. One by one, they each began to rattle, rolling across the shelves and bumping into one another, then clattering to the floor.

"Are you seeing what I'm seeing?" Eustace asked her.

Cordelia spun around and backed away from the shelf until she was at her sister's side, the humerus still in her hand.

"The bones," Eustace whispered, taking the humerus from her, starting for the corridor and the stairs. "Follow me!"

Cordelia rushed up the staircase behind her and pushed the bookshelf closed. The bones had gone quiet again.

In the study, Eustace laid the humerus next to the therimoire. "Look at the shape," she said. "This is what we think of when we think of bones. This long, tapered pillar that swells at each end, then branches into joints and connections with smaller bones."

"True," Cordelia said. "But what's your point?"

Eustace pointed to the journal. "It's kind of like the rune I was showing you, isn't it? And what better depiction of life *and* death? What if they're adding bone to all their spells and potions? What if that's their secret ingredient? It would explain the stockpile down there."

"The oven," Cordelia whispered, going pale. "In the basement room. They must burn them. It's the only way to get a fire hot enough." She took a step back from the desk. "Eustace . . . Our name. Are we Bone witches? Or are we *bone* witches?"

Eustace stared past her, eyes unfocused as her mind wheeled.

"I thought you said our name was French?" Cordelia reminded her.

"I thought it was," she said. "But it must be occupational, given as a result of what someone did in the community, or who they were. Like the surname *Smith* meaning someone was a blacksmith. They could have given our family the name *Bon* in Normandy because we were nice or . . ."

"Or?"

Eustace looked at her, snapping out of her distant stare. "Or we picked it up somewhere else along the way. *Bone* because of . . ." She grabbed the book and stared at it.

"So, which are we?" Cordelia asked her again. "The Bone witches or *bone* witches?"

"Both."

CORDELIA'S FINGERS STARTED itching—someone was soon to call. She buried them in her fists, surprised when the doorbell rang instead of her phone. "If that's Gordon, I don't want to see him."

Eustace frowned at her. "I'm not playing your games." She headed for the hall, and Cordelia quickly followed.

As she passed from the library toward the vestibule, Cordelia saw a shadow shift above her and knew that Morna was restless. The bracelet around her wrist suddenly felt heavier, and she closed a hand over it, disturbed.

Reaching the front door, Eustace opened it to the lanky form of Bennett Togers, his back to her as he looked out over the front lawn. "Mr. Togers," she said with a forced smile. "How nice of you to drop by. Did you bring the paperwork?"

Cordelia crumpled with relief—she wasn't ready for another showdown with Gordon. But she also felt a terrible pang, thinking he was well and truly gone. Her sister hadn't seemed nearly so upset as she by his secret notebook, a fact which left Cordelia feeling temperamental and impetuous, like a sullen child who's overreacted. But she couldn't shake the resentment she felt at being studied without her knowledge, or the sharp slice of betrayal at having it come from someone she trusted just when she was learning to truly open her heart.

Bennett turned to her and smiled wanly, stepping inside, a parcel of papers clutched to his chest. "I had other plans this afternoon, until one of your invitations fell into my lap. I believe you have them spread across town."

Eustace closed the door behind him and gestured to the parlor, but he turned promptly toward the library, settling himself against the back of the worn leather sofa. Both sisters followed him as far as the doorway.

"Is there a problem?" Cordelia asked.

"I left messages," Eustace told him. "We had every intention of inviting you. You're kind of the guest of honor, in fact."

He gave them a singularly patient look, as though they were children he had to explain things to. "As you are well aware, the estate is in legal limbo at the moment, as neither of you have officially taken up residence here and signed the paperwork to begin receiving your inheritance."

Cordelia coughed, the brandy still burning her throat. "But that's the whole point," she told him. "To sign. It's a celebration!"

Bennett scowled. "I saw something of the sort on the invitation. Then you are decided?"

"Of course we are," Eustace declared. "That's why I've been calling. We just wanted to make it official with all our new friends." She eyed Cordelia over her shoulder.

"Right," Cordelia chimed in. "We thought it would help our reputation in town to share the good news with everyone. We were going to really make a spectacle of it, bring you up in front of the whole town and sign it all together."

Bennett's scowl only deepened, causing his forehead to crease like paper. "Under the circumstances and as the estate's attorney, I must advise against this. I feel it is my duty to let you know that you would be taking on an immense amount of personal liability should something go wrong."

Cordelia crossed her arms, reminding herself the man was only doing his job; he would be a rather poor attorney if he didn't counsel them against it. But she was determined to have this party and learn more about the person who'd been sending them threats. Of course, she couldn't explain all that to Mr. Togers. "We could sign now if it made you feel better, do the bit at the party for show."

He cleared his throat multiple times, overcome with a sudden attack of phlegm, and cocked an eyebrow at them. "It appears I cannot talk you out of this. In which case, I will attend so that I may personally oversee the safety of the estate and its possessions."

Eustace smiled and patted his arm. "Your warning has been duly noted, and your work here is done. Any and all responsibility is on our heads, not yours. We'll see you in three days' time." Taking him by the elbow, she led him back to the front door. "You can rest assured that we will take great care before and during the event."

He stiffened at being suddenly and discourteously escorted out.

At the vestibule, Eustace plied the paperwork from him, then opened the door and stood aside. "My sister and I greatly appreciate your concern. You have proven yourself to be an excellent steward of our family's assets."

Bennett smiled coolly. "I pride myself on my service to this family."

"Of course you do," she told him.

"Mr. Togers?" Cordelia called, before he could depart. "I was rather hoping Arkin could make himself available to help with parking the night of the party. You did say he was at our disposal. Gordon has departed us, I'm afraid."

Bennett smoothed out his suit jacket and lifted his chin before stepping into the vestibule. "As you wish."

"Oh! And Mr. Togers!" she called again as he stepped onto the front porch.

"Please, Ms. Bone," he expressed with some exasperation. "Call me Bennett."

"Yes, Bennett. We do hope you'll come. There is a special surprise planned for the end." She dared not tell him what, considering his liability speech.

"Impertinent," she heard him mutter.

"What was that?" Eustace asked.

Staring them both down from the porch, he frowned. "This is not how things are done at Bone Hill."

To which Eustace gave him her sweetest smile. "Perhaps it's time for a change."

CHAPTER TWENTY-SIX

The Spell

CORDELIA PULLED ON her rubber boots and headed into the dawn. The party was tonight, and she wanted to get an early start on setup. It was still half-dark in the garden, with bands of purple, gold, and blue on the horizon. The birds were just beginning their morning song. Lulled by the subtle beauty, she walked to the promenade, where she spotted a cottontail near a patch of clover. The morning was peaceful and cool, a departure from the heat and turmoil she carried inside.

These last few days without Gordon made her feel like she were walking around without one of her vital organs. Something essential was missing. She questioned the way she'd reacted. Were roles reversed, she couldn't imagine how things might appear; that he'd trusted her at all was astonishing. But then she would circle back around to the possibility that he'd pretended to trust her in order to win her trust, and learn more from her. And the empty, discarded feeling of being used would return.

She wrapped her pink silk robe tighter at the waist and blinked back the threat of tears. She told herself the feeling would pass. She'd only known the man a month, after all. But her heart didn't buy it.

Closing her eyes, she called to the magic within her, feeling it stir in her core and unfold into her limbs, like warm sap rising to the surface. Her feet anchored her to the soil that was her protector as she breathed deeply, inhaling the beauty of this place like a favorite fragrance. For a moment, she felt whole, as if nothing and no one existed but her and the ground and the sky. She reached deep into herself, probing for this newfound truth. *I am a witch,* she thought, confidence holding. "I *am* a witch."

And then something flickered like a dying bulb, the course of power within her snagged and broke, retreating to a secret place. She stumbled, losing her balance, and just caught herself, knowing that it was in the hole in her heart—the one Gordon left behind—where her power was faltering.

Cordelia stared at the ground and sighed.

When she looked up again, she saw a woman in the distance. A fine mist stewed over the grasses, swirling around her skirts. Her hair was long and yellow-white, pulled back beneath a hooded cloak rich with fur trim, but hanging heavy over her shoulders. Layers of strung beads draped across her chest, her dress a brilliant blue trimmed in red. A brightly embroidered belt shot with gold thread wrapped her waist, hung with hide sacks. And she carried a tall staff with brass fittings that moved with her as she walked. The woman stood looking at Cordelia before slowly walking away, disappearing under the cherry trees.

"Hey!" Cordelia called as she began to gather her senses. "This is private property!"

But the woman just kept walking, obscured by the shifting hues of her cloak.

Cordelia wondered if this was the person her sister had seen—this older woman in strange dress, with her crooked staff that seemed to pull at Cordelia's mind and heart in a way she didn't understand. Maybe Eustace had been wrong about it being a man. It had been dark, after all, and she said herself she could make out very little. But how could a woman of this age outrun a nimble fox?

She tore across the grass toward the stranger, but as she crossed the halfway point of the promenade, she knew she'd lost her. Slowing, she kept on in the same direction, her ribs aching and her mouth dry, until she came face-to-face with the tomb. The mists parted and the iron gates stood open and the roses held their maddening color. The sun broke over the crest of the hill and spilled its blinding light across her.

"If you're in there, you need to come out," she called, shielding her eyes. "I've already seen you! And you're trespassing."

The wind stirred in the trees and the mouth of the crypt yawned open and silent. Cordelia took a step forward. "I'm serious," she said, a little louder. "If you come out now, we can talk. But if you don't, I'm going to go back to the house and call the police!"

No response.

She stepped to the doorway and peered in. "You can't hide in here," she said, trying to stand her ground. She looked around, but the crypt was empty. Her mother's box gleamed from the back, but even the shadows were flat and quiet, unable to hide an entire person.

Cordelia wrapped her arms around herself. The woman must have changed course, vanishing into the trees behind the hill. Or maybe she'd been a mirage, conjured by the mist and morning light.

She turned to go.

When the knock sounded—just like she'd heard that night with her sister, pounding from behind the stones of the back wall—she didn't stop or turn around. She ran all the way back to the house, losing the tie of her robe along the way.

CORDELIA HAD ALL but forgotten about her encounter of that morning. It was evening and she'd had a full day of setting up tables and chairs, stringing lights, and arranging things just so. It left little room for musing over recent troubles, including Gordon and the woman on the promenade. The busyness did her heart good, and she was glad for the distraction. Focusing on a doable task was far more satisfying than racking her brain with unsolvable mysteries.

The garden was too full for a large cluster of furniture, even with Eustace's recent attempts at pruning, so Cordelia worked each table and set of chairs into a nearby bed, stringing them along to draw the guests around every bend. The overall effect was pure enchantment—a banquet fit for a fairy procession, a magical winding landscape of secret niches and undiscovered beauty, every corner presenting another treasure. In the fading light, the rich colors seemed to luminesce, alive with their own luster, and everything twinkled under a canopy of newly installed garden lights. Cordelia had even sprung for a stone statue to be shipped overnight. The *Queen of Seasons,* she was called, and she was displayed where she could be seen from the solarium, by the small camera Gordon had hidden there.

The house took on a *Come hither* quality, its angles softening and its colors brightening. A splendid palace carved out of time, an American fairy tale. The tower loomed over all, its windows shining like a lighthouse in a dark harbor.

Cordelia stood back and looked up. She couldn't have achieved this with just simple pruning and good lighting. It was as if they were infecting Bone Hill, she and Eustace, their vision creeping into its crannies, making it their own. And something about that delighted her. She suddenly couldn't imagine ever leaving this behind.

Her sister burst through the door of the solarium, a rich green dress wrapped around her body. Her elaborate curls spiraled in dazzling silver and ebony rings. Even little Marvel had a lavender bow around her neck.

"You've outdone yourself!" Eustace exclaimed. "I don't recognize the place."

Cordelia clapped her hands together. "It's pretty good, isn't it?"

"It's magnificent," Eustace raved. "If this doesn't win Bellwick over, nothing will."

Cordelia swelled with pride. She couldn't help noticing how radiant Eustace was. This place had given her back her health, and Cordelia loved it for that alone. "You look divine."

Eustace gave a little twirl. All around her the shrubs erupted with additional blooms. "Did I do that?" she asked with a look of surprise.

"I think we're only just discovering what you can do," Cordelia said with awe. Her own party dress was printed with bright poppies and tied behind the neck, leaving her shoulders bare. A long ruffle at the hem gave it bucolic flair.

"You make this place look good," Eustace told her.

She started to smile, but it faltered on her lips. She choked on a sob and turned her face away.

"Honey, what is it?" her sister asked, concerned.

"I'm fine," she insisted, pushing the emotion back down. "It's stupid."

"Why don't you just text him?"

"I can't," Cordelia said for the fiftieth time, though she'd never been able to adequately explain why. A tiny flare of pain beat behind her right temple, but she chose to ignore it.

Her sister inhaled deeply and pinched her lips. "Stubborn as the day is long. Such a shame. He's the first good apple you've ever picked."

"Whatever he was, he's gone now," she said with finality. "And whatever it looks like, tonight is not about a party." She turned to Eustace. "Are you ready for this?"

"Almost," her sister answered. "Come with me. We have just enough time before the guests arrive."

"For what?" Cordelia paused when they reached the bookshelf door, already waiting open. "We'll get all dirty," she stalled.

"Where else are we going to cast the spell?" her sister said with an eye roll.

She followed Eustace onto the stairs. "*Spell?* What spell?"

"Follow me and I'll show you," her sister called up to her, rounding the corner toward the little room.

With a huff of exasperation, Cordelia did as she was told. As she neared the room, she heard the dull clank of wood against iron and felt a wave of dry heat. She stepped inside. Eustace had a lantern burning in the corner. She loaded more wood into the stove under a stainless-steel tray of something black and misshapen. She closed the oven door and moved a circular range on top to squirt in a stream of lighter fluid. Flames leapt through the hole, licking high into the air, and Eustace stepped back until they settled again.

"I've been cooking these for a while already. They're nearly ready." On the table beside her, the therimoire lay open.

"Cooking what?" Cordelia asked, noting a scent like burnt corn.

"Bone," she said matter-of-factly. "We can't do the spell without it."

Cordelia cringed. "We couldn't have been chocolate witches?"

Her sister laughed, but Cordelia noticed the slight tremble in her hands, the way her lips had gone pale. She regretted more than ever her decision to send Gordon away, if only for Eustace's peace of mind.

"There's a spell," Eustace told her, pointing to the book, "for added protection. It's like a blessing or an anointing. I've spent the last few days translating it."

Cordelia pressed her lips together. "You're nervous. I get that—" she started.

Eustace rounded on her. "I'm not nervous, Cordy. I'm terrified.

Whoever carved our mother up like a pumpkin, they were *here*. In *our* home. They want to do the same to us. Or worse. And now we're holding open the door, inviting them in. We could be inviting our death tonight."

"I'm sorry." Cordelia swallowed. She believed they were doing the right thing to try to draw their opponent out, but she hadn't quite allowed herself to face the gravity of it. Eustace clearly had. She pointed to the open book. "This will help?"

Eustace nodded slowly. "I think. In any case, it's all we've got."

Cordelia drew a deep breath. "I'm in."

"Good." Her sister pointed to a slew of odd ingredients already on the table. "Let's mix these up first—goose fat, elderberries, and the seeds of something called red orache, which I found in the solarium. I hope you don't mind—I took this from your room." She held up a small silver hand mirror. Finally, she picked up a sharpened twig. "Switch of an ash tree," she told Cordelia.

"What's that for?" Cordelia asked, a little concerned.

"You'll see," she told her, as she began crushing the fat, berries, and seeds together. "I looked into that word you mentioned—the one you heard upstairs. The one in our aunt's letter."

"And?" Cordelia stepped closer, curious.

Eustace sat the pestle down on the table. "*Volva* means *seeress* in Old Norse, a kind of Viking witch. They practiced *Seidr*, an old form of magic that means *to bind*. They traveled from place to place giving prophecies, casting spells, healing the sick, bestowing blessings and curses, speaking to the dead. They were revered but also feared. Even the gods respected them."

"The dead?" Cordelia placed a hand to her throat, the silver bracelet catching the firelight.

"That bracelet," Eustace added. "I told you the ends were different. This webbed style, like a duck's foot, was only found in the jewelry of *volvas*. Several burial sites have been unearthed throughout Scandinavia. They were entombed with great ceremony."

She carefully drew the steel tray from the fire with a pair of long tongs, dropping the bones into the mortar and grinding. "We must be descended from these women, and the gifts have continued to pass down. Though *how* I couldn't say. *Seidr* isn't exactly a common practice anymore, even in Nordic countries. It's been all but forgotten."

When the concoction had become a gritty, dark purple paste, Eustace stopped mixing. "There's one other thing they did," she told Cordelia as she picked up the ash twig. "They sang."

Eustace dipped the end of the twig into the mixture and swirled it around. "They sang to put themselves into a trance. They sang to call the spirits of the dead, who would answer questions and tell them things no one else knew. They sang to bind, to make their magic. And now it's our turn."

Cordelia swallowed. "Our turn?"

"The spell instructs us to sing as we draw on the bind runes. But I have no idea what." She raised the pointed end of the twig to Cordelia's face. "Be still. Only your lips are allowed to move."

Cordelia leaned back. "Why do I have to do the singing part?"

"Because you're the ghost whisperer, dummy. Besides, I made the potion." Eustace let the tip of the stick hover just over Cordelia's skin, between her eyes. "I'm waiting," she said after a long minute.

Cordelia racked her brain. "I don't know any songs. Mom gave me her music aversion, remember?"

Her sister frowned. "Surely you've heard something you can remember in a store or someone's car? We're running out of time."

Cordelia closed her eyes and tried to conjure a tune from her subconscious. After a minute she opened her mouth and uttered the only words that came, "*Rock on, Gold Dust Woman . . .*"

It came out unsteady and off-key, more of a warble than the throaty vibrato Stevie Nicks was known for. But it was the best she had under the circumstances.

Eustace raised one eyebrow in question.

Cordelia carried on, her husky rendition of "Gold Dust Woman" gaining volume as she continued.

"You do know this song is about cocaine, don't you?" Eustace said, but she twirled the stick in the paste again, and brought it out, one end gleaming violet against the bark. As she laid the tip against Cordelia's forehead, drawing out a thick line, Cordelia kept singing. Eventually Eustace's voice joined hers.

Together they sang verse after verse as Eustace painted the runes across Cordelia's cheeks and forehead, down her throat and arms. Partway through, Cordelia opened her eyes. The black wall behind them glowed faintly where their two names had been drawn, an inner fire igniting the letters. One by one, each name came to life in the darkness, catching the light, pulsing with power and the quaver of her voice, as if their ancestors were arriving one at a time, gathering at the sound of her song. Glancing down, she saw that the runes around the floor did the same, as well as the ones Eustace had drawn across her skin.

When she finished, Eustace held up the mirror so Cordelia could see how the runes were drawn and carefully copy them onto herself, making sure to remember they were backward in the reflection. More than once, Cordelia's eyes met her sister's as the song rose between them, their throats and hearts strengthening with every stroke. What felt silly and out of place at first now was full of energy and intention. Her tone-deaf warble had found courage and conviction and rang through the room with clarity and accuracy alongside her sister's. When the last rune was drawn, Cordelia set the stick down, and she and Eustace sang the final line together—"*Is it over now? Do you know how to pick up the pieces and go home?*"

The glow of the writing on the wall faded slowly, the runes on the floor flattened to black again, and the purplish ones they'd drawn across each other dulled, eventually disappearing altogether.

Eustace looked at her sister. "It's time."

Cordelia's fingers ached. "Someone's here."

CHAPTER TWENTY-SEVEN

THE PARTY

D ON'T GO OUT there," Cordelia whispered, grabbing her sister's hand. She stepped next to Eustace in the vestibule. In a matter of minutes, their home would be crawling with guests: a slew of semi-hostile strangers who wanted them off this land, and one murderer who was stalking them outright. She suddenly wasn't sure if she wanted Eustace to open that door.

"We'll go together," Eustace said, and Cordelia nodded, taking a deep, stabilizing breath.

They swung the door wide to find Arkin parking the old Mercedes. "My uncle sent me to help valet," he called to them shyly.

Cordelia smiled with relief. "It's good to see you again," she told him, even though she didn't exactly mean it. He'd been so looming and peculiar before, like he was a starving man and she a steak. But tonight, he was back to his usual state of idiosyncrasy—painfully unsociable, all arms and legs, few words, less chin. She was beginning to feel sorry for him.

He gave her a quizzical look, lumbering near the car, gawky and graceless.

"You were here the other day with your uncle," she reminded him. Surely he hadn't forgotten. He'd startled her so. "You surprised me on the third story?"

"Right," he said, cutting his eyes away. "Sorry. *Again*."

She waved it off. "Just glad you're back. Be sure to arrange the cars in rows across the lawn. And leave enough space for them to pull out, or it will be madness when everyone goes to leave."

He nodded once more, eyes cast to the ground.

"Have you ever done this before?" Cordelia asked him. His self-doubt was practically palpable. She was beginning to worry that she should have hired a service.

"Cordy, leave the poor boy alone," Eustace said, tugging at her shoulder. "He can park a car, for Christ's sake."

Arkin smiled tightly in their direction.

"We'll leave you to it then," Cordelia said as they went back inside. Once the door was closed, she asked Eustace, "You don't think . . . I mean, it couldn't have been Arkin you saw that morning? Could it? He is tall. And young. He could be fast. He knows the place."

Her sister laughed dryly. "Are you kidding me? That kid couldn't outrun a snail. He'd be too busy gawking at his own feet. The guy I saw was cocky. An arrogant bastard who knew he had the drop on us. Arkin doesn't know his own shadow from a turd on the ground."

Cordelia shrugged a shoulder and followed Eustace out back. She trusted her sister. When the man came, she believed Eustace would know him. And they had the cameras to pick up any suspicious activity.

The guests trickled in over time, a steady stream of curious busybodies and wide-eyed voyeurs, mouths agape as they marched through the vestibule and stair hall, the elaborate dining room and kitchen, out through the green maze of the solarium and into the twinkling gardens. Cordelia and Eustace took them in turns, escorting them primly from one feature to another, pointing out the house's many exceptional details—the carving of Winter Bone over the parlor door, the inlaid stair hall floor, the stunning stained-glass window over the stairs and its play of light—before releasing them outside, where they gasped with wonder at the labyrinth of flower beds and party tables under a darkening sky.

Cordelia shook so many hands and made so many introductions, she would never remember them all. It was a bigger turnout than they'd expected, and she had to admit that in this, Gordon had played his part well. She recognized a few faces: Gladys from the coffee shop scowled as she climbed the steps to the porch but kept her dark thoughts to herself. And Dr. Mabee brought his plump wife, Rebecca, but sadly could stay only a short while. Bennett Togers sauntered up behind them, face long and expressionless.

"I'm glad you made it," Cordelia told him. "I hope we don't disappoint."

But the attorney didn't smile or make small talk. "I'm here to see to the preservation of the property and the signing of the trust. That is all."

Cordelia grinned anyway as he strode off to find a drink.

By the time their last guest arrived, Cordelia was willing to bet money the town of Bellwick had been emptied out. Wandering bodies milled the gardens like herd animals set to graze. Couples shared benches beside the boxwoods. Even some children scampered across the promenade, their laughter ringing through the hills.

For the most part, they were polite, though they were often slow to take Cordelia's hand. And she noticed the occasional glare from a shadowy alcove of the garden. They kept their words few and their voices clipped, but she could see them relaxing over the course of the night, forgetting where they were. Shoulders rounded as they grew more comfortable, chatter escalated like the chirping of birds, smiles sprung onto their faces. The wine helped. And Cordelia kept it flowing. She'd been sure to order several crates for just that reason.

To her way of thinking, it didn't matter how they showed up; it mattered how they left. If they left easy and happy and ready for a good night's sleep, then they would remember this night—and more important, this *place*—fondly. And perhaps that would erase a little of the skepticism and wariness built into the bedrock of Bellwick. It would be a start, at least.

Even more important, if they let their guard down, it would be easier to detect the person she and Eustace were searching for. Who had been on their property? Who knew their secret? She kept her eyes peeled for someone who looked a little too familiar with the surroundings, a little too comfortable. Someone who didn't goggle at the chandeliers and fine moldings as if they'd never seen them before. Someone who strode with assurance across the polished parquet floors and the soft ryegrass outside. Someone who didn't look as out of place as everyone else.

But so far, she'd come up short. And there'd been little opportunity to pull her sister aside and find out if she'd had better luck. With such an overwhelming turnout, they could have really used Gordon to help corral guests and keep them occupied. Once again, Cordelia doubted her decision to send him away.

Still, the night wasn't a total bust. She'd made a few good connections thanks to the party, including a woman whose aunt told her stories about gatherings held at Bone Hill at the turn of the century: seances and other spiritualist practices that were fashionable then. People purportedly came from all over to attend, and a maid would bring their stories with her into town. Another woman said her grandmother claimed the house had been a den of gamblers and card players, where the wealthy occasionally won but more often lost. "Built their fortune on other's *mis*fortunes," she said blackly. "Cards and dice in the early years. Before that, darker, unspeakable things."

The best was an old man who looked like he could be a hundred if he was a day. He hadn't a hair left on his liver-spotted head, but he was still standing. His father had once been a groundskeeper on the property, filling his children with stories about Morna's natural prowess with the local wildlife and the kindness of Linden's wife, Hyacinth, who often baked treats for the man to take home.

"Sometimes she would send us medicines," he recalled. "Homemade cough syrup—stuff like that. Tasted something awful but worked like a charm. My father said it was Linden who made the medicine, but no one ever believed him."

"I've heard that Morna was troubled," Cordelia told him, nervous the name might conjure the ghost. "Dangerous."

"She was shy," he replied. "Misunderstood by those who didn't know better. They say she jumped," he told her, pointing to the house's tower. "But my father never believed it."

"Didn't he?" Cordelia quickly sipped her wine to conceal her surprise.

"She had a pair of ravens," the man said. "They were like her children. She fed them and talked to them. Ravens live an awful long time in captivity, you know. Smarter than chimps, they are. Something happened to them birds. Something awful. My father would never say what, but Miss Morna wasn't the same after that."

"How terrible," Cordelia said, glancing toward the tower, where the windows were empty, still glowing golden from inside. "She didn't harm them herself?"

The man stuck out a lip and shook his head slowly. "My father said she'd sooner hurt herself than them birds. Didn't have it in her to even swat a fly." He leaned toward Cordelia as he went on. "They set her up with a nurse. Sister to the town solicitor. But poor Morna only got worse in her care." He clutched at Cordelia's arm with a withered, shaky hand. "My father thought it was the nurse that done it."

Cordelia jerked back reflexively. She recalled that the article she read claimed the nurse had been in the tower with Morna that day, presumably to stop her. She spun to stare up at its glinting windows, half expecting to see Morna standing there now, a smudge behind the glass. When she turned back, a woman she didn't know was escorting the old man away.

Her sister slid an arm into hers, sneaking up from the side. "No sign of him yet," she whispered. "But he's here. I know he is. I have a feeling."

Cordelia looked at her, then up to the sky. The light was all but gone. "Come, let's get everyone to the promenade. It's time."

Eustace nodded, and together they made their way through the garden, rounding up guests as they went, ushering them onto the gently rolling mounds and wide-open grass beneath the sprawl of flowering branches. On their way there, Cordelia latched onto Bennett Togers, towing him along in earnest.

A table had been set up under two dogwoods, with a fountain pen and the necessary paperwork, held down by a brass paperweight in the shape of a hand that they'd taken from the study. Cordelia escorted Bennett behind it to stand beside her sister. Raising a silver dinner bell, she rang it loudly until she had everyone's attention. "My sister would like to say a few words," she told the hundreds of eyes blinking at her from the dusk.

Eustace cleared her throat. "It is with great honor that we ask you here tonight to witness the signing of our inheritance with Mr. Togers, steward of our family's estate for many years. When my sister and I first got the call about our aunt Augusta, we came expecting to find a little country house, perhaps a few sentimental heirlooms, and nothing more. You can imagine our shock when we pulled up to this place. The grandeur that is Bone Hill overwhelmed us in the beginning, but after many weeks here, we now know it as home. We missed the opportunity to truly know our family as we might have wished, and that gives us something in common with all of you. It is our great hope that, moving forward, you will share in the special magic that is this place alongside us, and allow us to share in the magic of community with you." She took up the pen and quickly scrawled her name on the final page, handing it then to Cordelia.

Coming around the other side of the table, so that Bennett was sandwiched between them, Cordelia also signed. She held the pen out to the attorney, whose placid mask slipped for a moment, his face suddenly dismayed, even panicky, as if he'd have liked to crawl under the table and escape them. But as soon as she saw the emotion there, it vanished, replaced by his veneer of calm. Taking the pen, he scratched his name onto the page.

"To many years to come!" Eustace finished, raising a glass, and everyone toasted the moment as the sky split with a squealing streak of light that burst into a thousand drops of colored fire.

The first of the fireworks had gone off right on time.

This was Cordelia's secret weapon—a grand show for the end of the night and a way to send them off with something rapturous still burning through their minds. A crew of three was on the far side of the promenade. They'd been setting up for the last couple of hours. But having failed to tell Mr. Togers what was coming, Cordelia noticed him duck as if a gun had been fired.

"Don't worry," she told him, placing a hand on his shoulder. "It's just some fireworks I ordered. Pretty incredible, right?" She looked up to see the sky flashing purple.

Bennett growled next to her. "Just some fireworks? Ms. Bone, this is precisely the kind of thing I warned you against. Fireworks are responsible for nearly twenty thousand fires a year. Would you like to burn the house down? A house that has been in this family for over a hundred years?"

"Relax," she told him, eyes glued to a sky lit with gold and green and red. "You worry too much for a man so close to retirement."

"A Togers never retires," he snarled acidly before stalking off.

Cordelia turned her face back to the sky. *What a funny old man,* she thought. *A moody, funny old man.* But she wouldn't let Mr. Togers or anyone else spoil this moment for her. They'd pulled it off. The papers were signed, the town appeased. Pretty soon, her accounts would flood with money and her financial worries would be over. And after tonight, she and Eustace would know who'd been leaving those curses. And they would deal with them.

She turned to her sister to congratulate her, only to find that Eustace, too, had disappeared. *No matter,* Cordelia thought, feeling the wine swim through her head. She was probably just restocking the madeleines. Or working over the crowd, looking for the man she would know once she saw him.

The sun had sunk fully beneath the horizon, and the woods echoed with insects. A pale sickle moon rose behind the spray of colorful gunpowder. It was a dark night, and dark nights were good for displays such as this one. Despite her earlier reservations, Cordelia didn't feel frightened or on edge. She felt alive, burning with magic like the sky above her, ready to burst with her power.

She stood silently as the fireworks eventually wound down. Turning, she noticed that Eustace hadn't returned, which meant it fell to her to herd everyone back toward the house so they could begin the shuffle of cars allowing people to leave. Once the sky was black again, she announced that if everyone would follow her through the gardens, they could wait inside where final mocktails—vanilla-bean toddies—had been prepared, while Arkin retrieved their vehicles one at a time.

It didn't take much more than that to get them all headed in the right direction. Cordelia snaked her way to the front of the crowd, nearing the house with a flock of guests at her heels. But just as she broke from the garden into the small clearing at the solarium, her eyes fell on a grisly scene.

Clapping a hand over her mouth, she quickly turned to try to stop the people behind her, but it was too late. Those just following were already getting an eyeful, their gasps and shrieks of terror bringing the rest running. She turned back, and a howl of unbridled horror ripped from her throat. Where was Eustace?

"Look away," she kept saying to everyone. "Look away!"

She had given them a show all right. Or someone had. One they would never forget.

Cordelia gripped the arm of the man nearest to her—a pharmacist she recalled, named Douglas something. "Tell Arkin to be quick with the cars! I need these people gone," she commanded.

She reached out to another, but he shied away. "Guide them around the side of the house!" she shouted at him, enraged by his reaction. Couldn't he see she was just as shocked as everyone else was? Couldn't they all see this wasn't her or Eustace's doing?

"Find my sister!" she yelled at a woman, who turned and ran away from her.

An abrupt wind had begun to kick up in frenzied circles around the house, lashing Cordelia's hair across her face, tearing at her skirts. She felt the rain coming, less a sensation in the air than a pressure building within. When she glanced up, a convergence of ugly clouds was streaking the sky, roiling like billows of smoke across the black, carrying the charge of a hundred storms.

Cordelia forced herself to take in the vandal's artistry, even as it turned her stomach and broke her heart, spiking her with fresh fear. Blood was splattered across nearly every surface—tables, ground, shrubs. Some had even hit the back of the house. It was haphazard and reckless. More about a show than a message. But the twisting pink cords that could only be entrails were different.

Driven into the ground between Cordelia and the house stood a tripod of wooden poles—two lashed together with cord, one leaning across those, its end driven deep into the earth. At the base of them, Marvel's intestines had been carefully arranged into a series of three runes, each identical to the next. Cordelia didn't recognize them, but they were instantly burned across her memory. Maybe Eustace would know what they meant, but she didn't want her sister to see the fox this way. It would crush her.

Marvel's head had been mounted to the pole emerging from the ground, thrusting toward the garden path, red with her blood. Her emptied husk was strapped behind, tied on with a long pink sash—the one Cordelia had dropped from her robe only that morning when she ran from the crypt to the house. The image of the old woman she'd seen blazed across her mind. If she was responsible for this, Cordelia would strike her down. She didn't care about her age.

The fox had been entirely gutted, and her hide drooped like an old glove. Blood matted her beautiful fur and stained the lavender ribbon she wore. Her eyes were dull with death. The pole had torn off part of her jaw, and emerged from her open mouth, jagged and wet.

The first time it happened, with the blood, Cordelia had felt only fear—icy and miserable. The second time, with the skin and ash, she'd felt dread and an answering power. But this time, her blood bubbled with the hot tide of rage swelling inside her, echoing in the angry crashes of sky overhead. This was not a storm she perceived; it was a storm she called. And once it broke, there was no halting it.

There would be no miracle for the fox this time, Cordelia knew. Even her sister's magic had its limits.

Above her, the sky crackled and split, raining her fury across them all.

CORDELIA'S STORM WREAKED havoc as the guests rushed to leave all at once, desperate to get out of the freezing sheets of rain and menacing lightning strikes, causing a congested knot of vehicles and mud while branches cracked and fell, flying through the wind, to smash windshields and terrify townspeople.

But Cordelia cared about none of it.

She let the energy rip through her and whip the air into chaos, let it catch fire to the treetops dotting the wide front lawn and soak the earth with a torrent the likes of which had never been seen in Bellwick.

She had only one thing on her mind—finding Eustace.

She tore through the house, drenched, screaming her sister's name, slipping in the hall as she dashed toward the stairs, grabbing the banister to steady herself as she ran up them. On the second story she threw open every door, calling as she quickly checked inside before moving on to the next door. With each empty room she felt a little more hopeless, a little more afraid that they had not only killed the vixen, but that whoever was responsible had also taken her sister.

She reached the room her sister had been sleeping in and threw open the door. The bed lay starkly empty, the coverlet drawn high, remade after the night before, the pillows fluffed and waiting. A dim light circulated from a lamp on a bedside table, causing the ravens to cast grandiose shadows up the wall. Eustace was not there, but someone was. Across the bed from her, the ghost of Morna wavered in the lamplight, her face an ashen blur, her dress a mess of black crepe.

"Where is she?" Cordelia questioned the spirit. "Where is she!"

Morna turned her sad, drooping eyes up to meet Cordelia's. Her mouth gaped open without sound. But her right hand tightened as her index finger extended, pointing down.

Cordelia had already swept the first floor, which left only one other place. She stumbled down the grand staircase into the library, skittering around the great desk to the hidden door. It was shut fast. Dragging it open, she grabbed the flashlight her sister had left on a nearby shelf and dashed down into the darkness. The narrow channels of the basement seemed to close in on her as she neared the little room.

Spinning into it, she held the flashlight out. It clattered to the floor. There, in the middle of the circle of runes, her sister lay unconscious, silver curls spread around her like a halo.

Cordelia rushed to her side. "Eustace!" she tried, turning her sister's face toward her, patting her cheeks frantically, checking for injuries. She laid an ear to her sister's mouth and felt the heat of her breath against her cheek. Relief swept through her, pulling up tears she'd been holding down. Cordelia sobbed as she tried to revive a stubbornly unresponsive Eustace.

"I'm going for help," she told her pointlessly, her own face a mess of salt and snot. "Don't leave me, Eustace!"

She raced back up to the first floor and out onto the porch, but the storm had soaked the ground so fast that many of the cars were now stuck in the mud, spinning their wheels uselessly, blocking everyone else as they sprayed them with sludge. A crosshatch of headlights cut through the dark, and the sound of horns honking filled the air between crashes of maddening thunder. In the confusion, Cordelia could no longer see Arkin, nor could she find Bennett or anyone else she recognized. She remembered Dr. Mabee leaving early, and knew what she had to do. She had no car—Gordon had taken his truck with him. But even if she had, it was doubtful she'd have gotten through this gridlock.

Instead, she ran. Once she reached the front of the property, she took off down the middle of the street. If someone came down that road, they would see her. Maybe they would stop. She could get a ride into town. She could find the doctor and bring him back to help her sister. It was their only hope. Calling an ambulance was out of the question. In a hospital, Cordelia knew, Eustace would surely die.

Her shins ached and her feet were likely bleeding, but she continued to belt down the asphalt, even as her breathing drew shallow and her head began to pound like an egg being cracked from the inside. Blood dripped from her nose, and she wiped it away hastily. *No,* she thought, the sound of her mother's body hitting the ground crashing through her. *Not yet. Not yet!* she called to the witch inside her—the seeress, the *volva*—begging her to hold on just a little longer, just until they could find help for Eustace.

When the brights of a vehicle finally glimmered in the distance, she waved her arms wildly and tore toward them, hoping the driver would see her in time to stop. The tires whined as the truck slowed and Cordelia went from a full sprint to a jog to a shuffle. Every step seemed to come with a cost now, and the light of the headlamps blinded her. Or was it the headache erupting behind her eyes like a volcano of torment? She wasn't sure, but she didn't care. She heard the driver's-side door swing open, and she managed to get the words out before the world dropped away.

"My sister," Cordelia said to the stranger she couldn't make out, shouting through the rain. "Please! You have to help us. Get Dr. Mabee!"

And then she let herself fall, and everything ceased to matter as a tide of black swallowed her whole.

CHAPTER TWENTY-EIGHT

THE NITHING POLE

CORDELIA WOKE WITH a start, sitting up so fast she nearly slid from the parlor couch onto the floor. "Where am I?" she asked as the scarlet furnishings and draperies came slowly into focus, the marble fireplace and lacquered table, the pump organ sulking in a corner. A vintage wool blanket in red and brown plaid lay across her lap, scratchy but effective. Her wet dress was still sticking to her skin.

"Take it slow," she heard a familiar voice say as a cup and saucer clinked on the table next to her.

Cordelia turned to see Gordon standing over her, his hair hanging in damp coils, a towel slung over his shoulders. He'd just set a steaming cup down.

"My sister," she said, throwing off the blanket and trying to stand, only to falter and end up back on the settee.

"Whoa," he reiterated, holding his hands out in case he needed to catch her. "Dr. Mabee is with her," he promised reassuringly. "She's gonna be all right. But you need to give it a few minutes. You can go up once you've recalibrated."

"Up?" Cordelia lifted a hand to her head, which was blessedly pain-free now that she was back on Bone property, but still reeled. She lifted the teacup with a wobbly hand and took a sip.

"When the storm kicked up, I jumped in my truck and headed this way. I was afraid that you were hurt or upset. I found you on the road and knew something terrible must have happened. I brought you back here and saw the basement door standing open. That's when I found your sister. I called the doctor and took her up to a bed once he gave the okay to move her."

"You saw the basement room," she said with a sigh.

"I waited with her for the doctor to arrive, just coming up once to make sure you were still okay," he confirmed.

"I can explain," she started, though she wasn't sure she could.

Gordon shook his hands at her. "You don't owe me anything, Cordelia. What happened to my mother had nothing to do with you or Eustace."

She bit her lip. "But I'd like to," she told him. "I'd like to tell you what we know, though there's nearly as much we don't. I want you to know the truth about me."

He smiled slightly. "You think I don't know the truth about you? You think it's been lost on me—the things you make happen? The way you've plugged into this place over the last week and a half, like a light bulb in a socket, and come alive?"

She gaped, making a point to set her cup down slowly and carefully. "I–I . . ."

He came and sat next to her, keeping plenty of space between them. "My *babci*—you remember I told you about her, the one from Poland?"

Cordelia nodded.

"She had a gift too. Not nearly so powerful or varied as yours. She called it *The Touch*. If she held something, put her hands on it, she could know things about it, about who owned it or touched it before. People in her village would bring things to her from time to time and ask her questions." He took one of her hands in his, toying gently with her fingers. "They respected her for it," he said. "So did I."

Cordelia didn't pull away. "I'm so sorry," she whispered. "About earlier. I didn't give you a chance—"

"You were right," he interrupted. "I should have told you. I was scared." He met her eyes then, his face open and honest. "Not *of* you. Of *losing* you."

She laid her free hand over his and smiled. "So was I."

A loud *ahem* broke them apart. Cordelia looked up to see Dr. Mabee standing in the doorway. She rose, and this time, her legs were steady. "My sister?"

"She's still unconscious," Dr. Mabee told her. "She went into shock, it seems."

Cordelia started forward, but the doctor put a hand up.

"Her heart rate and breathing have stabilized. I've already started an IV drip to keep her hydrated, and we can administer nutrition infusions if she doesn't come around in a few days."

"A few days?" Cordelia placed a hand over her chest. "What are you saying?"

Dr. Mabee peered at her. "I don't know what happened to your sister, Ms. Bone. Or how it managed to happen *here*. But the rest of her recovery is up to her. She must come around on her own, in her time, or not at all."

Cordelia stumbled back a step. "That can't be," she whispered. She couldn't do this without Eustace. Not any of it. Going on without their mother was one thing, and neither of them had ever known a father, but Cordelia could not go on without her sister at her side.

Dr. Mabee frowned. "I'm sorry. I truly am. There is nothing more I can do at this time. Keep an eye on her. Stay with her as much as possible. Your presence will be a comfort. There are reports that unconscious people can still hear those around them. Call me if anything changes. I'll be back tomorrow to change her bag."

Cordelia's mouth fell open. She couldn't believe he was just going to leave while her sister lay upstairs in some sort of comatose state. She followed him helplessly to the door.

"If you can figure out what caused this, maybe that will help." He gave her a bleak expression, all turned-down corners and glum eyes. "This changes everything, you know. Whatever happened here, I wouldn't consider myself impervious if I were you. Be careful, Ms. Bone." And then he was gone.

Cordelia shut the door and turned to Gordon. "I need to see her."

He nodded quietly. "You go upstairs. I'll help the last couple of people get their cars free of the mud."

She climbed the stairs slowly and found her sister lying in Morna's old room, an IV pole by her bedside, the ravens watching over her, mute and frozen. Eustace looked peaceful, as if she were only sleeping. Cordelia wanted to shake her. *Wake up!* she wanted to scream. *Don't you know I need you?* Instead, she took her sister's hand.

"What happened to you?" she asked quietly, but Eustace didn't budge. Her face was a still mask, with none of its usual sly expressions. Her chest rose and fell in a sleepy rhythm, everything working as it should. But Eustace was gone. And Cordelia feared she might never get her back.

WHEN SLEEP CAME for Cordelia, it came heavy and without promise. There were no trenchant dreams for her to ponder upon waking, no spectral visitors from her family to tell her what to do. Just emptiness and the resounding sense that she was utterly and wretchedly alone.

She'd stayed up with her sister well into the night, murmuring in Eustace's ear, telling her stories of when they were children, stroking her hair as the tears fell. In the end, it was Eustace's own draught of chamomile, skullcap, and valerian that eventually put her to sleep in the armchair by the bed.

In the morning, she woke feeling groggy, stiff, and hopeless. After checking that nothing had changed with her sister's condition, she made her way down to the kitchen, where Gordon was washing blood and dirt from his hands. The chrome flashlight sat on the counter beside him.

"You saw?" she asked.

He nodded, pointing his eyes out the window to the solarium. "It's sick. I can't believe that after everything your sister did for that animal, this is how it ended."

A sob caught in Cordelia's throat, and her hands balled into angry fists at her sides. She'd had no special bond with the fox as her sister did, but it was a part of Eustace and therefore a part of her. And it was an innocent, a walking miracle. Seeing something so callously butchered and discarded went straight through her heart. "Where did you put her?"

"She's beneath the statue," he said, sounding tired.

Cordelia hated that the garden ornament she'd splurged on had become a headstone. The *Queen of Seasons* would now remind them of only one thing. "Thank you," she told him as she readied the enamel coffeepot. "I didn't know if you'd stay."

He turned to her. "I won't leave you again. Not like this. It isn't safe."

She squeezed his hand in gratitude.

"I can stay in the carriage house if you want, but I'll feel better if—"

"No," she said. "My sister needs you. *I* need you. Please. You can take any room you'd like."

"I won't be doing much sleeping," he told her. "I don't trust them not to come back under cover of darkness. It seems to be their favorite way."

"We'll take shifts," she agreed. She let the coffee steep while she found a mug, then poured herself a large, strong cup.

"How was it?" he asked. "Before, you know."

She took a breath and let the memories of the night wash over her. "Perfect," she said. "Better than perfect. Until . . ."

Their party had been a runaway success, but now would be forever marred by the vision of blood and guts strewn across the garden and the epic storm that raged afterward, drenching their guests and backing all the cars into a muddy, motionless knot. Her hope had been to update their reputation. Instead, she had only sealed it.

Still, they'd had a couple of victories last night. The trust was signed and witnessed. She could wire the money to Busy by that night. And the gory scene had happened in full view of the back camera Gordon placed. If nothing else, they would have footage of who was responsible. They could press charges.

"The camera," Cordelia said to Gordon. "Have you reviewed the tape? Did you see who did it?"

Gordon hung his head, a heavy sigh on his lips. "About that . . ."

"Wasn't it on?" she asked, frantic. They needed this. "I checked before the party."

His lips tightened. "You should see it for yourself."

Accompanying her to the parlor, Gordon pulled up the back-camera footage from the night before, rewinding to a point just after the fireworks display. Then, he let it play.

Cordelia watched as the statue stood resolutely in view, pale against the night. Beside the *Queen of Seasons,* her shadow seemed to elongate, growing deeper and taller, until the shape of a man could be seen emerging from behind her, eerily reminiscent of Cordelia's dream of the shadow in the parking lot with her mother. The head turned toward the camera, wholly blank, and made a hissing sound. And then the lens cracked, and a moment later the footage zigged and zagged, rippling across the screen before turning to snow and finally going blank.

They knew. Their stalker had been watching the estate. They'd seen Gordon install the cameras. And they knew all along. But how they'd managed to stay concealed, to break the camera without ever touching it, were other questions entirely.

"They're all like this," he said. "I already checked. They all blink out at once."

Cordelia felt limp, a wilting stem with nothing and no one to hold her up. Their plan had failed and cost her far too much.

They walked slowly back to the kitchen, and Gordon sat down beside her at the table. "Do you know what happened to Eustace?"

"I've been thinking about it all night," she told him. "It's like Marvel's death ripped out her soul. It must have occurred during the fireworks. Eustace sneaked off somewhere. I thought maybe she was checking the food or talking to someone. After the fox, I found her like that. In the basement room."

Gordon leaned back in his chair. "Why would she be down there?"

Cordelia shrugged. "She'd been going down there more and more. We . . ." She met his eyes, hoping he wouldn't flinch at the words. "We cast a spell down there before the guests arrived. Something she found for protection. Obviously, it didn't work."

He tilted his head as he listened.

"When I found her, the secret door was closed. No one knows about that but us. I think she went down there and closed it behind her so none of the guests would see if they wandered inside."

Gordon nodded. "It wasn't locked? Like someone shut her down there?"

"No," Cordelia told him. "She could have gotten out as easily as I got in. She must have been up to something she needed that room for."

Gordon drank his coffee, thinking. "What your sister did saving that animal—it was special. Not like anything I've ever witnessed before. Impossible, even. If she saw what happened, do you think it could have put her into shock like that?"

Cordelia thought about what the old man had told her last night concerning Morna's ravens. "Maybe, but she wasn't out there. How would she see?"

Gordon looked at her. "You tell me."

Cordelia felt it land on her all at once, like a fist to the face. How she hadn't realized it before defied her. She must have been in a certain amount of shock herself. She moaned into her hands. "You're right. She saw it happen."

"How? If she was in the basement?"

"Because she wasn't in the basement," Cordelia told him. "She was in Marvel."

Gordon set his cup on the table and looked at Cordelia with intelligent eyes. "The fox? Your sister is the fox?"

"She could put herself—her senses, her consciousness— inside the fox if she wanted to. It had become a habit of sorts. The morning she saw the man on our property and chased him—"

Gordon's lips twitched. "She'd been inside the vixen. That's how she ran him down."

Cordelia nodded. "I think she wanted to look for the person responsible during the party *as* Marvel. We hadn't had any luck up to that point. She must have thought the fox's senses would give her an advantage. I bet she went into the basement so no one would find her in some kind of trance state and snap her out of it. She probably thought she'd be safe down there."

"The runes on the floor," Gordon said, eyebrows raising.

"Yes. They seal the space, apparently. It was a room used for workings. Spells and potions and things. She was just starting to put it all together."

"What did Dr. Mabee mean when he said he didn't know how it happened *here*?" Gordon watched her carefully.

Cordelia knew there was no point holding back the truth; he'd likely already guessed after her two fainting spells. "We can't leave the estate," she told him. "Something about the land protects us. Without it, we're doomed. But here, we don't get sick or hurt. At least we shouldn't. It hasn't always been that simple for me. But things had just begun to improve on that front before . . ."

She looked away. She didn't want to remind him of their fight, the terrible things she'd accused him of. "Anyway, Dr. Mabee doesn't know how or why, but he says it's been this way for generations. Somehow, our mother managed to hold off the effects for as long as she did. But even she succumbed eventually. Although, we think someone played a role in that. The same person who is hunting us now. Eustace and I were both suffering before we came here. I doubt we had long. But after my first trip with you to the store and learning about the legacy of the estate, we've been careful. Last night shouldn't have happened. The fox is one thing, but my sister should have been safe here."

He let the explanation ease into his mind. "That's why your aunt never left."

Cordelia gave him a tight smile. "It seems there's something to your children's rhyme after all."

He waited a minute before telling her, "We're going to catch him. Whoever it is, they'll pay for this."

"It had to be someone at the party." She finished her coffee and set the cup back down.

"Did you notice anyone odd?"

"Not in a way that really stood out," she answered.

"What about during the fireworks? Did anyone leave or sneak off?"

"My sister," she said, frustrated. "Otherwise, no. I mean, Mr. Togers stalked off in a huff, but he's old. Eustace said this guy was young—he was fast."

"And driving that pole into the ground would have taken some strength. A man like Togers doesn't have it in him. Plus he doesn't seem the type to bite the hand that feeds him. Did you tell anyone about the fireworks?" Gordon asked her. "Beforehand?"

Again, Cordelia shook her head. "Not a soul," she said, biting a nail. "They had to have known about the timing, but how? And the fox—no one knew about her but you and me and Eustace."

"You don't think the fox was a victim of opportunity?" Gordon asked.

"The first time, sure. But I think they knew exactly what they were doing when they killed her last night," she said. "I think she was just another message."

"What do you think it means?" he asked her now. "The intestines were—"

"Don't remind me," Cordelia told him. "I can't stop seeing them."

"Did you recognize the runes?"

"No, but I spent some time looking into it last night while I was sitting up with Eustace. I found some of her notes and books. It's called *Thurisaz*. It means *thorn*. Which is exactly as unpleasant as it sounds."

Gordon crossed his arms. "Why three of them in a row?"

"It's a way to curse," she said. "Or bless—to stack the runes in multiples, usually of three. The whole thing is a curse, in fact. I looked it up. It's called a nithing pole. It's an ancient Viking tradition, a way of directing malice. Typically, they used horses to make one."

"Like a Norse version of an upside-down cross?" Gordon asked.

"Black magic," Cordelia whispered, stretching her fingers to her throat, feeling for the runes they'd painted there that had failed them. "A supernatural way to cause harm."

Someone wanted to hurt them, to chase them off. Maybe someone bearing ill will from town. But Cordelia had heard different kinds of stories last night about her family, stories of kindness and vulnerability tucked in among the whispers of strange and illicit activity. The people of Bellwick might have been suspicious, but they came for the party just the same. She didn't think they were malicious.

She recalled again the old woman she'd seen in the fog, her gem-colored dress, her shining staff. Her appearance on the same day as the nithing pole couldn't have been a coincidence.

"What kind of harm?" Gordon asked specifically. "Did it have a certain method, like illness or starvation?"

"Disempowerment," Cordelia told him. "It desecrates the land, renders it spiritually or energetically dead."

Gordon leaned forward. "That's it then. You said something about the land protects you. And that *thing* out there is meant to destroy the land. They cut you off from your source, whatever it is, when they erected the pole."

"They're trying to weaken us," Cordelia whispered, her eyes finding his. "They're trying to weaken us for the final blow."

CHAPTER TWENTY-NINE

THE SEERESS

CORDELIA KNEW WHAT she had to do. She stared down at her sister's motionless body, brushing the ringlets of hair away from her face and clutching her hand. "You're going to wake up," she whispered. "You're going to wake up, and we're going to make things right."

The words in their aunt Augusta's letter clung to her—*There are many wrongs to right.*

Cordelia called for Gordon. When he entered the room, she told him, "Stay with her."

"Wait. Where are you going?" he asked.

"I can't answer that." She turned for the door.

"Cordelia!"

"I have to help her," she tried to explain. "Dr. Mabee said her recovery is up to her, but he's wrong. She can't do it alone. Neither of us can."

Gordon looked at her with pinched, worried eyes. "I don't understand."

"Neither do I," she told him. "But I'm beginning to."

She strode into the hall and climbed the stairs. The morning light was streaming through the stained-glass window, playing tricks with the snake's coils of blue and purple glass, the twists and turns of the tree's golden roots. The colored rays hit the floor below, shifting like a kaleidoscope across the inlaid medallion. Such a simple but peculiar star, she thought, like a snowflake. The longer Cordelia stared, the more the pieces of the design seemed to disconnect and reconnect before her.

It was so plain. How had she ever missed it? Their mother's tattoo. The scratches their aunt made in the wall. The symbol written on the cover of the book Augusta had left them.

Algiz, Eustace had called it. The elk rune. A symbol of protection. The medallion inlaid into the floor wasn't a medallion at all, but a bind rune. The elk rune repeated eight times in a circle, joined end to end.

She reconsidered the stained-glass window, with its depiction of the Garden of Eden—a common theme for Victorian times. But this was no forbidden fruit. It was Yggdrasil—the World Tree. Even she knew that story. And the serpent was no mere serpent, but a dragon. The very same that gnaws forever at the roots of the World Tree, trying to bring the Nine Worlds crashing down. How carefully her relatives hid their magic in plain sight. So carefully they'd hid it from themselves.

Certainty filled her, and Cordelia kept climbing until she reached and passed the third story. The house was quiet, the grand staircase empty. The tower held only a whisper of darkness, barely perceptible on the widow's watch. But Cordelia knew whom she'd find up there. Morna's disquiet was never gone, however still or bright the tower seemed. She was a hunger that never abated and a presence that would not rest. And she was waiting for something.

Cordelia was beginning to understand what.

She took the stairs two at a time, ready to confront the ghost that, like everyone else, she'd so misunderstood.

At the final stretch, she climbed to the widow's watch, keeping a tight grip on the railing. The narrow landing wasn't much to claim. The boards were rough and dry from sun exposure and the windows drafty. Bright light filled the space as the windows gave her a 360-degree view of the property. But above her, just out of reach, shadows brooded in the corners like cobwebs.

"I know you're here," she said carefully, turning in a slow circle. "And I know you can hear me."

Something darted by her field of vision. Cordelia spun but found nothing. "Hear me now," she said to the gloom. She raised her arm that bore the silver bracelet. "You want your revenge? Well, I want something too."

She gritted her teeth as a darkening mist began to gather in the corners, roiling against the pale glass, moving around her.

"I know what you are," she ground out. "I know what *we* are. And I know what someone did to you. Maybe not *who*. Maybe not *how*. But I know you're innocent. And you're angry."

The mist swirled before her, twirling in and out of the shape of a woman.

"Tell me," she commanded. "And if you can't speak, *show* me."

Arms pale as milk shot out from the mist and grabbed her about the head, pulling her into the spirit smoke. Cordelia's mind spun in and out of her own consciousness, crash-landing at last into a scene from another time. She was still in the tower high above the property, but she was no longer alone. Her vision fixed on the acrid face of an older woman she didn't recognize— stout and thick-shouldered with sloping eyes, heavy cheeks, and a nose like an osprey.

"Go on," the woman was saying through a voice like ground glass. "No one will miss you. They'll be relieved to be rid of you. You've brought nothing but disgrace to this house. And shame. You killed those birds, all those poor animals. And you blamed it on a ghost. They're going to send you away. And you and I both know what'll happen then. You won't live a day if you live an hour. And it'll hurt so much worse."

Cordelia's perspective shifted rapidly, and now she was facing a much younger woman, with a mess of auburn hair and weeping eyes of black, her face slick with tears, puffy and red and twisted in fear and confusion. The younger woman shook her head briskly, like she could shake the words free. "No. It isn't true. It isn't true! I loved them," she cried, backing away. "They were murdered! Why won't anyone believe me? Why are you doing this? Who are you?" She stopped choking on her tears long enough to stare darkly into the woman's eyes. "Who are you really?"

Cordelia spun to see the old woman smile, slow and greedy. "What's the matter? Don't you remember? I'm Martha Togers," she said with mock concern. "I'm your keeper, girl," she added wickedly. "I'm your death."

Morna shook her head dramatically, strands of wild hair sticking to her wet cheeks as she wept. "Please," she begged. "Please stop. Please help me."

The large woman stared her down. "I can't help you now," the woman told her. "No one can. Only you can help yourself."

Morna glanced back, her shoulders hitching with her sobs.

"Can't you fly, girl?" the woman asked her, taking a step forward. "Don't you remember how?" She stepped forward again, and Morna stepped back. "Time to fly," she was saying, like a skipping record, as Morna backed closer and closer to the window. *Time to fly, time to fly, time to fly . . .*

Morna cupped her hands over her ears and squeezed her eyes tight. When she opened them, they were still, like tops that had finally stopped spinning. She took a breath and propelled herself backward. Cordelia wanted to reach for her, but she was no more substantial than a beam of light striking the glass. The casement windows gave behind her weight, flinging open, and Morna tumbled into the day, her face slackening in a sudden wave of shock and understanding. But it was too late. Cordelia heard her body hit the drive below, a grotesquely hollow sound, the thud of a melon breaking apart.

The nurse smiled, like she was hearing a pure note being struck on a fine instrument. And then she mussed her hair, took a deep breath, and screamed at the top of her lungs.

Everything spun again, and Cordelia was rocking on her heels in her own time, gripping the rail to hold herself up in the glass box of the tower. She gasped for air, coughing and shaking her head, as the spirit let her go. And then she pulled the words up from her chest and gave them to the mist. "I want my sister, Eustace. Someone took her from me. And I want her back."

The mist spun around her, frenzied and looking for release. "Give me my sister," she told it. "And I will give you your revenge."

The bracelet on her wrist burned hot, and Cordelia hissed. The mist dove at her, parting to flow around her just before contact. Cordelia turned as it slammed into the casement window at her back, blowing it open. The garden twisted beneath her, and the wide promenade lay like a blanket of pink and green. Behind it, the great hill rose, stunted on top, the peak lopped off.

That's where the old woman waited.

She stood there staring back at Cordelia. Her sapphire dress rippled in the wind, her staff pierced the hill like a jewel on a spike. Cordelia watched her lower her hood, the shock of hair like a scarf of white, as if her head were permanently wreathed in clouds.

Cordelia blinked and stumbled back down the stairs, racing toward the first floor. When she hit the bottom, she was knocked forward to her knees, but she clambered up quickly and rushed through the dining room and kitchen, out the solarium, cursing the house's architect for not plotting a straighter route.

The poles they'd found in the garden had yet to be dismantled and hauled away to burn where Eustace would never have to see them. But the blood, at least, had been washed into the earth by the rain.

Blood and soil, Cordelia thought as she ran.

Every step that carried her closer to the crypt revisited her anger from the night before. If this woman was responsible for what happened to Marvel, to her sister, she would tear her to shreds on that hill. But she wasn't even out of the garden when the humming started, the earthy rumble that wrapped its way up her legs to her chest and throat, growing louder and louder by the beat. Her ears rang with the sound, a chorus so strong each note became a hundred, each voice a thousand. They drove her on like hooves pounding beside her. They called her to the den of her ancestors, and Cordelia felt the world around her slipping.

For a moment, beneath the pink shade of the cherry trees, she thought she saw them. A long line on either side of her—men and women, boys and girls, their mouths open, their throats reverberating, their tongues loosed. The words eluded her, and maybe they were not words at all, but their faces were plain enough, sliding in and out of being as she ran.

The song overwhelmed until her grip on reality loosened along with her throat. Something in her begged to join in, to let out a howl so great it would shake this place to its foundation. *Sing,* it seemed to whisper, then chant, then storm. *Sing, girl! Sing!*

Cordelia opened her chest and throat and mouth. And whatever came out was lost to her. Her body doubled on itself, bones popping in and out of joint as she ran, until she saw herself like a beast tearing up the ground, claws digging into the earth, propelling her forward, the woman fading in and out with the animal.

When she neared the crypt, she saw the doors waiting open, the roses swirling in the morning sun, the mists creeping from inside like the breath of a dragon, twirling in white curls. She hit the side of the hill and latched on, scrabbling for purchase. She clambered up the steep slope, clawing with her fingers and digging with her knees and toes. The soil stained her hands and feet and legs black, but she didn't care. She had only to reach the top and all would be as it should be. Her resolve pushed her up that slope like a madness, a fever of the soul. She ascended like a she-bear on the hunt, a lynx plowing through snow, with only her instincts to guide her.

As she rounded the crest and pulled herself onto flat land, she found the woman waiting. But behind her, the thicket of Connecticut's hills was gone, a vista of white-capped mountains in their place. An emerald valley shone between them. A wide-open sky frosted blue.

The air nipped at Cordelia's skin. Her hair blustered behind her. The woman's cheeks were red with cold. She smiled, and her teeth were waxy in the light.

"Who are you?" Cordelia demanded.

"The wand wed," the woman said, her voice gravelly, as if it hadn't been used in a very long time. "The speaker of truths and the seer of destinies."

Cordelia took in the large staff, the crooked form and the branching top—three arms with shiny brass decorations cast on them. *Algiz.* "What are you doing here?"

"I am where you brought me," the woman said plainly. "And you are where I have brought you."

Cordelia shivered and wrapped her arms across her chest. When she looked back, she could not see the house or the gardens. Just miles and miles of forest spilling onto a sparkling coastline in the distance.

"Do I know you?" she asked the woman, feeling a pull to her, a sense of home.

At this, the woman smiled again with wide, ruddy lips. "Your blood sings my name, daughter. Your soul knows me well. As does your mother's."

"My mother?" Cordelia took a step toward her.

"Magda of the bones," the woman hissed with wild eyes.

Cordelia's eyes narrowed; she took another step. "The *bones*?"

The woman leaned toward her, her grin as broad as her face and her eyes aflame with wisdom. "My bones, girl. And your bones someday. That is the beating heart of our clan. That is where the power lives."

"Power." Cordelia seized on the word. "You mean our magic?"

"I mean our gifts," the woman told her. "Healing the sick. Riding the minds of beasts. Reading the runes. But the greatest of these is our song."

"Singing," Cordelia echoed. "Like I heard in the ground? In my legs? Like what brought me here?"

The woman stood tall and proud. "The bones sing for you, girl. To stir you to your purpose. To rouse you from your ignorance. Our song calls the spirits close. It looses the tongues of the dead and sets them wagging. Do you know of what the dead speak, girl?"

Cordelia shook her head.

"Everything," she said slowly, beginning to circle Cordelia. "We sing to call the dead, and the dead speak our futures into being. Our power is not just our own but theirs. And we honor them for it."

"Aunt Augusta," Cordelia whispered, turning in place to follow the woman. "The runes across her face. The doves."

"The dead require many things to speak," the woman told her, pausing. Then: "Most of all, they require *company*. We are the company of the dead. And the dead reward us for it." She paused here and leaned forward. "Now, the dead require blood." She pointed at Cordelia's wrist, where the bracelet held fast.

"Blood?" Cordelia shivered at the word.

"Your blood," she said calmly. "To shed another's."

Cordelia shook her head. She was getting lost. "I don't understand."

"You will," the woman assured her. "When the time is right."

"How do you know my mother?" she asked the woman, returning to her earlier point.

"Magda sang for me," the woman said. "And I answered."

"She called you?" Cordelia tried to clarify.

"Her heart was sick with fear when her lover died," the woman told her. She began to circle Cordelia again. "She stood before me where you are now, and I spoke her fortune to her. *Stay,* and she would surely die. *Leave,* and face the same. But the babe . . . Leave, and *the babe* would live." The woman stopped and faced Cordelia, placing a hand at her womb. "She didn't even know she carried life then," the woman said. "Just as you don't now."

Cordelia froze. "A-a baby?"

The woman grinned. "My line is strong in you, daughter. Another *volva* to raise our clan, eh? Odin favors us well. But your fate is not your mother's. Leave, and both of you will die."

Cordelia shuddered, running a hand down her stomach to her navel. "And if I stay?"

The woman's lips drew back. "Ours is a tree with one root and two branches," she said cryptically. "But not for long. For the tree to survive, one branch must be felled."

Cordelia began to shake her head. "No. No that can't be." *Beware the pair,* Gordon's mother had said. *Beware the heir.* And now her sister lay dying. Cordelia didn't care what this woman said or who she was—it couldn't come down to her or Eustace. She wouldn't make a choice like that. "You're lying," she insisted. "You don't know what you're saying. Did you hurt her? Are you the one who took my sister?"

The old woman began to laugh. "You are much like her—your mother," she said. "She wanted to fight me too. But she knew better. She knew old Hella's tongue is made of pine and iron, arrow-straight and twice as sharp. And when I told her to keep one of my teeth next to her heart to protect her and the child, she knew

it was the only way. Your sister is my daughter, girl. As you are.
And your mother. And your mother's mother. I do not strike
my own." She peered into Cordelia's stormy eyes. "Teeth will not
save you," she said. "You need something sharper."

"What about my sister? What will save Eustace?" Cordelia
asked.

The old woman sneered. "Have you not been listening, girl?
Are your ears full of goose fat?"

Cordelia trembled at her ire.

"Bone pays for bone. Blood for blood." She glared at her. "If
you want to save your sister, bring her to me. The land may be
weakened by blasphemy," she uttered. "But *we* are strong."

"Who are you?" Cordelia asked her, wrapping her arms around
her waist.

"I am what lies behind," the woman said. "And I am what
lies ahead. Hella of the Bones. Speaker for the dead. I wield the
Seidr." She drew near to Cordelia, placing a finger between her
breasts. "And you are of my *völur*."

The word flowed into Cordelia like honey, unlocking secrets
along the way. This was the first *volva*, the original witch of
their clan. It was her power, her magic, her *blood* that flowed
through them. *Even the gods respected them*, Eustace had said.
Hella of the Bones—mistress of *Seidr*, singer of songs. They had
been *of the Bones* ever since. Her bones. Theirs.

The old witch drew back, her cold eyes resting on Cordelia's
shocked face as she tried to process everything she was learning.
"When the time comes," the woman said, "call and we will answer."
She gave Cordelia a hard look. "Do not forsake the bones, girl. Lest
the bones forsake you."

Cordelia gripped the bracelet on her wrist, cold as ice and hot
as fire, heavier than a two-headed ax and just as sharp.

"The dragon is waiting," Hella said. "Its hunger knows no

bounds." Her eyes hardened into blue stones. "Slay, girl, or be eaten."

She drew her staff high before her and drove it back down into the center of the mound, and everything around them vanished.

Cordelia was alone again, and the world was as black as obsidian and just as merciless.

WHEN CORDELIA OPENED her eyes, Gordon stood over her, his face stretched nearly beyond recognition with worry.

"Thank God," he cried, squeezing her shoulder. "I thought you'd never come around."

Cordelia blinked and sputtered, a dry cough tearing its way through her throat. She tried to raise herself on her hands. Gordon wrapped a burly fist around one arm to help her. When she sat up, the world swam. It took a few seconds for the vertigo to settle. She looked down to see black smears across her shins and palms. Thick arcs of dirt lined her fingernails and toenails. The oatmeal knit of her dress was streaked green and brown from her climb.

Cordelia placed a hand to the side of her head, remembering the strange run across the promenade, her scramble up the hillside, the woman's finger on her chest—*Hella of the Bones*.

"What happened?" she asked, wondering how much time she'd lost and what had taken place in the interval between the woman stabbing the mound with her staff and Gordon waking her up.

"I heard you tearing through the house," he explained. "There was this powerful noise. I know I wasn't supposed to leave your sister, but I was worried about you. I followed it outside. That's when I spotted you up here."

It was then Cordelia realized they were still on the hill above the crypt. "Noise?" Had he heard the voices too? Did he see Hella?

"It was you," Gordon told her gently. "You were . . . you were singing. But 'Kumbaya' it was not. It's like it was tearing out of your throat. I'm surprised you can talk."

Cordelia put a hand to her neck. That would explain the burn she sensed there—the shredding of her vocal cords.

"That's not all you were doing," he told her. "You were kind of—well, you were—" he tried. Finally, he got it out. "Levitating. You were suspended above the ground."

Cordelia looked up at him, barely comprehending, the photo they had found of her grandmother suddenly making its own kind of sense. "I was what?" She looked around, searching for the blue dress, the white hair. "Is she still here?"

"Who?" he asked.

Cordelia tried to get to her feet.

"Careful," he told her, helping her up, steadying her with his big arms.

"Did you see her?" she asked now, turning in a circle. But Hella was not there, and with her had gone the mountains and trees, that vast cerulean sky, the gleaming coastline.

"There was no one else." He looked at her softly, but Cordelia brushed off his concern.

"I wasn't up here alone. I was with someone. Her name is Hella. She's our—our ancestor. She was right here."

Gordon gave her a worrying glance. "Maybe you should sit back down," he said. "I think the fall must have confused you."

"What fall?" Cordelia asked, turning to face him.

His mouth tightened. "When I got up here, you were lying on the ground. I figured you must have dropped while I was climbing. I was afraid you hit your head. You could have a concussion," he tried to tell her.

"I'm fine," Cordelia snapped. "I just need to find her. She said to call when it was time, but I don't know what she means. She said we had one root but two branches, and that someone must be felled. She said they need my blood to shed another's. She couldn't mean the baby, so she must have meant Eustace. But that can't be right. She said she could save Eustace."

Beside her, Gordon's beautiful mouth went slack, his eyes wide like a spooked horse's. "Baby?" he whispered. "I think we should call Dr. Mabee."

But Cordelia ignored him, flailing and twisting to break his grasp. "I don't need a doctor," she said. "I need to find her!" Her eyes widened with realization. "And I think I know where she is."

Gordon tried to grab her, but Cordelia dodged him, starting down the hillside, half on her knees and half on her feet, much the way she'd come up. Gordon followed quickly, springing down as if he were part goat.

At the bottom, Cordelia bolted into the crypt, aiming for the back wall. She began to press and knock on the stones all around the bloody handprint, grabbing at corners to try to pry them loose.

"Cordelia," Gordon said, coming up behind her and grabbing her hands with his. "What are you doing? Let me help you!"

She stopped fighting and spun on him. "You want to help me?"

He stepped back. "Please."

"Then go get a crowbar and anything else you can think of. We're taking this wall down," she insisted.

He stood there a moment before nodding his consent. "Okay. I'll be right back. Just . . . stay here."

Several long minutes later, he came thundering back in with a crowbar in one hand and a pickaxe in the other. "Stand back," he told her as he approached the wall, swinging hard and hitting deep between the stones. "I'll loosen them and then you can pry them out."

They worked like that, side by side, until they'd managed to create a four-by-four-foot hole.

"Give me your phone," Cordelia told him as she tried to see inside.

He handed it to her, switching on the flashlight app as he passed it along.

When Cordelia shone the bright light through the hole they'd made, it streamed down a narrow corridor and a steep set of stone stairs. She started down. Near the bottom, the light sparked off a dozen surfaces, butter-white and smooth as alabaster. Cordelia found herself in a small room, shaped like a beehive—a cavity within the hill beyond the crypt itself. Every wall and surface was lined with human bones arranged to create elaborate designs, like a tiny chapel of death. Skulls stacked on skulls rose above them in sinister pillars. Femurs and humeri were piled like logs. Metatarsals and phalanges were pressed into thick mud, dried like spackle, in a circling pattern overhead. Many had been carved with runes.

Gordon entered behind her, brushing dust from his hair as he looked around. "Holy Bologna," he said, taking it in.

The center of the tableau was a skeleton in the middle of the room. She sat on a stool of oiled wood, with a low back and a wide base, a tattered but colorful cloth cast over it. A series of runes and swirls were carved around the edges. Her garment of pristine blue, rimmed in ruby trim, had not faded much despite its countless years. Even the fur lining of her cloak, though spare, still sported soft tufts. Strands of ash-white hair hung from patches of desiccated scalp still clinging to her skull. Her hands lay in her lap, near the brass-decorated staff leaning against her, a little crooked toward the top where it split apart into three branches. Every detail had been carefully arranged, perfectly preserved. From her hide pouches to her strands of glass beads. Every tiny thing in place. Except . . .

"Look," Cordelia said, pointing. "Her teeth. They're missing." All but a few of the woman's teeth had been pulled. And Cordelia knew why. To create the runes they'd found in the basement. Hella of the Bones was indeed still speaking for the dead.

Gordon studied the glimpses of wall between the stacked bones. "I've heard of these," he said. "They're dotted all over New England. Chambers just like this one, made of stone. They're believed to be megalithic. I've never seen one this large."

"It must have been here first," Cordelia said, staring at the figure seated in the place of honor before her. "They must have chosen this plot of land because they could house her inside of it."

"And then they built the crypt in front," he continued where she left off. "To hide it."

"No," Cordelia told him. "To keep them close. To enlarge it." She turned to face Gordon. "It was never blood and soil. It was always this. *Bone.*"

"Bone and soil." Gordon grinned. "I'll inform the neighborhood kids."

"This is why we can't leave," Cordelia said. "This protects us, feeds us. We're bound to these remains. It's why the dynasty trust exists. To keep this and us safe, *together*. To protect the bloodline."

Cordelia neared the staff, studying it up close. "I recognize this," she told Gordon. "It reminds me of Mom's tattoo."

"The rune?" he asked.

She nodded. "It was very crudely done. She must have made it herself. Hella told me our mother took one of her teeth to stay alive when she left. That she *kept it close to her heart.*"

Gordon approached her. "You can put ash in the ink," he said. "They do it for memorial tattoos."

Of course. She'd burned it first, ground it down. Like with all the recipes Eustace was working on.

"Who are they all?" Gordon wondered, turning in slow circles beside her, taking in the countless bones.

"Our ancestors," Cordelia told him. "Just like the ones in the crypt. Only older. Ancient." Cordelia knelt before the bones of Hella and gently touched one of the pointy digits on the hand. Bits of sinewy skin clung, holding each piece together. The dark blur of tattoos could still be seen on some. She rose and turned to face Gordon. "I need you to go get Eustace. Bring her down here."

He paused, staring at her. "But the IV."

She shook her head. "If I'm right about this—and I know I am—she won't need that anymore."

Gordon looked like he might argue again.

"Hurry!" she told him. "Please. You have to trust me."

He pressed his lips together and rushed out, leaving Cordelia alone in the dark of the crypt, with only the bones for company.

CHAPTER THIRTY

THE FALL

A BABY, SHE THOUGHT with wonder and fear standing before the mummified remains of Hella. *Gordon's* baby. Cordelia placed a hand on her womb. She'd never given motherhood serious thought before, but when she considered Gordon as a father, she couldn't help but smile.

Someone darkened the doorway they'd made, cutting off what little light traveled down the stairs. She took a step up. "Did you bring her?" she asked, assuming it was Gordon.

There was no reply.

Cordelia took another step up, and another. One more and the bit of light that remained reached her eyes. The shape, the face came into focus. And they were not Gordon's at all.

Arkin peered down at her, his eyes lit with a hungry fire.

"What are you doing here?" Cordelia spat.

He grinned, and she saw that his teeth were browning near the gums, the incisors longer and pointier than she remembered. Hella's words ran through her mind—*Teeth won't save you. You need something sharper.*

It was then she noticed the other, subtle differences in him. His white-blond hair was a touch longer, shaggier around the ears, his face leaner at the cheeks and temples. And there was a small mole beneath the lower lash line of his right eye. But more than these details, it was the fire burning in him—the leer and the loom—the way he looked like he could swallow her whole. He had none of Arkin's fear or reticence, and all the perversity and hubris of the man Eustace had seen.

"You're not Arkin at all, are you?" she asked, feeling the alarm begin to mount in her belly. "Let me pass, and I won't hurt you."

His smile only widened at that. But then, to her surprise, he moved aside.

She took another step forward, and a hand reached out. Cordelia grasped it, and was pulled into the crypt by none other than Bennett Togers.

"Mr. Togers," she gasped, shooting Arkin's look-alike a wary glance. "What are you doing here? You forgot the papers last night in all the madness. I can fetch them for you. They're just inside."

Bennett tucked his hands behind his back. His smile was that of someone who's just been told a silly joke. "We won't be needing those," he said.

"Get the staff," he told the young man. Turning back to Cordelia, he said, "You'll have to forgive my nephew. He has a tendency to unsettle people. We don't let him out all that often."

"Arkin's brother?" she asked, aware that she was in the crosshairs of something she didn't fully grasp. She needed to proceed with caution. "The resemblance is remarkable."

She could hear the young man bounding down the stone steps, shuffling around, and then stomping back up again. He emerged with Hella's staff in hand.

Bennett gestured for it, and the boy paused, something warring inside him.

"Han," he commanded. "To me."

Han handed it over reluctantly, barely hiding his gleam of resentment.

"Temper, boy," Bennett growled, snatching it from him with an agitated frown.

Cordelia watched them with interest.

"You were saying," Bennett said, turning back to her.

"You're Arkin's brother," she said directly to the young man, who glared at her and grunted.

"His twin, actually," Bennett told her. "He lacks Arkin's social graces," he said with a chuckle. "But he more than makes up for it with power and gusto. He has a real zeal for learning the family trade."

"You mean law?" Cordelia couldn't imagine this boy behind a book or a desk. She wasn't sure he could read. She wasn't sure he could speak.

Bennett smiled in that shit-eating way again. "Cordelia Bone, meet Han. My sister's boy. Your third cousin. Please say hello."

"Cousin?" Cordelia's mind reeled and her stomach lurched as several things came vividly into focus at once.

Beware the pair. Beware the heir.

Both boys had the same platinum hair she'd seen on Hella. And the many times Togers had said something about "*this* family," he'd really meant "*our* family." The way he'd known the house and their history, the secret compartments, the literal skeletons in their closets.

"Shall I give you a little history lesson?" he asked, gripping the staff in the crook of his elbow as he pried a pair of black leather gloves off one finger at a time. "Your great-great-great-grandfather, Erazmus, built this monstrosity for his simpering bride, Arabella Devall, after he'd made his fortune robbing graves and selling corpses to the medical trade. It was easy for him and his father and uncle. Too easy. When the dead tell you where they are, it's like shooting fish in a barrel."

Cordelia stepped back carefully as he watched her, unperturbed.

She wanted to call Gordon, to warn him somehow, but it was his phone in her hand. And there was nothing she could do.

"Of course, they graduated from that to other nefarious endeavors," Bennett went on. "Gambling. Rune casting. The selling of a few simples and charms. But the seances really put them over the top. And by then, they'd begun to make legitimate investments. The dead know many things," he told her. "Horse races . . . the stock market . . . They needed only to ask." He clucked his tongue several times. "Poor Arabella. She'd been raised genteel. Not at all prepared for her husband's dark business dealings or his stern hand. I'm afraid she found him rather repulsive. But he had a partner, you see. My dear ancestor Reginald, whose son— Arran—was a strapping lad by all accounts. Arabella was taken, and they began their affair in the carriage house."

The portrait Gordon had brought her suddenly made sense, the way she'd tracked Arabella's ghost to the carriage house that night, following in her footsteps in more ways than one.

Bennett looked bored as he continued. "When Erazmus found out, he was livid. He conjured a storm this county has never seen the likes of since. Not even your tantrum last night could compare—though I must say, I was a little impressed. Lightning struck the carriage house and burnt it nearly to the ground. Arabella survived, as did her lover. And the binding spell between our families held fast. Erazmus did not kill Arran, however much he wanted to, because he needed him. He sought revenge another way. He seduced Arran's wife and quickened her womb with his own seed. And thus, my great-great-grandfather was born— Tobias Togers."

Cordelia gawked. She took another step back, angling toward the open door of the crypt. Her gaze bounced between uncle and nephew.

Bennett smiled. "Of course, I'm using the term *seduced* lightly.

Love charms can be so tricky. Not quite rape. It's a gray area, I'm afraid."

Cordelia didn't think it was gray at all, but she didn't argue.

"When Arran learned of his wife's infidelity, he drowned Arabella in the pond as payback." Bennett shoved his gloves in a pocket. "Spouses do not share the same limitations, you see—or the same protections. We Togers have been Bone bastards ever since. Waiting and watching from the sidelines for our chance to take what is ours."

Hella's words to Cordelia that morning now made much more sense—*Ours is a tree with one root and two branches . . . For the tree to survive, one must be felled.*

Bennett Togers was the dragon, gnawing at the root of their family tree, trying to bring it down. How long had the Togers been trying to undermine them? It had been a Togers who coaxed her great-great-aunt Morna to jump from the tower, posing as her nurse. Cordelia's mind whirled over the possibilities. It wasn't one enemy they were facing; it was generations of enemies.

"*Binding spell?* What ties our families besides blood?" she asked, stepping back again. She bumped into a stone pillar behind her and carefully scooted to the side of it.

"Your ignorance is truly astounding," he said with a sneer. "And I thought your *mother* was stupid. I'm speaking of magic, girl! Your people fled here with what they could—a brother and sister, Omen and Sabina Bone. But they'd left much behind. This land was all they could afford, yet they were barely strong enough to work it. And so bound to their precious, hoarded remains that they could scarcely make a run to trade for sugar and flour.

"They scooped my ancestor up. A man by the name of Callum. A drunkard and dullard on the edge of death whom they promised the world. They used their power to restore his health, and their money to educate him. The binding spell between him and them reversed his pallid fortunes and tied ours to yours in perpetuity. As you cannot leave this land, so we cannot leave you. At least, not for long. We have been your bondsmen generation after generation. But no more."

Cordelia started to take another step back, and he glared at her. "Where exactly do you think you're going?" he asked, slamming the end of Hella's staff into the floor. It dented the stone slab, chips of rock flying.

"Please," she told him, not daring to move again. "I need to check on my sister."

"Yes," he said coolly. "That was a lucky break, I'm afraid. I didn't realize she'd be in the fox when we set out to erect it on a spike. Not that it matters. It's tidier this way, really. And of course, it's not the first time. My grandfather managed something similar decades back when he killed a pair of ravens your aunt was riding. What was her name again? The sad one?"

"Morna," Cordelia said darkly. All the fear she'd once felt suddenly shifted into anger on Morna's behalf.

Bennett smiled again. "Yes, her. Anyway, that's the problem with beast riding, I always say. You're vulnerable inside the animal. The birds flew too high, beyond the reach of any protection. And it broke her to be in them when they fell. She was never the same, didn't know up from down. It was easy to talk her out of a window after that. There are limits to what the bones can do," he said sagely. "We thought then we'd finally found the loophole we needed."

Cordelia heard approaching footsteps, and Gordon stumbled through the open gates, Eustace hanging limply in his arms.

"Ah, here we are," Bennett said.

"I came as fast as I could. I didn't want to hurt her, and I had to take the IV out," Gordon panted before noticing Bennett Togers and Han. His eyes shifted as his arms flexed to keep a firm hold on Eustace's body. "What's going on here?"

Bennett gave him a patient smile before answering. "A transfer of power, I'm afraid. One that's long overdue. Set her down just there, if you will, Mr. Jablonski. And back away."

Gordon looked to Cordelia, a glint in his eye. But Bennett was faster. A jerk of the staff, and Cordelia was flung toward him. He spun her around and held the staff to her throat.

"Please," she told Gordon. "Just do what he says." She'd already seen the staff dent stone; she didn't want to find out what else it was capable of. Not when her sister's life—and her own—hung in the balance.

Gordon laid Eustace down on the crypt floor carefully and took several steps back. He looked at Han. "Arkin, you've always been a good kid. You don't have to do anything here that you don't want to."

Bennett shook his head. "How very noble of you, Mr. Jablonski. But this is not Arkin, you see. This is Han. And Han, I'm afraid, has quite the appetite for destruction."

"His twin," Cordelia said to Gordon, the staff rough against her skin.

Gordon's eyes met hers, and she knew he was making the connections she already had. Connections that would explain his mother's death, her final words. *Beware the pair. Beware the heir.*

Bennett tensed behind her. "Your mother was collateral damage, regrettably. She was nosy, and we couldn't let our little family secret out," he said, glancing in Han's direction. "We take them out one at a time, you see. And no one's the wiser. But she saw them together, and the boys needed the practice."

Gordon's hands curled into monstrous fists.

"Ah, ah, ah," Bennett warned him, squeezing Cordelia. "Between the staff and my nephew, you'd never get close."

Han leaned toward them, his eyes fixated on Gordon's hulking form, and Cordelia watched helplessly as Gordon clutched at his head in agony, crumpling to the ground.

"Make him stop," she begged. "Whatever he's doing, make him stop!"

"Very well," Bennett said, and Han released his invisible grip on Gordon. "Shall we continue?"

"Please," Cordelia tried again. "Surely there's a way to break the binding spell. Without hurting anyone."

Bennett sighed behind her. "I'm sorry, but that's just not going to be enough. You owe us a debt. And we're here to collect."

Cordelia whimpered. In the cramped interior of the crypt, she didn't dare conjure a wind or a lightning storm. She would never be able to control whom it impacted, and she wouldn't take a chance on hurting her sister.

"You can blame your mother," Bennett told her cruelly. "When you meet her on the other side."

At that, Han let out a wretched laugh, sinister and dense.

Cordelia knew that laugh. She'd heard it in her dream. Han was the shadow in the parking lot, the one who cut her mother's protection away. They killed Maggie and probably hoped that Eustace and Cordelia would never make it long enough to find out this place existed. "My mother? What did you do to her?"

"What did *I* do to *her*?" Bennett questioned. "My dear, you have it all wrong. It's what *she* did to *me*. First, she was born. Something my father, Munro, worked very hard to impede. He jabbered endlessly in that foolish little ear of your grandmother's convincing her that a home birth would be the death of her. He convinced her that her boyfriend Alton, the future botanist who was pressuring her to deliver in a hospital, was a great man of science and knew better than her own family of simpletons and shut-ins, living in primitive seclusion.

"It took time, I'll give her that. But my father started early. We never thought your mother would survive the delivery. She surprised us all. And that iron-clawed auntie of yours made sure to bring her here as quickly as possible. Alton took his own life, the damned fool. I was ten years old at the time. Even as a baby she was beautiful, your mother. A selfish, beautiful, wide-eyed, empty-headed thorn in our sides.

"I loved her once. I tried not to, but I was weaker then. For a time, I entertained the idea of our union as another means to our end. I even proposed, but she refused. We could have fed the two lines into one, the way great rivers are born, but she had a lover, like her whore mother before her. A university man here for the summer. They rendezvoused in the stables like animals in rut. I watched them hump each other silly. Watched that cuckold plant his seed in her. And then I choked the life out of him. That was *my* initiation."

Before he could go on, her sister started to moan from the floor. Her head turned this way and that as she fought to find consciousness.

Bennett leaned down, his grip on Cordelia slackening. He pointed the staff at Eustace. "What's happening?"

Cordelia, seizing her chance, bolted from his arms. But he was fast for his age. Bennett slung the staff in an arc and the pillar beside her began to crumble, a great slab of stone threatening to topple from above.

Gordon threw himself against the pillar, using his shoulder and back to hold it in place just long enough for Cordelia to dash from the crypt, falling down the steps and racing across the promenade toward the house. Behind her, she heard a cascade of falling rock and prayed her sister and Gordon would be safe, but she didn't slow or turn around, because unless he'd been knocked unconscious, Bennett would come for her. And the boy—Han. And they were both far deadlier to Gordon and her sister than the caving crypt. She needed to lure them away. She pumped her legs with as much speed as she could summon, burning with the effort.

Tearing through the solarium and kitchen, she racked her

mind for anything that could help. All she could think of was the basement room, so she sped through the hall and library toward the secret door. Maybe, if she was lucky, that was one secret the house had not given up to the Togerses. Maybe she could hide. Maybe the runes would afford her some protection.

She heard the kitchen door bang against the wall as someone entered the house a moment later. Whatever had collapsed in the crypt as she'd fled was obviously not enough to stop Bennett or his nephew. One of them was in pursuit.

She neared the bookshelf door, hoping the basement would give her sanctuary, but her hopes were quickly dashed as it swung open. Arkin stood in the gap, staring down at her. Cordelia barely skidded to a stop before colliding with him.

He didn't have his brother's unnerving presence, but his eyes were flint as they met hers. He was not the simpering boor they'd thought. And he did not look kindly on her now.

"Arkin," she said through gulps of air. "I–I—"

A crash sounded from behind, and she spun to see Han at the study door. He'd bumped into a library table and sent the double-globe lamp careening to the ground.

"Uncle said to be careful," Arkin hissed.

Cordelia backed around the desk, trying to determine how she could wriggle out of being caught between the two of them at once. Her eyes tripped over the little pouch of rune-carved teeth, and she slipped a hand behind her, folding it into her fist.

Han glowered at his brother as if he might strike him.

"You might be stronger," Arkin told him. "But I'm smarter."

Han's eyes narrowed devilishly, and in that moment Cordelia thought Arkin a bigger fool than any of them.

She tried to slither back a few more steps, till she was past Han and could turn and make another run for it. But his eyes darted after her, and as soon as he moved in her direction, she stopped.

"My sister always thought she was the smarter one too," she said to Han, hoping she could distract him, keep him from boring into her with whatever infernal power he possessed. She still didn't understand why their gifts seemed so different from hers and her sister's.

"Don't speak to him," Arkin shouted.

Cordelia looked from one to the other. She'd never had the gift of reading people that Eustace did, but she saw these men for what they were—puppets. Keeping their secret had left them naive and uniquely gullible. They knew nothing of the world, groomed as they were to be servants of their uncle, who was groomed to be a servant of her family. Arkin, having gotten out more, was the better adjusted of the two, but weaker. Han, a channel of immense power, had paid a dear price for it. He had the temperament of a willful child.

It was her only advantage. She focused on Han. "You let him tell you what to do?"

He shook his head and made a guttural screech. She still didn't know if he couldn't speak or just chose not to.

"Stop it!" Arkin fussed at her. Above them, a light bulb burst. Arkin turned on his brother. "Don't! Uncle said not to break anything."

The bulb in the lamp on the desk exploded, and Cordelia jumped. Then the green glass shade shattered.

Cordelia slid one foot back, and then another. Han's eyes fell on her. "Must have been hard all these years. Always being the one stuck inside. Always being the dirty little secret. Must have been hard to watch him get everything while you did all the work."

"You shut your lying mouth," Arkin cried, stepping forward. Han's eyes darted away from Cordelia to him. "Don't listen to her," Arkin told his brother.

"There he goes again," Cordelia said, a sly slant to her lips. "Telling you how to conduct yourself."

Han looked at her, eyes glinting. He took a step in his brother's direction as he lowered his head.

"He's the weak one," Cordelia whispered. "He's always been weak. You're the real heir of this family. If *he* weren't around, you'd have all the power."

"That's enough!" Arkin lunged at Cordelia from across the massive desk as his brother lunged at him, but Han was the quicker of the two. They toppled back toward the open doorway to the basement as Han slammed into his brother, Arkin tearing at his own face and screaming.

Cordelia sent a sudden blast of wind spinning around the room. Papers went flying and books blew off the desk; with a boom, the bust of Homer hit the floor, where it split into pieces. It knocked both boys even further off-balance, and they tumbled down the steep, inelegant stairway.

Cordelia rushed to shove the door closed, pulling with all her strength to move the desk just far enough to keep the door from opening again.

She put a hand to her chest and turned around, running from the room and headlong into the chest of Bennett Togers.

Cordelia bounced off him, spiraling around the hall and hitting the floor before she finally regained her footing. She scrabbled back on hands and knees to the stairs, using the banister to pull herself up as he stalked toward her.

"What did you do to them?" he growled.

"It's what you did to them. I just gave them a little encouragement."

Bennett lunged at her, and she jumped back, stumbling up another three stairs. The sound of the bookshelf door striking the desk echoed through the house.

He smiled like he'd won. "You think a locked door can hold him? Tell me, what did your mother teach you about our gifts?"

Cordelia tried to stay calm. She needed to if she had any hope of surviving. But he still had the upper hand.

"We're witches," she said, though Maggie had never told her that.

Bennett cackled. "Is that what she told you?"

"We can heal," she stated more confidently, backing up again, taking another two steps. "And meld with the minds of animals. And tell fortunes."

"You idiot girl," he spat. "Witches are for costume parties. We're necromancers, born of an ancient, unsevered line. We are the death keepers. And we can do far more than you have been told."

Cordelia backed toward the landing of the second story as he advanced on her, climbing the stairs beneath her slowly.

"What is the opposite of healing?" he asked her. "Do you know how you unlock magic to take a life?"

She shook her head. If she could just keep him talking, keep him distracted while she thought of something.

"First, you must squeeze it out of something with your hands. Beat it out with your fists. Only then will the spirits tell you how to do it without. When I killed your mother's lover, I ran to the woods horrified at what I had done. I cried out with his blood on my hands, and the souls of our people found me there, broken by the creek. They whispered their darkest secrets to me. Ancient curses we've nearly forgotten. That's when I really began learning. Just as my father before me and his before him. Tobias killed his own wife in her sleep so he could learn the dark ways. But our line is newer, weaker. We couldn't overcome yours until now."

Cordelia took another step back, and another. She reached the second-story landing and turned to continue higher. "What did you do to my sister?" she begged him. "What did you do to Gordon?"

He ignored her pleas. "I had to start small, of course. Mice, bats . . . You're familiar with my work. This craft takes practice. Trial and error. But my skill set kept growing—madness, paralysis, pain, darkness. Those are my gifts. Your sister cures disease, and I grow it. But the boy, he's better than I ever was. His blood is strong. The strongest in our line. When your aunt weakened, he overpowered her with it. He held her down from afar. She stopped moving. Stopped speaking. Stopped eating. Eventually, she stopped breathing. Her heart stopped beating. Strong as she was, even she couldn't resist him."

"But the bones," Cordelia said, still climbing. Overhead, movement on the widow's watch caught her eye. Morna's shade darkened the air like a pillar of fury. "The crypt. It should have kept her safe."

Bennett smirked. "Only the blood of a Bone can bind another Bone."

The runes over her aunt's lips flashed through her memory, and Hella's words—*Bone pays for bone. Blood for blood.*

"That's where your fool family messed up. Han is not the first secret son in our line. They're easy to hide when you can never leave your own property. My ancestress's child by Erazmus—the boy, Tobias—was hid from his own father. All this time, we've been creeping up on you, and they never saw us coming. They never knew our blood was theirs."

Cordelia backed up again, glancing above her. She was nearing the third story. She felt the spirit's hunger as she drew closer. The runes her sister had drawn across her skin the night before burned beneath it, as if they'd been embedded with hot coals. The teeth in her hand began to rub against each other, heating up with the friction. Inside herself, the magic responded, pulsing and hot, eager to defend.

"None of that now," the old man said, twisting the staff, and Cordelia could feel the power inside her constricting as if it were being squeezed from her body. Her head began to throb.

A pounding sounded on the front door, a shaking of the knob, and Bennett flicked the staff. Cordelia could hear all the locks in the house click closed automatically. Gordon's voice sounded through the glass as he called for her; his fist slammed the wood. She breathed a sigh of inward relief that he was still alive. But where was her sister then?

"Why are you telling me all this?" she asked Bennett, if only to keep him talking. The staff in his hand sounded a dull thud on every stair.

"Because I'm so tired of pretending to be lower than you." He leered at her. "I want you to take the truth to them when you die. I want them to know it was *us*."

Cordelia squeezed her eyes closed and climbed back another two steps to the third-story landing. She was backing her way toward the widow's watch.

A terrific blast rocked the first story, and the sound of splintering wood rang up to them. Bennett smiled. "That will be my nephew now," he told her. "Not that I need his help. It's no wonder he's so strong. You and your sister are the weakest of your line by far. He must have gotten all the power you've wasted."

He pointed the staff toward her, and Cordelia stumbled up several stairs.

"You think that boy is strong," she spat at him. "But his mind is weak. He's never known love or affection. He only knows your thirst for power. He only knows what it is to be an instrument in your hand. He'll destroy you. And everything you've worked toward. He can't carry your line forward. He can't function in the real world. Whatever power he has, it's cost him. And the price is too great."

She edged her way onto the widow's watch now. There was nowhere else to go. Around her, the property sprawled in every direction. But she was trapped.

A horrible primal scream cut through the air, and Cordelia and

Bennett both looked down over the railing, where Han stood in the middle of the stair hall, glaring up at them.

"Where's your brother?" Bennett called down. But the boy only wailed and tore at his hair.

Cordelia looked at Bennett, whose face was drawn with fear and consternation.

"Han!" he shouted down again. "Where is Arkin?"

Han released a howl so potent it rattled the house on its foundations and blasted the glass out of the tower windows.

Cordelia tried to cover her face as shards sailed past her in every direction, cutting and nicking her across her cheeks, collarbones, and forehead. A large piece sliced right through the open palm of one of her outstretched hands. Slowly she uncurled as the glass fell at their feet and rained down over Han. Blood trickled from her gash.

"What did you do?" Bennett screamed down at him.

Before the boy could respond, the front and vestibule doors crashed open, sending pieces of door frame flying. Han ducked behind his arms as the black bear charged in, all five hundred–plus pounds of it, thrusting its open mouth forward in an ear-splitting roar. The boy had barely taken his arms from his face when the animal fell on him, ripping his throat out and tossing him like a rag doll across the parquet floor in a spew of blood.

"Eustace," Cordelia gasped.

Bennett lifted his eyes to hers, his mouth hanging open as if his jaw had been broken. His secret weapon had been destroyed. It had all happened so fast, so unexpectedly, that he'd not had a chance to react and save the boy. Slowly, his pupils constricted, his gaze refocusing on her. He jerked the wand back and Cordelia felt her throat tighten, constricted as if she were being strangled by an imaginary hand.

"It's time to end this," he snarled.

Cordelia's head thrummed with pain, the pressure in her

skull unbearable. She would have screamed had it been possible. Clutching at the base of her neck with her injured hand, she felt the runes they'd drawn on her ignite against her skin, trying to protect her. They were the only reason she was still drawing a sliver of air. She backed toward the window overlooking the gardens, then around again toward the front as Bennett climbed to her level. In a shadowy corner Morna's ghost was brooding, her face just beginning to materialize from the dark.

Bennett glared at Cordelia. The placid, congenial attorney was gone. Here stood a killer of sixty-plus years, a man who had tasted blood and liked it. "You'll be purple inside of a minute," he told her quietly. "And dead inside of two. And that bitch sister of yours won't be able to save you even if she rides in on a flying lion."

Below them, the throaty huff of the bear could be heard, and the wet, sinewy rip of flesh as it fed.

Cordelia reached to claw at him, but with so little air, her movements were jerky and off-balance. Blood trickled from her nose and ears and her eyes bulged; she knew her brain would bleed out if she didn't suffocate first. Outside, a strong wind was gusting in continuous circles around the house, as if they were trapped in a cyclone, a by-product of her own desperation, growing with every loop. But as her nemesis slowly choked the magic and air from her, she could manage no more.

Bennett smiled coolly. "Your pitiful storms can't save you now, girl. Not while I have this." He thrust the staff in her direction and her throat snapped shut. Whatever thin cord of oxygen she'd been drawing was undeniably gone.

Her palm burned from the teeth as they clashed against each other inside the pouch at a frightening speed.

"What's that sound?" he snapped, eyeing her, bending to see behind her back.

Cordelia flung them at him, unable to hold them a moment

longer. They sailed from the pouch like hot coals, sizzling against his skin where they hit his face.

"Arrgh!" He turned away, throwing a hand up to protect his eyes.

It was all Cordelia needed. She reached out and grabbed the staff he held with her bleeding hand, red streaking the wood and brass. "Blood for blood," she choked out.

A streak of lightning, jagged and sizzling, ripped its way through the roof and the tower, igniting the staff in their grip, bringing it to life with white fire. Bennett drew back, shrieking as she took it from him. All at once, every door and window in the house burst open, and the wind that had been billowing beyond reach blustered through from dozens of entry points, spiraling up the center of the staircase. Something traveled with it, barreling toward them in a torrent, and she moved the staff to her other hand, reaching out to snap whatever it was from the air as it flew past. Her fingers clutched clumsily at it, and she felt the cool, smooth surface nick her skin. It was the bone knife from the crypt, the same one Bennett had used to perform the burial ritual on their aunt.

She didn't hesitate. She flipped it blade-down and drove it straight into the old man's chest beneath his collarbone, into the soft flesh between ribs, gritting her teeth. "Bone for bone," she cried.

Bennett let out a dreadful howl, grasping at the smooth, white hilt emerging from his chest. Behind him, the mist was gathering, as if every shadow in the house had come together in one teeming mass.

"Take him," she told the spirit of her great-great-aunt. "My debt is paid."

The shadow moved with unnatural speed. In an instant, Morna had fully materialized behind him with eyes of black fire and violet glinting through her wild auburn hair. She wrapped her arms around his chest and her legs around his hips. Her eyes met Cordelia's for the briefest of moments—a flicker of acknowledgment in them—before she threw herself back, crashing through the tower window, jagged with broken glass.

Bennett's face contorted with fear. He flung out a hand and gripped Cordelia's arm as they fell, threatening to pull her down with them. But the staff did not budge, and Cordelia held fast to it as the old man's fingers slid down her skin, catching at the bracelet. For a split second, he thought he'd found purchase, but the silver band loosened against the blood from her cut, sliding easily off her wrist and hurtling toward the ground below as Bennett and Morna dropped like falling stones.

Cordelia stood gasping, eyes burning and salty, the wind still kicking around her. She forced her trembling feet forward and looked out the yawning window, creaking gently on its hinges.

Beneath them, Bennett's body had broken against the nithing pole, the sharpened lumber slick with blood as it protruded from his abdomen, cold eyes staring up, his mouth twisted in an open scream.

CHAPTER THIRTY-ONE

THE KNIFE

CORDELIA MOVED GINGERLY down the stairs, one hand on the crumbling brick wall, one on the swollen lump of her belly, which descended a full two steps ahead of her. She'd thought that by the third trimester she would have adjusted to the idea of being pregnant, of fat ankles and indigestion and having to roll to her side to sit up. But her fingers still danced over her growing abdomen with surprise, and every time the baby moved she froze, as if realizing for the first time there was something alive inside her.

Gordon, on the other hand, was a natural father. He rubbed her back and made Eustace cook her gobs of vegetables and read to the baby at night from an old copy of *Aesop's Fables* he found in the library. He rearranged Arabella's boudoir into a darling nursery, so their little one could be kept close. And he was already stripping the wallpaper from Opal and Theodore's turret room, so he could paint it sage green to match their daughter's name.

Sage had been Eustace's idea, but Cordelia loved it instantly.

Reaching the bottom step, she took a minute to catch her breath and vowed to have yet another discussion with her sister about spending so much time down here. She realized the grow room was Eustace's new obsession, but she was getting very tired of traversing these perilous stairs. At least the overzealous LED bulbs Gordon had installed chased the dark to the farthest corners, and the evidence of their family's past—the wooden shovels and coils of rope and old crowbars—had been relegated to the barn.

Cordelia wound her way through tray after tray of sprouts—bean and broccoli and alfalfa—and tower after tower of microgreens. Along the way, she picked a leaf or two to taste—the radish greens were her favorite, with their sharp, peppery bite. Bunches of herbs and dark, leafy heads of kale and chard lined the walls in hanging planters, and pots of tomatoes and peppers were caged wherever there was a free spot. Eustace figured she could grow just about anything under the right lighting, and so far, she was correct.

Cordelia noted, with a hint of annoyance as much as amusement, that her sister had started cultivating something else in the basement grow room behind the cruciferous vegetables.

When she couldn't find her among the plants, she made her way to the ritual room, where she found Eustace at the broad farm table on the back wall, pulverizing something that smelled like rotten garlic in the giant mortar and pestle.

Cordelia folded her arms over her bulging belly. "I thought we said no cannabis."

Eustace turned in surprise. "Cordy! You have got to stop sneaking up on me like that." She placed a hand over her chest. "You're like some kind of pregnant secret agent. The bigger you get, the quieter you get. It's unnatural."

"You're just upset you got busted," Cordelia told her.

"It's only one plant," Eustace argued.

Cordelia narrowed her eyes.

"Okay, okay. It's only one corner of plants. Purely personal. Medicinal, even."

"Mm-hmm." Cordelia stared her sister down. "This isn't Colorado, Eustace. They're not friendly to cannabis growers here. Not yet."

"I know," her sister grumbled.

"What are you grinding up now? It smells like ass and turnips," Cordelia complained.

Eustace cast her a sympathetic glance. "Sorry. It's stinkweed. As great for a broken heart as it is heat rash, asthma, or parasites."

"Is it good for malnourishment? Because that's what this baby is gonna have if I've gotta keep smelling that stuff."

"I told you not to come down here until *after* baby Sage is born," Eustace reminded her.

Cordelia stared at her sister. "Was that for my benefit? Or so you could cultivate illegal botanicals in our basement behind my back?"

Eustace set the pestle down and put her hands on her hips, turning to face her sister. "No one's going to find out, Cordelia."

She'd obviously struck a nerve if she was getting called by her full name. Cordelia arched her brows. "Let's hope not. We certainly don't need any more legal attention drawn in our direction now that the accident's behind us."

The accident is how Cordelia preferred to think of Togers and his nephews' untimely demise on their property. She'd been certain they would haul her down to the station once the paramedics and police saw the shaft of bone protruding from the old man's chest. How could she explain her presence in the tower with him during his fall? She could hardly expect them to believe that the ghost of her great-great-aunt had killed him in revenge for his family's role in her own death more than eighty years ago. But when she'd scuttled down the stairs and out the back door to see his body arched across the ghoulish nithing pole, she realized the knife had disappeared. And along with it, the oath ring she'd worn, her promise finally kept.

And then there was Han's body in the stair hall, or what little the bear had left of it. The authorities vowed to trap and shoot the bear within the week. They set their metal cylinders up in several locations around the property, but never found him. It helped that Eustace had driven him all the way to upstate New York, just to be sure. She couldn't endure his being slaughtered when he'd only done what she dictated.

She'd had to explain to Cordelia in great detail how, when Bennett had his nephews kill Marvel on the nithing pole, the trauma had flung her from the animal. For hours, her consciousness had wandered disembodied and confused, before she began to develop an understanding again of who and where she was, what had happened. But even then, she didn't know how to get back to herself.

The bear, it turned out, was the nearest and most willing host. Perhaps its previous contact with Cordelia and her had left a mark. She was able eventually to slide into its body. And then it had been only a matter of time, and the fight to drive the bear back to the estate from a few miles off without losing herself to the animal's instincts along the way. She hadn't arrived in time to warn Cordelia about the Togerses, but she had shown up in time to help protect her.

When Bennett brought down part of the roof of the crypt to try to stop Cordelia, Gordon had shielded Eustace with his own body, dragging her into the room of bones once the attorney and his nephew had taken chase, before digging his own way out to go after them. They'd found her afterward, fully restored and stumbling out on her own two feet. "I always thought I wanted a family reunion," she'd said sarcastically. "I've changed my mind."

Arkin's body was a different story. They found him lying at the bottom of the basement stairs. He'd suffered a hemorrhagic stroke, according to the coroner. Multiple brain bleeds at one time—something their office had never seen the likes of before.

His death was ruled natural, though Cordelia knew it was anything but. Han had killed his brother in a fit of rage. She felt responsible, but she couldn't see another way. Bennett had poisoned his nephews against them over many years. There would never be a world where both lines could exist side by side. Hella had confirmed it herself—for the tree to survive, one branch had to be felled.

Of course, there was plenty of questioning that followed. But a key to the big house had been found in the old man's pockets, and Cordelia explained again and again how she'd come in to discover the attorney already on the stairs, his speech deranged upon seeing his nephew's remains, refusing to come down or listen to reason. As evidence of his mental unrest, she pointed to the myriad doors and windows flung open around the house, something he must have done before making the slow march to the tower to leap to his death.

It all looked cut-and-dried enough. The two women appeared to have little reason to bring harm to the aging attorney. And everyone knew of Bennett's devotion to their great-aunt. There was an assumption that grief—and, possibly, unrequited love— had been compounded by the trauma of his nephew's mauling and driven him into a fit of temporary madness. And the people of Bellwick had developed a certain desensitization toward odd happenings at Bone Hill. This, no doubt, would become another in a long line of tragic tales that made up the Bone family lore.

Even the authorities were quick to write it all off, taking the easiest and most obvious explanation for all three deaths. For once, their family's haunted history served them well, and Cordelia was grateful for the nursery rhymes and superstitions. Though it was not a reality she relished for her daughter, being raised near Bellwick. She'd been holding Eustace and herself to the highest standards of cordiality and ordinariness ever since, in the hope that they might put some of the past to rest.

It helped that they were seen regularly in town.

Cordelia rubbed at her left arm.

"Still itch?" Eustace asked, nodding her chin in the direction of Cordelia's healing tattoo.

She looked down at the eight-pointed star marking the underside of her left forearm, just like the design in the stair hall. "Not really," she said. "It's healed remarkably fast thanks to your poultice."

"Mine too," Eustace agreed, raising her right forearm to expose the same design inked just below her elbow.

Cordelia pursed her lips, twisting them to one side. "There's a property for auction near Mystic," she told her sister. "It's a real mess, but the bones are good."

Eustace eyed her carefully. "You promised not to go farther than Bellwick with the baby."

"And I won't," Cordelia assured her. "I just thought, you know, maybe someone could go in my place. Bid by proxy. Gordon could really make a gem of it. We'd stand to double our investment."

Eustace frowned. "And what is this one saying? *Buy me, Cordy?*"

Cordelia gave her sister a dark look. "It's not like that. The whispers are . . . *informative*, not commanding."

Before Bone Hill, Cordelia had never heard them from so far away. But now, the whispers came to her across varying distances, rustles in her mind like dreams, waking her in the middle of the night, driving her to the computer to search listings—houses that needed rescuing, that begged to be seen, to be restored, to recapture their former glory. They were always historic. And always haunted. Cordelia found she had a heart for them. She liked to think she and Gordon were doing them a service—the houses *and* the dead.

"Can I take the dog?" Eustace asked reluctantly.

Cordelia burst into a wide grin. Gordon had adopted a blue

heeler mix a few months ago, which he named Asher. Asher had promptly adopted Eustace. He could hardly be pulled from her side most days. The only reason he wasn't down here now was because Gordon had taken him to the woods to gather firewood. "Sister, you can take anything you damn well please."

"The dog will do," Eustace told her. "But only if you promise to wait until after the baby is born on any more of these. I don't want to be gone when she comes."

"Done," Cordelia told her. "This is the last one, I swear." In total, they'd acquired four properties so far, and already flipped one. Cordelia's knack ensured they found the diamonds in the rough before anyone else did; Gordon's handiwork ensured they profited on the sale. Together, they made an unbeatable team. And the business gave them some normalcy in the community. It was important to Cordelia to provide that for the baby.

She knew full well that like her and her sister, like their mother and grandmother before them, her baby would be born a Bone—a witch, a necromancer, a *volva*. A speaker for the dead. A reader of runes. Sage's gifts would show themselves in time, and she would learn the secret history of their bloodline, the one she and Eustace were still unraveling, though much had been laid bare between Bennett Togers' revelations and Eustace's decoding of the rest of the therimoire. But until then, Cordelia wanted her daughter to have as normal a childhood as they could provide.

"Besides, Molly will be here next month. She can be my auction lackey after that," Cordelia said. Once the baby came, Cordelia and Gordon would need more help with the business. And even now they could never tear Eustace away from the garden or kitchen or basement long enough to do what needed to be done. Molly would stay in the carriage house and take over the day-to-day for a while. Cordelia was looking forward to seeing her again. She'd proved herself more loyal than Allison had ever been, even when she'd been forced to accept another job, and

Cordelia was thrilled to have an opportunity and excuse to hire her back.

Eustace sighed. "You think she can handle this place?"

"If she can handle John, she can handle Bone Hill," Cordelia said confidently.

Eustace frowned again.

"What is it?" she asked her.

"I need to tell you something."

Cordelia felt the baby kick and placed a hand to the right of her navel to still her. "Okay."

"There was a sighting," Eustace told her cautiously. "Of Diana."

It was Cordelia's turn to frown. "When?" she asked. "Where?"

Bennett's sister had fled town after the deaths of her boys, avoiding questions regarding the abuse and neglect of her son Han, who most people in town didn't know about, and a child endangerment charge by the state. Neither Eustace nor Cordelia was certain what she was capable of or what powers she possessed, or how the binding spell might impact her now that she'd left Bellwick—the last Togers alive no longer in their service.

Eustace took a breath. "Massachusetts," she said. "Far away."

"Not far enough," Cordelia mumbled.

"The PI said a waitress identified her near Andover," Eustace told her. "She turned up in a morgue in Boston shortly after."

Cordelia put a hand against the wall to steady herself.

"She came in as a *Jane Doe*." She looked pained. "The PI didn't correct them. I didn't want to upset you, but I figured you should know."

"How?" Cordelia asked.

"Hit-and-run," Eustace told her. "She was beat up pretty bad. But the hair . . ." She didn't need to say more. Her boys had inherited their blazing blond manes from their mother.

"I was afraid it would come to this," Cordelia whispered. She had no pity for this woman who'd allowed her sons to be used, who supported a brother that tried to kill her and steal their inheritance, but she also knew that Diana had been influenced by her family's long history of bondage.

Now, with Diana and Bennett gone, and both the twins dead, the Togers line had ended, and there was no one left to threaten them. "I guess it's for the best."

Eustace shrugged. "This binding business should have been put to an end generations ago. Now it's run its course, and we can all be free of it."

Cordelia hoped her sister was right—that they were truly *free of it*. She looked down at her belly. If her daughter was to survive, the twins could not. It was a dark irony she could not escape, and part of being a Bone witch. Not all their gifts were good. Death was their calling also, curses and sickness and blight. The dark half of being a *volva*. She comforted herself with the understanding that unlike Togers and his ilk, she'd use those particular powers only in self-defense.

They'd been something she'd been fully prepared to unleash on Busy Mazzello when he pulled up in front of the house the day after Bennett died, but fortunately didn't have to. She'd known him the instant he climbed out of the car—shoulders like smoked hams and a scar running from one eyebrow to his chin, a voice thicker than clotted cream. As her attorney's newest and wealthiest client, she'd had no trouble getting an advance on their inheritance, delivered *in small bills*.

"Pleasure doing business with ya," he'd said as he pulled the briefcase from her hands.

"Can't say the same," Cordelia had told him as she strode out onto the porch. She'd watched him toss the case into his car and start around the other side to leave. "Mr. Mazzello!" she'd called. "Just one more thing."

He'd paused and looked up, a triumphant grin parting his meaty lips.

"If you ever threaten me or anyone I know again, I'll destroy you," she'd said sweetly.

His brows had bulged then, and his face fell. For a second, he'd looked like he might start toward her, just before the massive oak limb came crashing down on the hood of his car, spider-webbing his windshield and missing his head by a hair.

What did they call drops like that? Cordelia remembered thinking. *Widow-makers.* She'd never seen such fear in a man's face before. Cordelia didn't expect she or Mrs. Robichaud would be hearing from him after that.

"I'm feeling tired." She put a hand to her head. "I think I'll go lie down."

"I can help you up," Eustace said, looking a bit guilty for being the bearer of difficult news.

Cordelia waved her off. "No. Stay. I'm fine on my own."

Turning for the door, she'd nearly made it out into Eustace's jungle of plants when her sister called.

"Have you thought of a middle name yet?" she asked. It had been the topic of much debate over the last few months.

Cordelia stopped and turned to face her sister. "Morna," she said quietly.

Since *the accident,* Cordelia hadn't seen the specter of her great-great-aunt haunting the tower anymore, but she'd felt a protective presence hovering over her as the baby grew. She liked to think it was Morna, though it could have just as easily been any of them. But she owed her life and her child's to the spirit she'd once feared, and this was a way to show her gratitude. One day, baby Sage would be old enough to ask about the meaning of her name, and Cordelia would tell her the story of the woman who haunted the tower and saved their lives. But for now, it was enough that she and Eustace knew and understood.

"Oh, I almost forgot," Cordelia said, stepping back into the room. Between the cannabis and the stinkweed and coaxing Eustace into house-hunting for her, she'd nearly forgotten why she'd come down. "I dreamt of her last night."

"Who?" Eustace asked. "Morna?"

"No," Cordelia told her. "Mom. I dreamt of Mom."

Eustace studied her. "Did she say anything?"

Cordelia shook her head. "No. But she smiled."

Her sister grinned. It was as good a sign as any that Maggie Bone was finally at rest.

"When I woke up," Cordelia continued, "I found this on the nightstand." She walked over and reached into the deep pocket of her wool cardigan, setting something gently on the table beside the mortar and pestle. It was the bone knife from the crypt. The one she'd buried in Bennett Togers' chest. The one that vanished before he hit the ground.

Eustace stared at it a moment, then turned and opened the door on the heavy iron stove and tossed the knife into the crackling fire within. A plume of flames sparked up in the oven's belly, and her sister swung the door closed, turning back to the table and her concoction.

"Leave it to Mom to leave a murder weapon lying around," she grumbled, but Cordelia could see the shine of tears gathering in the corners of her sister's eyes.

"Leave it to Mom indeed," Cordelia agreed.

ACKNOWLEDGMENTS

It takes a team to build a book, and I am eternally grateful for mine. From the moment the Bone sisters came strolling into my head, to the moment I held this book in my hands, each of these people were part of the journey. Their fingerprints are all over the pages.

My agent, Thao Le, who knew I'd always be down to write a book about witches. My editors, Monique Patterson and Vicki Lame, who steered the unwieldy vessel that was this novel beside me and helped me shape it into something far more palatable. The entire team at St. Martin's Griffin, from Mara and Vanessa, who stayed on top of every detail, to my exceptional copy editor, Tom, and proofreader, Ken. As well as Christina, Kiffin, Janna, Cassie, Anne, and every other individual who stuck their neck out for this book. My incredible cover designer, Olya Kirilyuk, who took all of my suggestions and turned them into something stunning to behold. And my publicist, Sara, and marketing coordinator, Kejana, who tirelessly answered my questions and dealt with my panic. My beloved family, who is the inspiration behind everything I do—Nathan, Zoey, Ben, and Evelyn. Always, always, Evelyn. My soul sisters, Tracey Lee and Sara, who show up daily in ways so few people are capable of. You are true heroines.

And to all the witches I've known, stood beside in circle, and tossed things into a fire with—Cynthia, Emmy, Sheryl, Tina, TL, Sara, Zoey, Ev, and so many more—you are beautiful, powerful women. I love making magic with you.

ABOUT THE AUTHOR

Zoey Sweat

AVA MORGYN grew up falling in love with all the wrong characters in all the wrong stories, then studied English writing and rhetoric at St. Edward's University. She is a lover of witchcraft, tarot, and powerful women with bad reputations, and she currently resides in Houston with her family, surrounded by antiques and dog hair. When not at her laptop spinning darkly hypnotic tales, she writes for her blog on child loss, hunts for vintage treasures, and reads the darkest books she can find. She is the author of YA novels *Resurrection Girls* and *The Salt in Our Blood*.